Daughter of Fate

A S Webb is the *Sunday Times* bestselling author of *Daughter of Chaos* and *Daughter of Fate*, the first two instalments of The Dark Pantheon trilogy. She holds a BA in English Literature and Theatre Studies from the University of Leeds and is inspired by stories rooted in history and mythology. She lives in London with her family.

Daughter of Fate

A S WEBB

MICHAEL  JOSEPH

PENGUIN MICHAEL JOSEPH

UK | USA | Canada | Ireland | Australia
India | New Zealand | South Africa

Penguin Michael Joseph is part of the Penguin Random House group of companies
whose addresses can be found at global.penguinrandomhouse.com

Penguin Random House UK,
One Embassy Gardens, 8 Viaduct Gardens, London SW11 7BW

penguin.co.uk

First published 2025

001

Copyright © A S Webb, 2025

The moral right of the author has been asserted

Penguin Random House values and supports copyright.
Copyright fuels creativity, encourages diverse voices, promotes freedom
of expression and supports a vibrant culture. Thank you for purchasing
an authorized edition of this book and for respecting intellectual property
laws by not reproducing, scanning or distributing any part of it by any
means without permission. You are supporting authors and enabling
Penguin Random House to continue to publish books for everyone.
No part of this book may be used or reproduced in any manner for the
purpose of training artificial intelligence technologies or systems. In accordance
with Article 4(3) of the DSM Directive 2019/790, Penguin Random House
expressly reserves this work from the text and data mining exception

Set in 13.5/16pt Garamond MT Std
Typeset by Six Red Marbles UK, Thetford, Norfolk
Printed and bound in Great Britain by Clays Ltd, Elcograf S.p.A.

The authorized representative in the EEA is Penguin Random House Ireland,
Morrison Chambers, 32 Nassau Street, Dublin D02 YH68

A CIP catalogue record for this book is available from the British Library

HARDBACK ISBN: 978-0-241-67640-0
TRADE PAPERBACK ISBN: 978-0-241-67641-7

Penguin Random House is committed to a sustainable future
for our business, our readers and our planet. This book is made from
Forest Stewardship Council® certified paper.

Author's Note

This book contains themes of a sensitive nature – please refer to the author's website, webbandpen.com, for specifics.

For those who carry the ones they've lost

And fate? No one alive has ever escaped it, neither brave man nor coward . . . it's born with us the day that we are born.

Homer, *Iliad*
(translated by Robert Fagles)

One Thousand Years Prior

Kronos lifted his torch, staring through sweat-stung eyes at the looming peaks of Mount Olympus. Banks of beech trees towered either side of him like verdant sentries, their leaves whispering in the wind. He drew a deep breath. Bushes of wild oregano clustered between the silver trunks, the herb's minty, earthen scent carrying on the chill breeze. Beyond the sloping swathes of forest, bare ridges of rock stood free of ice and cloud, silhouetted against a coal-dark sky scattered with stars. Watching, waiting.

'Father!'

Kronos looked back. His eldest son, Zeus, was climbing the trail behind him, his own flaming torch spilling streaks of light and shadow across his face.

Kronos sighed. 'You should not have followed me.'

Zeus stood firm: weary yet defiant.

Suddenly, Kronos saw not a man, but a boy. All gangly limbs and wide, sea-blue eyes, the same expression etched across his face as at the injustice of his younger brother, Poseidon, stealing the wooden cow he had lovingly crafted. Kronos wondered how Zeus had grown so fast. Sun-crinkled skin spread from the corners of his eyes, and his jaw was lean and bearded. He was almost thirty. When Kronos was younger people had remarked that they looked more like twins than father and son. He could not recall at what age his body had revealed the truth.

It felt strange now to contemplate the passing of time, when he was about to become ageless.

'Father, please . . .'

Kronos turned back to the path with an aching heart.

'You could save her.'

He froze, his chest constricting as he thought of the last time he'd seen his youngest daughter, Hestia, still only a babe, wrapped in blankets by the hearth, her wan little face looking up at his. He thrust the memory away. He could not allow himself to be drawn down that road. Once he tasted the sacred fruit, he would no longer be a father and a husband. He had been called, and all that he once was must be set aside. It was the greatest sacrifice and the greatest honour a person could ever hope for: to become a Titan.

'We have spoken on this. Go home, Zeus.'

'Do you not care?'

Kronos took a couple of steps.

'Father! Do not walk away from me.'

His son's words were arrows in his heart as he continued on, fighting the urge to glance back. Eventually, Zeus grew quiet, but Kronos could hear his son's ragged breath as he followed like a spectre behind him.

Kronos' progress was slow in the dark with the burden of his pack and torch, and the small stones that slipped under foot. For a while the trees grew so tall, he could no longer see the mountain's peak above him, only a sliver of star-flecked sky. The way grew tangled, thick roots lying like steps across his path, the vivid green leaves of beeches giving way to the jade spines of towering pines. Owls and other creatures of the night called to one another from the shadows. Then a rustling sounded up ahead. Kronos' eyes darted between the trees, lingering on a churned patch of earth between two pines.

Wild boar.

He paused, his free hand leaping to the handle of the knife sheathed in his belt. A tusk to the gut could be deadly.

After a while, the noise faded, and Kronos once more resumed his ascent.

He had not gone far when there was a cry behind him.

Despite himself, he spun around. Zeus, still following, had tripped on a root, his torch sputtering on the ground.

Kronos cursed under his breath. Damn the boy's stubbornness.

Fighting every instinct, he turned away from his son and pressed on.

He clambered over great channels of rock and long-dead trees that had been shaken free by storms to pour like rivers from the peaks. He did not slow as the way steepened and the pines thinned, the tufted earth replaced by loose grey stones. The wind grew fierce, whipping Kronos' thick woollen cloak and threatening to extinguish his fire. He was forced to scramble up the scree, using his free hand to steady himself on the lichen-stained boulders littering his way. The urge to glance back at his son gnawed at him like the cold air lancing across his skin. All the while the sky paled, the stars fading into the cold blue light that creeps before the dawn.

In the shadow of the highest peak, he came across a flat bank of rocks perched on the edge of a sharp ridge, falling in a sheer drop to the forested valley below. Beyond the trees and the grassy plain and sandy beach stretching away from the foot of the mountain lay the Aegean Sea: a dark foil to the brightening sky.

Kronos set his torch in the centre of a clutch of stones and heaped a few twigs and bracken onto the little fire. For a brief moment he thought Zeus had finally abandoned his pursuit. Then his son emerged from scrambling up the scree to stand at the edge of the light, his clothes smeared with dust, his eyes blazing brighter than the flames.

Kronos could not help the spark of pride that warmed his chest.

'Sit with me.'

Zeus added his torch to Kronos' fire and lowered himself onto a rock beside his father. Kronos delved into his pack and handed his son a couple of strips of dried goat meat, then took a swig from his waterskin. Zeus devoured the goat, groaning as he chewed.

A smile twitched Kronos' lips. He held out his hand. In the centre of his palm lay an almond.

Zeus swallowed his mouthful.

Kronos curled his fingers around the nut and blew on his knuckles. Then he opened his hand to reveal the almond vanished.

Zeus' brow darkened. 'I'm not a child.'

Kronos sighed, retrieving the almond from his tunic pocket.

'I care,' he said softly. 'You, Poseidon, Hades, Demeter, Hestia, Hera . . . You will always have my heart.'

Zeus leant forward, his voice nothing but a hoarse whisper, as though he feared the mountain might be listening. 'Once you have become a Titan you could come home in secret, use your power to heal Hestia, then return.'

Kronos shook his head. 'You know I cannot. You must be strong now. Take up the responsibility as head of your family.'

Zeus recoiled, the fire in his eyes cooling to ice. '*Our* family. You always said we came above all else. Was that a lie?'

Kronos' ribs tightened. 'I have never lied to you, son.'

'Then why will you not save your own child?'

Kronos gazed up at the mountain's highest peak, his heart aching. 'I have been chosen for a higher purpose. As one of the Twelve, maintaining the balance of the tapestry of life will be my responsibility. I cannot place my own loves above every living being on the earth.'

The look in Zeus' eyes was too painful to hold. So many words lay piled between them, and yet still he could not make his son understand.

After a long pause he added, 'I saw the face of creation. This is how it must be.'

Zeus' expression grew thunderous. 'My mother gave her life so Hestia could join this world. Do you care so little for her sacrifice?'

At the mention of his wife, Rhea, Kronos flinched.

'Your anger shames your tongue.'

'It is you, Father, who should be ashamed.'

Kronos clenched his jaw, swallowing the torrent of words he longed to hurl at his son. Silence raged between them. Drawing deep, calming breaths, Kronos let Zeus' anger wash over him until the tidal waves faded to ripples and the fight in his son's eyes ebbed away.

Zeus hung his head. The knot in Kronos' chest eased. Finally, acceptance.

Brightness crept along the edge of his vision. He looked to the east, where the sun crested the sea, spilling its rosy glow across the world. Then he turned to gaze at the ridge of stone behind him. Tears flowed freely down his cheeks as that honeyed light burnished the mountain, transforming its grey crags into golden rock and, below their stony ridge, its dark forests into swathes of gleaming emerald.

Then he heard it.

A melody sang to him that before, he had only heard in his dreams. Harmonies of bright birdsong, rasping leaves, whistling wind and the pulse of rumbling stone. The heartbeat of the world. The song of life itself.

The tangle of emotions roiling in his gut melted away.

'It is time. This is where I must leave you.'

They both rose to their feet, and the air between them grew tight as a drum skin. Then Zeus threw his arms around Kronos, clinging to him as though he were driftwood in a tumultuous sea.

'I'm sorry, Father.'

Something in his tone struck unease through Kronos. He tried to pull away, but as he moved pain seared through his back. He gasped, unable to fill his lungs as Zeus let go of him. Kronos fell to his knees, palms hitting the hard rock as he coughed blood onto the ground.

Zeus stood over him, Kronos' knife clenched in his trembling hand.

'W-why?'

'For *our* family.' Zeus' face twisted into a mask of grief. Then his shoulders broadened as he said, '*I* am Kronos, chosen to become one of the Twelve.'

Kronos' mouth stretched wide, tears muddling with the blood seeping between his lips.

'You cannot . . . the Mother will . . .'

'She will do nothing. Just like she did nothing when Rhea died, when plague took half the village, when our crops failed and whole families starved. The Mother does not care for us. Neither do you.'

Kronos no longer saw the boy he'd raised, but a wild thing that had stolen his son's skin.

Zeus' face glowed in the swelling light. 'I will use the apple's gifts to help those in need. I will be a saviour. I will be the coming of a new dawn.'

Then Zeus dragged Kronos across the stony ridge. Kronos struggled in vain, his hands slick with his own blood as Zeus hauled him to the edge, then pushed him down the mountainside.

PART ONE

1. A Skull and a Crown

Danae crouched in the shadows at the mouth of the cave. It was a cloudless night; the ink-dark sky swirled with stars and a sickle moon. Athens sprawled out beneath her vantage point, halfway up a hill opposite the acropolis. Even at this hour, the city pulsed with life. So many people, so many lives intertwining, colliding.

Three years had passed since her last visit to the city, but the memory of her eighteen-year-old self trying to find her way to Delphi lingered uncomfortably under her skin. She could still taste the fear of standing in chains before a theatre of men bidding for her life, recall the terrible sounds of King Theseus' hounds ripping apart his son's body, and feel the bone-crushing hopelessness of door after door closing in her face. Its stone buildings may look beautiful in the moonlight, but to her the city of riches smelt like desperation, shame and piss.

A bone-white feather drifted across her vision. Then the warm breath of Hylas the winged horse tickled her cheek. When she did not move, he gently nipped her ear.

'I know.' Her gaze lifted to the acropolis. The hulking outlines of the Temple of Athena and King Theseus' palace looked like two colossuses crouching under the stars. 'Time to go.'

Hylas was already saddled, Danae's meagre possessions stuffed into two pouches that hung down his flanks. She had stolen the saddle straight off the back of a nobleman's mare in a town outside Thebes and crudely fashioned it to fit around Hylas' wing joints.

She tucked her flyaway strands of hair into the rough braid that hung to the nape of her neck and pulled up the hood of her black seer's cloak. Its length hid the ill-fitting brown tunic beneath – another stolen item, this one from a Phrygian farmer's washing basket. It had been a long time since her clothes had seen a river. Hylas too was looking the worse for a year on the run, his once gleaming coat smeared with dirt, his tail knotted, his mane tangled.

'We're almost there,' she whispered, smoothing his neck.

She mounted the winged horse and cast a final look around the cave that had been their home for the past five days. It was the longest they'd stayed in once place since fleeing the Caucasus Mountains a year earlier. She thought of the griffin's cave that had been her shelter as she'd climbed the highest ice-encrusted peak to reach Prometheus, the Titan imprisoned for attempting to liberate mortals from the tyrannical Olympian gods. Even now, the words of his prophecy still echoed in her mind. *When the prophet falls, and gold that grows bears no fruit, the last daughter will come. She will end the reign of thunder and become the light that frees mankind.*

She screwed her eyes shut. She had travelled to the end of the world, betrayed her friends and dedicated all her strength to finding the man she believed would teach her how to fulfil her destiny. But the Titan had left her with nothing but questions. One, in particular, had consumed her. Eclipsing all else, it had driven her across rivers, mountains, cities and villages, while she fought to keep herself and Hylas concealed from the Twelve.

She opened her eyes. Tonight, she would finally get her answer.

Weaving her fingers through Hylas' snowy mane, she locked them into their familiar hold. It was a risk, flying over a bustling city on such a clear night. But she could delay no longer. She'd spent five days hiding in her cave so she could stake out the palace, learn the guards' patrol route and King Theseus' movements. Earlier that day, she had discovered that he was due to leave the city the following dawn to visit the King of Aetolia. It was now or never.

She dug her heels into Hylas' sides, and he cantered across the rocky ground beyond the cave, then launched into the air on his vast feathered wings. Her hood blew back, the cloak streaming behind as her cheeks stung with anticipation.

You cannot run from your destiny, said the voice that had awoken inside her along with her power.

She pushed the words from her mind with practised force and braced herself as Hylas descended. As his hooves clattered onto the palace roof, she slid from his back to land softly on the tiles.

'Don't move,' she whispered.

Hylas tossed his silky white mane, threaded silver in the moonlight.

'You'll have food soon, I promise.'

The horse eyed her then rippled his lips.

'And wine.'

At that, Hylas pressed his muzzle into her hand, gently nibbling her fingers. The ghost of a smile curled Danae's mouth. During their time together, she'd discovered the horse had a fondness for unmixed wine. No doubt a product of being raised on Olympus.

'I won't be long.'

She unpinned her cloak and stowed it away in Hylas' saddle bag, then checked her knife was securely tucked into the belt of her tunic. Lastly, she untied a coil of rope attached to a grapple hook and wound it around her arm. Moving as stealthily as possible across the sloping roof tiles, she crept towards the edge.

The streets of Athens spread out beneath her, a sea of winking brazier lights. The city was as loud as a storm-tossed coast. Kapeleia rumbled with merriment as their customers conversed over cups of wine and plates of victuals, and other late-night establishments beckoned patrons with the tantalizing glow of candles and the promise of blissful forgetting.

Danae padded along the edge of the roof, carefully measuring her steps. When she reached the correct spot, she hooked the grapple onto the lip of the palace roof. Once satisfied it would hold, she wrapped the rope around her thigh and slowly lowered herself past the stone pillars until she was parallel with a window on the second floor.

The shutters were closed, and arms of bronze filagree barred her way. This was the tricky part. She heaved her weight back and forth, until the swinging motion brought her within touching distance of the shutters. She collided with the wood and almost lost hold of the rope. They were bolted.

Of course they were. This was the king's bedroom.

She cursed her own stupidity. After all her planning, she'd failed to account for a lock. But she was not thwarted yet.

During the past year, she hadn't just spent her time running and chasing answers. She'd also been practising the skill of harnessing her powers. Wherever she and Hylas went, she had drained the life force from trees, bushes, livestock, every shimmering thread she consumed poured into better understanding her abilities and how to wield them with force.

As she swung back towards the window, she stretched out her arm and drew a tangle of life-threads into her hand. She'd left several trees withered and lifeless in the Athenian forest in preparation for tonight, but she hadn't planned on using her powers so soon. Gods know how many threads she would need to fight her way out.

Her hand collided with the shutters. Wood splintered and bronze twisted as the windows were blasted open. She landed sprawled on a tiled floor. The room was vast, dominated by a huge bed on the far side, guarded by painted pillars and silk curtains.

Without pausing for breath, she leapt to her feet and sent another surge of life-threads into her arms while pacing across the room, giving her the strength to drag a heavy ornate table along the wall to block the double doors.

She had barely finished moving the piece of furniture when something cold and sharp pressed against her skin. Slowly, she turned.

King Theseus held a sword to her cheek. Silver light poured in from the window, throwing the creases of his face into shadow. His nostrils flared, and the corners of his mouth curved with disdain. He stood naked, one foot in front of the other, his weight perfectly balanced. This was a man who knew how to wield a weapon, so confident of his own power he hadn't even called out for the guards. But then Theseus was no ordinary king. In his youth he'd been Greece's greatest hero, until Heracles, the mortal son of Zeus, had claimed the title with his courageous labours. However, there were whispers that Theseus had travelled to lands even the mighty Heracles had not braved, and if legend was to be believed, had almost succeeded in kidnapping the goddess Persephone from Hades' palace in the Underworld. Danae had good reason to hope this was true. The omphalos shard's visions, the last piece of an obsidian stone that granted images of the future, had led her to Athens. Finally, she might be about to discover the answer she'd spent a year searching for.

Danae flinched at a crash behind her. The doors bulged against the weight of the table as they were battered from the other side.

'My king! Are you hurt?'

Before Theseus could reply, Danae whipped a further clutch of life-threads into her hand and hurled him across the room. He crashed past the painted bed and smacked against the wall. Quick as she was, he still managed to cut her before his sword clattered away across the patterned floor. Blood dribbling down the front of her tunic, she leapt across the room and straddled him, her knife against his throat. Theseus looked dazed, his chest heaving.

'Where is the entrance to the Underworld?' Even as she spoke, she felt her energy wane. She'd mainly been reviving her powers with the life-threads of shrubbery and small animals. Even draining them from a couple of large trees didn't come close to how she'd felt after absorbing the life of the harpy. She longed to feel that powerful again, ached for it, more than anything else in the world.

The table screeched against the floor as the guards doubled their efforts. She had moments.

Theseus stared at her, his mouth slack. She couldn't believe this man had ever been called a hero. He was nothing like Heracles.

She pressed her knife against his jugular. The pressure of the blade biting into his skin brought clarity back to his stupefied face.

'C-Cape Taenarum.'

She had her answer, but she didn't let go.

'What's down there? Did you see the dead?'

'I . . . didn't get past the River Styx.' The boundary of the Underworld, whose waters were said to be haunted by unburied souls. Danae's heart sank. Theseus had never made it into Hades' kingdom after all.

Beneath her blade, the king's blood pulsed through his vein. It would be so easy just to flick her wrist. He would bleed out in a matter of moments. All those life-threads waiting to flee his body and be absorbed by hers. The memory of ecstasy shivered through her.

Do it, said the voice. *He deserves it. Remember what he did to his son.*

Danae recalled the sight of Hippolytus' lifeless body, battered and mutilated by Theseus' hounds. Retribution for the young man having an affair with his stepmother, Queen Phaedra. Danae bit the inside of her cheek so hard she tasted metal.

Another crash reverberated through the room.

She glanced at the window, then back at the quivering king. She kicked him hard between the legs. 'That's for Ariadne.' Another of Theseus' victims, Danae had met the Maenad woman on her home island of Naxos. Many years earlier, Theseus had taken Ariadne from her home on Crete, lain with her under the false promise of marriage, then abandoned her on the island.

Theseus groaned like a wounded bull as Danae leapt from the bed. She was halfway across the room when the doors flew open, sending the table crashing onto its side, and blue-cloaked Athenian guards poured in. Three or four she could have taken, but there were eight, all of them armed.

She dived for the window, but one of the guards grabbed her leg, dragging her back into the room. She twisted onto her back and, summoning her life-threads once more, slammed her hands into the floor. The tiles shattered, shards flying up into the faces of the guards. The man let go, and she lunged again for the window, scrabbled onto the ledge, then grabbed hold of the rope.

Her palms burned as she heaved herself upwards, muscles screaming with the effort. Teeth clenched, she poured every drop of strength into reaching the roof. The grapple hook glinted in the moonlight above her; she was almost there. Then the rope jolted. Danae clung on as the cord swayed violently, tugged by a guard leaning out of the window below.

Then the hook gave way.

The rope slipped from her fingers, and she plummeted past the second-floor window, screaming into the darkness as the ground came rushing up to claim her.

But instead of bone-shattering stone, she landed with a thwack across Hylas' back. The horse dipped violently, whinnying as he beat his snowy wings towards the moon. Winded, she clung on to the saddle, her legs dangling in the air. When she'd regained her breath, she heaved herself to a sitting position and wrapped her arms around Hylas' neck.

'Take us to Cape Taenarum,' she whispered.

Below, the palace blazed, braziers igniting from room to room as guards raced through the corridors, raising the alarm.

Danae cried out as an arrow grazed her leg. Glancing back, she saw several guards leaning from the upper windows, bows aimed at the sky.

'Higher, Hylas, higher!' she urged, as another flurry of arrows shot past them.

The winged horse surged up towards the moon, until finally they were out of range, no more than a shadow on the sphere's pearly face.

Dawn seared the clouds, their underbellies glowing like hot coals. Hours after they left Athens, Danae and Hylas soared over the waters of the Saronic Gulf, alighting in a forest in the Argolid region of the Peloponnese. They were only halfway to Taenarum, but both she and her steed sorely needed rest.

Tiredness had become as familiar to Danae as breathing.

She barely registered the ache in her thighs and back as she slid from Hylas' saddle. She staggered towards the stream of silver she'd spotted snaking through the canopy as they flew over the forest. She fell to her knees, and both she and the winged horse lowered their heads to the river, the cold water numbing her mouth. Once her thirst was quenched, she delved into Hylas' saddle bag and hooked a small sack of barley grain on a tree nub for him to eat.

While Hylas chomped, Danae melted into the forest. She kept him in her sights, but ventured far enough that her companion would not witness what she must do.

Placing her hands on the trunk of a large oak, she reached for the tree's life-threads. She was met with the usual resistance – the tree was strong and healthy – but eventually it bent to her will, just as they always did. A gasp slipped from her lips as the oak's life-threads rushed into her, banishing the pain of her bruised ribs and healing the arrow wound on her leg. Energy surged through her veins as all around her, brown wilted leaves fell like tarnished snow, and the first budding green acorns shrivelled and tumbled to the forest floor, never to become trees.

Danae turned from the dead oak, her body lighter, her heart heavier. She only did what she must to survive, yet the corpses of the trees and animals she left in her wake fed the knot of shame ever-writhing in her stomach. She was like a plague, bringing death wherever she went.

She returned to kneel at the bank of the little river, taking two waterskins, one from each of the saddle bags. Her wavering reflection scattered as she pierced the surface of the water, refilling the vessels. Warped and dirty as it was, her face had not changed since she left Naxos three years ago.

There are no gods. Her hands trembled as the voice repeated Prometheus' words, spoken just before his death atop the

Caucasus Mountains. *There were only ever mortals, and those mortals chosen to become Titans . . . You are a Titan.*

A familiar argument unfurled in her mind. She, the gods and the Titans could not be the same, as Prometheus had claimed. Yes, the Twelve had lied when they painted the Titans as monstrous giants – Prometheus had looked human, just like her. And even if the gods were in fact Titans, like the foe they had defeated in battle for the dominion of the earth, she could not be. Prometheus and the Olympians had lived for centuries, they were immortal.

No, whispered the voice. *Not immortal.*

The gods and the Titans might be ageless, but Prometheus' death had proved that they could be killed.

She shook her head. Even so, she was not like them.

Her youthful reflection stared back, mocking her. Both Phineus, the father of her loyal friend Manto whose sacrifice had saved her from the harpies, and the priestess of the oracle at Delphi had become wizened with their constant use of the prophetic omphalos stone. But not her. She raised a wet hand to her face and traced the skin around her eyes, her mouth, her cheeks. Smooth. Unchanged. No matter what she did or where she went, she was stilled in time.

She wondered what her sister would look like now. Alea would be in her twenty-second year. If she had lived would she have grown to further resemble their mother? Or would their father's likeness have been drawn out with each turn of the sun? Then Danae's thoughts crept to Arius, her little nephew, stolen from her sister's bed on his first birthday. Alea had been convinced he was Zeus' son, her heart irreparably shattered when Arius was taken by a shade, and his all-powerful father did nothing to prevent it. Danae had no idea what had become of him, if he was dead or alive.

The voice interrupted her thoughts, repeating more of

Prometheus' final words. *Apollo does not drive the sun across the sky. Hades rules the Underworld, but there is no afterlife there.*

'Enough!' She stood abruptly and stormed back to the saddle bags, roughly stowing away the swollen waterskins.

The voice was wrong, Prometheus was wrong. Alea must be in the Underworld. And she was going to prove it.

Hylas lifted his muzzle from his feed, nickered softly and trotted towards her. He lay his head over her shoulder. She wrapped her arms around his neck, breathing in the scent of his mane. Behind him, the sun gleamed through the trees, rippling golden light across the river.

She didn't realize she was weeping until Hylas drew back his head and licked the salt from her cheeks.

'I'm not crying. You just smell awful.'

Hylas snorted, and Danae smiled. He was the most intelligent beast she'd ever known. He seemed to genuinely understand human speech, as well as having an ingrained knowledge of the land. She hadn't shared more than a passing sentence with another person since her encounter with Prometheus, let alone touched one without violence. Without her realizing it, the horse had become her closest friend. She liked to believe he too felt their bond, and that was why he hadn't abandoned her and flown back to Olympus. But whatever his reason for remaining at her side, she was grateful. She didn't know what she would have done without him.

She removed Hylas' saddle to give him some respite from the chafing leather and sat down beside the river.

In her haste to escape Athens, she'd barely given herself time to revel in how close she was to finally finding a doorway to the Underworld. She'd known it was going to be difficult, but she hadn't expected it would take this long.

She had not been able to divine the first two visions the

omphalos shard had shown her when she asked it how to enter the kingdom of Hades. The third vision it revealed to her, a twelve-pointed sun floating above a crowned skull, had led her to Athens. It wasn't common knowledge that King Theseus had ventured into the Underworld, the journey not being one of his heroic deeds immortalized in song or pottery. But after lurking in enough kapeleia and asking the right questions, she'd teased out the tale.

She glanced at the saddle beside her. Hylas was now lying down in the shadow of the trees, his head tucked into his breast. Danae ran a hand over her face. She should rest. Tomorrow they would continue on to Cape Taenarum, and she would need every crumb of strength for what awaited her there. Even so, her fingers twitched towards the left-hand saddle bag.

Just once more.

She slipped her hand beneath the leather flap and drew out the wrapped omphalos shard.

There was another question she had asked of the stone, besides seeking the location of the entrance to the Underworld. It had not given her the answer she sought. Even now as she contemplated asking again, her pulse quickened and her palms grew clammy.

She unwrapped the obsidian rock and let it roll, naked, onto her hand. Immediately, her life-threads shot into the stone, her consciousness soon following.

As she floated, suspended in the void of nothingness, she asked, 'Where is my sister's soul?'

Her ephemeral self vibrated with the hope that this time it would give her a different answer.

She deflated as the tapestry of life-threads began to weave into the same vision she'd been shown the first time she asked the question.

Twisted branches laden with apples. A glowing, ever-moving sketch of the tree. It towered above her, shimmering as shining threads drew the outline of its trunk, its leaves, its branches and those ripe, golden orbs.

She was ripped from the vision as Hylas knocked her hand with his muzzle. The omphalos shard tumbled across the grass and she retched, her head spinning as she fought to orient herself. Hylas stood over her, wings splayed, whinnying and rearing onto his hind legs.

A moment later she realized why he'd dragged her back to the physical world.

Behind him in the ever-brightening sky, two dark shapes soared towards them.

In an instant, Danae was on her feet, a clutch of life-threads tingling in her hands. She'd known the risks of choosing to linger for five days in Athens, but she had been careful. She had been so careful.

Even so, the harpies had found her.

2. A Familiar Song

Danae hurled her life-threads into the air and shot a blast of wind at the harpies, sending one tumbling into the trees on the far side of the river, while the other dodged her torrent of air, tucking its leathery wings into its sides and streaking towards her like a javelin. The creature expelled a blood-chilling shriek as they collided, its taloned feet raking Danae's thighs. Pain stabbed through her legs, but she remained upright and with another surge of power threw the harpy from her, sending it crashing into a nearby tree trunk. Hylas brayed triumphantly and emerged from the forest to kick the harpy in its scaly chest.

'Hylas, stay back!' Danae staggered forwards, her legs screaming. She could not risk the horse being injured. She could mend herself by consuming the life-threads of another living thing, but she could not heal others.

She leapt on the fallen harpy before it had a chance to rise as Hylas disappeared back into the trees. Its jagged teeth were stained with blood, its yellow eyes bright with fury. Danae pulled the knife from her belt and plunged it deep into the creature's shattered chest. As its wings stopped flailing, she placed her hands either side of the blade and called the harpy's fleeing life-threads towards her.

Yes, crooned the voice. *Yes!*

Suddenly, searing pain ripped through Danae's shoulders and before she could drain the harpy's life force she was dragged backwards. The second harpy lifted her into the air, talons digging into the flesh below her collarbones.

She gasped, barely able to draw breath as the harpy carried her higher and higher. Haphazardly, she hurled blasts of air upwards, but none found their target.

Pain beat through her like a battle drum. She was running out of strength, the river beneath her an ever-narrowing vein of shimmering water.

The *river*.

Danae gathered her life-threads and channelled them downwards in a glowing rope that cut through the air to plummet into the water. Then, with an agonizing roar of effort, she pulled them back towards her, bringing the current upwards as though it were erupting from a spring.

The churning column of water smacked into them both. The harpy's talons retracted from Danae's shoulders as they tumbled downwards like seeds blown through the sky, the harpy desperately flapping, one wing hanging limp.

Danae fell into the embrace of the river and hit the bed, lungs swelling with liquid as she tried to draw breath. She spluttered, unable to command her body after the shock of the fall.

Then she was jerked to the surface, Hylas dragging her tunic between his teeth. The pain in her shoulders was so great she could barely raise her arms to heave herself onto the bank, but her need for breath forced her to push. She hit the earth like a speared fish, retching and coughing until her lungs filled with sweet, life-giving air. Rolling onto her back, she stared up and watched the lone harpy falteringly flying away across the sun-bleached sky.

Hylas let out a soft whinny and gently nudged Danae's back. She groaned and rolled onto her front. Forcing herself to her feet, she staggered towards the nearest tree and threw her arms around its trunk. The moments where the tree fought to retain its threads felt the longest of her life, a century of agony stretched into each one. But finally, the familiar surge of energy tingled through her limbs, and her flesh repaired itself. She detached herself from the withered tree. Her tunic was still shredded and bloodstained, but her body was whole once more.

Hylas stood watching her, a bloody stain across his snowy muzzle, his dark eyes tinged with sorrow.

Danae suddenly found she could not look at him. She scanned the ground and spotted the omphalos shard nestled in a scatter of leaves. Her heart skipped with relief, and she stooped to retrieve it, carefully wrapping it in the hem of her cloak.

'We have to go.' She stowed the stone away in Hylas' saddle bag and attempted to lift it onto his back.

Hylas retreated, tossing his head.

'I know, we both need rest, but we can't stay here. The harpy that got away will report to its master. The Twelve will come for me . . .' Her voice wavered. Despite her newly replenished life-threads, a wave of tiredness crashed over her. 'Please, Hylas.'

The horse blinked, then took a step towards her.

'Thank you,' she said softly as she lifted the saddle over his wings and buckled it beneath his belly. Then she grasped a fistful of her sodden tunic and attempted to scrub the blood from his nose. Her efforts only spread the stain deeper across his white hair. She winced.

'Sorry.'

Hylas nipped her ear, harder than usual, but still within the realms of affection. He lowered his right wing so Danae could hoist herself into the saddle. Once on his back she wound her fingers through his mane.

'Take us to the Underworld.'

*

There was little in the way of shelter on Cape Taenarum, a hardy, rugged stretch of land situated on the tip of the southernmost peninsula of mainland Greece.

The sun soared high in the sky by the time Danae brought Hylas down on a rocky slope out of sight from the walled town. There were no beaches that she could spot, just the deep, dark sea on all sides, crashing against the cliffs.

She looked at Hylas, torn between her reluctance to leave him alone and exposed and the knowledge that she couldn't walk into a strange town with a winged horse. She retrieved her purse from his saddle bag, then unclasped her cloak, shivering as the wind lanced across her skin. She set about securing the obsidian fabric to Hylas' saddle and draped the material over his wings. It was a poor disguise, but hopefully it would be enough to give a passerby the impression of an ordinary horse.

Hylas let out a weary nicker.

She smoothed his neck. 'I won't be long, I promise.'

Hylas blinked, his white lashes stark against his large mahogany eyes.

Her chest twinged as she turned away from him, but as she clambered over the tufted earth towards the town of Taenarum, her thoughts narrowed to her task: find food and discover the location of the entrance to the Underworld. With no military fortifications, the stone wall around Taenarum was simple enough for a seasoned rock climber, like Danae, to scale.

Taenarum was famous for its green marble, and the town reverberated with the clanging of stonemasons' chisels. As she and Hylas had flown in, Danae spotted several mining sites dotted around the cape. Despite the modest size of the town, the wealth this resource brought in was evident. The buildings were all fashioned from polished stone, their facades pristine and the roads swept clean. Many of the dwellings sported talismans above their doors crafted from the local stone: dolphins, miniature hammers, the all-seeing eye of the Twelve. Most of the people walking the streets appeared healthy and well dressed, the women favouring long, layered peplos in rich colours. It was a welcome relief that, even in the middle of the day, Taenarum was quieter than Athens at night, the pulse of the town more an amble than a sprint.

Once inside the walls, Danae clung to the shadows. At the end of the fourth street, she spotted the wooden sign of a kapeleion. She paused. Like in Athens, she would most likely find the information she needed from loose-lipped patrons deep in their cups. However, she was already garnering unwanted attention in her bloodstained, talon-torn tunic and doubted she would be welcome in the establishment dressed as she was.

She veered east, up a sloping road towards the heart of the town, until she reached a market square. Many of the shops displayed groaning stalls beneath their colourful awnings. She scoured the various merchants' wares until she found what she was looking for.

A moment later, a rainbow of cloths arced through the air as she hurled a blast of wind to upend the table of a fabric seller. The woman screeched in dismay, hurrying to scoop the materials from the dusty ground. While several other shopkeepers clustered to her aid, Danae snatched a roll of navy woollen cloth and ran. She had enough coin to buy the wares, but with an ever-dwindling purse she had decided to only pay where she could not steal.

Once free of the bustle of the square, she darted into an alley and folded the fabric at the top, then wrapped its length around her before removing the tattered clothing beneath.

Fixing it in place with the pins and rope belt from her old tunic, she fashioned herself a similar garment to the one exhibited by the women of Taenarum. Her disguise complete, she retraced her steps to the kapeleion.

The gloom inside was a welcome balm to the brightness of the day. It was a small establishment, quiet except for a group of men dominating one corner. The remnants of a plate of salted fish, flatbreads and small dish of olive oil lay between their cups. Another man sat beside the hearth, idly strumming a seven-stringed kithara. On the far side of the fire was a lone patron, the hood of their faded emerald cloak pulled low over their face, their feet twitching in time to the melody.

Danae approached the proprietor, a slight man with ebony skin. She drew an obol from the purse tucked into her belt and proffered it to him.

'A cup of wine.'

The man eyed her, then pocketed the silver. 'Right you are.'

She ensconced herself at a table in the corner farthest from the group of men while the barkeep poured her cup. When he brought it over to her, she said in a low voice, 'I've heard Taenarum is not just famous for its marble . . . it is said there is a gateway here.'

The proprietor's hand trembled as he set the cup down. He looked at her for a moment, touched his forehead, then turned away.

'Wait.' She reached beneath the folds of her peplos and slid a golden drachma across the table towards him. 'There's more where that came from,' she lied.

There were now only three obols left in the purse she had been given in exchange for Queen Phaedra's ring back in Corinth. She'd planned on spending the last of her wealth on a fine amphora of wine for Hylas, but this was too important.

The proprietor snatched up the coin. 'Talk to Antigonos, he might be foolish enough to take you.' He nodded at a bald, middle-aged fellow with a complexion like cracked leather, sat amongst the group of men. 'But no good will come of it,' he muttered as he shuffled away.

Danae sighed, then drained her cup. It seemed a swift return to Hylas was not to be. Summoning her mettle, she approached the group.

'Good afternoon, gentlemen. May the Twelve see you and know you.'

They blinked, staring at her as though she were a statue that had just come to life, until they remembered themselves and touched their foreheads in the sacred gesture.

'You looking for someone?' asked a man with dark hair and bloodshot eyes.

Danae addressed the man the barkeep had pointed out. 'Are you Antigonos?'

His chest swelled. 'Who wants to know?' Like the barkeep, his accent had the broad resonance of the south.

'I'm told you can take me . . .' she lowered her voice, 'to the place beneath.'

The kapeleion fell silent. Danae glanced behind her to see the musician clutching his kithara, eyes stretched wide. The emerald-cloaked stranger had grown so still, they could have been cast from Taenarum's green marble.

'You don't know what you're asking . . .' Antigonos growled.

'I know exactly what I'm asking.' She drew herself up, wishing she still had her black seer's robe. It was much easier to command respect when people believed she had the power of the gods behind her. 'I'll make it worth your while if you show me.' She flashed her purse beneath the navy folds of her dress, hoping the men couldn't tell how empty it was.

Another of the group, a younger man with sandy hair, pale cheeks and watery blue eyes, placed a hand on Antigonos' arm. 'No one ever comes back from that place. I've heard the ghosts of all those who died haunt the tunnels. Their tears streak down the walls, and if you touch them, you lose your mind, and there are disembodied red eyes that follow anyone who –'

'Oh, hush, Georgios,' an older man beside the lad knocked him over the head, 'you've been paying too much heed to your grandma's tales.'

'Tell me where the entrance is, and I will go alone.'

Antigonos barked out a laugh and licked his teeth, eyes raking over Danae. 'You'll die down there without a guide, girl.'

'I will have to risk it, if none of you are brave enough to take me.'

Antigonos bristled. 'You calling me a coward?'

Danae shrugged. 'I am not the one who is afraid.'

The men looked to Antigonos. He ground his teeth then said, 'Fine, I'll show you the way. But it will cost you.'

'I can pay.'

Antigonos sat back and folded his arms. 'How much?'

'Three drachmas.'

With the swiftness of someone with far less wine inside him, Antigonos lunged forward and grabbed her purse. He scattered her remaining obols on the table.

'Liar.'

Danae remained still as the man rose from his seat and drew so close she could smell the fish and fermented grapes on his breath.

'Tell you what, I'm in a charitable mood. So, I'll let you pay another way.' He slipped an arm around her waist, pulling her towards him.

Her body tensed beneath his touch, but before he could strengthen his grip, she punched him in the chest, engorging the force of the blow with a small clutch of life-threads. Antigonos flew back, crashing through the table, scattering his companions and smacking into the wall beyond. He slid down the stone, leaving a floor-to-ceiling crack in his wake.

Her rage died as quickly as it had flared. She had used too much of her power. No mortal save Heracles could send a man flying like that with a single blow.

'What . . . a-are you?' stammered the barkeep, a stool held out in front of him like a shield.

Danae backed away. She was such a fool. It would only be a matter of time before someone told a local priestess what they had seen. Then the Twelve would find her once more, and she would never discover what had happened to her sister.

She fled from the kapeleion, pacing through the winding streets until she was sure no one was pursuing her. She slowed, turning into a narrow alley, then leant against the wall to catch her breath. The sun had already begun its afternoon descent. She'd left Hylas too long and had nothing to show for it. Biting the inside of her lip, she tried to focus on what to do next.

Her thoughts were interrupted by a flash of green at the end of the alley. Her eyes darkened, and she paced towards it. When she turned the corner, she found the emerald-cloaked stranger who'd been sat in the corner of the kapeleion seemingly very interested in a pair of white shutters.

She grabbed them, dragging the stranger into the shadows of the alley, and rammed them against the wall, her forearm pressed against their neck.

'Why are you following me?'

'Daeira, i-it's me.'

Her heart stilled. It had been a year since she'd heard the false name she used aboard the *Argo*. She dropped her arm and took a step back.

The stranger removed their hood. It took Danae a moment to place the man standing before her. His once round face was pinched and had lost its youth since she'd left him with the other Argonauts outside the city of Colchis.

'Orpheus?' she breathed.

The musician managed a strained smile. 'I almost didn't recognize you back there, but when you used your power –'

Danae whipped out her knife and held it to his neck. 'Who are you with?'

His eyes bulged. 'N-no one.'

'Do not lie to me,' she pressed the blade against his flesh.

Orpheus gasped.

'The Argonauts, are any of them here?'

'I-I'm alone.'

'Then why are you here?'

'The same reason . . . you are.' He drew a stuttering breath. 'To find the entrance to the Underworld . . . and I have. I-I can take you there.'

She released him, her pulse drumming in her ears as the musician coughed and massaged his neck.

'If you know where it is, then why were you idling away the hours in that kapeleion?'

Orpheus blinked, his hands laced protectively around his neck. 'I thought if I listened to the locals I might learn something useful. The way will not be easy. No mortal has yet succeeded in breaking into Hades' kingdom.' Danae thought of Theseus and his claim that he'd never made it past the River Styx. Orpheus managed a half-smile. 'A better approach than yours, I'd wager. People tend to be looser with their tongues if you don't throw them against a wall.'

Danae watched him, searching the creases of his face as though they were a map that would lead her to the truth.

It was unnerving that an Argonaut had appeared in Taenarum at the same time as her, seemingly by coincidence. Unless it was no such thing . . .

Wild assumptions tore through her mind. She had abandoned Jason and the others without a word, leaving them under the cover of darkness to wake and discover Dolos, the healer and Heracles' closest friend, slain and Danae vanished. What must they have concluded? Perhaps Orpheus thought her a murderer, and he had been ordered by Jason to seek her out and deliver retribution. Or the musician had been lurking in Athens, and King Theseus had charged him to snare her, and, despite Hylas' speed, he'd somehow reached Taenarum first. Or he was an agent of the Twelve, sent to ambush her where the harpies had failed.

Or perhaps the fates might be smiling on her at last.

3. The Art of Pále

Dust swirled from the arena floor, glittering through the wisps of cloud trailing across the stadium carved into the rock of Mount Olympus.

Hera perched on the edge of a golden throne upon a shaded dais. Her back was straight as a javelin, hands laid neatly across her lap, her face impassive as the stone platform beneath her feet. Only her kohl-rimmed eyes betrayed the fury simmering in her soul.

Reclining beside her on an even larger throne was her husband, Zeus. Hera stole a glance at him. His face was as smooth and youthful as the day he'd left their old mortal village for Olympus. Only his eyes, threaded with gold like a lightning-cracked sky, betrayed the god he had become. His right hand lay upon the head of the mortal boy sitting at his feet, his fingers twisting idly through Ganymede's mahogany curls. The boy cradled a golden goblet of ambrosia wine in his hands. Zeus' goblet. He was the official cup bearer to the King of Heaven, and Zeus would drink nothing that had not first passed those sweet, mortal lips.

The hours Hera had spent fantasizing about slipping a drop of poison into that goblet. But the victory would be short-lived. Zeus would only install another soft-lipped mortal youth in his chambers to mock her with.

Zeus shifted and began conversing with his brother, Poseidon, seated on his other side. The unintelligible murmur of his words scraped her ears like the drone of a fly on a blistering summer's day. She set her jaw and looked to the empty throne at the end of the row beside the God of the Sea. There was another unoccupied seat to her right. Five thrones for the senior Olympians, that unfilled pair a constant reminder of the two absent deities: Hades and Demeter. One banished below the earth, the other confined to the sky palace, broken beyond repair.

Hera sighed. It had been too long since she'd last spent time with Demeter. She had been distracted of late, her days plagued by a lingering fear that followed her around the palace like a dog.

A child could have been conceived and birthed in the time her husband had failed to erase the greatest threat the Olympians had ever faced. Yet here he sat, seemingly free from the worry that endlessly gnawed at Hera.

It had been a year since she'd confronted the girl from Prometheus' prophecy, the mortal who was foretold to end her husband's reign. Yet despite Zeus vowing to find her, she seemed to have disappeared like smoke. Hera shivered at the memory of battling her atop the snow-swathed Caucasus Mountains, the girl's power so like her own. The altercation had almost claimed her life. When she had returned to Olympus, she'd expected a call to action. Instead, Zeus and Poseidon had sworn her to secrecy. Her husband had impressed upon her that of all the Twelve only the three of them, and Hades, knew of the Titan's prophecy and that was how it must remain. The children must go on believing the so-called 'last daughter' was in fact a creature from the Underworld, created by Hades to plague them. Hera had known she must obey, but what troubled her more than the command was that neither Zeus nor Poseidon could tell her where the girl had come from or how she had gained her powers.

A drumbeat burst into life, joined by the steady clap of the nymphs ordered to fill the stadium's seating. At Zeus' decree, once a year, his children fought in the old way. They were forbidden to use their powers, relying only on the strength of their bodies, as mortals must.

The rhythm raced to a frantic pulse as the first pair of Zeus' divine children ran out onto the arena. Hera and Zeus shared two sons; the rest were the result of Zeus' dalliances with other women. Their eldest son, Ares, the God of War, was followed swiftly by his half-sister, Athena, the Goddess of Wisdom and Warfare. Ares had inherited Hera's fine features and was built like a warrior, his muscle-corded limbs gleaming in the sunlight. But Athena had been blessed with their father's piercing blue eyes, a feature Zeus prided above all. Hera's son had toppled kingdoms, and still Athena, the offspring of Zeus' other great love, was his favourite. Hera smoothed a hand across her brow. After all this time, there remained barbs in her husband's heart she could not loosen.

Ares turned to the gathered nymphs, gesturing for them to cheer louder before he prostrated himself before his parents. Below the dais sat the rest of the royal children, who today played the part of spectators. They were all there, save Dionysus, the God of Wine and Pleasure. He had forsaken the comforts of Olympus, choosing to waste his endless life cavorting with a commune of mortal women.

Ares winked at someone below, and Hera glanced down to see Aphrodite, the Goddess of Love, married to her younger son, Hephaestus, lean forward, teasing her tumble of auburn curls across her bare shoulders. Hera pressed her lips into a thin line as Hephaestus stiffened. Hera knew that the God of Craftsmen despised these ceremonies, forced to watch his wife fawn over his brother, whom she had taken as her lover. The whore had abandoned her husband when he needed her most, and for that Hera would never forgive her. Just as she would never forgive Zeus for what he had done to Hephaestus.

Hera's attention was drawn to the youngest member of the royal brood seated at the far end of the row. Hermes, the Messenger of the Gods, reclined against the stone in full armour, his ridiculous winged boots resting on the back of the bench in front, his hands locked behind his helmet.

'Hermes has no respect,' she hissed.

Zeus followed her gaze and chuckled, which only inflamed her more.

As the years had passed, Hera hoped she would forget the faces of the mortal women Zeus had lain with, but they haunted her in the visages of their children, in every favour the King of Heaven bestowed on his offspring that were not hers.

Zeus lifted his hand. The drumbeat slowed. A pair of nymphs ran across the stadium to Ares and Athena, swiftly removing their golden armour until they stood barefoot, both dressed in nothing but a short leather kilt. The drumbeat shifted again, now swifter and sharper, as Ares and Athena dusted their hands and began to circle each other. Hera's jaw tightened as Hermes flitted amongst the rest of the divine children, gathering bets on who they thought would emerge triumphant.

'Brother,' said Zeus to Poseidon, 'who shall be the victor?'

Poseidon considered. 'Athena. She has the greater skill.'

Hera laughed sharply.

Zeus raised an eyebrow. 'My wife does not agree.'

'Physically, Ares is Athena's superior.' Hera appraised her son's muscular frame. 'He is undoubtedly the stronger contender.'

'You are blinded by your womb,' said Poseidon.

'You are just blind.'

Zeus raised his hand to quiet them. 'What say you, Ganymede?'

The boy at Zeus' feet tilted his head to look up at the King of Heaven. He blinked, his thick lashes fluttering over his cow-like eyes.

'I could not possibly pass judgement, my lord. I am but a mortal and they are gods.'

'Even so, choose.'

The mortal's throat bobbed. He lowered his head to survey Ares and Athena. 'The God of War will surely live up to his title.'

Zeus smiled and petted Ganymede like a dog. 'See, wife, you have an ally.' Then he turned his attention back to the arena. 'Ares is strong, but my Bright Eyes is cunning. She may best him in the end.'

Hera fought the urge to roll her eyes.

Ares and Athena continued to circle each other, raking the imported earth of the arena floor and coating their hands with dust. Hera's stomach tightened as she watched them, the desire to see Athena's blood spilt wetting her mouth. Guttural grunts burst from the pair as they clashed together, grappling each other's flesh.

Poseidon popped an indigo grape into his mouth, its sweet juice gleaming on his lips. 'Ares will soon grow bored and try to end the match with brute strength, that is when Athena will strike.'

Hera shook her head as Zeus' hand drifted to Ganymede's shoulder, and the boy lifted the goblet to his master. Zeus took a deep drink of the fortified amber wine, his eyes never leaving his children.

After less than half an hour of wrestling, Ares pulled back, then with a roar launched himself at his sister. Hera leant forward in her seat, afraid to blink as Athena darted around him.

Not swiftly enough.

Catching her around the waist, Ares hurled her to the ground and twisted her arms behind her back. There was a crack and Athena shrieked, her left arm bending at an unnatural angle, but Ares did not release her. The drumming rose in a crescendo, then fell silent as Zeus raised his goblet.

'Ares is the victor.' He looked at his wife. 'You were right, my wise queen.'

Hera relaxed, warmth spreading through her body as Ares released his sister and clicked his fingers at one of the nymphs sitting in the front row. The girl paled, trembling as she rose and walked across the arena toward the gods. Ares grabbed her and pushed her down to her knees before his moaning sister.

The nymph closed her eyes, tears trickling beneath her lashes as Athena reached out with her good arm and clutched the nymph's thigh. Then Ares took the nymph's head in his hands and twisted. His sister gasped, her broken arm shuddering back into place through the power of consuming another's life-threads. The nymph's body slumped to the ground. As Ares and Athena took their seats, two more nymphs sprinted onto the arena floor, lifting the corpse and carrying it out of the way.

Hera gazed triumphantly at Poseidon. 'You see, my boys are not so easily bested.'

The God of the Sea inclined his head and for a moment, all was right with the world.

Next, the twins, Apollo and Artemis, were stripped of their armour.

The two divine children launched themselves at one another. They were well matched, both tall and lean, yet their similarity was also their greatest disadvantage. Where Apollo dived, Artemis dodged, and where she struck, he predicted her blow. They knew each other's every move even before the thought had sparked.

The pair not being her blood, Hera's attention drifted. But she was soon drawn back to the arena when one of the nymphs screamed, the cry echoing around the stadium. Hera's brow creased. No blow appeared to have been landed by either Artemis or Apollo; they were still locked together, arms wrapped around one another as they struggled for dominance.

But the nymphs were not watching the match.

Something was falling from the sky, a dark tangle of wings and talons. Zeus rose to his feet as it crashed into the arena to lie twitching where it fell. Hera paced behind her husband as he ran down the stadium steps.

'Get back!' Zeus shouted as his children clustered around the creature.

A harpy.

Up close Hera could see that one of its wings was broken, its torso a bloody mess of lesions.

Her husband knelt beside the beast, tilting his ear to its leathery lips. A rasping sound issued from its mouth, but she could not catch the words. Zeus nodded once, then placed his hand over the harpy's heart, and the creature stopped moving.

He stood, his palm stained with blood.

'Leave us.' The drum of feet echoed through the arena as Ganymede, the children and the nymphs fled from the stadium. 'Poseidon, stay,' Zeus added as his brother turned to follow.

Hera waited for the last nymph to vacate the stadium, then turned to her husband. 'This is *her* doing, isn't it?'

Zeus' eyes burned like the blue heart of a flame. 'Leave.'

Hera blanched. 'I fought her, I can help you –'

'I said, leave.'

'I am your wife. I deserve to be here as much as he does.' She gestured towards Poseidon.

'You are not my blood.'

The breath hitched in her throat. Cheeks burning, she turned on her heel and strode towards the archway that led out of the stadium and up into the palace. But once the sun no longer warmed her skin, she melted into the shadows, pressing her back to the stone wall of the passageway. Calming her breath, she strained to listen.

'That was cruel, brother.'

Zeus ignored his comment. 'The second harpy would have returned with her sister if she could. She must have perished.'

Poseidon hissed out a breath. 'You must bid Hades craft more to send after the girl.'

'No.' There was a pause. 'I knew the harpies would fail to destroy her. But with its dying breath, the one that returned revealed where she is. She will run, but her trail is fresh. I will have her soon.'

'Will you kill her yourself?'

Another pause. 'I will send one of the children.'

Hera's heart thrummed against her chest, her body aching with the memory of the wounds she had carried from facing the girl atop the Caucasus Mountains.

'You would risk sending the children after her again, now we know how powerful she is? Have you decided to tell them the truth?' asked Poseidon.

'No,' Zeus replied sharply. 'The prophecy must be kept a secret . . .' He continued so softly Hera could barely hear him, but she did catch a name. '. . . Hermes.'

'You really think the boy is a match for her?'

Another silence, swollen with Hera's racing heartbeat.

'If he is not, I will send another.'

Hera clasped a hand to her mouth. Not waiting to allow Zeus and Poseidon time to discover her, she ran down the dark passage, the terrible truth of what she'd learned searing through her veins.

Expendable, whispered the voice that had lived in her mind ever since Zeus bid her bite into a golden apple, all those years ago. *To him, the children are expendable.*

4. Seekers

'Tell me where the entrance is,' Danae demanded.

Orpheus' lips parted. He stared at her for a moment, then his face crumpled. He slid down the wall to sit like a child on the ground, head hung between his knees, his shoulders heaving.

Danae clenched her teeth. Her nerves were screaming at her to run. For all she knew, this was a trap, and Orpheus had created this display to stall for time. But there was something in the rawness of his pain that felt honest, as though it held a mirror to her own. And if he did indeed know where to find the entrance to the Underworld, he might be her best chance of discovering the truth of what had happened to Alea's ghost. Her breath quivered at the thought.

She stepped towards the musician and lay a tentative hand on his shoulder. He flinched at her touch.

'I'm not going to hurt you.' She crouched to his level. 'Orpheus, look at me.'

He lifted his bruised eyes to meet hers. 'I'm sorry . . . I've been so alone . . .'

'Come on,' she said gruffly. 'Let's get out of here.'

Orpheus wiped his face and heaved himself to his feet. They walked in silence to the end of the alley, then Danae turned left, Orpheus right. They paused and looked back at one another, speaking in unison.

'My horse is outside the town –'

'– my belongings are this way.'

A beat fell between them.

'My lodgings aren't far,' said Orpheus. 'And I have food and wine.'

Danae hesitated. 'Good wine?'

'Decent enough . . . nothing fancy.'

Thinking of Hylas she replied, 'All right, but we must be quick.'

They paced down the quiet street, out into a square dominated by a large water fountain crowned by a statue of Aphrodite, the Goddess of Love. The Olympian's likeness was carved from Taenarum's pale green marble and painted in bold colours. She was leaning forwards, reaching for someone, her voluptuous curves draped in a thin cloth buffeted by an imaginary breeze. Bright flowers floated in the water, and the sweet scent of rose and beeswax drifted across the square, from where the locals had anointed the marble goddess's feet.

As they walked past the statue, Orpheus' eyes swept over Danae's makeshift peplos and lingered on her braided hair.

'Why aren't you dressed as a seer?'

Danae frowned. Of course, Orpheus had known her when disguised as Daeira, the seer, one who divines the will of the gods. She countered his question with one of her own: 'Why are you seeking the Underworld?'

Orpheus' eyes shimmered. 'My Eurydice.'

Danae recalled the name from the musician's songs aboard the *Argo*. 'The girl from your village?'

Orpheus nodded. 'She waited for me and when I returned home from Colchis, she agreed to be my wife.'

'What happened to her?'

'She . . .' he drew a wavering breath. 'Not long after our wedding – she liked to walk in the forest, and one day a man followed her . . .' his voice cracked. 'She fought him off and ran. My brave girl was swift, but in her haste, she was bitten by a snake.'

'I'm sorry.'

Furiously Orpheus wiped his face. 'I'm going to get her back.'

Danae said nothing.

They walked on a little longer in silence, then he asked, 'What happened to you?' When she did not reply he continued, 'Were you kidnapped by the shades that killed Dolos?'

She released the breath that had been locked in her chest. He did not know what she had done. It had happened nearly a year ago, yet her body still tensed at the memory of that night: the snow crisping the trees, blanketing the world in deafening silence, Dolos' dark blood staining the white ground as it dripped between the healer's lifeless eyes. It had been self-defence; she had discovered Dolos meeting with a shade to procure more of the strength elixir he'd secretly been feeding to Heracles on Zeus' command. When she'd threatened to return to the camp and tell the hero the truth, Dolos had stabbed her. Her powers and her fury had saved her, but they had also taken the healer's life.

'Yes,' she forced herself to lie. 'Dolos and I spotted a shade skulking around the camp. We chased it into a clearing, where it attacked us. Then more appeared. I managed to take one down, but there were too many ... They killed Dolos and kidnapped me.'

'Poor man,' whispered Orpheus. 'It was a terrible shock when we found him dead along with the shade.' He paused. 'Heracles was distraught.'

Danae swallowed, her throat thick.

'Did he find you?' asked Orpheus.

'What?'

'Heracles. He, Telamon and Atalanta left the Argonauts after we discovered Dolos' body ... We thought you'd been kidnapped and they went to search for you. Jason was furious.'

Her pulse quickened as she grasped for more threads to weave into the fabric of her lie. 'No . . . I managed to overpower the shades and escape.'

She could feel Orpheus' eyes on her as they turned down another street. 'What did they want with you?'

'I don't know . . .' Her heart fluttered like a fledgling bird. But she was saved from further interrogation as the musician stopped in front of a row of marble workshops and pointed to a narrow street behind them. The air rang with the peal of hammers.

'My lodgings are just down there.'

He led her down the passageway, halting at a shabby entranceway, before unlatching the cracked oak door.

To call the room lodgings was generous. There was barely enough space for the small table, stool and pallet that filled the entire left-hand wall. The marble dust from the workshops had even found its way through the cracks around the door, coating everything in a fine green powder. It simultaneously gave the place a feeling of abandonment and disease.

In the silence punctuated by the dull hammering of metal on stone, Orpheus dusted off his bag and began filling it with the meagre items scattered around the room.

Scanning the place, Danae frowned. 'Where's your lyre?'

'I sold it,' Orpheus replied as he picked up a small amphora of wine from the table.

She stared at him. When they'd travelled together aboard the *Argo* the lyre was like another limb to the musician. When the instrument had almost been destroyed by the storm that wrecked the Argonauts on Lemnos, he'd been devastated. It was his soul in physical form. She couldn't believe he would ever willingly part from it.

'Why?'

'I needed the coin to travel here.'

'Couldn't you have played for payment? You're the finest musician in Greece!'

Orpheus looked at her with hollow eyes. 'I cannot play without a heart, and mine was dragged to the Underworld the day Eurydice died.'

She couldn't argue with that.

The musician lifted a spare tunic from his stool, rubbing the fabric between his fingers. 'It feels as though the whole world has been poisoned by her death. This terrible war . . .'

'What war?'

'Surely you must have heard? Prince Paris of Troy and Queen Helen of Sparta have eloped. Rumour has it Paris was a guest at the Spartan court and while King Menelaus was called away he seized the chance to take Helen back to Troy. In retaliation Menelaus and his brother, King Agamemnon of Mycenae, have declared war on Troy. Half of Greece has pledged to come to their aid.'

It was testament to how little time Danae had spent in human company over the past year that she had not heard the news. She recalled a fleeting conversation aboard the *Argo* about Helen, allegedly the most beautiful woman alive. Then she remembered something else.

'Eurystheus is King of Mycenae, not this Agamemnon.'

Orpheus shook his head. 'After Heracles chose to join the Argonauts rather than return to Mycenae, the brothers Atreidai attacked the city and deposed Eurystheus. Agamemnon took the crown, and his younger brother Menelaus, by way of marriage, took Sparta.'

Danae blinked. Kingdoms had fallen in the time she had been searching for the Underworld. The ordinary people would suffer the most, but she had no space in her heart to care for other people's wars.

'So, where is the entrance to the Underworld?'

'In an old abandoned mine to the west of the town.'

Danae nodded. 'Good, we'll head there as soon as I've retrieved my horse.'

Orpheus hurried to stuff the last of his belongings into his pack.

Danae turned to leave the room and, as she did, the chill breath of fear prickled her neck. She had forgotten, just for a moment, that she did not know if she could trust him. It had been so easy to fall into conversation like they used to on the *Argo*, when the wind bloated the sails, and the oarsmen rested their arms and exchanged idle chatter. But they were Argonauts no longer. He may not know that she had killed Dolos, but Orpheus still might be an agent of the Twelve. He was desperate to bring his wife back from the land of the dead, and desperate men will do anything for that which they desire.

She rubbed her eyes. It would be the cruellest fate of all to fall into the Olympians' clutches when she might be so close to seeing her sister again.

As she thought of the Underworld, the voice echoed Prometheus' final instruction in her mind: *Go to Delos. Seek out Metis.*

'Be quiet,' she muttered.

You cannot run from your destiny.

'I said be quiet!'

'I didn't say anything . . .' Orpheus stood behind her, wearing an expression of concern. 'Are you all right?'

'I'm fine.' She balled her trembling hands into fists. 'Let's go.'

*

Danae and Orpheus made their way out through Taenarum's gates and clambered down the rocky slope to where she'd left Hylas.

The familiar hand of dread squeezed her insides when she found no alabaster horse waiting amongst the grey stones and sun-crisped grass. Had he finally left her? Had someone taken him?

She clicked her tongue. Nothing.

'Hylas, I've got wine!'

She was answered by the mournful call of the wind. Then a dash of white appeared from behind the cliffs, and Hylas soared through the sky like the moon escaping a clutch of clouds.

Grinning, she ran to the horse as he landed and threw her arms around his neck. Hylas' mane was encrusted with salt. She drew back. 'What have you been doing? And where's my cloak?'

Hylas ignored her and sniffed in Orpheus' direction.

The musician gaped.

'What? Never seen a flying horse before?'

Slowly, still staring at Hylas, Orpheus shook his head. When he'd recovered enough to speak, he said, 'How did you . . . where did you . . . it's called Hylas?'

'Yes.' Danae set about unbuckling one of the saddle pouches and retrieved a small bowl from within.

'Hylas, not Heracles?'

Her cheeks flushed. When the winged horse approached her atop the Caucasus Mountains, it had felt right to name him after the friend who had saved her life and in return lost his own to the Earthborn on the Doliones' shore, rather than the lover she had stolen from and abandoned.

'Give me the wine.' She avoided the musician's gaze as she walked over and snatched the amphora from his hand.

Pulling the cork with her teeth, she slopped the liquid into the bowl and set it on the ground. Hylas lowered his head and drank greedily, flecking his muzzle with drops the colour of blood.

'Did everyone know about us?' she asked quietly.

Orpheus shifted a stone between his feet. 'It wasn't spoken about, but the way you looked at each other . . . it seemed obvious to me.'

The air grew stiflingly thick. She wished she hadn't asked.

'Got any food in that bag?'

Orpheus nodded.

'Good. We should eat, keep our strength up. Gods know what's waiting for us in that mine.'

The musician delved into his pack and proffered her a hunk of bread. She tore it, giving one half to Orpheus, the other she tore again, dropping one piece into Hylas' bowl, shoving the other into her mouth. She folded her arms around herself as she chewed. Despite the bright sun, the wind felt like it blew from the depths of winter. She wished she still had Heracles' lion hide.

On her journey to discover the entrance to the Underworld she had passed through Corinth, where she'd first met Heracles and his crew. She knew it wasn't safe for her to carry the fur, let alone wear it. Useful as it was to have a hide impenetrable to any blade, Heracles' famous lion skin was as recognizable as the man himself. So she'd buried it under the stars, leaving nothing but a small mound of earth. She'd sat before it, her hands smothered in dirt, recalling the scent of the oiled wood of the *Argo* and the chatter of the crew's voices as they rowed, woven with the rasp of the ever-constant waves. Lastly, she allowed herself to think of Heracles, of his lips on her skin, and the warmth he'd teased from her body. She had sobbed until her tears ran dry, cradled in the exquisite ache of remembering what it felt like not to be alone.

She swallowed her mouthful of bread and turned to Orpheus.

'We should go before we lose the light.'

The musician nodded.

'Lead the way.' As he walked past her, she added, 'Remember what I am, Orpheus.' And for good measure she sent a flurry of life-threads into the earth so the stones around her feet danced. 'If this is a trap, you will not live to regret betraying me.'

Orpheus looked back, his eyes bloodshot and weary. 'I don't know what I've done to earn your mistrust. We were comrades once.'

'It's not personal. I don't trust anyone.'

The sun descended towards the ocean as the three of them trudged towards the western side of Cape Taenarum. Danae drew in deep lungfuls of the salty sea breeze. Soon they would be underground and gods know when she would next smell the waves. If she ever would again.

'Did you learn anything about the mine from the locals?' she asked. There were places on her home island of Naxos that no one would tread, superstitions ingrained over the years through whispered fireside tales. Yet there was often a kernel of truth within these stories. Perhaps it was the same here.

'They say there is a vast bed of green marble beneath the mine, buried deep. Many years ago, when the mine was built, the crest of the rock was discovered by chance. To reach it, the foreman ordered the shaft to be dug deeper than they'd ever gone before. It was dangerous, but the marble was worth so much the miners took the risk. Soon they began to return to the surface with stories of invisible beings and floating crimson eyes.'

'Shades,' breathed Danae.

'Exactly. Then, three decades ago, the shaft collapsed. Twenty-one miners were killed. People said it was punishment for burrowing too close to a place where the living did not belong, and no one dared reopen the mine for fear of it being cursed.' Orpheus stopped and pointed across the undulating coast to a mound of stones further along the headland. 'There.'

They paced along the cliff edge until the mouth of the old mine yawned open before them. The red earth within the exterior shell looked to Danae like the fleshy caverns of a great mouth. The stone walls were strengthened by beams of timber and a litter of ropes and pulley systems lay discarded around it. Above the entrance, carved into a stone above the lintel, was a likeness of the god Hephaestus. He was the smith of the gods and patron deity of all blacksmiths, builders and craftsmen. He was depicted here without the usual armour and regalia of the Twelve, clothed in a simple tunic, wielding a chisel and mallet. Below the image an inscription read: *Lord of stone and metal, guide our tools to strike true.*

She took a step towards the darkness then turned at the sound of Hylas braying behind her.

'Shhh.' She returned to the winged horse, smoothing his coat, but he only grew more agitated, rearing on his hind legs and flexing his wings.

She grabbed at his mane. 'Hylas, please!'

Her heart rattled in her chest as his hooves left the ground. He was going to fly away, abandon her when she needed him most.

'*Sorrow is the song love sings . . .*'

Danae glanced back at Orpheus in surprise. She had forgotten the power of that voice. It cracked with disuse, but still flowed with the sweetness and purity of a fresh mountain spring.

'*Mournful, she cries to the gloom,*
Her teardrops form pearly rings,
On blood-red anemone's bloom . . .'

As the melody curled around Danae's mind, she was struck by a sudden realization. Before the vision that had led her to Athens, the omphalos shard had shown her a songbird singing alone into an empty cave. Only, now she realized it hadn't been a cave. It was a mine. A flare of hope swelled in her chest, another grain of proof that, despite what the voice believed, fate was on the side of finding her sister.

With Orpheus' song, Hylas calmed and returned to the earth, the panic fading from his eyes.

The musician tailed off, his singing stifled by tears. 'I told you, my voice is not what it was.'

'It's still beautiful,' she whispered. 'Thank you.'

Orpheus wiped his eyes. Then he delved into his bag, brought out a torch and bashed two stones until the end, wrapped in oil-soaked rags, burst into flame. He proffered it to her.

'You keep it. I'll need my hands free for whatever we meet down there.'

Orpheus paled but he nodded. 'You never told me who you're looking for.'

Her instinct was to lie, yet the musician's song had disarmed her.

'My sister.'

'I hope you find her.'

'And you your Eurydice.'

She might be making a grave mistake, but what else could she do? Kill him? Bind him in rope and leave him helpless in the mine to starve? Like her, he walked a life strangled by grief. Who was she to deny him the chance to find his wife?

They shared one last look then, side by side, walked into the darkness.

5. The Mines of Taenarum

As they entered the mine, Danae kept her hand on Hylas' neck, drawing comfort from his warmth in the cold darkness.

'It's all right,' she whispered, attempting to soothe herself as much as the horse.

Her skin prickled as they stepped further into the murky depths of the cavern, the light behind them dwindling, replaced by the fire of Orpheus' torch. The air grew increasingly dank and stale, trapped by the tightly packed walls of earth. The torchlight illuminated the remains of several campfires scattered about the abandoned mining equipment. Travellers perhaps, desperate for shelter, or local children daring each other to prove who could last the longest before the ghostlike shadows sent them fleeing for home. In their youth that was just the sort of thing Danae's brothers, Calix and Santos, would have done.

The spacious cavern narrowed at the rear, funnelling into a passageway just large enough for Danae and Orpheus to walk beside Hylas. There were track marks on the floor, an abandoned cart lay turned on its side, and gleaming chunks of green marble spilled across the ground. The locals must have truly feared what lay ahead if they had left this much valuable stone to gather dust.

Danae caught sight of a roughly daubed mark across the passage's lintel that looked as though it had been hastily scrawled. The all-seeing eye of the Twelve. A desperate attempt to protect the town of Taenarum from the horrors the locals feared had been set loose inside the mine.

The air grew colder as the passageway sloped downwards. The walls here were made of sheer rock, rather than packed earth, and they glistened with silvery condensation tracks – the supposed tears the local lad, Georgios, had spoken of.

Hylas huffed out a misted breath, his tail flicking his flanks. Danae glanced back over her shoulder, her neck twinging from continually checking the length of tunnel in their wake. Every few yards she imagined red eyes looming out of the darkness.

'Do you think there's any truth to it? What the locals believe about this place?' asked Orpheus.

'That it's haunted?' Her own voice sounded strange, distorted by the blood thrumming in her ears. 'It's not the dead I'm worried about.'

The torch trembled in Orpheus' hand. 'I pray Hades will be merciful. I would give anything to bring Eurydice back home, even if it means taking her place.'

Danae remained silent. She had grown up believing, like everyone else, that there was an uneasy alliance between Olympus and the Underworld. It was said, at the birth of the world, Hades was begrudgingly forced to rule over the land of the dead while Zeus gave their other brother, Poseidon, dominion over the seas. Even if the tales were false, like so much of what she'd been told, he was still one of the Twelve and the younger brother of Zeus, King of the Gods. The deity whose reign she was destined to destroy. She must avoid Hades at all costs.

'Do you think he will look kindly on us because you are his niece?' continued Orpheus.

'What?'

'Poseidon is your father, is he not?'

The lie she had told aboard the *Argo*. She cursed silently to herself. Try as she might to fit effortlessly into her old disguise, she could not help bursting the seams and tearing the fabric.

'Of course, but I do not count on Hades' favour. We should tread carefully. Hades might be angry that we have entered his kingdom uninvited. If we can, we should avoid him altogether.'

Orpheus shook his head. 'He is the only one who can give me my Eurydice back – I must petition him. Besides, they say Persephone, his wife, is a sweet, caring goddess, I know I can convince her to take pity on our plight; me a mourning husband, you a loyal sister . . .'

When Danae did not reply, he continued, 'Do you think the stories are true about the creature that guards the entrance to the Underworld? I've heard Kerberos is a monstrosity, more terrible than anything Heracles ever faced and –'

'Orpheus, be quiet.' An ache throbbed behind Danae's eyes.

They continued in silence, save for the clip-clop of Hylas' hooves and the trickling water running down the walls.

Suddenly, Orpheus stopped. 'Look there,' he breathed.

Danae crept forward into the pool of firelight and crouched to investigate what lay across their path. It was a skeleton, the flesh almost entirely wasted, just a wisp of hair and an old grey tunic clinging to mouldering bones.

She pointed to the corpse's shattered legs. 'Probably broken by the collapsing shaft.' Or something else, she thought, but did not voice it. Marks stretched from the body into the blackness of the tunnel. 'They tried to drag themself out,' she murmured.

'Gods . . .' Orpheus paled.

'Come on.' Danae walked past the body, gesturing for him to follow. The musician picked his way around the bones. When the sound of hooves did not follow, she called, 'Hylas.'

The horse wouldn't move.

'Hylas, come here.'

The horse sniffed at the body and tossed his head. Danae sighed, walked back to the corpse and moved the bones to the side of the passage.

'What are you doing?' Orpheus looked horrified. 'You can't just shove them aside, what if their ghost takes offence?'

Danae dusted the dirt from her hands. 'They've been left here to rot. I doubt they'll care about being moved a foot.'

'Wouldn't you care if someone treated your sister's remains like that?'

A surge of rage burned her throat, but as she opened her mouth to voice it, Hylas trotted towards them and nibbled Orpheus' ear. The musician smiled and patted his neck. As Danae watched them, her anger cooled.

'Aren't you at least going to say the funeral rites?' prompted Orpheus.

Of course, she was supposed to be a seer.

She huffed a breath through her nose, then swiftly intoned, 'May the Twelve see you and know you, may the Keres spread their wings over you as you walk the path of judgement. May your soul find peace across the final river.' Finally, she touched her finger to her forehead.

Once the ritual was performed, Hylas stalked ahead as though nothing had happened. She shook her head. Sometimes it seemed like the winged horse riled her for sheer enjoyment.

The tunnel continued to descend, the torchlight licking up its gleaming walls until the orange glow spilled over a ledge.

'This is where the shaft must have collapsed,' said Orpheus, peering into the darkness.

They stood on the edge of a vast ravine. Veins of green marble snaked through walls of solid rock, falling away into the blackness below. The remains of a wooden platform with a rope pulley system clung to the ledge, the rest of the contraption lost to the ravine.

'What do you think, Hylas? Can you take us down?'

The horse eyed them both, then lowered his head. Danae helped Orpheus climb onto Hylas' back, his legs behind the horse's wing joints, then she swung herself up in front. She gave Hylas' neck a last smooth before winding her fingers through his mane and whispering, 'Go slow, we can't lose the light.' She looked back at the musician. 'Hold on to me. Flying can be a shock the first time.'

Orpheus wrapped his free arm around her waist.

To his credit, he only let out a small gasp as they soared into the air. Danae had grown to love the motion of Hylas' body in flight. It reminded her of being at sea. In the past year, between the bouts of running, stealing and life-thread training, on a cloudy day, she'd urge the winged horse higher and higher until they broke through the barrier of mist into the boundless sky beyond. It was like being suspended in a vast ocean of air. There was only stillness beyond the clouds, in that never-ending blue. And when the sun rose in the east and spilt its light across the white carpet beneath, the whole world looked golden. Up there she felt detached from the earth below. All the pain, the fear, the longing.

The torch stuttered as Hylas flapped his wings.

'Easy now,' Danae called as they jolted down past the marble-threaded rock. A bitter coldness enveloped them, the air so oppressive it felt as though it had not been disturbed for several lifetimes. Hylas took them lower and lower and still she could not see the bottom. She began to wonder if there was an end at all, if the poor miners who'd been caught in the collapse were still falling endlessly into the darkness.

'Look, below on the far wall!' shouted Orpheus.

She peered down, her eyes raking across the rock until she spotted a horizontal split, just wide enough for Hylas to alight.

The horse landed on the ledge and once she and Orpheus had dismounted, Danae took in their surroundings. The cleft in the stone gave way to another passage, similar in size to the first, yet here the walls were smooth and rippled like a seabed, as though they had been worn down by the elements, rather than chiselled by man.

They did not have to go far before encountering their first challenge. A fork in their path. The passage was revealed to be part of a series of natural tunnels that burrowed into the rock bed, splitting into a labyrinth.

'Which way?' asked Orpheus.

As Danae gazed at the passages, she glimpsed a dash of movement in the one on the left. She grabbed the torch from Orpheus and ran a few steps into the tunnel. The undulations in the stone threw pitted shadows along its length, but the passage appeared empty.

'Did you see that?'

'No.'

'There was movement, I saw something . . .'

'There's nothing there, Daeira,' he pressed, then repeated, 'Which way do we go?'

She turned slowly to look at him. Orpheus' face was drawn in the flame light. Unease crawled up her spine. Was he deceiving her?

'How did you discover there was an entrance to the Underworld in Taenarum?'

The musician's brow furrowed. 'A farmer in the neighbouring village to mine said he'd heard there was an entrance at the furthest point of mainland Greece. He could tell me little else, but I had to try . . .'

Danae stared at him, wishing her gaze could pierce those red-rimmed eyes and lay bare what thoughts swam beneath.

She looked back at the tunnels and forced herself to make a choice.

'We go this way.'

Their path split again and again. Each time they were forced to choose, Danae tried not to think of the odds mounting against them. Orpheus followed at her heels like a child, always looking to her to decide the way. She cursed herself again for not extracting more information from Theseus. A map for a start.

Her mouth had grown parched. They could have been below ground for hours or days, without the sun she could not tell.

'Take this,' she proffered Orpheus the torch and drew out a waterskin from Hylas' saddle bag, along with his bowl. She poured the horse a drink, took a draught herself, then offered the skin to the musician. 'Don't suppose you've got any more food in that bag?'

Orpheus shook his head, took a glug, then handed back the skin.

They only had enough water between them to last another day or two. After that it would be a slow, painful death by dehydration.

'Before, you said you wanted to bring Eurydice home,' Danae said as she packed away Hylas' bowl. 'How will you do that?'

'I will convince Hades to fashion her a new body, just like the old one.'

Danae's chest tightened. 'You believe he has that power?'

'Yes,' Orpheus said simply. 'The gods can do anything.'

She thought of Hera, the Queen of the Gods, blazing

in golden majesty, as she had hurled spears of ice at Danae atop the Caucasus Mountains. Fear, all-encompassing as the darkness around them, threatened to consume her as she imagined what would happen if she fell into Hades' hands.

The musician will not find what he seeks. Nor will you, said the voice. *There is no afterlife in the Underworld.*

A wave of weariness crashed over her. It was much harder to battle the voice when she was sleep-deprived and ravenous.

She tucked the waterskin back in the far saddle bag, but as she reached for the strap the horse jerked away from her, tossing his head.

'Shh now, it's –' Something dry and scaly clamped over her mouth. Instinctively she jabbed her elbows backwards, hitting whatever was behind her. A burst of hot breath was expelled on the back of her neck, but her assailant didn't let go. So, she twisted, pummelling with all her strength.

Orpheus cried out as behind her the air shimmered under her blows, punctuated by a pair of crimson eyes with pupils of deepest midnight.

Memories hurtled through her mind. Her nephew Arius' cries as he was ripped from Alea's bed, the charcoal-cloaked shade staring at her in the Athenian flesh market, the dull grey body of the dead shade she had killed outside the city of Colchis.

Some of her punches landed, and at last one of her kicks uprooted the shade. They tumbled together, smacking into the rocky ground. Hylas was braying and Orpheus shouting, but the sounds blurred into the drum of blood in her ears as she scrabbled to locate the shade.

Then everything went dark. Orpheus must have dropped the torch.

'Orpheus!'

The musician did not reply, but she could hear groans. With the loss of her vision, every noise was intensified; the clatter of Hylas' hooves on the rock, the panting of breath.

To her left, she could hear heavy breathing. She stretched out until her fingers touched leathery skin. Gripping onto what might have been an arm or a leg, she dragged the shade towards her. The creature flailed, trying to smack her away as she clambered on top of it. She worked her way up to its head and smashed it into the ground until she felt the shade's muscles slacken beneath her. Something warm and wet seeped beneath her fingers. It was near death, its life-threads beginning to flee back into the earth. She had a limited window to consume them; once the life force left its body, the power of the shade's threads would be lost.

Just as she was about to drain the creature, she was interrupted by braying from somewhere far away.

'Hylas!' she screamed, leaping up and stumbling in the darkness towards the sound. She tripped on something lying across her path, and Orpheus yelped as she crashed down on top of him. 'Hylas!' she cried again, but she could no longer hear the horse, not even the click of his hooves on the rock.

'Hylas . . .' she whispered, choking on the realization that he was gone. Her faithful companion, her one true friend. How could she have been so selfish? She should have let him go at the entrance to the mine, told him to fly away and be free. He had been scared; he knew something was wrong before they even set foot in the place and yet she'd forced him to come with her.

'Daeira,' Orpheus grabbed hold of her. 'The torch . . . I'm sorry, something knocked me down . . . Are they gone?'

She pulled him to his feet. 'We have to find Hylas. The other shades must have taken him.' Then she dragged the musician in the direction she'd last heard the winged horse.

She stretched out her free hand until her fingers touched cold stone and began treading carefully along the passage, wary at any moment of a hidden drop.

'They will have come from the Underworld,' she said with more confidence than she felt. 'That's where they'll have gone.'

Orpheus did not voice his reply, but his fingers tightened around hers.

As they felt their way together in the pitch darkness, she hoped with every life-thread in her body that she was right.

6. Gates of Bronze

It was difficult to gauge their progress with no light to guide them. Danae had given up counting the twists and turns in the passage, struggling to adjust to the sightless world of touch. Every sound was amplified, Orpheus' ragged breath grating on her ears. She could no longer visualize the rocky tunnel around her, could not tell if the walls were narrowing or widening. The darkness itself seemed to take on a viscous quality, its heaviness weighing on her chest, squeezing her breath. If she had not been so aware of her body, it would have felt like being drawn into the omphalos shard's vision realm, her consciousness suspended in the void of nothingness.

Suddenly, she stopped moving.

'What is it?' Orpheus' grip tightened on her hand.

She groaned. In the aftermath of the shade attack she had been so distraught by Hylas' capture, she'd not given thought to the horse's saddle bag being taken with him. She'd lost the omphalos shard.

'All my belongings were with Hylas.'

'Don't worry,' Orpheus squeezed her fingers, 'I have enough coins for the ferryman to take us both across the River Styx to the Asphodel Meadows.' This was the realm of the Underworld supposedly populated by the virtuous dead, where Alea and Eurydice should be.

You should never have come here, said the voice. *You should have turned back, while you still could.*

'Shut up,' she spat.

Orpheus flinched.

'Not you, I meant . . . it doesn't matter.'

Strangely, now she couldn't see Orpheus, her suspicion of him waned. She could feel the truth of his terror through his grip, the way he clung to her as though she were saving him from drowning. He was a man willing to walk into the jaws of death because he couldn't live without his wife. Surely he was no agent of the Twelve.

'We'll find them, Orpheus. Eurydice and my sister.'

His grip softened a little as they continued to feel their way along the passage.

After several paces he asked, 'What's her name?'

Danae hesitated before answering. 'Alea.'

Her heart ached. She had not spoken her sister's name aloud for a very long time. She hoped her family still talked of Alea; she could not bear the thought that her sister might be forgotten. Or remembered only as a whore who danced with the Maenads.

'That's a lovely name. It means "she of the sweet voice", does it not?'

'Yes,' Danae whispered.

'She's lucky to have a sister like you.'

Danae could not bring herself to reply.

They trudged on, a pair of pounding hearts and echoing footsteps in the darkness.

After a while Orpheus squeezed her hand. 'Can you hear that?'

They both grew still and Danae strained to listen. There were vibrations rumbling from somewhere far away: a low rhythmic humming.

'Daeira, I think . . . it's a song.'

'How can you tell?'

'It sounds just like an old Thracian tune my grandfather used to whistle.'

Danae's pulse quickened. 'Let's follow it.'

As they felt their way towards the vibrations, the darkness seemed to fade from an inky black to a grey gloom. Then something shifted across her vision. She froze, imagining it was a shade, but then the movement came again. A pulse of white light up ahead.

'Orpheus –'

'I can see it.'

The quality of the air had changed too. It was ripe with a mildewy musk.

They stumbled towards the faint light like moths to a flame. After being in the dark for so long, when the bursts came Danae was forced to squint against the sudden brightness.

When they grew close enough to make out the source, it was revealed to be tiny pulses of light travelling along strands of hair-thin roots laced over the tunnel wall.

'The music's stopped,' said Orpheus.

Danae did not care. They had found light. She reached out with her free hand and touched the rock between the strands. It was damp. Tentatively she prodded one of the strings. The light changed direction, darting from her touch back along the network of roots, like a ripple across a pool.

'They're beautiful,' breathed Orpheus.

'The wall's moist. There must be water coming from somewhere. Perhaps we're near the Styx.'

As they walked on, the roots thickened, and the beats of light became bright enough to make out the shape of the widening passage. Even so, she and Orpheus kept hold of each other's hand. Soon, they found themselves clambering over twisting roots as thick as human limbs. Then, all of a sudden, the tunnel came to an abrupt end.

Ahead of them was a space so vast, it felt as though they had travelled to another world. For a moment Danae thought they had somehow reached the surface, for far above their heads were lights that shone in the blackness like stars. But these heavens were not the ones she knew, their constellations as alien to her as the strange glowing roots.

Below this unfamiliar sky, the pulsing tendrils peeled away from the mouth of the passage, entwining over the rocky ground, leaving a clear pathway towards a pair of gigantic bronze doors at least forty feet high. On either side of these metallic gates, the roots knotted together, mounting into a tangled wall, so tall it was impossible to see what lay beyond.

'This must be it.' Orpheus let go of Danae's hand and took a step towards the doors.

She grabbed his tunic and drew him back into the relative gloom of the passage. Then she crouched down, searching the ground. When her fingers found a loose stone, she hurled it into the middle of the pathway and waited.

Save the gentle throbbing of the roots, there was no movement. No shimmering distortions in the air.

After lingering for what felt like an age, Danae nodded to Orpheus, and they both re-emerged from the tunnel. With each step along the tendril-lined path, her heart fought harder to escape the confines of her chest. If this was the entrance to the Underworld, why was it apparently left unguarded?

As they drew nearer the bronze door, she could see it too was webbed with finger-thin roots. There were no markings or any sign of a knocker or handle. Below the glowing strands, the great doors seemed to be just slabs of plain metal.

The surface world was littered with statues, murals and effigies of the Olympians. She had expected a vast likeness of Hades to preside over the entrance to his kingdom, something to state his ownership. But the Lord of the Underworld seemed surprisingly unostentatious.

'How do we get in?' whispered Orpheus.

Danae ran her hands over the crease in the doors, then pushed. Unsurprisingly the bronze did not move.

'Get back.'

Orpheus did as she bid him. She summoned a swell of life-threads into her hands and hurled a blast of wind at the doors. The bronze shuddered, ringing like a great bell, but remained in place. The roots recoiled where the concentrated air had struck them, then slowly snaked back into place.

'Gods, it's like they're some sort of creature,' breathed Orpheus.

Danae glanced behind her, searching for any crimson eyes looming from the passage. None came.

'Keep a look out for shades, I'm going to try and climb over.'

She waded through the roots to the right of the door, then began ascending the twisted wall, all the while trying not to think about the surprisingly warm, flesh-like quality of the coils.

'They're holding my weight. Come on,' she called to Orpheus when she had almost reached the top. 'I'm coming, Hylas,' she murmured under her breath.

Then the tendril beneath her moved. Quick as a heron darting for its prey, the root whipped from under her feet and, before she hit the ground, caught her around her waist. She barely had time to cry out before it had tossed her into the air to land in a heap back on the path.

'Are you all right?' Orpheus ran over to her.

Danae sat up, bruised but otherwise unharmed. She took the musician's outstretched hand, and he heaved her to her feet.

'I'm really starting to hate those roots.'

*

Danae sat on the path, sweat prickling her brow as she glared at the bronze doors. She and Orpheus had made several more attempts to climb the root walls and each time were unceremoniously tossed back to the ground. She had returned to trying force, rumbling the earth and whipping torrent after torrent of air into the glowing tendrils, but each time she cleared a hole, they immediately wove back into their original pattern. And no matter how many life-threads she flung at the doors, the bronze gates remained steadfast.

Weariness began to weigh heavy in her limbs. She couldn't keep using her finite supply of life-threads, not with the risk of more shades appearing at any moment. She had given thought to draining threads from the network of roots, but they were so strange and otherworldly, she was afraid of what they might do to her if she consumed them.

Orpheus crouched beside the tangled tendrils, gazing at their undulating lights and giving them the occasional prod.

'We could wait for someone else to open the door?' he offered. 'There must be someone behind there who needs to come out at some point.'

'Gods know how long that will be.' Danae pressed the heels of her palms into her eyes. This was almost worse than being lost in the dark.

'Daeira!'

She jerked her hands away from her face.

Orpheus was on his feet, his face shining with excitement. 'It's the roots!'

She opened her mouth to question his meaning, then realized she could hear the vibrations again.

'They're making the music.' Orpheus grinned, staring at the tendrils like they were the chorus of a play.

As she watched him, her eyes widened. Force evidently wasn't going to work, but charm might.

'Orpheus, sing!'

'What?'

She pushed herself to her feet. 'My powers evidently aren't much help here. If the roots can make music, they may respond to it. We've got to try. Or we can sit here and wait for more shades to come through those doors and kill us.'

He stared at her, then nodded. 'All right.' He cleared his throat.

His voice rasped on the first few notes, then the rust fell away, and a pure, unwavering melody spilled from his lips. It was the same song the roots had been humming, and in response to his tune their lights raced faster and faster until every tendril seemed lit up from within.

'Keep going,' Danae urged.

Was it her imagination or was there a quiver of movement from the doors? Her hopes lifted further at the unmistakable screech of metal on stone, and sure enough the great bronze doors began to creak open.

'Yes!' Danae's heart soared.

Then Orpheus' voice cracked. He stopped singing.

The gates froze, then began to close.

'No, no, no, Orpheus, keep going!'

The musician struck up his tune once more, the doors stilled, then he faltered.

'I . . . I can't remember the words.'

With a groan, the bronze gates continued to close.

'Shit.' Danae grabbed hold of Orpheus' hand. 'Run!'

They sprinted forwards, hurtling towards the ever-narrowing gap, and threw themselves through the crack a heartbeat before the doors crashed shut.

They remained sprawled on the ground while they caught their breath. Danae looked at Orpheus and smiled with relief. They were lying on sand, black as a midnight sky, that rolled away from the bronze gates in undulating dunes towards the bank of a wide river, the water beyond inky as the obsidian shore.

The River Styx.

Hope swelled in Danae's chest. She hadn't wanted to admit to herself how terrified she had been of what she would find when she reached the Underworld, that the river of death and the three realms – Elysium, the Asphodel Meadows and Tartarus – might not exist at all. That Prometheus would be proven right.

'Where are the souls of the unburied?' asked Orpheus as they rose to their feet and dusted off the black sand.

Like all mortals, they had been brought up to believe that when a person died their body must be buried and the proper funeral rites performed, or their ghost would be doomed to wander the banks of the Styx for all eternity. But there was no one here, nothing but the sand, water and the darkness beyond.

There is no afterlife in the Underworld, repeated the voice.

Danae ignored the sudden sinking sensation in her stomach. 'Perhaps they don't wander this part of the river.'

Her sandals melted into the sand as she walked towards the water, the itch between her toes a familiar comfort. She glanced back at Orpheus. 'Do you think it's strange that we've not seen any more shades since that ambush in the tunnel?'

Orpheus looked about, his face grey under the sickly light of the strange Underworld stars. 'I suppose . . . Perhaps they found what they were seeking.'

Danae's gut twisted as she thought of Hylas, and what those creatures might be doing to him. She must find him, as well as Alea.

'Daeira, look!'

Orpheus pointed to where the river curved away into the distance. A sleek barge fashioned from dark wood was being punted against the current by a charcoal-cloaked figure, a light similar to the ones in the sky glowing at the end of its staff.

'The ferryman,' breathed Danae.

Orpheus hastily drew his purse from his bag and pressed two obols into her hand.

A heartbeat later, the coins slipped from her fingers to be swallowed by the midnight sand. The ferryman had almost reached the bank, his barge floating through the dark current like an autumn leaf on a slick of tar. He was close enough now for her to see what lay beneath the charcoal cloak.

A pair of crimson eyes.

She was transported through time, her feet no longer held by sand but melded to the stage in the Athenian theatre, bound in chains, the air ripe with fear and piss. She could feel a sea of eyes bearing down at her, but only saw one pair shining scarlet beneath a charcoal hood.

Wrenching herself from the memory, she regained control of her body and backed away.

The ferryman reached the bank and drove his staff into the sand, pulling the tip of the barge up onto the shore.

Orpheus approached. 'Please,' he called, 'take us to Hades!'

'Orpheus!' Danae cried, as the ferryman reached out an arm sheathed in a black hide glove and turned his palm to the sky. The musician proffered his silver coins then froze, his eyes widening as he caught sight of what lay beneath the charcoal hood.

Danae's pulse thundered. If she set foot on that barge, it would all be over. She had revealed her powers in the passages. The shades that took Hylas might well have warned the other denizens of the Underworld. The ferryman would surely hand her over to Hades and then he might give her to Zeus . . .

Orpheus staggered back, just as the ferryman turned his hooded head towards her.

The shade lowered his hand then reached beneath his cloak. Before he could reveal whatever weapon it concealed, Danae summoned a clutch of life-threads and hurled a blast of wind at the ferryman. The shade careered back and tumbled into the inky waters of the Styx.

'Come on!' she shouted to Orpheus and sprinted towards the barge.

The musician sprang into action, racing behind her. But just before they reached the vessel a long, piercing note ripped through the air.

Danae turned to see the ferryman half emerged from the river, an ebony horn held to his lips.

Then the ground shook.

Danae crashed into Orpheus and the pair fell together onto the black sand. The earth rumbled again, as though it was being pounded by a giant. The tremor dislodged the barge, and it slid back into the water, floating out of reach. Then a shape emerged from the gloom far along the bank. The creature was vast, the thud of its great feet accompanied by a cacophony of hissing. The nearer it drew, the quicker it ran, as though it had caught the scent of its prey.

Despite herself, Danae screamed.

Charging towards them was the largest hound she had ever seen, as long as the *Argo* and as tall as an oak. Its coat was as black as the sand and from its thick neck sprouted three snarling heads, ropes of spittle dangling from teeth the length of her arm. Like the shades, its three pairs of eyes burned like red-hot coals. With another jolt of terror, she located the source of the hissing. From the scruff of its three necks sprouted over a hundred snakes, their serpentine bodies writhing over each other like a scaled, living mane. Finally, as if the beast wasn't terrible enough, a scorpion's tail curved up behind its back, a sting as long as her leg poised and glistening.

This must be the beast Orpheus spoke of: Kerberos, Hades' three-headed hound who guarded the River Styx.

Recovering herself, Danae scrambled onto her feet, whipped a cord of life-threads into the sand and flicked a wave of grains at the hound. With no blade to fight with, she had no hope of killing it without weakening it first. She would have a better chance if she blinded its eyes. All six of them.

Kerberos' central head roared, tossing furiously as its other two snarled.

Two down, four to go.

As though connected by one mind, the snakes stopped writhing and stretched into the air, fanning out like a spray of deadly peacock feathers around the creature's neck.

'You just made it angrier!' called Orpheus.

Danae ignored his comment and shouted, 'Run!' before throwing another torrent of life-threads into the air and hurling them towards Kerberos. The force of the gale sent the beast stumbling back, then its scorpion tail darted forward. She had to fling herself across the sand to avoid being impaled by the stinger. She twisted onto her back just in time to see the dog lunge towards Orpheus, who was running across the shore. Summoning more life-threads, she hurled another concentrated blast of air at the beast's belly. The hound was caught mid-leap and slammed into the sand. She staggered to her feet and ran towards it, cursing herself for wasting so much energy trying to open the bronze gates.

Just as Kerberos pushed its sinewy body off the sand,

Danae leapt. She wrapped her limbs around its scorpion tail and clung on. Digging her thighs into the groove between two segments, she held on tight as the beast roared again and thrashed its tail. Screaming with the effort, she thrust a hoard of life-threads into her arms and with all her strength, twisted.

A bellow of pain exploded from the hound. Danae crashed onto the sand, falling from the severed stinger. She was soaked in something warm and sticky. She prayed to the fates it was blood rather than poison. Barely able to fill her heaving lungs, she staggered to her feet, ready to face Kerberos. But the beast was bounding away from her.

She heard Orpheus cry, 'No, no!' and looked round to see him pelting along the shore, desperately trying to catch up with the floating barge, the hound pursuing him.

Danae bolted after them, her legs screaming.

Then Kerberos pounced.

Orpheus turned, at the last moment raising his fists as the giant hound bore down on him. Then one of Kerberos' heads snapped its jaws around the musician's torso.

Danae staggered, falling to her knees as Orpheus' body was ripped between the beast's three maws like he was nothing more than a scrap of meat.

Her mouth stretched into a silent scream. She could not look away, could not move.

Then something cold and hard closed around her neck.

She gasped and fell forward onto the sand. It was as though someone had leached all the colour from the world, along with every drop of warmth and hope. Like her insides had been scraped out and all that remained was an empty hollow.

Her hands flew to her throat, and her fingers met a collar of metal. She tugged at the ring, but it would not give.

The sodden hem of a dark cloak swayed into her line of sight. She looked up to see the ferryman standing over her.

Stretching an arm towards him, she reached for the power of her life-threads.

It did not come.

Panic exploded through her. She tried again and again but each time she searched for her threads, she felt nothing.

'What have you done to me?' she rasped.

The shade tilted his head.

'Help me,' she begged the voice.

It did not answer. Her mind echoed with silence.

Then the ferryman struck her, and darkness fell.

7. A Burning Promise

Hermes, Messenger of the Gods, stood before the moving mosaic sprawled across the wall in the megaron corridor. The precious stones scattered into a flowing rainbow, swirling into the same scene that was triggered each time he passed.

An infant Hermes sat upon a grassy knoll, surrounded by a peach sky sliced through with golden rays. In his tiny hands he held a lyre, fashioned from a hollow tortoise shell. Amongst mortals it was believed that he had created the first version of the instrument on the day of his birth, a lie fed through his priestesses for generations until the myth became truth. The other Olympians all had scenes celebrating real achievements, but Hermes had no cities named after him, no wars had been fought in his honour, and, unlike his father and uncles, he had battled no Titans. When constructing the mosaic, his half-brother, Hephaestus, had said he wanted to commemorate the one thing that gave Hermes joy: his music. It was a gesture born of kindness, something he would never see from his other siblings, but to Hermes it only highlighted his lacking.

He turned away and paced towards the megaron. Better not keep his father waiting.

As he paused before the great doors, inlaid with mother-of-pearl clouds, his thoughts returned to the harpy. The unnatural angles of its bleeding, shattered body as it lay twitching on the stadium arena only hours earlier. He shuddered at the thought of what kind of creature could have wrought such destruction on one of his father's pets.

The groan of the megaron doors opening wrenched him from the memory, and he hurried into the throne room.

The sightless marble eyes of his family stared down at him from the empty thrones encircling the curving wall. Zeus alone sat at the feet of his statue, so still he too might have been cast from stone. Hermes flinched as the doors closed behind him, the guards leaving him to a private audience with his father.

He swallowed, then walked forward to stand on the yellow mosaic of the sun in the centre of the floor. Dropping to his knees, he bowed his head, the clatter of his armour echoing around the vast room.

'Come here.'

Hermes rose, willing himself not to tremble as he approached the steps that led up to the thrones. Once level with his father, he prostrated himself and stared at Zeus' feet. He racked his brain, trying to recall what he might have done to incur individual attention from the King of the Gods. The last time he had been summoned alone to the megaron was because he'd stolen his brother Apollo's prize cattle and hidden them in a cave in the Peloponnese. He could still remember the agony of his lip splitting under his father's gauntlet. But surely Zeus did not blame him for the death of the harpy?

'Look at me.'

Hermes sat up. Meeting Zeus' gaze was like staring into the sun: his father's eyes were so swollen with life-threads his cerulean irises burned gold.

'Do you remember the day I made you a god?'

'Yes, my lord.'

Hermes would never forget it. He had just seen fourteen summers, living with his mortal mother, Maia, in a village on the slope of Mount Cyllene. When the shades came for him, she told him he must be brave, although her own cheeks shone with tears. That was two hundred years ago. He never saw her again.

Hermes had never truly believed he was the son of the King of Heaven until the moment he was brought to this very room. The divine family had been seated on their statue thrones, and there, at the end of the semi-circle, waited a giant likeness of Hermes carved in marble. It had felt like a dream, walking amongst the living, breathing gods of Olympus. They all seemed so much larger than him. So much older. There must be a mistake, he had thought, but then Zeus himself descended from his throne and bade Hermes kneel in the centre of the sun mosaic, as he had done with all Hermes' siblings before him, and produced a wrinkled, golden apple.

He had never seen a fruit like it, shining with a strange glow and soft with decay as though it had been left on its branch far too long. Zeus had bade Hermes take a bite. Reluctant as he'd been, as soon as he sank his teeth into the puckered golden flesh it was as though he had spent his whole existence in a dark cave and was only now emerging into the light. He'd felt the power of his life force pulsating through him and suddenly seen the glowing strands of energy rushing around the bodies of the gods. His new family. His father had placed a hand on his head and said, 'By my power, Hermes, blood of Zeus, you are now divine.' And he had wept without shame, for surely this state was what mortals called paradise.

Hermes flinched at the sound of his father's voice, his focus returning to the present.

'Do you know why I chose to make you divine?'

It felt as though Zeus had somehow read his mind. The question was something he had wondered many times himself. He was the last of Zeus' children to be elevated to godhood, and yet his father continued to spawn mortal children with earth-bound women below, some going on to achieve far greater things in their short lives than anything Hermes' legacy had yielded.

He shook his head.

'I saw you, my son. The man you truly are. I knew you were destined for greatness.'

Hermes' jaw slackened. 'Me?'

Zeus smiled, and suddenly the room felt brighter. Hermes wished the other Olympians were here to see this. His father leant towards him, his voice heady and velvet like incense smoke. 'I have a secret to tell you. A secret you must reveal to no one. Do you understand?'

Hermes nodded eagerly.

'Do you recall the Underworld creature disguised as a mortal girl?'

'The one with strange powers created by Hades for my siblings to hunt?'

Zeus nodded. 'She is still alive. And it is no game she plays.'

Hermes' breath became shallow as he waited for his father to continue.

'I am going to tell you something your siblings do not know. My brother created her without my approval.'

Hermes' eyes widened. Despite their strained alliance, there was one thing his father and his uncle had always agreed on. Dominion over mortals. For centuries Hades had created creatures and sent them up to the surface to wreak havoc on humanity on Zeus' command. The King of the Gods would then dispatch one of his bastard mortal children to take care of them, reminding people the Olympians watched over them and kept them safe. So long as their faith never wavered.

Unease crept up Hermes' spine.

'Father . . . does Hades wish us harm?'

Zeus sighed out a long breath. 'That is the right question. I knew you were the child of mine to entrust with this task.'

Hermes' cheeks flushed.

'You remember why your uncle is forbidden from ever stepping foot above the soil?'

He nodded.

'Hades does not suffer his captivity gladly, and like a caged bird his beak can be vicious. Now, listen carefully.' Zeus leant forward. 'The creature he has made is cunning. She is dangerous. She not only looks like a mortal but thinks like one. Your siblings failed to kill her because they were brash and careless. Power alone is not enough; you must employ your cunning to snare her. I hear mortals call you the God of Tricksters. Perhaps you can succeed where your brothers and sisters have failed. And when you do, bring me her head.' The King of the Gods sat back on his throne.

A myriad of questions burst into Hermes' mind. Normally, he would never dare interrogate Zeus' orders, but he was drunk on his father's flattery. 'Why must I keep it a secret? Last year, we all took part in tracking her. And Athena said she has powers like ours, how can that be? Uncle Hades doesn't have the ability to make gods, only you do, so why –'

Zeus' gauntleted hand twitched, and immediately Hermes fell silent. The warmth had leached from his father's expression, his eyes darkened like thundering clouds.

Hermes dropped his head, unable to bear the anger sharpening the angles of Zeus' face, but his father forcibly lifted his chin.

'I gave you everything.' Zeus spoke so softly his voice was barely more than a whisper. 'I raised you up from the dirt and made you ageless. You are blessed. My own father betrayed his family. He was a good man once, but he forsook all that was dear to him to become a twisted and monstrous Titan. Tell me, Hermes, what did he force me to do?'

'Kill him,' Hermes breathed.

Zeus nodded. 'I threw him from this sacred mountain and made war on the Titans, so their kind would never again threaten my family.' Zeus released Hermes' chin. 'Mortals do not bestow faith easily, my son. Even after I saved them from the Titans, gave them cities and riches beyond imagination, their love was hard won. You have been worshipped since the dawn of your divinity because of me. Everything you are, your very existence, is granted by my grace. And you question me.'

'I'm sorry,' Hermes whispered. 'Please forgive me.'

The chill of his father's stare cut him to the marrow. Tears seeped beneath the cheek plates of his golden helm. 'I will make you proud. I will bring you the head of the Underworld girl, I promise.'

Zeus surveyed his son. 'The harpy tracked her to the Argolid region. Begin there.'

'Yes, my king.' Hermes bowed again, descending the stairs and shuffling backwards towards the megaron doors. 'Thank you for entrusting me with this task.'

As soon as he passed the mother-of-pearl clouds, he turned and ran.

A shower of sparks greeted Hermes as he stepped into Hephaestus' forge. The cavernous room was carved into the mountain rock below the palace of Olympus. Nymphs with soot-encrusted faces rushed around the workshop, manipulating the bellows and tinkering with various mechanical contraptions.

Hephaestus was the second child born from the union of Zeus and Hera, the King and Queen of Heaven. He was, in

Hermes' mind, far superior to his brutish older brother, Ares. It was Hephaestus who had created the Olympians' armour, having discovered a way to smelt the gold while imbuing it with life-threads so it could channel, store and amplify the wearer's power.

The God of Craftsmen leant over a central workbench. He wore a leather apron over his large torso and a bronze mask protected his face. As Hermes bounded down the stairs, his half-brother set down the axe he was grinding and slid up his face-covering.

'What do you want, Pip?' It was a pet name born from Hermes' diminutive stature and his love of playing the pipes.

Hermes pointed to the golden wings attached to the ankle of his left boot. 'I need you to look at the wing joint. Something's not right when I fly long distances, I keep veering off at an angle.'

Hephaestus raised a grizzled eyebrow. 'Nothing wrong with the boots, it's your flying technique.'

Hermes scowled. 'It is not.'

It had been a devastating blow to Hermes to discover after his divinity ceremony that he would remain as he was forever: an ageless man trapped in the body of an undersized youth. He had isolated himself in his chambers for weeks, until Hephaestus visited with his newly forged armour. His brother had told him that his suit was special because it had wings, and if he were any larger, they wouldn't have supported him. The very next day, Hermes had left his chambers to practise. It had taken a good year and many broken bones before he conquered the agility of flight. And that was before testing the boots outside of the safety of Olympus' walls, where he was at the mercy of the wind. But what were years to a god? Now he could soar higher than any bird, any winged horse. He alone was master of the sky.

Hephaestus made a dismissive grunt, flicked down his visor and turned back to the axe. 'I'm busy, come back later.'

'What's that?' Hermes pointed at the weapon.

Once more, Hephaestus pushed back his face-covering. 'It's called an *axe* and you use it to chop —'

'You know what I mean.' Hermes stepped closer. An axe crafted by Hephaestus was never just an axe.

His brother's face stretched into a lopsided grin, and he grasped the weapon in his left hand. He clicked his fingers and beckoned to a couple of nymphs, the bronze brace supporting his right arm reflecting the firelight of the forge.

Hundreds of years ago, Hephaestus had tried to steal a golden apple from their father and uncover the secrets of its divine gifts. As punishment Zeus had thrown him from the palace walls. When Hephaestus had crawled back up the slope of Mount Olympus, Zeus had forbidden him access to the mortals kept prisoner in the Olympus vault. So, without draining the life-threads of another, Hephaestus' body had mended with all the agonizing twists and aches of a mortal recovery. After years of rehabilitation and self-designed apparatus to support his damaged muscles and broken bones, he had taught himself to walk again, but his body could not be remade as it once was.

Hermes swallowed as he thought of how close he'd come to incurring his father's wrath that morning. Hephaestus' disability was a permanent reminder of just how hot Zeus' anger could burn.

His brother spun the axe between his fingers as the nymphs carried over a plank of wood, stopping in front of him to hold it at waist height. Hephaestus pulled down his visor then swung the weapon over his head. The blade sank into the wood with a soft thud. Hermes frowned. Hephaestus hadn't even tried to break the plank, and the nymphs barely even staggered under the blow. How disappointing.

Then the wood exploded.

The nymphs cried out as thousands of needle-sharp splinters shot across the room, embedding in their unprotected flesh.

Hermes grinned. 'Nice.'

Hephaestus returned the axe to the workbench then picked several shards of wood from his scarred forearms. 'Before you ask, no you can't. It's for Ares.'

Hermes' elation soured. 'You could make it faulty . . .'

Hephaestus chuckled. 'As much as I'd like to blow him up, I don't think Father would approve.' He removed his metal visor and ran a hand through his sweaty hair. 'I must get on. Come back tomorrow.'

Hermes drew himself up. 'Ares can wait. Father has tasked me with a secret mission.'

Hephaestus paused. 'You? A secret mission?'

'Yes.'

A strange look crossed his brother's face. 'Fine,' he sighed. 'I'll take a look at the wing now.'

Hermes grinned and set about tugging off his boot.

Hephaestus set it on the workbench and hunched over it. Hermes waited while his brother tinkered, twisting his fingers behind his back to prevent himself fiddling with things he shouldn't.

After several minutes Hephaestus held out the boot. 'Done. One of the feathers was out of place.'

'Ha, I knew it!' Hermes slipped his foot back into the boot and rose into the air, the metallic wings vibrating at his heels. 'Thank you.' Then he added, 'Father will be most pleased.'

As he soared across the workshop Hephaestus called, 'Take care of yourself, Pip.'

Something in his tone made Hermes turn back, but his brother had already returned to grinding Ares' axe.

*

Hermes landed on the steps of the aviary: a stone tower built onto the western wing of the palace. He really should have set off on his father's quest by now, but he'd left his pipes here and he loathed long journeys without them.

He heaved open the oak door and was greeted by a cacophony of caws, chirrups and coos. Wings ruffled and beaked heads twitched at the disruption, feathers drifting through the cavity of the room like blossom shaken from a peach tree. Hermes looked up to the large window at the top of the tower, where the birds entered and exited to relay their messages. Nearest this portal of sky, resting on perches secured to the walls, were Zeus' eagles. Below them were Artemis' buzzards and Ares' falcons, and beneath them an iron grate sliced the tower horizontally in two to prevent the birds of prey attacking their smaller cousins below. Great care had to be taken with the comings and goings around the tower to protect the more vulnerable birds. The eagles were particularly aggressive.

Hermes stepped around a fresh pile of droppings splattered across the stone floor. As he took the steps that curved upwards along the wall, he strummed the chains of the dangling homing medallions, leaving a chiming discord in his wake. The pendants were emblazoned with each of the Olympians' sigils, given mainly to kings and priestesses so they could convey messages to the Twelve.

He stopped still. He'd been so absorbed in his thoughts he hadn't noticed the figure sitting on the ledge of one of the barred windows further up the steps.

Aphrodite's face glowed in the sunlight, her undulating copper hair dancing like flames in the breeze, her white dress pouring over her curves to drape across the steps below. She held a dove in her hands, smoothing the creature's feathers.

What Hermes would give to be that bird.

Aphrodite was married to Hephaestus, but Ares was the one who shared her bed. It was one of life's greatest cruelties that a bastard like the God of War got to lay his hands on the sweetest, most beautiful woman who'd ever breathed.

Hermes found being in her presence rather like being tugged in several different directions while a fire was lit beneath his feet. It was too much, trying to hold loyalty for Hephaestus, hatred for Ares and desire for Aphrodite inside him all at once.

His cheeks flushed beneath his helm as Aphrodite's emerald eyes met his. She smiled.

'Hello.'

'Hello,' he replied, hating the way his voice always cracked up an octave when he was in her presence. He coughed and tried to think of something clever to say.

'You weren't at the feast today.'

Aphrodite sighed. 'I doubt I was missed.'

Tell her you *missed her,* whispered the voice.

Hermes clenched his jaw. The voice inside his head that had awoken the day he was made divine had grown quieter with the passing years, yet Aphrodite's presence always seemed to aggravate it.

'Have you . . . er . . . been to earth recently?'

Aphrodite's eyes flashed and she looked pointedly over his shoulder. Hermes glanced back. He spotted a shimmer where the staircase curved up the opposite wall. A shade. He'd noticed more of them lurking about the palace recently.

'Aren't you allowed to go anywhere on your own?'

Aphrodite let out a tinkle of joyless laughter. 'You know I'm not.'

She looked so sad. If he hadn't been so self-conscious, he'd have embraced her. For twenty years the Goddess of Love had been kept under a guard of shades, ever since she stole from the sky palace and ran away with a shepherd. Ares had discovered her living with her mortal lover at the base of Mount Ida. They'd had a child. The God of War had forced her to return to Olympus, leaving her son and his father behind. For a while Aphrodite had her priestesses send her word of the herder and their boy, but the King of the Gods soon put a stop to that. As far as Hermes knew, the child was last known to be living in the city of Troy with his father.

Aphrodite released her dove into the air, where it fluttered up to an empty perch.

'Hermes,' she whispered, her eyes glistening like two green lakes, 'will you do something for me?'

He allowed himself to step closer. 'That depends . . .' he said in his huskiest voice.

'Will you take a message to my boy?'

His heart sank. Not that, anything but that.

'I . . . I'm sorry. You know I can't.'

Aphrodite stared at him for a moment, then blinked the tears from her eyes. She took a last lingering look out of the window, before rising to her feet. Hermes felt a familiar tingle in the base of his stomach as she swayed down the steps towards him. The breeze carried her scent: rosewater and sandalwood.

Wouldn't you like to make her smile? Wouldn't you like to make her moan?

Hermes clenched his fists.

Aphrodite placed a hand on his arm. 'I understand.'

The tingle became an ache.

He wasn't a fool. He knew Aphrodite didn't see him in the way he wished. He didn't blame her. He was forever trapped in the body of a youth, doomed to remain on the cusp of manhood. But perhaps, if he became someone she relied on, someone she trusted, then one day she might look beyond his wanting exterior.

He would have to be thorough in his search for the Underworld creature. So thorough it would be remiss of him not to at least pass through Troy.

'Perhaps . . .' he glanced over his shoulder at the shade, then whispered, 'I could try.'

The smile that spread across Aphrodite's face was dazzling. Hermes gazed at her, only blinking when the Goddess of Love pressed something into his hand. His pipes.

'I found these. I believe they belong to you.'

'Yes,' he rasped, staring as she moved past him down the steps.

When she'd gone, and he noticed the edge of a curled piece of parchment tucked inside one of the barrels, Hermes realized that she must have known he was going to say yes.

8. The House of Hades

Danae came to with the tang of blood in her mouth. Her head ached as though it had been cracked open, and her right eye was swollen shut. She groaned, recalling the ferryman's fist connecting with her face before she lost consciousness. Then her hands flew to her neck, and she gripped the iron collar encircling her throat. Through the pulses of pain shooting across her skull, she searched for her life-threads, desperately hoping her disconnection had been a momentary lapse.

She felt nothing.

Feebly, she tugged at the metal ring, feeling for weak points. There were none. The breath hitched in her throat.

She was alone. Truly alone.

The voice was gone. Hylas was gone. Orpheus was gone.

Orpheus.

The memory of the musician caught between Kerberos' jaws swallowed her, twin serpents of grief and guilt binding her chest. If she hadn't attacked the ferryman he might never have summoned the beast, and Orpheus would still be alive.

She curled into herself, sobbing until the pain in her head was sickening. It was only then that she took in the vast bed she lay on, its frame constructed from dark, polished wood, and the softness of the sheets, made from wool so fine it felt as though they had been spun by spiders.

Peeling herself from the bed, she looked around a room that was twice the size of her family's hut on Naxos. Its walls were made of smoothest obsidian marble, cracked through with pale veins. The only other furniture was an oak table with a small silver jug, goblet and a dish with a beeswax candle resting upon it. No frescos adorned the stone, no carvings or mosaics. And there were no windows. She had no way of knowing how much time had passed, only that her mouth ached with thirst.

She hauled herself up and pushed herself off the bed. She staggered as her head throbbed with the movement but managed to steady herself on the bedpost. Sucking in deep breaths, she inched her battered body towards the table, lifted the jug and sniffed.

Water.

It might be poisoned. But if her captor wished her dead, they'd already had ample opportunity. Ignoring the goblet, she tipped the jug to her lips. Its contents were surprisingly sweet and fresh. She gulped, her stomach aching as it filled with cool, delicious water. Once she'd drunk her fill, she wiped her mouth on the back of her hand and realized that her skin, while bruised, was clean. She looked down and saw that her sandals and peplos were gone, replaced by a gown of ink-dark silk. She yanked it above her legs. Someone had scrubbed her head to toe.

Clenching her teeth she flung down her skirt.

She would find whoever was responsible and make them pay. But first, she needed to get her powers back.

She forced her aching legs into motion and strode towards the ebony door. Bracing herself for it to be locked, she tugged at the handle and almost fell back as it swung open without protest. Gathering herself, she crept forward and peered out into a high-ceilinged corridor lined with more beeswax candles nestling in bronze bowls.

Tentatively, she took a step beyond her room. The candlelight shivered up the dark marble walls, chasing shadows into the corners. Like in her chamber, no art adorned the corridor, no murals or statues, just sharp lines of polished stone. Her breath echoed down the vast passage, accompanied by her footsteps and the dripping of candle wax. At the end was another door set into the stone. She tried the handle. This one was locked, and she had no power to force it open.

She had never felt weak before she'd discovered her sister's sea-bloated corpse floating in the waves, dragged it onto the beach near their home and watched an apple tree sprout from Alea's still heart. The day she'd tasted the golden fruit, and her powers had awoken. In her youth she'd delighted in her body, relished the exhilaration of running across the sun-baked earth, sparring with her brothers and clambering over sea-slicked rocks. But now those pleasures seemed feeble to her. It was as though she had grown wings, only to have them torn from her back.

Beyond this second door, the corridor turned abruptly, and she found herself stepping out onto an open square walkway, surrounding a large chamber below. Pillars crafted from the same obsidian marble stretched up from the ground to support the upper level. To her left, a grand sweeping staircase descended to the lower floor. She looked up. Instead of a roof, the ceiling became one with the jagged rock above. She realized that this building must be carved out of a vast bed of marble beneath the earth. And there, prising through great cracks in the raw stone, were more of the glowing roots, these thick as tree trunks, snaking down to the floor below. She crept forward, trying to get a better view of an object that seemed to be suspended from the ends of the tendrils.

It looked like a table, fashioned from another slab of marble and held in the air by the roots curled around it. Benches carved from ebony were stationed beside it, and on its polished surface lay silver platters of food.

Her stomach groaned. It felt like days since she and Orpheus had shared that meagre hunk of bread.

Roasted meats, freshly baked cakes and sweet citrus fruits called to her like lovers. As she crept through the shadows towards the staircase, her body thrummed with anticipation, any moment expecting to be ambushed. But she remained alone.

As soon as she reached the lower floor, she ran to the table and snatched up a flatbread, tearing the still-warm dough then submerging a piece in a dish of luminous olive oil. The bread was almost at her lips when she noticed a bowl of pomegranates. They had been sliced in half, their seeds glistening like blood-red jewels.

She dropped the bread and took a step back. So much of what she had been taught about the world was a lie, yet the tale of Hades tricking Persephone to remain in the Underworld by feeding her six pomegranate seeds was ingrained in her being.

She must not allow herself to become distracted.

Her eyes darted across the table and settled on a small knife next to a bowl of russet apples. She snatched it and pushed the blade beneath the metal collar, wincing as it caught her skin.

'I wouldn't do that if I were you.'

She pulled the knife from her neck and spun around.

A figure emerged from the darkness beside the staircase. A man clothed in a long black robe that seemed to melt into the floor at his feet.

Danae had never seen a likeness of the God of the Underworld, but she knew without doubt that this was he. As Hades moved, she caught a faint whisper of Heracles in his face, but where his nephew was built for power, he himself was slight. He seemed young and ancient all at once. His pronounced cheek bones tapered to an angular jaw, and his midnight hair was cut unfashionably short and brushed away from his face. His skin was so pale it was almost blue, his face smooth and hairless, except for two lines etched between his dark brows. His eyes too appeared bleached from lack of sunlight, his irises more grey than azure, like a dying sky clinging to the last vestiges of light.

Danae's fist tightened on the handle of the blade.

Hades prowled to the far end of the table, trailing a bone-pale finger across the edge of the marble slab.

'You might accidentally slice your jugular. Death would follow in three heartbeats.' He spoke softly, but his voice rasped as though it were not often used. His pallid eyes lingered on her collar. 'It is unsettling, I know, but necessary after what you did to Kerberos.'

Danae stared at him. He almost looked pleased.

Her free hand flew once more to the collar around her neck, and a sudden realization dawned. She remembered that when she had discovered Prometheus chained atop the Caucasus Mountains, he too had been shackled with a ring of iron. His had rested on his shoulders, loose around his emaciated neck. Now she knew why. Imprisoned for centuries on his icy crag, cut off from his powers; no wonder he had not been able to escape his chains. Despite the anger she'd nursed for the Titan over the past year, she felt a pang of pity. Prometheus' final revelations may have destroyed everything she thought she knew about the world, but to feel like a hollowed shell for centuries was a cruel punishment indeed.

'You leashed me. Like a hound.'

The ghost of a smile played across Hades' mouth. 'And, like a hound, I must train you.'

She tensed.

'Please, sit.' He gestured to the opposite end of the table as he lowered himself onto one of the benches.

The blade still in her hand, Danae remained where she stood. 'Why haven't you killed me?'

Hades straightened the knife that lay beside his silver plate. 'Why would I want to do that?'

She did not answer.

'If I were Zeus, I would certainly wish to eradicate you. But I am not my brother. Now . . .' he gestured again to the table, 'please eat.'

She did not move. 'You know who I am?'

Hades poured himself a goblet of amber wine. 'Zeus' children may believe his lie that you are one of my creations, but I know the truth. *When the prophet falls and gold that grows bears no fruit, the last daughter will come. She will end the reign of the thunder and become the light that frees mankind.*' Danae's blood chilled to hear those words trip softly over Hades' tongue. The Lord of the Underworld smiled. 'If you wished to hide the fact that you are the one prophesied to end my brother's reign, you should have been more careful about displaying your powers. And perhaps arrived on a less conspicuous animal than one of my own creations.'

Hylas.

'What do you mean, one of your creations? Where is my horse?'

Hades took a sip of wine, then dabbed the corners of his mouth with a pristine cotton cloth. 'The beast is quite comfortable in his old paddock. Now tell me, how did you steal a Hesperides apple?'

Danae frowned. 'I didn't steal anything . . .' The name of the fruit was strange to her, yet as the memory of her sister's chest cracking open and the golden apple tree bloomed in her mind's eye, it did not seem important. In the chaos of her capture, she had become distracted and forgotten the only thing that truly mattered. 'I will tell you anything you want to know, if you take me to my sister.'

The lines between Hades' brows deepened. 'Who?'

'My sister, Alea. She's dead.'

He sighed. 'Please, sit. You must eat.'

Her skull felt tight, the pressure in her temples mounting. 'She died three years ago. I need to see her ghost.'

Hades reached for an apple and sliced the fruit precisely in two. Then again and again, arranging the pieces until twelve perfect segments sat side by side on his plate.

'Let me rephrase my previous question.' He crunched a segment between his teeth, staring at Danae as he chewed. 'How did you gain access to the tree with golden apples?'

'It just appeared.'

'You're going to have to do better than that.'

Danae swallowed. 'If I tell you, will you promise to let me see my sister?'

Hades smiled. 'A truth for a truth. All right.'

Every instinct cried out for her not to reveal how she had gained her powers. But what choice did she have?

'My sister drowned herself. I dragged her body from the ocean, then her chest split open, and a tree with golden apples grew from her heart. I . . . I was compelled to eat one.'

Hades stared at her, so still he could have been cast from white marble. When he did not speak, she continued, 'Is Alea in the Asphodel Meadows? Is her soul here, in the Underworld, with the other virtuous dead?'

'Gold that grows bears no fruit . . .' he murmured, as though he had not heard her. 'Yet here you are.'

'Is there an afterlife in the Underworld?' Danae pressed.

Hades blinked, then sighed once more and popped another slice of apple into his mouth.

Danae could contain herself no longer. She slammed her fists onto the table and screamed, 'Tell me!'

Hades stretched out a hand. Danae gasped as her fingers took on a life of their own and clenched tight around the knife, lifting it to her neck. A sickening realization crashed over her: he was using his life-threads to control her.

'Remember to whom you speak, little Titan.' He released her hand, and the knife clattered to the ground. 'I was led to believe you spoke with Prometheus, yet you seem as ignorant as every other mortal.' His voice was laced with irritation.

Little Titan.

'He was a liar,' Danae rasped.

Hades surveyed her and for a while neither of them spoke. Then he lifted a hand into the air. Danae flinched, but this time it was not his own power he used. She was grabbed by several pairs of rough hands. The air around her shimmered, and four pairs of crimson eyes loomed out of the darkness.

She lashed out, but they were ready for her, leathery hands pinning her arms to her sides.

'Take her to the ferryman. Instruct Charon to show her my kingdom of Erebus.' Hades met her gaze. 'You will find the answers you seek. I hope you may be of use to me when you return.' He snapped his fingers and as the shades dragged her past the table he added, 'A word of advice. Stay close to the ferryman, however inquisitive you may feel. The creatures of the Underworld know not to harm Charon, but you are something new . . .' He turned back to his plate.

'Will Charon take me to my sister?' Danae called as the shades hauled her towards a doorway beyond the root table.

The Lord of the Underworld did not answer, continuing to eat his apple as though she had already left the room.

9. Erebus

The shades marched Danae through a wide hall punctuated by obsidian pillars and emerged onto a large stone platform. She glanced back and saw that her assumption had been correct. Apart from the rectangular crevice harbouring the columns they'd just walked through, Hades' palace was completely hidden within the rock. She shivered. It felt as though she were standing on the lip of an eyeless giant.

A winding staircase snaked down the rock face from the platform to the ground below, illuminated by those strange lights glowing in the ever-dark sky. The shades pushed her down the steps, and when she finally reached the bottom, her bare feet sank into cold earth.

Danae blinked. Ahead of her stood a grove of trees. How they grew without the light of the sun, she could not fathom. Their bark shone white in the pale glow from the imitation stars, like bones protruding from the soil. As the shades walked her between the neat rows of trunks, she noticed their leaves were almost translucent, the veins visible, like jellyfish whose insides could be seen through their skin. They reminded her of how she saw the world when consuming another being's life-threads.

The emptiness inside her groaned.

Ever since the ferryman had collared her, she'd felt disconnected from her body, as though her soul had been imprisoned in an unfamiliar cage of flesh and bone, heavy and thick as clay.

As they left the grove behind, her toes sank into black

sand. They trudged on until the rush of the river roared beyond the dark ground and there, waiting on the shore, was the barge.

Danae stiffened, her feet digging into the grains as Charon, the ferryman, stepped from the vessel, his glowing staff in his hand.

Then the shades let go of her. She was frozen with indecision, with no voice to guide her. After what the ferryman had done to her, her instinct was to run, but going with Charon might be her only hope of finding Alea.

A shade to her left began to sign, its shimmering hands distorting the air. Charon nodded, then his hood twitched towards her. She wondered how the shades could understand one another; perhaps their skin was more clearly visible to their crimson eyes than hers.

She swallowed and took a step forward, then another. When she reached the shore, Charon gestured to the barge and held it steady for her to step onto. She glanced back at the ghostly grove. The shades had already vanished into the gloom. Clenching her fists to prevent her hands from trembling, she stepped onto the vessel. The planks were cold and slippery beneath her feet. The boat bobbed as the ferryman climbed on after her. She could still feel the imprint of his fist against her temple. The skin around her swollen eye was painfully tender. She knew that if she had a mirror, she would look as unrecognizable as she felt.

Danae lowered herself onto the little bench at the far end, eyeing Charon as he drove his staff into the river and steered them out into the current of the Styx.

'What does your master want with me?'

Nothing but rushing water answered her, echoing off the rock ceiling high above.

'Where are the dead?'

The shade continued to punt the barge along the river as though he were just a spoke in an ever-turning wheel. She knew he could understand her – he was able to take orders from his master well enough – but perhaps he did not have the power of human speech.

As they continued, the Styx swelled around the vessel, fed by tributaries trickling like glistening veins from cracks in the rock. The banks of sand became wider, until it seemed like the barge travelled through the heart of a black desert. She looked down at her feet and the obsidian grains trapped between her toes. She was reminded of the oracle at Delphi, and the dust that had covered the chamber once she destroyed the omphalos stone that lay inside a crevasse in the depths of Apollo's temple. Back then, she'd journeyed to the sacred city believing she was cursed. She'd had no idea how powerful she was.

She could not shake the sensation that she was dreaming, despite the stale, cold air that raised the hairs on her skin. The Underworld was so vast, she struggled to comprehend that the world above managed to exist without collapsing into the cavernous kingdom beneath it. Without daylight or the familiar constellations to guide her, she could not orient herself in time or space.

At some point she must have fallen asleep. Her head jolted from her chest as the vessel rocked, and she opened her eyes to see Charon dragging the barge onto the shore. Once the boat was free of the water, he stood to the side, staff in hand. For a breath they both looked at each other, then the ferryman turned and began to stride up the side of a vast dune. Her legs clumsy from disuse, Danae staggered after him.

Soon, her body ached with the effort of wading through the fine sand. The desert rolled around them; jet waves frozen in time. There was no wind here, no breath of relief. The footprints they left behind would linger, perhaps for ever. Despite her mounting exhaustion, Charon did not slow, did not seem to grow weary at all, continuing to trudge with his staff held aloft. After a while she no longer noticed the ferryman, her gaze fixed on the shining crystal bobbing at the tip of his staff. At one point the little sphere of light moved so far ahead she was no longer caught inside the ring of its glow. She began to see things in the periphery of her vision, eyes staring at her from the darkness. She remembered what Hades had said, that she must stay close to the ferryman for her own safety. She forced her aching legs to move faster.

They might have been walking for hours, or days, when the ferryman abruptly came to a halt. Danae sagged behind him, falling on all fours and burying her hands in the grains, her back heaving as she sucked in air.

A gloved hand appeared in front of her face holding a waterskin. She grabbed it, hurrying to remove the stopper and gulp down the sweet water. It spilled over her chin, dribbling down her front, but she did not care, only relinquishing the skin when Charon tugged it from her fingers. She wiped her mouth on the back of her hand, watching him like a wolf watches a lion.

The shade delved into the depths of his cloak and drew out something wrapped in cloth. He proffered it to her.

She took it and peeled back the material to find two pieces of flatbread. She raised them to her nose and sniffed. The bread was stuffed with olives. Her insides twisted, nauseated with only water bloating her stomach. It would do her no good for her body to fail before she found the Asphodel Meadows.

Her weak, powerless body.

She fell upon the bread, almost choking as she swallowed half-chewed mouthfuls.

When only crumbs remained, Charon whipped the cloth from her hands and continued to walk. Danae groaned, heaved herself to her feet and followed him.

She tried to count the peaks of the dunes they traversed but gave up somewhere in the eighties. She began to wonder if they were walking in circles, the hills of sand looked so similar. Her mother had told her a story of King Ixion, who had been most honoured amongst mortals and invited to Olympus to dine with the gods. His pride was so swollen at the prospect of walking amongst the Twelve, he made it known that he lusted after Hera, the Queen of Heaven, and intended to fulfil his desire. As punishment for his hubris, Zeus strapped him to a burning wheel, forever condemned to spin through Tartarus, the skin melting from his flesh for eternity.

Perhaps she had died of exhaustion, and her torment was to believe herself alive, endlessly trudging towards a destination she would never reach, the faint flicker of hope that she might see her sister again as painful as a sea of ravaging flames.

She stopped walking.

Her feet no longer stood on sand but on earth. It was rippled, like a parched seabed. Ahead of her was a vast plain of ochre soil, covered by a film of mist. Sparse clutches of pale plants protruded through the fog, reaching the height of her knee. They were tall and spindly, their colour almost entirely faded, like a painted amphora left too long in the sun. A coronet of delicate flowers clustered atop their stems. White touched with the palest blush.

Movement caught her eye, and she looked to her right to see a herd of roaming cattle, pausing occasionally to chew on the plants. As they moved closer, she realized that they were not cows at all. Their bodies appeared bovine, but their heads were those of red deer. Some were even crowned with twisted horns.

'Which realm is this?' she called after the ferryman.

Silence.

She didn't know why she bothered to ask.

Ahead, Charon grew still and stretched an arm out, indicating her to do the same. He pointed at something on the ground. Danae crept forward. The plant looked like any of the others they'd passed. Then the stalk bent beneath an invisible weight, and a small patch of air around it shimmered.

Breath held, she leant closer, straining to see through the fog. Then, as though materializing from the misty vapour, a pair of crimson eyes stared back at her. Reptilian pinpricks of red, just like the eyes of a shade.

Danae stretched out a hand, but whatever it was scurried away. As the air shivered she made out a small, lizard-like shape before the creature vanished into the trailing fog.

She looked up at the ferryman. 'What was that?'

Charon blinked then turned, leaning on his staff as he continued to walk across the plain.

She pursued him. 'Its eyes and skin were just like yours . . .'

More silence.

'Gods be damned, enough! I know you understand me!'

The ferryman paused and his hood twitched as though he might look back. Then he carried on walking.

From some reservoirs deep within her, a swell of anger propelled her forward. She ran, lunged at the shade and brought them both crashing to the earth.

She landed two blows before Charon had her pinned beneath his staff. She squirmed, trying to free herself, but his grip was like a vice. She had been good at this once. On

Naxos she had often bested her brothers in a furious flurry of fists. But now her body was weakened by pain and hunger, and she had become too reliant on the power of her lifethreads to win a skirmish.

Charon's hood had fallen from his head during the scuffle, and at the sight of the iron collar around his neck she stopped fighting.

Unlike the other shades, the ferryman had visible markings upon his skin. Silvery scars sliced through his invisible hide like a patchwork of glass. From these lines she could make out the shape of his nose, his jaw, his mouth.

'Why are you wearing a collar like mine?' she rasped.

The ferryman blinked again. Once, twice.

'Are you a captive?'

Something shifted in Charon's crimson gaze, and he eased the pressure of his staff across her chest. Then he stretched open his mouth.

Danae flinched.

It was pink and moist, full of creamy square teeth, just like hers. But where a tongue should have been was a scarred stump, severed at the root.

The ferryman closed his mouth and released her, pulling his hood back over his head. He pushed himself up and continued to trudge across the misted earth.

10. The Mists of Mourning

With no moon or sun parading their endless dance across the sky, Danae had nothing to mark the flow of time except her own weariness as they continued to trudge across the fog-bound plain. Her mind still reeled from the sight of Charon's mutilated tongue and the collar around his neck, but she was too exhausted to attempt to divine what had happened to him.

Her feet were blistered by the time the ferryman stopped in the shadow of a large black rock, rearing out of the ground like a curved claw.

Charon drove his glowing staff into the earth, so it stood tall on its own, then sank down to sit cross-legged on the soil beside it. Danae followed his lead, tugging the length of her dress over her legs. She shivered. She felt so small in this vast sea of earth and mist.

From the folds of his cloak, Charon pulled out the waterskin and another cloth-wrapped parcel. He placed both on the earth and nudged the skin towards Danae. She took it and drank. Charon then passed her a strip of cured meat that tasted like salted beef. She chewed, watching the shade lift a piece to the mouth beneath his hood.

She thought back to a night before she'd joined the Argonauts. She'd broken her journey in a mountain village with Heracles and his crew, where she'd followed a shade carrying the unconscious barkeep's boy to a cart she now realized had been driven by Charon – or another shade wearing the same charcoal-grey cloak. A cart full of drugged bodies. The Missing, stolen from their families, never to return.

'I know shades take the Missing. Two years ago, I saw one take a baby from Naxos. Was the child brought here, to the Underworld?'

Her body felt taut as a trapped strand of hair as she waited for a response.

Charon shook his head.

A sip of breath slipped from her lips. 'Do you know where the shade took him?'

Again, the ferryman shook his head.

The air sagged from her lungs, and she turned away from him, curling up on the chill ground.

She drifted in and out of fitful sleep. At one point she dreamed the ferryman lay his cloak over her, tucking its soft corners under her limbs.

Danae woke suddenly. She stared across the misted earth, her breath heavy in her chest. In the distance, the pale plants swayed despite the lack of wind, as though disturbed by an unseen current.

Weary as she was, sleep could not be recaptured, so she sat up and wiped the damp soil from her cheek. As she gazed across the misty plain, she thought she could see figures moving in the haze. She rose silently, Charon's cloak sliding to the ground with a hiss. She glanced at the ferryman, but he was as still as the rock he slept against, his staff laid beside him like a fallen warrior put to rest with his sword.

She took a step away from the rock, then another. The mist drifted around her ankles, like she was walking on the surface of a cloud. Her eyes remained fixed on the horizon and the dark shapes moving in the dim light. As she walked, she thought she could hear music. Strange lilting sounds that were a medley of hissing and clicking, tangled with a harmony of soft notes sung from human throats.

Her heart began to beat a rhythm of hope in her chest. Were they ghosts?

As she drew closer, the forms solidified until she could make out two hooded figures drifting across the plain, stooping occasionally to pick the plants. Their cloaks were as pale grey as the mist, tattered lengths rasping across the soil.

'Are you dead?' Danae asked tentatively.

One of the figures turned.

She gasped, throwing her hands over her eyes as she looked into the face of a beautiful woman, her mouth stretched by a pair of ivory tusks, her hair a mass of writhing snakes.

Gorgons.

Danae's heart thundered as she waited for the cold creep of her limbs turning to stone. Everyone knew the tale of Medusa, the woman Poseidon had raped in the temple of Athena. Enraged at the violation of her holy sanctuary, the Goddess of Wisdom and Warfare had transformed Medusa into the third gorgon and, like her sisters, cursed her to turn anyone who met her gaze to stone. She was said to have been slain by the hero Perseus, while her sisters lived on in the Underworld.

Danae kept her hands clamped over her face as the hissing circled her.

'We will not hurt you, creature of flesh,' said one of the gorgons, her voice a silken caress.

'There are tales within tales, and very little is what came to pass,' said her sister, her words creaking like timber.

Danae wriggled her toes. She had not been petrified yet. Perhaps, like so many of the stories she had been told, the power of the gorgons' stone-sight was only myth.

She lowered her hands.

The gorgons had removed their hoods. Danae stared at their hair, marvelling at the tangle of scaled bodies sliding over their scalps. The first woman's snakes were green as the hills of Thessaly, her skin a deep hazel, her lips full and questioning. Her sister's serpents were ebony, her tusks stained with age, her skin creased and pale as the moon.

'Were you made?' asked the elder of the two.

Danae frowned. 'What?'

'Were you made or were you born?' pressed the younger.

'Born,' she said hesitantly.

A breath fluttered from the elder's lips, and she moved forward, clutching at Danae's arms. Her hands were cold and rough.

'We have been made before and we will be made again,' she muttered, her snakes hissing like the tragic chorus in a play.

Danae cringed away from her. 'What do you mean?'

'More flesh,' whispered the younger, stepping close on Danae's other side. 'He is never sated, always changing, always cutting.'

They grabbed hold of her arms. Their snakes became more frenzied, writhing and hissing, their tiny forked tongues licking the gloom.

'Get off me.' Danae struggled, but their grip tightened.

'We miss our sister,' cried the elder. 'We miss her ever-so.'

Then light blazed across the plain.

The gorgons let go of Danae and shrank back, throwing up their hands to shield their eyes. Their snakes too cringed away, flattening themselves down their mistresses' necks.

Danae turned to see Charon striding through the mist. He held his staff aloft, the crystal atop it a miniature sun, blazing away the creatures of darkness.

When she looked back, the sisters had disappeared, once more swallowed by the mist.

The ferryman's vermillion eyes were bright with rage. He

reached out a gloved hand and prodded her sternum. Then pointed to his own.

'I understand,' Danae said, still breathless. 'I won't wander off again.'

Charon nodded once, then led her back to their makeshift camp.

After a few more fitful hours of sleep, Danae woke again, this time to the drumming of hooves. The ground trembled as she pushed herself upright. Charon stood a few feet away, his staff clutched in his gloved hand as he gazed at the horizon.

A cloud of dust lingered between the misted earth and night-dark sky. Shapes moved within the haze. They appeared to be men on horseback, charging towards them like an invading army.

She was tempted to cry out and beg their aid. As though sensing her thoughts, Charon grabbed the back of her dress and yanked her into the shadow of the rock. She struggled against him, but he held her against the stone, clamping a gloved hand over her mouth.

The pounding of hooves grew loud as thunder as the horses neared them. Then, like a storm-whipped wave, the riders crashed past the rock.

Danae's eyes widened despite the stinging dust as she saw that it was no army, but a herd of centaurs.

She had once seen their likeness on an amphora, the torso of a man mounted on the body of a stallion. The mighty creature had been in the throes of death, poisoned by an arrow shot by Heracles. Centaurs were said to dwell in the mountains of Thessaly and Arcadia and feast on raw flesh.

She stopped struggling as their powerful bodies raced past. Their long hair streamed behind them, blending with the fur that traced the length of their spines all the way to their gleaming tails. They were all the colours of an autumn forest: auburn, mahogany, bright russet and darkest ebony. Not one turned back to look at Danae or Charon; they cantered on, as though chased by an invisible swarm of gadflies.

Once the dust began to settle, the ferryman released his grip. She swiftly moved away from him, staring after the centaurs. When she looked back, Charon had already begun to trudge onwards.

Danae followed him. After what felt like several hours, her foot caught on something hidden in the mist, and she fell to the ground. Roots had bubbled up to the surface, pulsing with the same ethereal light as the ones surrounding the bronze gates. She clenched her jaw as she scrambled to her feet and was forced to hop over the glowing coils to keep up with Charon.

The air too had changed. It felt closer somehow, the moisture rattling in her lungs. Sure enough, when she looked up, she could make out the crags of the rock ceiling above and the crystals of the glowing stones set into its crevices to mimic the stars. The world was growing smaller.

She flinched as something drifted past her face. A butterfly. For a moment she was held in memory as its large cherry-red wings transported her back to a similar insect on Lemnos. But, like so many things she'd encountered in the Underworld, the butterfly was not as it seemed. The creature before her may have the same vibrant wings, but its body was squat and hairy like a spider, its eight legs dangling like claws ready to curl around its prey.

She continued on and soon the roots became so thick, she and Charon were forced to clamber over them hand to foot. A flock of birds flew overhead, their feathers shimmering like spilled oil, their necks longer than their bodies. A little while later, Danae could have sworn she saw a crow with no head at all. Flowers too began to appear between the roots. She recognized none of them, their jagged petals splashed with echoes of colour as if an artist had spilled all their dyes at random. A creature that resembled a bee, with the horns of a beetle, landed in the centre of one of these plants. She watched it rub its engorged abdomen on the pale-yellow pistil until the petals suddenly snapped together. A moment later, something dark trickled between them.

She wondered if she still slept on the misty plane, trapped in a fever dream.

She was drawn from staring at the carnivorous flower by the sound of running water. She hurried after Charon and found the shade standing at the edge of a large lagoon, the glowing roots trailing into its depths. It seemed they had finally reached the end of the vast cave that contained the Underworld kingdom of Erebus. On the far side, a waterfall tumbled from the rock face, masking the current that flowed beneath it out through a cave. On the surface of the dark water floated plants that were round and as milky pale as fallen moons. Between them, tiny silver fish darted through the lagoon, glowing antennae protruding from their heads. Danae's gaze darted between their little shimmering bodies, then her eyes were drawn to movement by the waterfall.

Someone was swimming in the lagoon.

It was a girl. Her back was to Danae, so at first all she could see was the girl's auburn curls trailing in the water. Time seemed to catch in the ripples left in the swimmer's wake as she reached the far bank and leant her white arms on the root-twined rock. From what was visible of her torso, she seemed to be naked. She was so very pale, but then most creatures in the Underworld seemed to be leached of colour.

The girl turned her head, the edge of her mouth and

outline of her nose emerging from behind her swathe of wet hair. Strange as she was, there was something achingly familiar about her features.

Danae's heart tightened, then soared through her chest. She could barely form words, her body calcifying with hope, as the girl extended a slender hand to twist a lazy finger around a protruding root at the edge of the lagoon.

Finally, with colossal effort, Danae regained control of her voice and rasped, 'Alea?'

11. Child of Love

Hermes trod the woodland path, battling the tempest of his thoughts. He wore only his winged golden boots and a simple blue tunic. The rest of his armour was stowed away in a bag slung across his shoulder. In his other hand he carried a basket of fresh bread, figs and a pot of honey.

He'd spent the past week visiting his temples in the Argolid region and the surrounding territories, hoping one of his priestesses might have heard whispers of a strange girl with god-like powers. But his search had proved fruitless. In his desperation, he had flown across the Aegean Sea to the outskirts of a small town in the kingdom of Lydia called Hypaepa.

The trees rustled as he stepped into the familiar clearing. As he approached the little hut nestled in the centre, his brow darkened. The vegetable patches he'd planted were overgrown, and many of them had gone to seed. He would have to pay a visit to the local boys he'd instructed to tend it and remind them what happened to those who disobeyed the Messenger of the Gods. But his heart lifted as he heard a warbling voice from within the ramshackle dwelling. The singer was not skilled, but she sang with the unbridled joy of one who does so purely for their own entertainment.

Hermes pushed open the crooked wooden door. The singing stopped.

'Who is it?'

'Just me,' he called as he stepped inside.

The hut was a shambles. A three-legged table propped up on a barrel was heaped with spools of thread and an array of pottery; most of which had been broken then glued back together incorrectly, the artwork a cracked, nonsensical jumble. Several chairs and stools were littered throughout the single room, twine wound around them to create pathways leading to a table, hearth and a single pallet pushed against the far wall.

'Don't move anything. I've got it all just where I want it.' An elderly woman sat in a corner of the room on a stool working an old loom, thread coiled in little coloured heaps beside her.

Hermes smiled. 'The next time I visit, I'll find you with a broken leg from tripping over all this mess.'

The old woman lifted her hands from her weaving. 'The next time you visit I'll be dead if you leave it so long again.'

Hermes' grin faltered. 'How long has it been?'

She sighed. 'Two years give or take.'

Hermes' frown returned. He set down his bag of armour by the door and picked his way through the obstacle course of furniture to draw up a chair next to the old woman, placing the basket of food down beside him. She looked smaller than the last time he'd seen her. He burrowed his head between her hands and lay it on her lap.

'Did you miss me, Arachne?'

She smoothed his hair, her twisted fingers raking across his scalp with just the right amount of pressure. She always knew how to relax him.

'No, you're a damned nuisance.'

Hermes smiled, then sniffed. He closed his eyes as she groomed him.

'You always sound the same,' she murmured. 'Such a youthful voice.'

Hermes sat up and leant across her to inspect the tapestry. He cocked his head.

'What's this one meant to be?' He could make out no discernible shapes in the design.

'A horse making love to a donkey.'

Hermes laughed. He had once asked Arachne why she continued to weave after her sight was taken. She had replied that it was the making, the texture of the thread beneath her fingers, rather than the finishing that gave her pleasure. Hermes didn't understand. Arachne had been brilliant once, a weaver possessed of a skill so beautiful it was almost divine. But her talents with thread were matched only by her wicked sense of humour. She had created a series of works depicting the gods' debauchery and philandering that became very popular in her town, then swiftly the rest of the kingdom.

When it came to Athena's attention that there existed a tapestry of her amorously chasing a bull, she had put out Arachne's eyes and destroyed all her work. Well, most of it. Hermes had managed to save a couple of tapestries. He kept them hidden far from Olympus, and it amused him to look at them from time to time. In his opinion they were finer works of art than anything in the marble sky palace.

'What did you bring me then?' A glint appeared in Arachne's milky eyes.

'Goat droppings and tree sap.' Hermes lifted the basket onto his lap, took the lid off the honey pot and dipped one of the indigo figs into its gooey interior. 'All disgusting, I'm afraid.' He lifted the honeyed fig to Arachne's lips and watched the golden syrup drip languidly down her chin as she bit into the fruit.

'Absolutely disgusting.' She chewed for a while. 'Go on then, what is it?'

'What do you mean?'

'You only ever come to me when you want something.'

'That's not . . .' Hermes twisted another ripe bulb between his fingers, the word 'fair' dying on his lips. He could never hide his feelings from Arachne. 'You remember I told you that my father is a very powerful man . . . well, he's ordered me to do something for him.'

Arachne nodded. 'Go on.'

Hermes wondered how much he dared reveal. 'It's a secret task he's entrusted only to me . . . I have to find something for him that doesn't want to be found, and I'm afraid if I fail he might . . . No, failure isn't an option.' He sighed, squashing the fig between his fingers. 'I've not had any luck so far, and then to complicate things, there's this woman –'

'Ah!' Arachne reached for his hands and when she found them, plucked the fig from his fingers. 'You *like* her . . .' She popped the fruit into her mouth.

'Yes,' Hermes said quickly. 'And *she's* asked me to do something too. She's so sad, because someone precious was taken from her, and if I find him and give him her message, I could make her happy. I would like that very much. But if my father finds out he'd be furious to know I'm not fully focusing on his quest.'

'Hmmm,' Arachne nodded sagely. 'This woman, you like her a great deal, don't you?'

Hermes flushed crimson. He was glad Arachne could not see him.

'You love her,' the old woman said softly.

He swallowed. It felt reductive, simplifying the knot of desire, guilt, shame and hope he felt for Aphrodite into one little word.

'I think,' he croaked, 'this might be my chance, for both my father and this woman to finally see me as a man.'

'You care too much about what others think, my young friend.' Arachne wiped her mouth on the back of her hand. 'For what it's worth, when I am trying to find something, I think about where I would be if I were that thing. A pot of honey doesn't like the window, you see, because it melts in the sunlight. But a dark shelf, or a cool patch of floor? Perfect. And as for your love, I'd be wary of setting such high hopes on the outcome of giving her what she desires. Seems to me she's gaining a great deal from your friendship, and you not so much. But then what do I know? I'm just a mad old woman who made fun of the gods and lived to regret it.'

Hermes scowled but laid his head back on Arachne's lap, his face tilted to look up at her. 'Do you really regret it?'

Arachne's lined lips spread into a smile. 'Not for one moment.'

Hermes pelted through the sky, the clouds beading his armour with dew. He turned Arachne's words over in his mind. Where would he go if he did not want to be found? Where in all of Greece would he hide if he were fleeing from the gods? If he were, like his father had said of her, a creature from the Underworld transformed to appear mortal?

Hermes halted so abruptly, he almost tumbled down to earth. Fighting against the buffeting wind, he trod the air.

How could he have been so foolish?

'She has returned to her master!' he proclaimed to the sky.

He was about to turn and fly back across the Aegean, when the wind parted the carpet of cloud below. The stone fortress of Troy reared out of the landscape beneath him. It looked as though another city had been erected across the bay, at the edge of the sparkling sea. A labyrinth of tents and standards stretched out for at least a mile, and lining the coast were rows of triremes, the great warships flying flags from all corners of Greece.

Hermes sucked in a breath. Aphrodite's boy dwelt within the city of Troy. He wondered how she felt about her lover, Ares, orchestrating a war that could very likely end her son's life. He revelled in a sharp stab of satisfaction as he imagined the rift tearing open between them.

You could have it all, said the voice. *Your father's respect and Aphrodite's love.*

Indecision tugged at him for a heartbeat, then he tilted his body and flew down towards Troy. As he passed over the Greek encampment, the stench of unwashed bodies wafted up to greet him. He wrinkled his nose and beat his ankle-wings faster. Soon, he was soaring over the vast stone walls of Troy, lined with bronze-helmeted centuries, before continuing on over the city.

Hermes landed on the flat roof of a dwelling that wasn't overlooked. It was always a dangerous thrill, venturing this close to so many mortals. He chewed his lip as the clamour of the city pressed in on him and decided what to do next.

He walked to the edge of the roof and peered down to the street below. It wasn't long before he found what he was looking for.

Leaping from the roof, he glided above the street. It was amazing how few mortals remembered to look up as they went about their little lives. He reached down towards a passerby, and the man below let out a strangled cry as Hermes yanked his cloak from his back. There were gasps from the people surrounding him, but Hermes flitted away so swiftly, he had vanished before they could fully comprehend what they'd seen.

He alighted in a deserted courtyard and removed his helm and gauntlets, stowing them away in a folded bag he pulled from a pouch on his belt, then pinned the cloak around his neck so the rest of his golden armour was covered. One advantage to not looking like a god without his armour was that he could pass inconspicuously through a crowd.

Glancing around once more to check no eyes spied on him from the shadows, he slung his bag over his shoulder and darted out of the square.

Hermes picked his way through the narrow streets until he spotted the faded awning of a kapeleion. Priestesses were the main fountains of knowledge for mortal goings-on, but kapeleia owners were renowned for being veritable honeytraps of secrets. Most fiercely guarded the details of their patrons' lives – their reputations were built on it – but every man had his price. Or pain threshold.

The first seven establishments proved fruitless, and by the time Hermes entered the eighth kapeleion, he was sweaty, his feet sore, and he was very close to draining the life-threads of the next person who breathed too heavily.

Inside the dusky room men sat on stools, staring darkly into their cups. A middle-aged barkeep was busy pouring a tray of wine, topping up the glasses with an extra dash of water while no one watched.

Hermes marched up to him, keeping his cloak tightly drawn around his armour. He grabbed one of the cups, downed the wine in one gulp, wiped his mouth on the back of his hand and grimaced.

'What kind of horse piss do you call this?'

The barkeep reddened. 'You'd better pay for that, boy.'

Hermes rolled his eyes, reached across the bar and grabbed the man by the neck. A few patrons glanced over at the commotion with mild interest, though many carried on drinking as though seeing their barkeep assaulted was a common sight.

'Where can I find a man named Anchises?'

He loosened his grip slightly to allow the barkeep to speak. The man coughed. 'Old Anchises the shepherd?'

'That's him.'

'He's . . . dead.'

'What?'

'They buried him a couple months back.'

Hermes swore. He wondered if Aphrodite knew that her mortal lover had perished. 'And his baby?'

The barkeep spluttered. 'You mean Aeneas? He's no babe. A man near twenty.'

Hermes frowned. Of course he was no longer a child. Mortal lives were so fleeting.

'Where is he?'

The barkeep told him where Aeneas lived, and for this trouble Hermes tossed a drachma at the crumpled proprietor as he downed another cup of the terrible wine on his way out. He may be in disguise, but he would never let anyone claim he was not a benevolent god.

The barkeep's directions took Hermes to an unsavoury part of town. Men with dirt-stained faces and hungry eyes leered from shadowed doorways, and women with exposed breasts and glazed expressions leant against peeling murals.

Hermes found the door he was looking for, barely more than a painted piece of driftwood rammed over the entrance, and knocked.

'Who goes there?' said a robust voice.

'A friend.'

Footsteps echoed from inside, then the door creaked ajar. A young man pressed his face into the sliver of light pouring in from the street. A dark-brown eye framed with thick lashes appraised Hermes.

'I must speak with Aeneas.' He cursed inwardly as his voice creaked on the name. So much for sounding authoritative.

The face retreated, and the door opened to reveal a tall, lithe man, radiant with the first bloom of manhood. Hermes' stomach twinged with jealousy. Then he took in the shape of the man's eyes, the freckles peppering his nose and his shock of thick copper hair. His mother's hair.

'What can I do for you, lad?' Aeneas asked.

Lad.

Fighting the urge to send him crashing through the interior of his hovel, Hermes strode past him.

'You live here?'

Aeneas' house consisted of a single room, a pallet on one side, a small hearth on the other, a single bowl and amphora resting beside it. He wrinkled his nose; the child of a goddess should not be living in a place like this.

'Take off your cloak, friend,' Aeneas closed the door. 'I would offer you wine, but I'm afraid I have none.'

'It's fine,' Hermes muttered. 'I've had enough terrible Trojan wine for one day.' He ignored Aeneas' outstretched hand and reached inside his cloak. He retrieved the message Aphrodite had stowed in his pipes and pressed it into Aeneas' hand.

'The Goddess of Love watches over you, Aeneas.'

The young man unfurled the parchment, eyes widening as he read. 'This cannot be. My father would have told me . . .'

'It is true. You are the son of Aphrodite.'

Aeneas looked at Hermes, his face full of wonder.

'Now,' Hermes tapped his boot on the filthy floor, 'you must leave the city at once.'

Aeneas pressed the parchment to his chest. 'I cannot.'

It was then that Hermes noticed the shabby armour laid out on the pallet. His heart sank.

'If you don't come with me, you will die.'

The mirth left Aeneas in an instant. 'Is this a test?'

Hermes sighed. 'Look, either you're going to starve behind these walls or be slaughtered in the dirt outside your city. I promise I can get you out safely, give you gold, a horse, whatever you need. You can go anywhere you want, be anyone.'

Aeneas drew himself up to his full, irritatingly tall height. 'I would proudly die for Troy and noble King Priam. It will be the honour of my life to defend my kingdom.'

There was only one thing for it. Hermes rose into the air on his winged boots, spreading his arms to reveal his golden armour.

'I am the god Hermes, Messenger of Olympus. I command you to come with me.'

Aeneas gasped, then fell to his knees, prostrating himself below Hermes' feet. He always loved it when mortals did that.

'M-my lord Hermes, forgive me. I did not know it was you.'

Hermes floated back to earth. 'Good. Now we need to hurry. I have places to be.'

Aeneas sat up, his eyes glistening. 'I cannot come with you, even though you are a god. I have sworn myself to Ares. It is my destiny to be a soldier, fall by the sword then spend eternity in Elysium.'

The poor, stupid fool. Never had Hermes been so sorely tempted to reveal that the dream of reaching paradise following a noble death in battle was a lie. But the punishment laid out by Zeus for telling a mortal that the three realms of the afterlife were a fantasy was execution, with no exceptions. There were rules even gods could not break.

Hermes sighed once more and ran a hand over his face. He must continue his search for the Underworld girl. He had spent too long in Troy already.

He could always force Aeneas to come with him. Knock the man out and fly him away from the city. But that was risky. If they were seen by a shade or one of his siblings' priestesses, Zeus would surely kill Aeneas, and he dreaded to think what punishment he and Aphrodite would face.

Struck by a sudden idea, he reached beneath his cloak and pulled a golden homing medallion from the pouch on his belt. The amulet was embossed with a rose in full bloom. He had taken it on a whim, wanting to keep something of Aphrodite's for himself.

'Think on what I have said, for I will return. In the meantime, find yourself some better armour. And if war does come before you see me again, place this around the neck of a bird with a message. It will reach your mother.' He paused. 'I know she would wish to hear from you before your end.'

'I will not forget your kindness, Lord Hermes,' Aeneas replied, his face shining with tears.

Hermes shook his head, wrapped his cloak around him once more, and stepped out into the street, muttering, 'Mortals.'

When the coast was clear, he flew up to a nearby rooftop, tossed the cloak aside and pulled the rest of his armour from his bag. Once fully clad in gold, he launched into the air. He would need to replenish his life-thread supply before the flight back to mainland Greece.

He swooped low, grabbing a woman from where she sat weaving on a balcony. Choking the breath from her lungs, he drained the life-threads from her dying body mid-air before dropping her corpse over the wall of Troy into the sea.

The mortal's life force streaked renewed vigour through Hermes' limbs, and he kicked up into the sky, cutting a path through the pale herds of clouds drifting above the ocean, towards the Black Sea entrance to the Underworld.

12. The Asphodel Meadows

Alea's name reverberated around the rock walls of the lagoon. Time slowed, and the air grew as thick as tar as the girl in the water turned to reveal the rest of her face. The lily pads shuddered as ripples fled across the water.

Danae fell to her knees.

It was not Alea.

Luminous green eyes stared back at her from a face framed with gills, which before had been hidden by the girl's hair. Silver scales snaked up her abdomen to circle her pale breasts, muddling with the freckles speckling her chest. She tossed her auburn curls over her shoulder and stretched back her mottled lips to reveal sharp, pointed teeth.

A Nereid. Danae had seen their likeness depicted in a mural on a wall at the trade office in Naxos Port.

She did not move as the creature swam towards her, the joy that had filled her now drained away. She saw how foolish she'd been, trying to fit the imprint of Alea's face onto the Nereid, anchoring her hope to a few fleeting similarities. As the sea-creature reached the edge of the lagoon she realized that she could no longer remember her sister's face as a whole, only in fragments. Despite her best efforts, Alea's memory was fading, and Danae was losing her all over again.

She did not flinch as the creature launched itself from the water, bone-white arms outstretched, jaws open wide. But before the Nereid could snare her in its clutches, Charon yanked Danae back from the water's edge. She fell to the ground as the Nereid hissed, then dived beneath the water, a large, shimmering fish tail breaking the surface as her torso disappeared.

Danae scrambled to free herself from the tangle of roots and rock, the impact of slamming into the earth shaking her from her reverie.

Charon watched her, still and grey as stone.

'Where are the Asphodel Meadows?' Each word was punched from her gut.

The ferryman raised a gloved hand and pointed all around them. Danae twisted, scouring the misty plain, then turned back in confusion.

'This can't be ... Where are the dead?' she shouted. 'Where are they?'

When he made no further attempt to answer, she clambered back over the twisted roots crying, 'Alea!' over and over again.

She did not know if Charon followed her. She did not care.

She ran across the plain, pushing herself back up each time a root tendril tripped her, still calling her sister's name. Flocks of strange birds soared up from the fog at the sound of her cries, and the marvels that had fascinated her on the journey to the lagoon were blurred into meaningless smudges by tears. After a while her sister's name became a barb in her throat, rasping out as a pitiful croak.

For a time desperation sustained her, driving her onwards across that vast, misted desert, until she tripped again, and this time her body failed her. She lay on the red earth, the fog a blanket of grey around her, unable to do anything but suck in one ragged breath after the other. Then she felt a hand on her shoulder, and the ferryman heaved her off the ground.

'Please ...' she whispered, 'this isn't the Asphodel Meadows. It can't be.'

Charon reached into the mist and plucked one of the pale flowers.

'Where are the . . .' The words faded on her tongue as she looked at the white petals tinged with pink, like drops of blood melted into fresh snow.

Asphodel.

They had spent hours traipsing past the very plants that gave the meadows their name, and she had not realized. She'd always envisioned the Asphodel Meadows as rolling green hills peppered with vibrant flowers – the way her mother had described them. But like everything else she'd been taught, it was a lie.

'There are no dead here,' she murmured.

Everything she'd seen was alive. Strange and unnatural but *living*. Not a single ghost, not a whisper of those who had come before. She could barely bring herself to voice the words, but she knew she must.

'Are there any dead in the Underworld?'

The ferryman shook his head.

She felt as though the rock above them had crumbled and the entire weight of reality was crashing down upon her.

Prometheus had been right. There was no afterlife in the Underworld. Hades' kingdom was the same rock, dirt and air as the land above it.

She had fought the Titan's truth with every breath, had spent almost a year constructing walls of adamant in her mind, protecting her hope that somehow, someday, she would be reunited with her sister. Now, in a single heartbeat, her fortress vanished like a sandcastle toppled by the tide. Alea's soul was gone, and Danae would never see her again.

She lay down on the earth and let the mist swallow her. A moment passed and then what felt like a lifetime.

She was aware of the ferryman tugging at her arms, but

it did not matter. Nothing mattered any more. She felt as though her chest was slowly peeling open from the inside out. She was capable only of lying on the ground, unable to form any thought as she waited for the pain to end.

Charon eventually gave up trying to pull her to her feet and scooped her into his arms, carrying her like her brothers had carried Alea home from Demeter's temple all those years ago.

The landscape changed around them. Creatures clustered to the edge of Charon's light as the ferryman trudged on, Danae watching it all through glazed eyes, unable to sleep despite her body crying out for rest.

She no longer wept. What use were tears, when she had already drowned?

Alea had never liked going out in their father's boat because she suffered from sea sickness. The concept was strange to Danae, who often felt more at home on the water than land. She had once asked her sister what it felt like. 'As though my insides have become untethered,' Alea had replied, 'and while the waves surge beneath me, I cannot imagine ever feeling well again.' Now, Danae finally understood.

Eventually, they reached the curved rock that had been their camp, and Charon set her down against the obsidian stone. He lay the waterskin and a piece of flatbread in her lap. She remained unmoving, staring ahead. The ferryman nudged her. She did not respond. Then he picked up the waterskin, removed the stopper and tipped it to her lips. Water dribbled down her chin, soaking the bread in her lap.

He stopped trying to feed her after that.

Finally, weariness overcame her, and she slipped into sleep. Alea ran through her dreams, her sister's laugh a song Danae could never catch. When she woke, she wished she could fall unconscious and never again open her eyes.

When he judged it time to leave, the ferryman lifted her

again and carried her across the midnight dunes. He stopped only once, setting her down to draw the waterskin from beneath his cloak and drink. Then, before Danae could protest, he grabbed her hair and pulled back her head. She gulped on instinct as he poured the liquid over her mouth. He released her and she fell forward onto the black sand, spluttering and coughing. When she had regained her breath, she wiped her spittle-flecked mouth with the back of her hand. Charon knelt on his heels, watching her. A tiny spark of rage flared in the cavern of her misery.

'Why did Hades want me to see this?' she croaked.

The ferryman remained still. She knew he could not speak in a way she understood, but he could give her some indication.

Charon made no effort to answer her question, but instead held out the flatbread she had refused to eat back at the rock. She took it from him and hurled it across the sand.

The ferryman sighed then lifted her again and carried her the rest of the way across the obsidian desert, only setting her down again at the edge of the River Styx, where his barge waited for them.

When they arrived at the riverbank leading up to Hades' palace, Charon did not linger to see if Danae would follow him out of the barge but scooped her into his arms and hastened through the ghostly grove. His ribs were heaving by the time they reached the pillared entrance hall at the crest of the winding staircase.

The feast chamber was deserted and Danae did not see another soul as the ferryman carried her to her room. She rolled towards the wall once he lay her on the bed, her face inches from the veined marble, the iron collar cold against her skin.

Sleep came and went but brought no relief. At one point she heard the door open and something being placed upon the table. The smell of freshly baked bread wafted across the room.

She did not move. Hunger and thirst had become nothing but notes in a symphony of suffering. She understood now why the Twelve had created the fiction of unburied souls wandering endlessly across the banks of the River Styx. It was a frightful punishment to go on existing when one had nothing to live for. Like those lost ghosts, now she knew the truth, she would never again know peace.

The world was a dark and terrible place, and she wanted no part of it.

In a few quiet moments during her year of searching, she'd allowed herself to escape into fantasy. She had imagined walking up the dusty path to her hut, the smell of her mother's honey cakes wafting from the yard. Eleni would wave at her as she pushed open the gate and scold her for staying away so long. Her pa would have just returned from fishing, and his nets, still wet and gleaming from the sea, would be piled on the table inside. Alea would be there too, bouncing Arius on her hip, asking their father about his day as he lowered himself into a chair by the hearth. Both would smile at Danae as she entered, then carry on chatting about the tides and the mercurial nature of red tunny. Danae would be happy just to stand there and let the ordinariness of them wash over her.

Allowing herself to remember her life before came at a heavy price. When she returned to reality, the pain was almost too terrible to bear. Yet she kept remembering. Like an old drunk who cannot stop themselves reaching for their cup. Now, in that dark, windowless room beneath the earth, she closed her eyes. Perhaps, this time, she would not have to come back. Perhaps, if she concentrated hard enough, she could stay in her dream forever. But as she trod the familiar path to her family's hut, voices drifted through her mind that had no place there. One, cold and aloof, she recognized, the other, lilting and boyish, she had not heard before.

'Where is the creature you sent to plague us?'

'Which creature?'

Slowly, she began to regain her senses and realized that the voices were not inside her head but wafting from beyond her room. Her bones grating with effort, she opened her eyes and rolled away from the wall. Her door had been left open.

'The one with godlike powers you disguised as a mortal girl.'

A harsh, brittle laugh: Hades.

'You flatter me, Hermes. I wish it was in my power to craft such a creature, but alas even my talents do not stretch that far.'

'But she is from the Underworld. Father said . . .'

'If it looks like a lion, roars like a lion and has a lion's teeth, then perhaps it is a lion.'

'I don't understand . . .'

'Your father is a liar.'

The sound of crashing furniture reverberated through the palace.

'How dare you slander the King of Heaven —' Hermes suddenly fell silent, and Danae heard a faint choking sound, then in a strangled voice, 'If you give her to me, I will do whatever you ask. Name your price.'

A pause.

'The girl you seek is not here. Fly home, messenger boy, and discover the truth. Now go, before I decide that Persephone could do with some company.'

Danae heard a clink, followed by a humming sound like the rapid beating of wings.

Somewhere, in the ruined caverns of her mind, a question echoed.

Why was Hades hiding her from the Olympians?

Her gaze drifted to the candle on her table. It had burned down to a waxy soup in its silver dish. She squinted at the brightness of the little flame, her eyes unused to the light after staring for so long at the dark wall.

There was a story her mother had told her and her siblings when they were children. The tale of Pandora, the first woman made by the gods. It was said that she was given a wedding gift by Zeus: a jar she was told never to open. But Pandora was curious, and one day, while her husband was away, she opened the lid. A terrible, blood-curdling shriek ripped through the air, and the daimons of worry, sickness, jealousy, greed and all the evils that now plague the mortal race came pouring out. Pandora fell back, covered her face and wept at the terrors she had unleashed. Then a gentle hand came to rest upon her head, and a soft voice said, 'Do not mourn, child. Despair can never rule your heart while I am here.' It was Elpis, the spirit of hope.

Danae closed her eyes. She was so tired, so very, very tired.

Then she thought of what Manto had said in those final moments before they pushed her over the side of the ship to save her from the harpies.

I know you're scared, but you must believe me, you are the last daughter. You are the hope of mankind.

Danae opened her eyes and whispered into the gloom, 'When the prophet falls, and gold that grows bears no fruit, the last daughter will come. She will end the reign of thunder and become the light that frees mankind.'

She thought of all those who had died at the hands of

the gods. All those mortals suffering in despair beneath the Twelve's tyranny, slaving under the false hope that one day they would be reunited with their loved ones.

If Prometheus was right about the afterlife, then he was right about her.

She must become the flame and light her own way out of the darkness.

With a colossal effort, she curled her legs over the side of the bed and pushed herself to standing. She took one small step, then another, until she stood before the table, looking down at the silver tray of bread, olives and cooked meats.

She picked up a piece of bread, lifted it to her lips, and took a bite.

13. The Creator

Danae had not long eaten her fill when the shades came.

Without protest, she let them escort her from her room, down the labyrinthine corridors of Hades' palace. From what she could gather, the feast chamber seemed to be the heart of the building, the other rooms and corridors snaking away like arteries flowing from it. She tried to commit the route to memory, but she could not hold the layout in her mind. It felt as though the corridors and pillared passageways were part of an endless warren burrowing into the earth.

Finally, they arrived at a thick marble archway, another ebony door cracked ajar beneath it. Danae glanced over her shoulder. The shades lined the corridor behind her, their bodies forming a wall of shimmering, translucent flesh.

Summoning her mettle, she walked through the doorway.

The chamber resembled the inside of a giant beehive. A honeycomb of shelving curled around its width, right up to where the ceiling domed high above. Thousands of scrolls were crammed into the square compartments, bronze numerals glinting at each cross section beside more symbols she did not recognize. A great shard of crystal, the size of a cart, was embedded in the roof, casting an eerie, cold light on the tiled floor below. A mosaic of an emerald serpent was coiled around the circumference of the room, twisting in on itself to bite down on its own tail. It was the only piece of artwork she had seen in the Underworld. At the centre of the chamber was a mahogany desk, scrolls of parchment laid out in perfect lines upon its polished surface. And poring over an unfurled roll, was Hades.

'Do come closer. I won't bite.'

Slowly, she approached the desk. Behind Hades, another archway cut into the shelving, mirroring the doorway she'd just passed through. Not much of the room beyond was visible except a stone slab raised up from the floor.

The God of the Underworld surveyed her. 'What do you think of my kingdom?'

'There's a lot of life in the land of the dead.'

The left corner of his mouth twitched.

'You could have just told me the afterlife isn't real.'

Hades blinked. 'Emotions can be deafening. Some things need to be seen to be believed. But now you know the truth, we can speak plainly. We shall begin with you relaying what Prometheus told you about your prophecy.'

Danae fought to keep her expression calm. 'Or we could start with why you lied to Hermes about my whereabouts.'

Hades did not seem surprised to learn that she knew about their conversation. She wondered if her door had been left open on purpose.

'I would have thought that was obvious. I want to help you.' He stepped out from behind the desk, the sharp angles of his body at odds with the smooth ripples of his dark robe. 'Tell me, are you happy with how my brother rules the mortal world?'

She did not trust herself to speak. Hades might have kept her alive and guarded her identity from Hermes, but he was still one of the Twelve.

He watched her intently. 'I am not like them. I did not choose this role. It was not my desire to craft the fiction of an afterlife hidden beneath the earth. But Zeus believed that to truly win mortals' devotion, he must first ensnare their souls.

After all, it is the great human obsession – what becomes of their ghosts after their bodies perish.'

'What does happen when we die?' Her voice sounded small in the vast room.

'Oblivion.'

Danae opened her mouth, but no words came. She could feel the weight of the earth above her, the soil packed with empty husks that had once been people. Alea was gone, erased. Everything she had been burned away like morning dew. The world carried on as though she had never existed, the only evidence of her life the crater she'd left in Danae's heart.

A bemused expression settled on Hades' face. 'There's no need to look so concerned. You will no longer face the body's slow creep towards death. To wield the powers you have, you must have tasted the Hesperides fruit. Therefore, from the moment the apple passed your lips, you ceased to age.'

There was that strange name again. 'I . . .' Once more she tried to argue and found she could not. The evidence had been plain ever since Prometheus revealed to her that she and the gods were the same. But until now, she had not been ready to see it.

She was ageless. Just like the gods.

She did not know which was worse, the prospect of watching all those she knew and loved grow old and perish or facing the terror of one day ceasing to exist.

'Of course, your body may still be wounded like a mortal's,' Hades continued. 'You can be killed.'

Danae stared at him, unable to form words.

Hades waved a hand, as though weary of this vein of conversation. 'In the centuries since gaining control of Mount Olympus, my family have become preoccupied with mortals' worship, as though it is their love that makes us gods. They have forgotten the true nature of divinity: creation.'

Finally, Danae found her voice. 'You are not gods,' she spat. 'Prometheus told me the truth. There were only ever mortals, and those mortals chosen to become Titans.'

Hades raised an eyebrow. 'How would you define a god? One who has power over life and death? Over creation itself?'

She did not answer.

'Come.' Hades beckoned her closer to the desk. 'I want to show you something.'

Tentatively, she stepped forward.

There were two drawings sketched upon the parchment Hades had been examining. Spindly writing and numerical calculations were detailed around them, filling the rest of the page. The first diagram was that of a man and beside it a smaller creature with a hooded head and a squat, reptilian body. Each likeness was painstakingly detailed. A straight line spliced the man's body in two, the left side revealing the sinews and muscles beneath his skin as though it had been peeled away. Heart pounding, her eyes trailed to the lizard-like creature. An image flickered across her memory. A pair of crimson reptilian eyes darting away across the Asphodel Meadows, the creature's body invisible. Then she thought of the patchwork of scars lacing Charon's otherwise similarly invisible skin and the gorgons' strange questions. *Were you born or made?*

Bile nauseated her insides, bubbling its way up her throat. Her knuckles turned white as she gripped the edge of the desk. Without it, her legs would have given way.

'I discovered the Aether lizards when my brother exiled me down into the bowels of the earth, and I thought how marvellous it would be, for a man to have such changeable skin. So, I made it be. Charon was mortal once, then he became the first of the Oneroi, my dream children. The ferryman is an ever-constant reminder of how far I have come since his creation.'

Blood roared so loud in Danae's ears she could barely absorb what Hades was saying. He had fashioned the shades out of people and the hides of these Aether lizards.

'In my mortal life I was a healer. But once I ate the Hesperides apple, the world opened to me like I was the sun and it a budding flower. I never dreamed what miracles would be possible if I applied the power of life-threads to my work. I made Charon my protégé and allowed him too to taste the golden fruit so we might carry on our work together without the inconvenience of death taking him from me. But in time I came to realize that when one is ageless, one has no need of a successor. And so, my apprentice took on a different role.' Hades' eyes shone with a brightness she had not seen before.

'I am a creator. All the beings that roam this kingdom were made by me. I take ordinary creatures and turn them into something magnificent. The harpies my brother, Zeus, commissioned to do his bidding, the Earthborn you faced in the land of the Doliones, even the creature you arrived with is my child. I bred the most intelligent horses for centuries until foals were born that could understand human speech, then I gave them wings. But I do not just make beasts. You have seen my botanical work on the island of Lemnos. The territory was a gift for my niece, Artemis, grown before my brother forbade me from setting foot above ground.' His expression hardened. 'I am called the Lord of Death but in truth I am the God of Life. Just think what we could achieve together once you eradicate my brother.'

Danae backed away from the desk. 'You ... mutilated them. All those creatures ... the shades ...'

A note of irritation clipped Hades' voice. 'I do not grow my creations as the great Mother does, from seed or egg or womb, but I elevate that which is already alive.'

She did not know who this Mother was, but there were other questions that clamoured to be voiced. 'The shades . . . they were all human once?'

Hades nodded. 'They were mortals plucked from a group known as the Missing.'

The irony was bitter: the people who vanished every year from all across Greece were transformed into the very beings who kidnapped them.

Danae felt as though every drop of blood had fled her body as realization crashed over her. 'A baby . . . One of your shades took my nephew from Naxos three years ago. What have you done to him?'

The furrows deepened between Hades' dark brows. 'I do not work with infants; their bodies are weak, they require constant care —'

'But a shade took him.' Panic strangled her voice. 'If you don't have him, where is he?'

Hades was silent for a moment. 'A baby, you say . . .'

'Yes,' Danae urged. 'His name is Arius. He was taken on his first birthday.' She drew a breath, fortifying herself to say the words she had not yet been brave enough to utter to anyone since Alea died. 'My sister believed Zeus was the father.'

She expected Hades to laugh, but instead a strange expression rippled across his face. 'Indeed . . . the fates work in mysterious ways.'

She stared at him, her entire body trembling. 'Is it true?'

Hades watched her like a falcon. 'Every generation my brother chooses a mortal woman to impregnate. He has them drugged and brought to Olympus.'

Every heartbeat was agony, her blood so hot it seared her veins. Zeus had abducted and raped Alea. Another truth she had fought so hard not to believe. Her beautiful sister had been right all along.

'Please . . .' she rasped, barely able to form words. 'If you know where Arius is . . . tell me.'

Hades seemed to wrestle within himself, then his gaze grew as sharp as a javelin.

'The child is gone. Most likely killed.'

Danae barely felt the blow. There were only so many cracks one heart could sustain, and hers had shattered in the Asphodel Meadows.

Hades' eyes gleamed. 'Destiny is not set in stone. The fates delight in twisting the future men think they have seen. Hold on to your anger, little Titan. You are not yet ready to face my brother, but after I'm finished, you will be.'

Danae stepped away from him. Her back met something cold and leathery. She turned as a sea of crimson eyes surged towards her, falling into a swarm of hands as a cloth soaked in something pungent and bitter was forced over her mouth.

Danae woke to bone-shattering pain pulsing through her skull. She was lying on something hard and flat, the iron collar cold against her skin. She tried to move her limbs and found herself restrained. Her jaw ached. There was something hard between her teeth; her mouth stretched around it. She probed the invading item with her tongue. It tasted like wood and seemed to be tied around the back of her head. Fighting the nauseating ache across her temples, she prised open her eyes. A domed ceiling of polished black marble loomed above her.

Twisting against her restraints, she took in the rest of the room. Along the majority of the walls were floor-to-ceiling shelves of glass potion bottles, containing liquids in myriad colours. Benches supporting strange metal contraptions with intricate pulley and lever systems were positioned between pots of pale plants she did not recognize. Crystal lights hung over their troughs suspended by chains, and beside these was a black marble plinth, with several slim metallic objects glinting on its surface.

Knives.

Fear rippled through her. She had seen blades like this in Dolos' healer's bag; silver slivers, some thinner than her little finger, designed to slice flesh. Her eyes slid up from the assorted knives to the shelving above, and her stomach lurched. There were more glass vessels, much larger than the potion bottles, some as thick as the trunk of an oak. There were creatures suspended within the liquid. Squirrels, goats, rats and some so grotesquely misshapen she couldn't tell what they had been in life. She was reminded of Polyxo's hut on Lemnos, yet where the old woman's workbench had been a chaotic jumble of spices, herbs and dried animal skins, everything in this room was precise and ordered.

At the sound of footsteps, Danae's head snapped around to see Hades emerge through an archway to her left, the shelving of the library chamber visible behind him. She must be lying on the stone slab she had glimpsed before.

He wore a bloodstained butcher's apron.

Her heart thudded so fast she barely registered that Hades was speaking as he moved towards the podium of knives.

'You reeked of desperation when you arrived in my kingdom, consumed with seeking the afterlife just like every mortal that survives the journey to Erebus. I had hoped, given what you are, you would be different.' His fingers lingered over the blades; then, as though changing his mind, turned away empty-handed. 'My wife Persephone was like you once. So full of feeling. Utterly incapable of ruling her own heart.' He pressed a finger into Danae's breastbone. She tried to scream, but all that came out was a muffled moan through her wooden gag.

'In the days of old, before my brother ruled Olympus, the Mother's chosen mortals had to forget their worldly desires, their wants, their dreams, their loves, in order to become Titans.' Hades traced his finger over Danae's chest, up her neck and beneath her chin. 'Zeus may have taken control of the holy mountain, but for all his power, he is still bound by human weakness. To defeat him you must shed your mortality.'

Danae trembled as his fingers tripped over her cracked lips, then traced upwards following the curve of her nose.

'The human mind is so wonderfully easy to break and reshape. Take the harpies, for example: their bodies – especially those tricksome wings – took months of labour. By the time I came to conditioning their minds, they had almost forgotten themselves and were wonderfully pliable. Charon, on the other hand, took five years to succumb to my methods after I changed his skin.' Hades' finger reached her hairline and began tracing invisible pathways across her scalp. 'I wonder, little Titan, how long you will take?'

His hands stopped moving, and Danae jolted at a twinge above her left ear.

'Did you know that pain originates not from the wound site, but here in the brain?' Her wooden gag muffled a shriek as Hades tapped her skull and a bolt of agony seared through her right arm. 'Like the roots of a tree, you have a network of nerves throughout your body, all signalled from your cranium. All I have to do is send a life-thread to press on just the right piece of the organ and . . .' She lurched as another burst of pain spiked through her left foot.

Hades continued to tap away, a musician strumming a melody of agony from her body. She thrashed like a beached fish, her vision darkening with every bone-cracking whip of pain.

Eventually, Danae's eyelids fluttered, but before her consciousness fled, the Lord of the Underworld relented. Relief washed through her, dragging her back to the room. She stared at the obsidian marble ceiling through blurred eyes. He could torture her body until she passed out, but he could not reach her mind. She would not let him.

Then Hades' fingers continued to move, parting her hair like a predator stalking through long grass. 'But the marvels of the brain do not end there. As darkness is twinned with light, the mirror of pain is pleasure.'

An odd sensation spread through her abdomen, down between her legs. For a moment she didn't understand what was happening, then she was transported back to a moonlit beach, the touch of Heracles' hands, his mouth on her skin. A muffled moan, half pleasure, half despair, slipped from her lips.

Not this. Surely Hades did not have the power to drag forth this innermost part of her?

She fought the feeling, tried to fill her mind with something, anything, to quell the ache building inside her. She gripped the guilt of stealing Heracles' lion hide, the blood of his closest friend staining her hands. She wrapped herself so tightly in shame she could barely breathe, but still the surge came. Silently, she screamed as her treacherous body shuddered against her will.

'There,' Hades removed his hands from her head. 'You see, it's all just little pulses of energy. All those feelings, all those desires that weigh you down and keep you tethered to your mortality: just sparks and signals. Ecstasy and agony: none of it is real.'

A lone tear trickled down her temple. She could see it gleaming silver in the light of the crystals glowing about the room. It was strange; she knew she was still bound to the table, yet she saw the scene as though watching from above. Like she had become untethered from her body, spirited away on an unseen breeze.

Perhaps Hades was wrong, she thought. Perhaps oblivion was not what awaited her. Perhaps this is what it was like to die.

14. Tartarus

Danae sat on the bench opposite Hades as Charon guided his barge through the inky waters of the Styx. The river rushed past them, the glowing crystal at the end of Charon's staff casting oscillating ribbons of light across the dark water. The Lord of the Underworld sat in silence, brooding amongst the folds of his midnight robe. Danae stared at the ferryman's back, her mind blank as the fabric of his grey cloak.

Every day for what felt like weeks she had been brought to Hades' laboratory and strapped onto the cold, marble slab. Sometimes he'd leave her alone for hours, sometimes moments, before returning to channel more pain or pleasure through her unwilling, powerless flesh. Her life became a cycle between sleep and torture, punctuated by the trudge down the corridor that connected the two. Then one day it was not the laboratory the shades escorted her to but the river.

'Would you like to know where we are going, little Titan?' asked Hades.

Danae did not reply.

'We are journeying to Tartarus. You will know it as the realm of everlasting torment, but before the age of Olympians, it held no connotations with the afterlife and was known simply as the deepest region of the world.'

Hades' words were met with more silence. He cocked his head, surveying her. 'What is it that you want?'

Danae blinked. What did it matter? What did any of her wants matter now? After what Hades had done only one desire burned within her, a single flame warming her cold husk. Every heartbreak, every tormented breath, every tear of her spirit could be traced back to one event. The night Alea was taken from the Thesmophoria on Naxos.

She wanted vengeance.

'To kill Zeus.'

Hades nodded.

'I will make you a deal. When we reach Tartarus, I will ask you to complete one simple task. If you do it, I will know you are ready. I shall remove the collar, and together we will storm Olympus with an army of Underworld creatures and kill my brother. Do you accept?'

Still staring unfocused at Charon's cloak, she whispered, 'Yes.'

A smoke-dark mist, thicker than the one that lingered on the Asphodel Meadows, had crept across the sandy banks, lacquering Danae's skin with a clammy sheen. After a while she noticed a scent she recognized. It was like hearing a stranger hum a familiar tune.

Salt water.

The echo of a memory sounded in her mind. A man's voice; warm and rough and kind. *All seas are the same beast. When we're riding her, no matter how far apart, we're riding together.*

She blinked, properly taking in her surroundings for the first time. 'We're not on the Styx any more, are we?'

'No, we are not,' said Hades. 'This is the Acheron. There are three rivers that feed the Underworld, but this is the only one that flows directly to the sea.'

A river that ran to the ocean in the world above. When she had first arrived in the Underworld it felt like a dream. Now she could barely remember what sunlight felt like on her skin.

They travelled on in silence. Eventually, the mist became so thick she could no longer see the banks on either side, only Charon's light bobbing ahead of them.

'When I was a child,' said Hades, 'my father used to entertain my siblings and me with a magic trick. He would hold an almond in his palm, then close his fingers and blow upon them. When he opened his hand, the nut would have vanished. When I asked how he did it, he said he made the almond invisible. I was disappointed when Zeus told me that it was a lie and our father had merely hidden the nut through sleight of hand. He became lesser in my eyes that day. But I never forgot the wonder he stirred within my soul. The idea that anything is possible.'

It was strange to hear Hades talk of his father and brother as though they had been part of a family like any other. Once, they had been innocent children.

'Why did Zeus banish you to the Underworld?'

Hades was still for a while, a pillar of chalk and ash blurred by the fog. Then he muttered, 'My brother has no imagination.'

Danae gripped the wooden seat beneath her as the barge knocked against the rocks to the right of the river and Charon wedged his staff between two crags, steadying the vessel. She had not noticed in the mist, but the soft midnight sand had given way to hard banks of stone.

Hades stepped onto the lip of rock and turned to Danae. He stretched out a thin, pale hand and helped her onto the rocks.

Danae and Hades walked in silence across the mist-dampened stone, following the ferryman's light through the dank fog. A dull ache had spread through Danae's legs and back by the time they arrived at the entrance to a cave. A faint orange glow pulsed from within.

The head of a giant snake had been carved from the rock, its jaws stretched open as though the cave entrance was a vast mouth. Gleaming eyes, forged from sparkling emerald stone, had been sunk into either side of the serpent's head. A forked tongue flicked over the lower jaw to form a walkway down to the rocks below, and from above two fangs, each as long as Danae was tall, stretched down like stalactites towards the ground.

Hades approached the stone reptile, the mist swirling about him with a lover's caress. He paused on the threshold of the forked tongue and glanced back at Danae.

'Welcome to Tartarus.'

The fog receded as they pressed on through the tunnel, the copper light brightening with each step. Danae became aware of noises, the clash of metal on stone and the rumble of what sounded like wheels. The clangs and crashes intensified as they proceeded through the smooth passage. She stumbled on a patch of uneven ground and looked down to see that parallel grooves had been carved into the rock walkway, similar to the cart tracks in the old mine far above.

They were almost halfway through the tunnel when a blast of heat rippled down the passage, stinging her cheeks and drawing tears from her eyes.

'What's down there?'

'Patience, little Titan,' Hades glanced back, his pale skin glowing in the burnished light. 'Soon all shall be revealed.'

At the end of the passage they stepped through another entranceway, supported by a thick wooden frame, and emerged onto a large platform on the edge of a huge pit, lit by hundreds of flaming braziers fixed to the curving rock wall. It was the size of a town, its jagged, circular interior a warren of caves. Twisting around them, stone staircases were threaded like veins across the rock, joining several walkways that stretched across the void. Carts attached to pulley systems that seemed to move of their own accord ran beside the stairs, their bellies glistening with hunks of precious metals, gems and slabs of rock. From this angle Danae could not see the bottom of the pit, only the steam that billowed up from below.

'It's a mine,' she breathed.

'Minerals, metals, marble, jewels,' said Hades. 'The earth's riches are bountiful.'

'What do you do with it all?'

'Most goes to Olympus. Some to the favoured kings of men.' His voice tightened. 'On the command of my brother.'

A deep bellow echoed up the pit. She moved forward to see what had uttered the sound and gasped.

Something huge emerged from one of the larger passageways. A creature over thirty feet tall, shaped like a man but bound in solid muscle, its leathery skin as grey as stone.

It was a giant, like the one Heracles was famed to have slain during his labours.

As she watched, a second emerged behind it, then a third. There was a whip crack and another bellow. The giants were all manacled at the wrists and ankles by thick metal chains, their muscular arms full of rocks they heaved into waiting carts.

Following her gaze, Hades said, 'Mortals may be the Mother's favourite children, but they were not her first. Once, we shared the earth with these creatures. Zeus wished to destroy them all, but I convinced him to let me imprison some in my kingdom. The giants have been invaluable to my work. Not only are they powerful, they age so slowly they are capable of living for thousands of years.'

Danae could not draw her eyes from them. These must be the beings the Olympians had fashioned the tales of the Titans after.

'Who is the Mother?' she asked.

'She is unimportant. As mortal children outgrow their parents, so we have outgrown her. Come.' With a flare of his dark robe, Hades strode across the platform down one of the flights of stairs cut into the rock. Danae and Charon hurried after him.

Danae was about to press Hades further, when several oddly shaped creatures, seemingly without heads, emerged from the same cave as the giants. It took her a moment to realize that they were shades, dressed in fortified leather armour, armed with whips and spears. One lashed out at the nearest giant, drawing a roar from the creature. Then another gust of steam boiled from the depths of Tartarus, and Danae was forced to cover her eyes.

They pressed on, deeper into the bowels of the cavern.

Danae slowed again as the clink of axes drew her attention to another of the caves. Here, the workers were not giants, they were mortals.

The rest of the Missing.

Like their larger fellow miners, these people were shackled together, their clothes so torn and filthy it was impossible to discern who they once might have been. They did not look up from their work as Hades, Charon and Danae passed them by, their eyes hollow as the cavern around them.

Danae thought of their families left behind, with no graves to mourn at, and no answers to sate their desperate longing.

She dragged her eyes from the mortals and forced herself to keep moving, pacing after Hades and the ferryman.

Eventually, their winding staircase reached the bottom of the cavern, and Hades paced towards a vast iron grate set into the rock bed beneath their feet. Metal tubes burrowed into the stone around it, feeding up to the cavern walls and into the pulley systems that operated the carts. Another burst of steam issued from the grate, the tubes vibrated, and the carts heaved into motion. Danae's lips parted in amazement.

'Check the locks,' Hades barked at Charon.

The ferryman obeyed, running between the eight metal locks holding the grate in place. Condensation glistened on the bars. As Danae drew closer, the heat burned her lungs and lanced sweat from her skin, but curiosity drove her forward. When she reached the edge, she looked down.

Dark water shimmered at the bottom of a vast well. Ripples scurried across the surface, then the liquid seemed to shatter as something huge emerged from the water.

A great reptilian head coated with emerald scales and black spines reared up. Eyes, like two burning suns slit through with obsidian, blazed up at Danae. Then jaws that could have swallowed her whole opened.

She threw herself back just in time to avoid being caught in the plume of steam soaring up through the cavern. It seemed Charon had known what to expect and had already moved back. Once the cloud of hot air had dissipated, he carried on testing the locks of the creature's cage.

Danae turned to Hades, who stood further back from the pit, his brow creased, arms folded.

'What *is* that?'

'It is the dragon, Typhon.'

'The *what*?'

'An ancient creature, possibly the oldest in existence, blessed with the gift of flight and fire. And it is mine.' Hades' lips stretched into a strained smile. 'Its containment is simple, yet effective. By keeping it submerged in water without the space to stretch its wings, the dragon's fire is neutralized.'

She felt a twinge of pity for this magnificent creature, imprisoned in a pit in the deepest part of the earth. Her hands flew to the collar around her neck. Both of them gelded, one by water, one by iron.

Charon hurried to his master's side and signed his report.

Hades' scowl deepened. 'Are you sure?' Then almost to himself he muttered, 'The stone does not lie.'

The ferryman nodded.

'Hmm.' The Lord of the Underworld stared at the grate. For a moment, Danae could have sworn she caught a whisper of fear in his pale eyes.

'Come.' Hades turned and strode towards another staircase that snaked up to one of the passageways burrowed into the rock. 'It is time for your task.'

Once more Danae disconnected from her surroundings, retreating into the innermost part of herself. After this, Hades had promised to take off her collar. That was all that mattered: regaining her power so she could fulfil her destiny.

They left the main chamber of Tartarus, Charon's glowing staff leading the way through a roughly hewn tunnel until they reached another grate guarding a cave beyond. The ferryman withdrew a ring of keys from beneath his cloak, undid the lock and heaved the door open.

Filthy, gaunt faces stared out from the darkness. The chamber was rammed with people. It was difficult to tell in the dim light but there must have been at least fifty mortals imprisoned in the cave. Like their fellows working the mine, their clothing was torn and covered in dirt. There were people in the first flush of adulthood all the way to the very elderly. At the sight of Hades stepping into the chamber they cringed back, pressing themselves against the rock walls.

'This is my vault. The weak specimens are useful for replenishing life-threads, the rest I put to work, or elevate into shades.'

Her heart stammered.

'Let them go.'

Hades turned to her.

'Free them and the mortal workers in the mine, then I will do whatever you ask.'

'That was not our bargain.' His expression darkened. 'Perhaps the rot of your humanity has not yet been weeded out. We should return to my laboratory.'

Her mouth dried.

'No,' she rasped. She forced herself to think of all the future generations she would save from the tyranny of the Twelve once she had defeated Zeus. She had to hold on to the greater good. The lives of the many over the fate of the few. 'What is my task?'

Hades snapped his fingers.

Several of the Missing whimpered as Charon stepped amongst them and pulled an emaciated man from their midst.

Danae drew a short, sharp breath.

The man was dressed in nothing but a grime-encrusted kilt. His mahogany hair hung in tatters, shrouding the sharp angles of his face. He was tall, his shoulders broad despite his wasted frame, his bruise-mottled skin stretched over long, spindly limbs. Danae wouldn't have recognized him had she not seen him this way once before, lying unconscious in a cave beneath a tree adorned with the bodies of dead men. A sacrifice to Artemis from the hunters of Lemnos.

A once powerful hero starved of his strength elixir.

Heracles.

'What would you give, little Titan, to have your powers restored? To destroy Zeus? It begins here. One little life. It should be easy; he looks so like his father.' Hades withdrew a bronze knife from inside his midnight robe. He laid the blade flat on his palms and held it out to Danae, like the temple hands used to do before the sacrifice at the Thesmophoria.

'The time has come for you to shed the last shackles of your mortality. As soon as you have completed your task, I will remove the collar, and your powers will return.'

She took the blade by its bone handle. Under Hades' tutelage she could become more powerful than she had ever dreamed possible. Just like him.

An old ache, a memory of ecstasy, rippled through her; of life-threads thrumming through her veins. Perhaps her humanity was already lost, left behind in the mists of the Asphodel Meadows. Her heart was barren, any remnants of feeling burned up by grief and fury. She had made so many agonizing choices, put aside what she wanted over and over again. She could do it once more. She had to. She was just a thing of flesh, with nothing but Prometheus' words where her soul should have been.

The air felt as thick as honey as she turned the knife in her hand. It was so light, such a small thing. A tiny destroyer of worlds.

Charon forced the man to his knees, pulling his head back to bare his neck.

Her gaze met his.

Heracles' cerulean eyes were bloodshot, devoid of anger or fear, filled instead with the stone-patient look of a man waiting to die.

Danae loosed a long, slow breath and raised the blade above her head.

15. Imperial Purple

Objectively, Hera knew she was flawless. As a mortal, she had been blessed with perfectly symmetrical features. She could no longer remember how old she had been when she became divine. Thirty perhaps? Time moved differently for her now; it was almost impossible to contemplate such a limited number. She had lived endless lives, and she would live endless more.

She sat in her chambers in a gilded chair, appraising herself in the bronze mirrored wall. Once satisfied with the shape of her hair, she lifted a golden headdress from the marble table in front of her and placed it on her oiled curls. It was a simple design, just a band with rods of gold shooting from it, but on her it was spectacular. The shining metal crowned her head just like the rays of the sun.

As she gazed at her reflection, she methodically recalled the wounds she'd suffered over the years, some at the hands of her enemies, some inflicted by those she loved most. She imagined what she would look like if she did not have the power to heal herself by consuming the life-threads of others, if Zeus ever denied her access to the lives of the mortals held in the Olympus vault. She was plagued by a terrible fear that one day she would wake up with all the livid scars, burns and mutilations she had ever suffered visible on her skin.

Two weeks had passed since she'd overheard Zeus and Poseidon's plan to send Hermes after the girl from Prometheus' prophecy. Two weeks of agonizing waiting. As far as she knew, the boy was still out there, searching. If Hermes failed, she had no doubt her husband would send another child. Possibly one of her own sons.

She smoothed the silk of her gown, banishing the fear threatening to curl around her heart. The colour was particularly special. The specific shade was imperial purple, the dye harvested from a rare species of sea snail. To create one dress required tens of thousands of the little creatures. The labour wasn't easy either; the snails resided on the ocean bed and had a fondness for human flesh. As a result, it often took decades to make a single garment.

Only the best for the Queen of Heaven.

A princess of Mycenae had once commissioned an imperial purple dress. The mortal had debuted it at the unveiling of a new temple dedicated to Zeus, no less. The bare-faced nerve of it. Hera had made sure the woman's body was cold before the arrogant creature had the chance to wear the gown again. Imperial purple was Hera's colour and hers alone.

She traced the little stoppers of each of the potion bottles lining her dressing table, the glass chinking under her fingers. Some were perfumes she'd concocted from flowers in the sky palace gardens. Some were medicines to help her sleep and calm her nerves. And some were poisons so deadly a single drop would asphyxiate an Olympian before they'd had time to grab the nearest nymph. Her son, Hephaestus, chided her for keeping them all together. It would be so easy to make a mistake, he'd said. She'd told him she never made mistakes.

The door to Hera's chambers opened, and one of her nymphs entered.

'Your son, Hephaestus, my queen.'

Hera nodded, and the nymph retreated through the door. Hephaestus entered the room and bowed to his mother.

He was still wearing his forge clothes, his face smeared with soot.

Hera's brow creased. 'You could have changed.'

'The nymph said you wished to see me right away.'

He lowered himself down onto the cushions at the edge of Hera's vast bed. She winced as he rested a grubby hand on one of the draped pillars that stood at each corner.

She rose, snatched a tasselled shawl from one of the many beautifully crafted pieces of furniture that littered her chambers and strode over to him.

Hephaestus pulled away as she began scrubbing soot from his rich brown skin.

'You should take more pride in yourself. You can't walk around the palace like this, you're a prince of heaven.'

'Stop.'

Hera sighed and relented from wiping.

'Don't look at me like that,' grumbled Hephaestus.

'Like what?'

'Like you pity me.'

'I don't pity you,' Hera said softly. 'I just don't see you enough.' She placed a hand on his cheek.

He knocked her arm away. 'Why don't you summon Ares? You could wipe my wife's pleasure off his lips.'

Hera flinched. She loathed it when he spoke so crassly. Almost as much as she loathed the copper-haired whore who'd poisoned her boys against each other.

She dropped the shawl and stalked over to the balcony, gesturing for her son to follow. Hephaestus grunted and heaved himself to his feet as a nymph darted from a far corner of the room to retrieve the shawl. He stepped through the billowing gossamer curtains and joined Hera outside.

She leant against the marble balustrade, the clouds

clustering around as though waiting to hear her secrets. As Hephaestus followed her, Hera's umber eyes darted over his shoulder, then she whispered, 'Has your father asked anything of you recently? Entrusted you with any special tasks?'

Hephaestus frowned. 'Nothing out of the ordinary. Why?'

The knot in Hera's chest eased slightly. 'I just had a feeling. You know how secretive your father can be.'

'Is this to do with Hermes?'

'Oh?' Hera smoothed her face into an expression of mild curiosity.

'He came to me to fix his boots, said Father had entrusted him with a special mission.'

Hera laughed. 'Zeus does enjoy creating games for you children. How is he getting along?'

'Not well. He returned to the palace last night. I heard him playing his pipes up on the north tower. He hides up there when he's unhappy.'

'Really?' He must not yet have found the girl.

Hephaestus scowled. 'Why are you so interested?'

'I take an interest in all the divine children.'

Hephaestus raised an eyebrow. 'You hate Hermes.'

Hera's jaw tightened. 'That's not true.'

'You hate all my siblings that aren't your blood. Stop trying to pry for information because Father is shutting you out.'

She pressed her lips together, wounded by the accuracy of the barb.

'It is important, in the current climate, that we stay close as a family.'

'What's that supposed to mean?'

She knew he loved her. She was the one who'd brought him into the world and nursed him back to health when Zeus flung him from Olympus. But his father's blood was potent. She could see the King of the Gods in the shape of his eyes and the movement of his lips. Beyond the physical, Zeus held a power over his children that Hera struggled to emulate. Even after what Zeus had done to Hephaestus, the pain her son would bear for the rest of eternity, he was still in his father's thrall. She couldn't trust him. Not yet.

Hera smiled and kissed her son's cheek. 'Never you mind.'

Hera ascended the twisting narrow steps leading up to the north tower. As she neared the top, she heard music echoing off the marble walls. A sweet, sorrowful tune. A smile tugged at her lips. She must admit Hermes had talent, despite his common mortal mother.

Hera's birth parents had been textile merchants, murdered on the road for their wares when she was an infant. With no other family to shelter her, she had been given to another woman in their village, Rhea, a fisherman's wife with four children of her own. It had been difficult at first, to be suddenly ripped from her comfortable life and forced to reside in a squalid hut that perpetually stank of fish. Zeus alone had given her reason to rise each dawn. A blue-eyed star in the darkness.

Rhea used to say it didn't matter that they did not share blood. *'We are all the Mother's children, and I love you as much as any babe from my womb.'* Hera wondered sometimes if that would still have been true, if she had been Rhea's husband Kronos' daughter with another woman.

Hera paused at the pinnacle of the staircase and lingered in the doorway. It was beautiful up here. It had been so long she'd forgotten. Between supporting stone pillars, the walls and ceiling were fashioned from mosaics of coloured glass. Another of Hephaestus' marvels. Swirls of light stained orange, teal and yellow draped over Hermes where he sat cross-legged on the floor, his helm next to him. His eyes were closed, a set of pipes at his lips, his mind borne away on the wings of his song.

Hera took a step towards him, and his eyes flew open. He dropped his pipes with a clatter, scrabbling to shove his helm back over his face. His armour clinked as he hurried to his feet.

'My queen.' Hermes bowed hastily.

Hera tilted her head in return. She never ceased to find it unsettling that Zeus had chosen to give his youngest divine son a golden apple at such an early age. But then, he was only a couple of years younger than the mortal boys the King of Heaven installed in his chambers.

She brushed the thought away. After centuries her anger had cooled to a glacier, each new offence just another splinter of ice.

Her face bloomed into a radiant smile. 'Don't stop on my account.'

Hermes didn't move, his arms hanging stiffly at his side. Hera wandered into the glass room, bent down and retrieved the boy's pipes, then proffered them to him. He accepted with a trembling hand. She turned from him and trod a path through the rainbows scattered across the floor. Beyond, the clouds swirled around them, every now and then a shaft of sunlight piercing the sanctum.

'Please, don't tell Father I'm here,' he blurted.

Hera smiled. 'I won't breathe a word.'

Hermes swallowed, then made a move towards the staircase.

'Wait.' Hera wafted between him and the doorway. 'It's you I've come to see.'

Hermes paused, unable to hide his surprise. 'What can I do for you, Divine Mother?' His voice cracked on the final word.

'I thought it would be nice for us to spend more time together. Hephaestus always speaks so highly of your company. Come,' Hera sank to the floor, 'sit with me.'

Her stepson dithered for a moment, then lowered himself down next to her. Hera shuffled closer to him, fanning the hem of her purple dress over her legs.

'Are you happy, Hermes?'

'Y-yes.'

'Good.' Hera leant back and sighed. 'I hope Ares hasn't been too cruel of late. I know he can be difficult when brewing a war, and the invasion of Troy has been his largest undertaking yet.'

Hermes' brow darkened.

Hera's eyes softened with practised sympathy. 'I love my son, but he can be awful when the mood takes him. He's always been that way, I'm afraid.'

The corners of Hermes' mouth twitched below his golden helm.

'He would be furious if he knew I'd told you this . . .' She leant forward and lowered her voice. 'When he was a child, he had a little toy horse called Horris. He used to sleep with it every night – refused to be parted from it. He'd even take it to bathe with him.' She laughed. 'When he was twelve, your father destroyed it. He told Ares that he was a man now and should no longer play with toys. Ares cried about it for months.'

'Months?' asked Hermes gleefully.

'*Months*. I think that's why he loves war so much. All those horses.'

The stiffness eased from Hermes' limbs as he gazed at her, cow-eyed. *Gently does it*, she thought.

'Darling, I know it isn't easy for you with the others. But I want you to know that you can always come to me.'

Hermes' expression faltered. As much as she could tell the

boy craved her approval, he was in thrall to his father. She must be careful.

'I know what Zeus has asked of you.'

Hermes' eyes widened. 'You do?'

Her pulse quickened as she leant closer. 'I have faced the girl. I fought her atop the Caucasus Mountains. I can help you.'

Hermes recoiled from her. 'I-I can't discuss it. With anyone.'

'Of course.' Hera sat back and folded her hands primly across her lap. 'I'm sure your father has given you all the information you need.'

He stared at her, his face contorted with indecision. Then he whispered, 'Hades said Father is a . . .'

'Go on,' Hera breathed.

'*Liar*,' Hermes mouthed.

'Did he now . . .' Hera's heart beat quick as a hummingbird's wing. 'What else did Hades say?'

'He said, if it looks like a lion –'

At the sound of footfall on the stairs, he abruptly fell silent.

Hera's head snapped towards the doorway, and she caught the telltale shimmer of a shade lurking in the shadows. A shiver scuttled down her spine.

'I won't hear of it, Hermes,' she said loudly. 'You *will* play me another song.'

The boy's face had turned grey with fear, but he rallied himself and lifted his pipe to his lips.

Hera's breast heaved as he played, barely hearing the music as she watched the doorway out of the corner of her eye. Finally, the distorted air shifted and moved back down into the gloom of the staircase.

Her lips parted, breath hissing between them. The thrill

of her transgression made her feel more alive than she had done in centuries.

Hermes abruptly stopped playing. 'I must go.'

As he rose, Hera grabbed his arm. 'Return to the Underworld. Press your uncle to tell you more.'

Hermes backed away from her, eyes stretched wide, then practically fled down the steps.

Hera remained where she sat, watching the shattered rainbow of light from the stained glass dance across the floor. She had come so close to winning Hermes' confidence. Yet this might be the perfect solution. If he was to defeat the girl, and keep Ares and Hephaestus from being thrown into her path, he must learn her real identity. Although Zeus had forbidden the elder gods from revealing Prometheus' prophecy to the children, Hades did not always obey his brother. He had almost cracked once. By the sound of it, he had been on the verge of telling the boy everything. She hoped another visit from Hermes would break him open. If the Lord of the Underworld was the one to spill the truth, neither she nor her boys would incur Zeus' wrath.

Hera closed her eyes and loosed a long, slow breath. Her husband was their captain, their guiding star; he'd forged a path for them into the heavens, and never once had she doubted him.

Until now.

16. A Titan's Choice

Danae paused, the knife raised above her head.

'Do it,' Heracles croaked.

During the long year she'd spent searching for the Underworld, she'd sometimes tortured herself by imagining how the hero would react if he ever saw her again. She had expected hatred, fury, even violence. Some proportionate response to her betrayal of all they'd shared. She had killed his closest friend, stolen his lion hide and abandoned him outside the city of Colchis.

She'd never dreamed she would be met with acceptance. It was almost as though he was trying to make this easier for her.

Hades must have broken him too.

Time moved like a ponderous drip of honey, and as she gazed into Heracles' gaunt face, the last words of Prometheus' prophecy echoed in her mind.

Become the light that frees mankind.

If one brief walk upon the earth was all mortals had, she owed it to every living soul to fight for them. Every single one.

Hades smiled as Danae plunged the knife down.

At the last moment, she twisted, Hades' mouth distorting as she sank the blade into his heart. The God of the Underworld staggered back, his pale face stretched in an agonizing grimace, the bone handle protruding from his chest.

She could never hope to become the light if she allied with the darkness. Hades might have promised to give her an Underworld army to defeat Zeus, but he was one of the Twelve, and under his reign mortals would never be free.

Heracles sagged onto all fours as Charon let go of him, sucking in desperate lungfuls of air, eyes stretched wide in disbelief. He stared up at Danae as though seeing her for the first time. The ferryman stood still as the rock around them, his crimson gaze locked upon his wounded master.

Danae ran to Heracles and tried to help him to his feet.

'I'm sorry, I'm so sorry.'

He flinched beneath her hands. He felt so frail, like he might shatter at any moment. A world away from the last time they had touched. A memory jolted through her: strong, calloused fingers, tugging the clothes from her body, warmth spreading through her. Then a cold slab hard against her back. She shuddered.

Like the ferryman, most of the Missing looked on in paralysed disbelief as their master, their tormenter, bled onto the floor of their cell.

Danae had almost helped Heracles to his feet when there was a scream behind her.

Hades, his chest heaving with the last vestiges of life, had grabbed the nearest mortal by her ragged tunic and dragged her down to the floor with him. With a guttural moan, he ripped the knife from his chest, slashed it across the woman's throat, then wrapped his fingers around her neck.

Time seemed to halt, then, like a river rushing towards a waterfall, suddenly regained speed.

'No!' Danae let go of Heracles and lunged towards Hades as he drained the woman's life-force. She had aimed too high: the knife had pierced the flesh above his heart, and, aided by the mortal's life-threads, the wound healed in the space of two breaths.

Danae made it halfway across the cave before Hades

straightened up and conjured a gust of wind that hurled her back against the far wall. She cried out as her bones cracked against the rock, her limbs pinned under the pressure of his life-threads.

Heracles staggered and once again fell to his knees as the rest of the Missing cringed back, clustering into the depths of the cave. Charon stood between Hades and Danae, his crimson gaze flashing between them.

The Lord of the Underworld's pale eyes burned with icy rage.

'How disappointing,' he spat through blood-flecked teeth.

Her heart thundered as he advanced, his arm outstretched as though he would drain her just like he had the mortal.

But before Hades reached her, Charon unleashed a guttural cry and charged his staff upwards, ramming its crystal end into the ceiling. There was a blinding flash of pure white light, then part of the cave collapsed.

Danae slid down the wall, no longer pinned by Hades' life-threads. Then a gloved pair of hands grabbed her. She coughed, her lungs full of dust, unable to see as the ferryman dragged her out through the doorway, leaving Hades, Heracles and the Missing trapped in the cave on the other side of the fallen ceiling.

'Wait,' she spluttered, as Charon pulled her down the passage, 'Heracles . . .'

But the ferryman only increased his speed.

Danae dug in her heels. 'Stop!' she coughed. 'Why are you helping me?'

This could be a trick, another of Hades' tortures designed to dangle hope in front of her only to snatch it away.

Charon grunted in frustration, turned towards her and held his staff aloft, then touched the glowing crystal to her chest.

Danae's brow furrowed. 'I don't . . .'

Frantically, the ferryman nodded towards the crystal.

'The light?'

He nodded again, then once more pressed the glowing rock to her sternum.

She drew a sharp breath. 'I . . . I am the light.'

The ferryman continued to nod emphatically.

'You know about Prometheus' prophecy. You know who I am.'

He nodded once more, slower this time. A heartbeat passed between them, her oak-brown eyes staring into his crimson orbs, then he continued to tug her along the tunnel, away from the heart of Tartarus.

'But Heracles . . . I can't leave him.' She tried again to pull back, but Charon tightened his grip on her arm and forced her onwards. Try as she might, she did not have the strength to fight him. His panic betrayed his thoughts without him having to voice them. The rockslide would slow Hades down, but it would not keep him trapped for long.

They stumbled through passage after passage, the rough stone walls glowing with the same light-pulsing roots that laced the tunnels leading to the entrance of the Underworld. After a while the ferryman eased his grip on Danae's arm. They had taken so many twists and turns, she would not have been able to find her way back to the Missing's cave without him.

Then she heard it.

The roots were singing again. It was the same song Orpheus had serenaded the tendrils with at the bronze gates.

They reached another fork in the passage, and Danae stopped moving. Charon tugged her arm, gesturing towards the left tunnel, but her head twitched to the right, following the source of the vibrations. They were growing louder.

The clatter of a stone echoed in the passageway behind them. Charon let go of her, raising his staff aloft.

Something about the strange music called out to her. Compelled, she took off down the right-hand tunnel, following the song as the roots hummed louder and louder.

At the end of the passage she came to an oak door, half hidden in the shadow of an alcove. She tried the handle. It was open.

She stepped through it and found herself at the bottom of a staircase. The walls were cracked and the steps roughly hewn, wispy lengths of roots prising through the gaps like strands of hair, vibrating with the Thracian tune.

Another door waited at the crest of the stairs, twisted with more of the pulsing tendrils. Danae slowed as she approached, her heart hammering as the hum of the song grew louder. She went to turn the bronze handle, but the door opened of its own accord.

The room was devoid of furniture or belongings of any kind. Like an ancient structure left to the ravages of time, the dark stone was ruptured with roots, across the floor, walls and ceiling. And all of them, however large or small, led towards the same central point.

Danae's mouth fell slack as she stared at the far wall.

It was difficult to determine where the roots ended and the woman began. She hung above the ground, her limbs held flush to the wall by a web of tendrils. They even wound around her tawny locks, splaying them against the stone like she was floating underwater. Her skin was deathly white, and through a binding of roots, the iron ring of a collar like Danae's was visible around her neck. But the tendrils were not just holding her in place, they were part of her. Like veins that had escaped her body, tiny roots pierced the skin of her wrists and ankles. They burrowed their way into every crevice; her ears, her nostrils, her mouth. And above her heart, twig-like branches sprouted from her chest, their bark decorated with pale leaves and delicate blossom.

This must be the Queen of the Underworld. Persephone.

Danae's throat thickened as images whirled through her mind. The young priestess who had dressed as Persephone for the Thesmophoria back on Naxos, her white dress fluttering, bright eyes gleaming as her feet pounded the earth, dancing with another priestess dressed as her mother, Demeter. In the tale Danae had been told, Persephone was stolen away to the Underworld by a lustful Hades, allowed only to return to the world above for six months of the year. But the woman before her looked as though she had not seen daylight in centuries.

Persephone's lips were parted, moving as though singing the words to the song the roots hummed, her eyes rolled back in her head.

Hades must have done this to Persephone; mutilated her just like the shades. Danae could see it would be fruitless to try and extract the goddess from the roots. She and the tendrils were one.

Behind Danae, the door crashed open, and Charon ran into the room.

The last line of music settled in the air, and Persephone's eyes spun back to reveal irises of milky white surrounding ink-black pupils.

'You brought the lark to my gate.' Her voice was thin and strangled as though there were roots wound around her vocal cords.

'It was you singing.' Danae stared at the web of roots splaying out from the goddess like lace-woven wings. She had suspected the tendrils had a higher intelligence; she never dreamed it was Persephone who was controlling them. That they were part of the goddess.

'Your companion's song reminded me of sunlight, and birdsong, and the grass beneath my feet. I had forgotten, but I was glad to remember.'

'His name was Orpheus. He's dead.'

'Ah . . . they all perish in the end. All my little pets.' Persephone blinked. 'Will *you* sing for me, like the lark did?'

Charon grabbed Danae's shoulder, pulling her back.

The goddess let out a strangled cry. 'I did not bid you leave! I will have you caged, little bird.'

Little bird. *Little Titan.*

Danae looked at the ferryman, eyes sweeping over the ring of jangling keys hooked into his belt, and the knife sheathed beside them.

She reached for the blade. Charon did not stop her.

Danae gripped the knife, the whites of her knuckles pressing through her skin as she turned and walked towards Persephone.

She wanted to take something from Hades. Just like Alea, Arius, Manto and her horse's namesake, Hylas, had been taken from her. In that moment, she did not see a woman, only a false god, kin to those who had destroyed her family.

Danae reached up and slashed Persephone's thigh in a place she knew death would follow moments later.

Blood sluiced down the wall, and a great surge of light ran through the network of roots as the goddess's threads returned to the tapestry of life. Persephone gasped, the roots across her lips trembling, then the tendrils went dark.

Danae was still as the blood pooled across the floor. Only when Charon once more grabbed hold of her arm and tugged her towards the door did she allow herself to be moved.

She had taken lives before in the heat of battle. The heady rush of fighting for her own skin had never left much space to contemplate the consequences of her actions. This should be different. She had extinguished a life knowing it would cease to exist. She had killed the Queen of the Underworld. But she felt nothing.

They continued on through the passage at the bottom of the stairs, Danae's blood-stained feet slapping against the floor, their way lit only by Charon's staff.

They hadn't gone far when cries echoed from further down the tunnel, accompanied by the clang of metal.

'Aim for the eyes!'

'I'm trying! Where the fuck did the light go?'

Danae's frown deepened. One voice was full of flint and honey, the other resonated with timber and bronze.

Breath hissed between her lips. Perhaps it was her torture-addled mind deceiving her, but she could have sworn she recognized those voices.

17. A Step into the Mist

Danae pushed past Charon and ran towards the voices. Behind her, the ferryman sounded what might have been a warning, his staff-light chasing her heels.

She skidded to a halt as she turned round a bend in the passage, Charon's light throwing the scene ahead into sharp relief.

Encircled by shades stood a knife-wielding woman dressed in battered silver armour, a bow and quiver of arrows slung across her chest, back-to-back with a flame-haired man, his sword raised before him.

Atalanta and Telamon, Heracles' faithful companions who'd travelled with Danae aboard the *Argo*.

They froze when they caught sight of her.

'You,' hissed Atalanta, her expression torn between surprise and fury.

Like a river bursting its banks, a surge of feeling flooded Danae's chest. She had never been more relieved to see two people who looked like they wanted to kill her.

'Call the shades off!' Danae urged Charon. 'These two are friends.'

The ferryman swiftly raised his staff, driving its end into the ground, beating a frantic tapping against the rock. The shades cringed back. Charon then signed an instruction and the shades' shimmering bodies vanished as they melted into the shadows.

For an agonizing moment no one spoke. All four of them stood so still, they might have been figures in a painted fresco, the air thick with the weight of all that had passed since they last saw one another.

'So,' Telamon's lip curled, 'you abandoned us for Hades.'

Danae's mouth dried. She had left them both, along with Heracles, asleep in the Argonauts' camp while she scaled the Caucasus Mountains in search of Prometheus.

'No, I'm a captive, look,' the words tripped over her tongue as her hands flew to the collar. She took a step towards them. Telamon did not lower his sword, eyes sliding over her to settle on Charon.

'The ferryman's on our side,' Danae added quickly. 'He helped me escape.'

'We are *not* on the same side,' growled Atalanta.

Like feeling prickling back into a numb limb, the urgency of their situation returned to the forefront of Danae's mind.

'Hades has Heracles imprisoned in the depths of Tartarus. We have to save him.'

Charon laid a hand on Danae's arm, his crimson eyes pleading as he shook his head. She shoved him off.

'Why do you think we're here?' said Telamon.

Atalanta's dark eyes burned beneath her scowl. 'Why are *you* here? To do Hades' bidding?'

'I told you, I'm a prisoner. I came to the Underworld to find my sister, but Hades, he . . .' her chest tightened, and she suddenly found it difficult to breathe.

'Forgive us if we don't believe a word that passes your lips,' said Telamon, his voice full of a cold disdain that sounded alien from his tongue. He turned to Atalanta, 'Come on, we'll find our own way.'

But Atalanta did not move. She stared at Danae as though if she glared hard enough, she might be able to burn straight through her.

'Why did you leave?'

'I . . .' she tried to find the words, but where could she even begin? As she recalled the night she'd left the Argonauts a year earlier in the forest outside the city of Colchis, shame roiled in her stomach. She pictured the blood trickling between Dolos' eyes, Heracles' lion hide propped on the stake outside his tent, the image the omphalos shard had shown her of a lone figure climbing the Caucasus Mountains.

The omphalos shard. Hades had it, along with Hylas and her other possessions that had been stowed in the horse's saddle bag, probably somewhere in his palace. The barge journey to Tartarus felt as though it had taken an age — even if Charon could guide her, it would take too long to go searching for it.

'There's no time to explain, but I will if we get out of here, I promise. Just know that if I could have done things differently, I would have.'

Atalanta's knife clattered to the ground. In two heartbeats she crossed the space between them, her fist slamming into Danae's jaw.

'Atalanta!' called Telamon. 'Remember what she can do!'

Pain blossomed across Danae's face as she hit the floor, but she stayed limp as Atalanta rained down blows upon her.

'Fight back, gods damn you!'

The onslaught ended as Charon dragged Atalanta away. The warrior shoved him off, panting, gaze still fixed on Danae.

'What the fuck is wrong with you?' she spat in between breaths.

'The collar,' Danae winced as she pushed herself to her feet. 'It cuts me off from my powers.'

Charon made an urgent motion with his hands, gesturing to the passage ahead with his staff.

'Atalanta,' said Telamon, taking a couple of steps in the other direction. 'Come on.'

Neither woman moved.

'I left because of Dolos,' said Danae.

At her admission Telamon grew still.

'You know what really happened to him, don't you?' growled Atalanta.

Danae drew a breath. 'I followed Dolos the night I left. I discovered him meeting with a shade in the forest. I killed it, thinking it was going to attack him, but it was bringing him Heracles' medicine from Olympus. He revealed that Heracles isn't a demi-god. Not in the way we think. His strength comes from that blue potion Dolos fed him under Zeus' instruction. I left the bag of strength elixir by his tent because Dolos told me that without it he'd be dead within a year.' Her pulse raced at a sickening speed, but she forced herself to continue. 'Dolos stabbed me to prevent me telling Heracles and I . . . I killed him.'

She felt giddy. It was liberating, after all this time, to finally tell the truth.

'You killed him,' repeated Atalanta, her voice low and dangerous.

Danae held her gaze. 'It was self-defence.'

'If any of that is true,' said Telamon, 'why didn't you return to camp and tell us? Why steal Heracles' lion hide and flee?'

Because I am prophesied to destroy Zeus, because I saw a vision of myself alone climbing the Caucasus Mountains, because I am a Titan. Whatever that means.

'I didn't know if I could trust you.'

Atalanta stooped to retrieve her knife. 'I've heard enough.'

'I know where Heracles is. The Missing too. We can save them.'

Atalanta advanced, her blade raised. 'Liar.'

'Wait.' Telamon stared at Danae. 'If she can take us to Heracles we should go with her.'

The warrior spun to face him. 'You believe her now?'

'No . . . I don't know,' he ran a hand through his flame-red hair, 'but what choice do we have? The Underworld is vast, it took us long enough just to find this place.'

'She murdered Dolos!'

'I have ears!' A muscle pulsed in Telamon's jaw. 'But it makes sense . . . the strength elixir. Atalanta, Heracles hasn't been the same since he had the last of that potion. For months now he's been growing weaker every day.'

'I will not put my life in her hands.'

'Gods damn you, woman, there is more at stake here than your pride.'

Danae's head snapped between them as they argued, her heart beating in her throat. Then the pair fell silent and glared at each other, the battle continuing without words. Finally, Atalanta loosed a grunt of frustration and kicked the rock wall of the passage.

'Fine,' she pointed her knife at Danae. 'Take us to Heracles, but if you so much as think about betraying us, I will slit your throat.'

Danae almost smiled. After everything she'd been through, being threatened by the warrior was strangely comforting.

She turned to Charon. 'We have to go back.'

The ferryman shook his head.

'I'm going with them, whether you come with us or not. If you really want to help me become the light, show us the way.'

Charon gazed at her, crimson eyes pleading beneath his hood. Danae remained defiant. The ferryman's shoulders sagged, and he turned back the way they had come, raising his staff to illuminate the gloom.

'There's something you should know,' said Danae as they hurried back down the labyrinthine tunnels. 'Down in the depths of Tartarus, Hades tasked me with killing Heracles. I stabbed Hades instead, and while he healed himself, Charon and I escaped. I imagine he will be angry.' Her blood chilled at the thought.

'Perfect,' grunted Atalanta.

'How is Heracles? Is he injured?' asked Telamon, his sword flashing in the crystal staff light.

'He's not in a good way.' After a breath she added, 'I really am sorry –'

'Not now,' Telamon cut across her. 'Since you failed to kill Heracles, will Hades have harmed him?'

'I don't know . . .' The hero's gaunt face blazed in her mind, blank with resignation as she raised Hades' knife above her head. 'It wasn't really about Heracles . . . it was a test.'

'Where are Heracles and the Missing being held?' asked Atalanta.

'A cell at the end of this passage. You should know, Tartarus is not like the stories. It's a mine. Hades has creatures working down there, giants and shades . . .' Danae wondered how much to reveal. How much they'd believe. 'They're not what they seem either. Shades are mortals, taken from the Missing. Hades replaces their skins with that of an Underworld lizard that can make itself invisible in its surroundings, then they're tortured until –'

'I think I hit her too hard,' said Atalanta.

Before Danae could argue, a terrible stench wafted through the tunnel. She gagged.

'What the fuck is that?' asked Telamon.

Immediately the ferryman gestured for them to be quiet and draw back towards the rock walls of the passage. Then he hid the glowing end of his staff beneath his cloak.

As darkness descended, another wave of putrid air hit them. Danae fought the urge to wretch again, bile stinging her throat. Her heart thudded against her ribs as she strained to listen.

From somewhere far away, she thought she could hear a high, cold laugh.

Then, much nearer, something growled.

Breath, warm and ripe with the tang of rotting flesh, raised the hairs on her neck. Whatever it was had scented them.

Coming to the same realization, Charon unleashed his staff, casting light on the passage. A creature hovered above them. It had the wings of an engorged bat, the body of a lion with blood-red fur, and, like Kerberos, a curved scorpion's tail. Its face resembled that of a man stretched over the skull of giant cat, slashed ear to ear with a hideously wide mouth, its blood-stained lips peeled back to reveal three sets of knife-sharp teeth.

'Manticore,' breathed Telamon.

Another creature of legend. Another of Hades' monstrous creations.

Charon jabbed his staff at the manticore, yet unlike the beasts on the Asphodel Meadows it did not recoil. The ferryman faltered and tried again. The beast roared at him, blowing the hood from Charon's patchwork head.

'Oh gods,' breathed Danae.

The manticore landed before them, its claws scraping across the rocks, spittle dangling from its jaw.

'Use your power,' hissed Telamon between his teeth.

'I can't, remember?' Danae called back.

The creature's eyes narrowed. Then it leapt forward, chomping Charon's staff between its jaws. The wood splintered, the crystal orb rolling away down the passage.

They clung to the tunnel walls as the manticore sprung at them, its claws screeching on the rock as they sprinted doggedly after the glowing end of Charon's staff. Danae's bruised ribs screamed in protest as she sucked in breath, forcing her body to move faster and faster. The stone passage shook beneath their feet as the manticore pursued them; every moment Danae expected the sudden agony of claws scraping down her back.

Then suddenly it stopped. There was no pounding of claws on the rock, no rancid breath billowing behind them. Nothing.

The four slowed, huddling together as they panted.

'Where did it go?' asked Telamon.

Danae grabbed the light crystal from where it had rolled into a nearby crevice. Holding it aloft, she took a step towards the darkness.

Like a lion springing from long grass, the manticore lurched from around the bend, its dark wings beating the stagnant air. There was nowhere to go. Danae flung her arms over her head, the crystal clattering at her feet.

But the death blow did not come.

She looked up to see a streak of white crash into the manticore, knocking it into the tunnel wall.

'Hylas!' Danae shouted, as the winged horse bore down on the creature, pummelling the beast with its hooves. A broken rope tether dangled from one of its forelegs.

In a heartbeat, Atalanta had drawn her bow and was sending arrows into the soft flesh beneath the manticore's jaw. Then Telamon ran forward, launched himself onto its back and buried his sword in its skull. He twisted the blade until the beast stopped twitching and fell still.

Danae ran to where the flying horse had landed. She flung her arms around his neck and buried her face in his coat. He was missing his saddle bag, with all her belongings and the omphalos shard, but in that moment she did not care.

'Thank you,' she breathed. 'Thank you.'

Atalanta approached, arms folded across her chest. '*Hylas?*'

Danae straightened up, too overjoyed to feel embarrassment, a protective hand smoothing the horse's neck. 'He's been a loyal friend, just like his namesake was.'

Atalanta's gaze softened at the mention of their old companion and fellow Argonaut. A man who had saved Danae's life more than once and had sacrificed his own to carry her to safety when fleeing the murderous six-armed Earthborn on the Doliones shore.

'You and this Hylas have a lot in common,' said Danae as she removed the dangling tether from the horse's leg.

The warrior raised an eyebrow. 'Me and a flying horse?'

'He has a fondness for undiluted wine. Although his tastes are a little finer than yours.'

Atalanta's scowl returned. Just for a moment, Danae thought she saw a spark of amusement, a glint of their old connection beneath the disdain etched on the warrior's face.

'One of Hades' creations?' Telamon yanked his sword from the manticore's body and wiped it on its crimson fur.

'I think so,' said Danae, staring at its ruddy face, so human save for its terrible jaws.

Telamon looked grim. 'It would be wishful thinking to hope we won't meet other creatures like this. We must keep alert. Which way now?'

Charon stooped down and retrieved the glowing crystal, holding it aloft by the shattered end of his staff. Pulling his hood back over his head, he signalled down the right-hand tunnel.

'You came back,' Danae whispered to Hylas as they hurried after the ferryman.

The winged horse huffed a breath through his nose, then gently nipped her ear.

Despite her surroundings, despite walking back into a nightmare to confront one of the Twelve, Danae smiled.

She was no longer alone.

18. A Life for a Life

Dust swirled through the rock passage, hazing the light from Charon's crystal.

Danae lay a hand on the ferryman's shoulder. 'We're close, aren't we?'

Charon nodded, trembling beneath her touch.

'You're afraid?'

He shook his head, but his crimson eyes betrayed him.

Danae's own heart fluttered as they turned a corner to find the tunnel ahead narrowed by fallen rocks: the wreckage of their escape.

She looked at Hylas, then back at the sliver of passage squeezed by the rubble.

Her heart sank. 'The way ahead is too narrow for you. Turn back, fly out of here.'

Hylas nibbled her ear.

'I'll find you. I promise.' Despite the certainty in her voice, she felt as though she might crumble as she smoothed his coat, then stepped away from the ice-white horse. 'Go on.'

Hylas blinked, then tossed his mane and turned back the way they had come. Danae swallowed the lump in her throat at the sound of his hooves echoing down the passage.

'We need to hide the light,' said Telamon. 'Or Hades will see us coming.'

Danae nodded.

Carefully, Charon once more wrapped his crystal in the folds of his cloak and moved towards the narrowed passage. Feeling their way in the darkness, the others followed, easing their bodies between the cavern wall and heap of fallen rocks. As they pressed on, the tunnel narrowed until the rubble blocked their path. Scrabbling in the blackness, they heaved the stones as silently as their straining limbs and lungs would allow, until finally the opening was large enough to squeeze through.

Hello, little Titan.

Danae froze. 'Stop,' she whispered. 'Did you hear that?'

'What?' breathed Atalanta.

'That voice.'

'I heard nothing,' replied Telamon.

They carried on clambering around the rocks, Danae's limbs heavy with dread.

She blinked as they emerged on the other side of the rubble, the passage lit by a dim orange glow bleeding from the braziers illuminating the pit of Tartarus.

Wide, terrified eyes glinted at them from the clefts of what once had been the Missing's cave. Debris was strewn across the ground, as though Hades had blasted his way out of the collapsed cell. Six bodies lay on the floor, not a mark on them, but clearly dead.

The God of the Underworld was nowhere to be seen. Danae took no comfort from Hades' absence. Surely he would have pursued her if he thought there was a chance she might escape?

'Heracles?' Telamon crept forward.

'Gone,' rasped a voice behind them.

A woman crept from the shadows, dressed in the ragged remains of a peplos. She was undernourished, like the rest of the Missing, her age indeterminate under the layers of grime encrusting her skin.

'He took the hero.'

'Hades?' whispered Danae.

The woman nodded, pointing down the passage towards the belly of Tartarus.

Atalanta and Telamon immediately set off, following her direction.

'Wait,' hissed Danae.

They paused and looked back.

'We can't leave them.'

Telamon ran a hand through his flame-red hair. 'There's forty-odd people, we'll never get everyone out.'

'We came for Heracles,' said Atalanta.

Danae drew herself up. 'What would he do?'

The two companions looked at one another.

Telamon sighed. 'You'd better have a plan.'

Danae chewed her lip. 'There might be a way to save everyone. If I can create a distraction to draw out Hades, you can grab Heracles and lead him and the others out of Tartarus.' She turned to the Missing. 'You all need to come with us.'

The woman who'd spoken and a couple of other people moved towards them; the rest remained cowering in the cave.

Danae clenched and flexed her hands. They didn't have time for this. Every moment they waited might be Heracles' last. 'If you come with us now, you might die, or you might live to see the sky again. If you stay here, you will perish in this mine. The choice is yours.'

The Missing gazed at one another, then slowly, like anemones appearing from their shells, they emerged into the passage.

Danae, Telamon, Atalanta and Charon led the way, creeping towards the cavernous heart of Tartarus. When they neared the end of the tunnel, Danae gestured for the Missing to linger behind them as she, Atalanta and Telamon peered around the corner.

'Fuck,' breathed Atalanta as she took in the vast mine above them and the hulking forms of giants moving across the walkways between the caves. 'Those things are huge.'

'You've fought a giant before, haven't you?' asked Danae.

Atalanta shook her head slowly. 'Geryon was a mouse compared to these.'

'There are more Missing working in the caves above. If we can make it up to the top entrance, there,' Danae pointed past the walkways snaking up the sides of the mine to the platform where Hades first led her into Tartarus, 'we can free more people on our way out.'

'Anything else we should know?' asked Telamon.

'Ah, yes,' said Danae. 'Hades has a dragon imprisoned beneath that . . .' Her tongue stilled as an icy wave of horror sluiced through her body.

Someone was lying across Typhon's grate, their limbs bound to the iron bars.

Heracles.

'No, no, no!' Without thinking, Danae drew Charon's knife and pelted towards the grate. Heracles appeared to be unharmed, but if the dragon breathed its steam before she freed the hero, he would be roasted.

She fell to her knees, sweat stinging her eyes as she slashed at his bindings. Heracles appeared to be unconscious. She was surprised to find he was tied with roots severed from the walls, grey and dull without their pulsing light, but easy to break. With a grunt of effort, she pulled his limp frame away from the iron grate, just before a billow of steam erupted from below.

She collapsed, gasping as the hot air seared her lungs. Atalanta and Telamon hurried to her side, Telamon scooping his arm around Heracles' torso.

'No,' Danae croaked, 'stay back . . .'

'What do we have here?'

Her head snapped round.

Above them, standing on one of the lower stone walkways, was Hades. A golden gauntlet gleamed on his right hand, bright against the midnight dark of his robe.

Fear, raw and immobilizing, spread through Danae's limbs.

Telamon crouched low, curling his torso over Heracles. Atalanta twitched her hand towards her bow, and with a lazy flick of his wrist Hades hurled her into the cavern wall, her armour clanging against the stone. She did not get up.

Danae forced herself to stagger to her feet.

'It's me you want. Leave them be.'

Hades descended the stairs, his obsidian robe rippling like a poisoned stream.

'Like you let my wife, Persephone, be?' His voice was calm, but his pale eyes burned with white-hot fury.

'I . . .'

In a heartbeat, Telamon twisted, flinging his sword straight at Hades. The Lord of the Underworld reached out his gauntleted hand and turned his fingers. The blade halted mid-air, crumpling in on itself, then plummeted to the floor below. With another flick, Hades threw Telamon across the cavern to crash into a barrow of gems.

In the commotion, shades had emerged from their caves and clustered to the walkways, peering down at the scene unfolding below. Danae dared not look towards the passage where Charon and the Missing hid, praying with all her soul they remained out of Hades' sight.

Suddenly, she was hoisted from the ground, held by a vice of life-threads she could not see.

'You murdered my wife.'

Danae gasped, the invisible rope around her ribs squeezing the air from her lungs. Hades stepped down onto the cavern floor, his chest heaving, his grey eyes full of wild anger. It was the most human she'd ever seen him look.

'I see now how deeply your mortal sensibilities cripple you,' said Hades. 'You will never be free of them while you live in this form.' He paced across the space between them, reached up and closed his gauntleted hand around her throat. An intense dragging sensation ripped through her, as though her organs were being torn out through her skin. So, this was how it felt to have the life-threads drained from one's body. 'Don't worry, little Titan,' he whispered, 'I will cut you a new one.'

Suddenly, Hades' grip slackened, and she crumpled to the floor as Charon leapt at the god from behind and brought him crashing to the ground. The ferryman straddled his master, the knife Danae had dropped gleaming in his hand as he stabbed Hades again and again. Danae crawled towards them, knowing once the shock wore off, Hades would kill Charon in a heartbeat.

Then a bone-rumbling crash shook the vast cavern.

Both slick with blood, Hades and Charon paused their tussle, as the iron grate to the dragon's pit shuddered, rising out of its open locks.

'No,' Hades moaned, eyes wide and dancing with brazier light.

The ferryman grinned, reached below his cloak and jangled his keys.

Danae gasped as the dragon's head bashed against the metal, momentarily lifting it off its hinges.

Hades was on all fours, his gauntleted hand stretched towards the grate. Danae knew he was manipulating a stream of life-threads in an attempt to contain his prisoner.

There was a crack so loud it sounded like the breaking of the world.

Even with Hades' life-threads holding down the grate, the dragon's next attempt to break free ripped the iron cage from its hinges and sent it smashing into the cavern wall.

Danae stared in slack-jawed amazement as a head the size of a ship reared from the pit. Wreathed in steam, water sluiced from its great emerald snout. A ridge of obsidian horns ran like a small mountain range down its nose and up between its eyes: two umber orbs glowing like the heart of a forge. Then it opened its jaws to reveal a mouth packed with teeth the length of Danae's legs, each wickedly sharp, and she was blasted with a gust of heat from the great furnace of its belly.

She crawled towards the ferryman, lying prone on the ground.

'We have to move,' she rasped, 'Charon.'

It was then she saw the knife protruding from his chest.

'No . . . please.'

Blood poured from the wound, his life seeping into the charcoal fabric of his cloak.

'Come on, we have to go.' She tried to drag him, but Hades had drained what little strength she had.

Charon took hold of her fingers and squeezed them tight. With a shaking hand he touched his chest, then pressed his palm to hers.

His crimson eyes swirled into a blur as tears flooded her vision. She felt his arm grow limp, then his breath stilled.

'I will be the light,' she whispered, 'I promise.'

Across the cavern, Telamon had Heracles slung over his shoulders and was leading the Missing up one of the stone staircases. Danae looked back at the grate to see Typhon rising out of its watery prison, the dragon's taloned front legs clawing the edge, its great wings straining against the walls.

Hades cowered before it, arm still outstretched.

Suddenly, Danae was yanked backwards by a rough pair of hands and dragged away from the pit. Atalanta hurled her against the cave wall and shielded her with her armoured torso.

Then came the blaze.

Danae was forced to hide her face as flames roared from Typhon's throat. The fire was so hot and bright, it felt as though the sun itself had emerged in the deepest realm of the world. Then the blaze darkened. She lowered her arms and through the lights bursting across her vision stared at the blackened rock floor, her gaze settling on a charred mound of scorched flesh and bone.

The smouldering remains of a man who had thought himself a god.

19. Flight and Fury

The dragon lifted its great head and unleashed a roar that shook Tartarus to its foundations. It had hauled itself halfway out of its watery cage, an orange glow simmering in the cracks between its emerald scales. Then the dragon drew another breath and chased its freedom cry with fire.

The heat was blistering, as were the screams from above. Danae's head snapped up, eyes searching the spiralling stairs. Relief rippled through her to see Telamon still with Heracles and the Missing, frightened but uncharred, fleeing up the stone steps.

She looked back at the leviathan whose body was swiftly expanding into the cavern. Atalanta's hand tightened around Danae's arm as Typhon's wings bashed against the circular wall, the dragon's obsidian spines grating against the rock.

'Come on!' shouted the warrior, dragging Danae towards the steps.

Danae's legs shuddered beneath her. She felt stretched, like a frayed rope held by its last strand, but she forced her body to keep moving. Atalanta did not look back at her as they climbed, but she did not let go of her either.

The cavern trembled as Typhon finally writhed free of the water, claws scraping the rock, wings and tail bashing into the walls.

The stone steps beneath them shook again, but this time it was not the dragon. During its reaches for freedom, Typhon's claws had ripped through several of the giants' chains, freeing a clutch of the hulking creatures. Now they fled, thundering up the steps, sending a torrent of dust and loose stones raining down on Atalanta and Danae. The warrior grunted and increased her speed, taking the stairs two at a time, dragging Danae with her.

Danae's lungs felt like they were tearing. She couldn't get enough hot, acrid air into her chest.

'The other . . . Missing,' she gasped, pulling on Atalanta's arm as she slowed to stare into the caves. Shades pelted past them, whips and weapons abandoned as they fled towards the entrance.

The warrior glanced back, her jaw tight. 'We can't save everyone.'

Then one of the giants above them tripped, breaking through a chunk of the staircase and sending a slew of rocks crashing down on Typhon.

The dragon bellowed and launched itself into the air, attempting to climb, the spines on its sail-like wings raking through the staircases below, obliterating them. Danae's eyes widened as its shimmering emerald belly moved past them, so close she could have reached out and touched the burning-hot scales. Then a claw came crashing through the stairs ahead of them, leaving gouge marks the width of Danae's head across the cavern wall.

'Shit!' Atalanta flattened herself against the rock, her arm thrown out in front of Danae as the dragon slipped back down towards the pit.

There was now a gaping hole where the next four steps should have been.

'We have to jump.'

'What?' Danae rasped.

'You'll get there, just put your legs into it.'

She did not give herself time to think as she summoned the last of her strength and ran, then leapt into the air.

She landed with a thud on the other side, her legs dangling towards the pit. Gasping, she dragged herself fully onto the step and rolled out of the way to clear a path for the warrior to jump across.

Time seemed to slow as Atalanta soared through the air. She was like a gazelle, all power and grace, her dark braids flying out behind her.

Then Typhon launched upwards again and the force of the dragon's cramped wings beating the cavern shuddered the rock. The impact hit just as Atalanta landed and she was thrown backwards.

'Atalanta!' Danae lurched forward, hurling herself towards the gap, her fingers closing around the warrior's wrist as she tumbled over the edge. Danae ignored the pain searing through her shoulder, her entire being focused on the hand clutching Atalanta.

The warrior clung to Danae, her deep brown eyes flecked with fear.

'I will not let you fall.' Danae reached her other arm down, bracing her torso and legs against the steps. Atalanta swung up her free hand and grasped it.

A glow, like the blaze of dawn, swelled from the depths of the pit as Typhon opened its jaws.

Danae's heart thundered. She heaved with all her might, her vision crackling with the effort, as a ball of fire billowed up through the cavern. As Danae pulled Atalanta onto the steps, the warrior roared, smacking her sandals against the rock to put out the flames licking her feet. Her lower legs were streaked with raw, blackened flesh.

'Are you all right?' asked Danae.

Atalanta moaned.

'Can you climb?'

The warrior looked up at her, jaw clenched. 'If you help me.'

Danae slipped her arm around Atalanta's waist and hoisted her to her feet. Battered and bleeding, the two women clambered the length of the last coil and stumbled towards the entrance passage. Danae could feel Atalanta's body tensing beside her with each agonizing step.

When they finally reached the entrance passage, she said, 'I could carry you on my back?'

'I'm not a child,' grunted the warrior.

Danae was torn between frustration and relief. She didn't know if she'd have had the strength.

It looked as though some of the giants had made it out despite the fire and crumbling steps. Chunks of rock had been ripped from the walls, and rubble littered the floor, all covered in a film of black soot from Typhon's fire.

Halfway through the passage, Danae felt a swell of warmth at her back and glanced over her shoulder. The entrance to Tartarus was brightening.

'Run!'

With a last burst of strength, they sprinted, Atalanta roaring in pain. Danae felt the skin on her back blistering as they reached the mouth of the entrance passage and threw themselves to the ground, just as a great tongue of fire licked from the stone serpent's jaws.

She lifted her head, peering around through smoke-stung eyes. The Missing lingered in a cluster at a safe distance from the entrance. With them was Telamon, kneeling beside the prone body of Heracles. There seemed to be far fewer mortals than there had been in the chamber. At a glance only around two dozen had made it out. Some stared at Danae and Atalanta, others at something behind them.

Danae turned and let out a sob of relief.

Hylas trotted towards her, his white coat gleaming through

the mist. The horse nibbled her ear then whinnied, tossing his head.

Danae began to push herself to her feet but was sent thudding back to the ground by another earth-shattering quake. She rolled onto her back as the roof of Tartarus cracked open like an egg, and from its depths emerged Typhon. Finally free of its rock cage, the great dragon unfurled its wings, each one the length of the *Argo*, and launched itself into the air with a deep, sulphurous roar.

The mist around them was blown away, revealing the River Acheron barely a yard from where they stood. For a heartbeat the air was filled with fire, the waters of the river stained with burning light as the dragon soared away across the plains of Erebus.

Before the brightness faded, the hulking forms of four giants could be seen thundering away along the riverbank. She stared after them, wondering what havoc they would wreak if they found their way to the surface.

A moan drew her attention. Atalanta lay on the scorched ground, curled into herself.

Telamon paced towards them. 'Is she wounded?'

'Her legs are burned. They need to be cleaned and bound.' Danae cast around, but there was nothing save blackened rock.

'What do we do now?' The woman who had spoken in the mine detached herself from the Missing.

'How do we get out of here?' A man in a once fine teal cloak joined her, wringing his hands.

Danae opened her mouth, then her gaze settled on his cloak. She thrust out an arm. 'Give me that.'

The man started but did as he was bid.

The fabric clutched in her hand, Danae turned to Telamon. 'I need a knife.' Charon's blade lay with his body, down in the depths of Tartarus.

After a heartbeat of hesitation, the flame-haired man slipped a slender knife from his belt.

A small gasp escaped from the Missing man's lips as Danae set about shredding the cloak. She handed Telamon back his blade and gathered the strips of material in her arms, hurrying to the bank of the Acheron. As swiftly as she could, she plunged the fabric into the salt water, then hastened back to Atalanta's side.

'This is going to hurt. A lot.'

The sound that Atalanta made as Danae washed the filth from her burns struck through her like a spear. The salt water would double the pain, but it would hopefully stave off infection. Atalanta jerked at each contact with the sodden rag until Danae was forced to ask Telamon to hold her still. Once she'd cleaned the wounds as best she could, Danae removed Atalanta's charred sandals and wrapped her feet and calves in the remaining wet strips. When it was done, the warrior lay still, her breathing shallow.

Danae wiped her hands on her dress and straightened up. A sea of soot-encrusted faces gazed at her expectantly. She thought of the labyrinth of tunnels she and Orpheus had traversed, and the ravine they flew down to find them. They would never be able to get the Missing out that way.

She looked at Telamon. 'How did you enter the Underworld?'

'Lake Lerna. We discovered the entrance back when we slayed the many-headed hydra.'

She nodded, her brow creased. 'Can we get back out that way?'

'I'm counting on it. Although we might have to wait for the tide. The entrance is hidden in a sea cave.'

'All right.' She thought for a moment. 'Heracles and Atalanta can ride on Hylas, everyone else will have to go on foot. You lead, I'll bring up the rear.'

A whistling wail whined across the rocks.

Danae's heart thudded, but she could see nothing except the inky waters of the Acheron and the rocky banks stretching away into the mist.

Telamon frowned, every muscle tense as he too scoured their surroundings. Then he turned to Danae and nodded. 'Good plan.' He eyed her collar. 'Let's get that off you.' He began to pry at the metal. A spark of hope flickered in Danae's chest. But, after several moments Telamon drew back. 'There's no join, no lock. I can't remove it here.' He held out his knife once more. 'You should keep this. Without your powers you might need it.'

Danae accepted the blade, her heart heavy. Then she turned to the Missing. 'We know a way out, but it is imperative you stick together and stay in a line behind Telamon, here.' She thought of the creatures she'd seen roaming Erebus; the gorgons, the centaurs, the manticore. 'We don't know what other dangers might be out there, and we can't defend you if you don't stick together, got it?'

The Missing looked to one another, then nodded.

Danae called Hylas to her, and she and Telamon set about heaving Heracles across his snowy back. The hero was so light. Guilt hollowed her insides as she stared at his gaunt, unconscious face.

When they brought the horse to Atalanta, the warrior grimaced and pushed herself to standing.

'I'm fine . . .' she winced. 'Don't need to ride.'

'For the love of the gods just get on the damned horse,' said Telamon, offering her his hand. She glowered at him but took it, breath shuddering as she climbed up behind Heracles.

At Danae's direction, the Missing formed a line behind Telamon, and he led the way towards the River Acheron, Danae, Hylas, Atalanta and Heracles bringing up the rear.

As they walked, Danae glanced back at the stone serpent. A couple of shimmering shades that had survived Typhon's blaze, only visible by their leather armour, fled over the rock tongue away from Tartarus. She wondered what they would do now their master was dead. Now they were free. If they could even remember what that word meant.

The bedraggled group trudged along the rocky bank of the Acheron, the wreckage of Tartarus smoking in their wake. Danae's hand rested against Hylas' flank, the warmth of him anchoring her like a life-thread tether in the void of nothingness. Heracles hung over the horse's back, his head bobbing with Hylas' gait. He had not regained consciousness since their escape. Every so often Danae would check he was still breathing. Behind him, Atalanta had grown clammy and pale, her lips clenched tight as she clung to the horse's mane.

For the most part they walked in silence, the Missing trailing behind Telamon like sheep. The mist had curled back in around them, a breeding ground for the imagination to conjure danger from every angle. It was heartless, but Danae was glad most of them seemed too frightened to speak. Her mind was filled with Charon, replaying the moment the light faded from his crimson eyes.

Danae looked up at Atalanta. 'How long will he last?'

The warrior was gazing at the ridges in Heracles' spine. 'He ran out of that potion six months ago.' She winced as Hylas flexed his wings, and she was forced to adjust her legs. 'He kept getting weaker . . . we thought he was sick.'

Danae's heart felt heavy as iron.

'Why did he come down here alone?'

'Eurystheus. When we returned to Mycenae, we found the king living on a patch of farmland outside the city. While we were aboard the *Argo*, he was deposed.'

'I heard.'

'Heracles still had one more labour to perform, so the bastard sent him down here to kidnap Kerberos. Wanted to use the beast as a weapon to reclaim his kingdom.' Atalanta sucked in a sharp breath as she shifted to check Heracles' pulse. Satisfied, she drew back.

'Why didn't you go with him?'

Atalanta's scowl deepened.

'We told him he wasn't up to it, so he left without us.'

Shame swelled inside Danae until she could contain it no longer. 'I'm so sorry,' she blurted, 'for everything that's happened. Please believe me, I never wanted to abandon you, I feel –'

'I don't care what you feel.'

Neither woman spoke for a long while after that.

The fog grew dense, blanketing the hard ground up to Danae's knees by the time the warrior rasped, 'Where are the dead?'

Even though she'd known this question would come, it still threatened to crush Danae. She owed Atalanta the truth, but not yet. Not here.

'Elsewhere. The kingdom of Erebus is vast.'

She was relieved when Atalanta did not press her further.

Silence fell once more, punctuated by the rush of the river, the staccato clip of Hylas' hooves against the stony bank and the dogged footsteps of the Missing. The rock walls were narrowing, now close enough that Danae could see the roots twisting through their cracks, some finger-thin, some as thick as fully grown cypress trees. All were dull, their light extinguished when Persephone died.

'How far until we reach Lerna?' Danae called ahead to Telamon.

'Not long now, judging by how narrow the cave walls are,' he shouted back. 'Hopefully we'll emerge in daylight.'

Light. Real sunlight. She could barely remember what it felt like to have warm rays kiss her skin.

She suddenly remembered Hylas' pack, her belongings, the omphalos shard, presumably hidden away in Hades' palace. They had come too far to retrieve them now. The prophetic stone Phineus and Manto had guarded, her link to the future, the compass that had guided her for the past year was lost forever.

Ahead, Telamon stopped walking and held up a fist. Behind him the Missing staggered to a halt.

'I'll find out what's going on,' Danae said to Atalanta and jogged along the line to Telamon.

'What is it?' she whispered.

The flame-haired man was squinting into the gloom ahead. 'Thought I saw movement.'

Danae followed his gaze but could see nothing.

Then there was a scream behind them.

She swung around as the Missing scattered like a shoal of fish.

'Something took Leon!'

'It grabbed him –'

'– I couldn't see.'

Danae ran back to Hylas, knife drawn, cursing the dim light from the crystals above. Atalanta drew her bow, grimacing with the effort of clinging to the horse with her injured legs. The rocks encasing the vast passage were jagged, full of large nooks and crannies for creatures to hide.

A smudge of black smoke hazed through the air, momentarily shadowing the light from the glowing crystals.

Then something fell into the midst of the Missing. Atalanta clung to Heracles so he would not fall as the horse brayed and backed away from the broken body lying bleeding on the rocks.

Danae and Telamon approached. It was Leon, the man who had been snatched. His limbs were broken, his heart torn out through the bones of his chest.

Dread seeped through her as she thought of Manto's death; their torso ripped open, their heart stolen. But this brutality could not have been executed by a harpy. They did not have the speed or stealth to pluck a man from the ground without being seen. But if it wasn't a hound of Zeus, then what other creature would rip out a person's heart?

'Everyone, keep together,' shouted Telamon. 'Those of us with weapons — Atalanta, bring Hylas round and flank the head of the group, Danae stay to my right — we'll form a triangle.'

As they moved into position, Danae's blade trembled in her fist. The knife seemed like a twig in the face of what might be attacking them.

A rattling wail ripped through the air.

'Oh gods,' murmured Telamon. 'I think . . .' he swallowed, 'I think it's a fury.'

Danae was about to press him to explain, when a memory surfaced. A story told around a crackling hearth in the depths of winter. Her mother had spoken of three creatures that lived in the Underworld. Ethereal beings born of night and vengeance, brought forth from the oozing pits of Tartarus. A trio of spectres cloaked in darkness whose sole purpose was to avenge the wrongs done to their master, Hades. They were said to torment the dead and tear reparations from the flesh of the living. There was no one alive who had seen them and lived to tell the tale.

She had hoped, like so many things she once believed, that this tale was a fantasy dreamed up by the gods to terrorize mortals. But if this nightmare was real, Danae had just set free the dragon that killed their master.

An act worthy of deadly revenge.

20. The Path of Fate

They came like a howling wind.

The furies hurtled around the group in a hurricane of blade-sharp talons, slicing at their flesh. Accompanying the creatures' unearthly rattles were the screams of the Missing, cries of pure terror pealing through the rocky passage. Through them, Danae could hear Hylas whinnying and Atalanta grunting in pain as she shot arrows into the maelstrom, but skilled as she was, the warrior could not find her target. Danae, too, thrust at the nightmarish shapes with her knife as they shot past, but it was futile. Then she felt a sudden gust of air beside her. She glanced to her right to find the woman who'd stood next to her gone. There was a splash, and something that looked like a body bobbed away on the waters of the Acheron.

Danae clenched her teeth and tightened the grip on her blade. She would not allow them to be picked off one by one like hares snatched by falcons. Not when escape was almost in their grasp.

She lunged again and again at the swirling blackness until her knife connected to something solid. There was a shriek, like the grating of metal on bone, then she was whisked into the air.

Up close, the fury smelt like death. Though the world around Danae tore past at a sickening pace, she could finally see the creature that held her. It was shrouded in a midnight cloak, so thin and ragged it looked like smoke billowing through the air. Its wings were like those of a huge dragonfly, vibrating at such a pace they could barely be seen. And its face ... was eyeless; nothing but a gash of a mouth containing three sharpened rows of teeth, and two small slits above it that flared as it sniffed Danae. She cried out, her arms pinned to her sides as its impossibly sharp claws dug through the skin of her chest as if it were soft cheese.

Then an arrow whistled past her ear and tore through one of the fury's wings. It shrieked and let go of her. The air was punched from Danae's lungs as she hit the ground. Mercifully, the body of a slain Missing broke her fall onto the hard rock, but pain still ripped through her torn chest as she gasped, desperately fighting to breathe. She struggled to sit up and saw Telamon, his sword bloody, standing in front of a group of around ten Missing and Hylas, Atalanta and Heracles still atop his back, the warrior continuing to shoot arrows at furies.

Suddenly, like hounds with the scent of a stag, the furies turned and streaked down the riverbank as the hulking form of a giant came into view. The creatures surrounded the giant, and a roar like the great horn of a warship echoed through the cavern. The giant lifted its arms, battering the furies with its fists. Even in the poor light Danae could see the blood pouring down its mottled skin. She felt a twinge of pity.

Then Telamon yanked her to her feet.

They ran, pelting along the riverbank of the ever-narrowing passage, Hylas cantering with them. Danae's legs felt like they were disintegrating, and she was not sure she would make it to the entrance before her body gave out. With each step the collar weighed heavier around her neck, threatening to drag her to the ground. Only the sight of Atalanta atop Hylas, her arms wrapped tight around Heracles, kept her tethered to her strength. The warrior was in more pain than she. If Atalanta could hold on, she could too.

She blinked. Her eyes must be playing tricks on her. Then she looked up, and a sob lodged in her throat. There were no more glowing crystals embedded in the cavern roof. The light bleeding through the gloom ahead must be coming from outside.

And there was wind. She breathed in a deep lungful of salty breeze, revelling in the fresh, cold air. Then she heard the crash of waves. She pressed on and caught up with Hylas. The horse paused, hoofing the sea-slicked rock. It had become too narrow on either side of the river for him to continue along the bank, and the passage was too small for him to fully flex his wings and fly.

She crouched down, slipped her legs into the salty flow and lowered herself in.

'What are you doing?' shouted Telamon as the Missing clustered behind him.

Danae clung to the rocks as the cold water lapped over her wounded chest, stinging as though the fury was clawing at her afresh. Then her feet hit the bottom.

'We can wade through,' she gasped. 'Hylas, come into the river!'

The horse backed away, flexing his wings. With a grunt, Atalanta pulled Heracles up into a seated position, the hero swaying violently.

'Look, it's safe,' Danae let go of the rock and lifted her arms into the air, bracing herself against the pull of the current. She stayed rooted to the spot.

Hylas rippled his lips, hoofed the bank, then tentatively lowered himself down into the river. Atalanta cried out as the salt water washed over her legs, but she kept herself and Heracles astride his back. Telamon helped the rest of the Missing into the river, and with Danae at the helm they strode with the current.

As they waded further, the swells grew, crashing against Danae's chest, sometimes up to her chin. Each agonizing wave threatened to sweep her away, but there was nothing in the world that could stop her now.

Then they turned a bend in the river and she stopped moving, tears streaking her sea-dampened cheeks.

Ahead of them, through the mouth of a cave that was just large enough for a small fishing tub to pass though, was the sky.

It was day: glorious, bright day.

The sky seemed to reach towards her with azure arms and wrap her in soft swathes of cloud. Despite the collar, despite all the horrors she had endured, for a heartbeat she was weightless, nothing but a pearly drop of water warmed by the sun.

Then Hylas nosed her between the shoulder blades. She smiled and wiped her face, wading forwards to ease herself out of the water onto a stony outcrop at the base of the cave's entrance. Gazing up, she saw they had come out at the base of a shallow cliff.

She looked to the Missing as they emerged from the cave and began to pull themselves up onto the rocks behind her.

'We need to get to higher ground before the tide comes in.'

'Can the horse take us up?' asked Telamon.

Danae looked at Hylas. The steed's muzzle was flecked with spittle, his coat gleaming with sweat. 'He's exhausted. He'll have to fly Atalanta and Heracles up, but the rest of us can climb.' She weaved her way between the Missing to where the horse waited at the mouth of the sea-cave and smoothed his neck. 'One last push, Hylas.'

Atalanta did not have time to protest as Hylas surged through the water, finally able to spread his magnificent wings after the confines of the passage. The warrior's eyes bulged and she clung to Heracles as the horse soared into the air. The Missing stared after them, clinging to the rocks like barnacles.

Telamon pulled himself out of the sea beside her, his sword sheathed in the back of his belt. 'We climb?'

Danae looked up at the plethora of crevices and grooves in the cliff's surface. 'We climb.'

Telamon went first, the Missing following. Danae was relieved to linger for a moment, rest her aching body and watch the sunlight dance across the waves.

She was free. She was alive.

She turned back to the rocks and, as the last Missing scaled the cliff face, forced her weary limbs to move. Once her hands found the first few rivets, instinct took over, and the pain in her chest became just another note amongst the whistle of the wind and the crash of the waves. She had been good at this once, and she would be again.

At last, her fingers curled around a grassy ledge and with one final burst of effort she heaved herself over the edge of the cliff. Pulling herself forward on her elbows, she slumped onto her stomach, breathing in the verdant scent of the grass and dry earth.

'Is she the last one?' A voice she did not recognize, harsh and clipped.

Danae's head snapped up. A group of about a dozen men stood around the cliff edge. All carried weapons, most in battered mismatched armour that had seen better days. Several tents were erected behind them. The Missing were huddled together, eyeing the strangers with fresh fear. Telamon stood with Atalanta, supporting the warrior. Both of their wrists were bound. Danae's pulse quickened at the sight of two of the men holding onto Hylas' wings, Heracles still slumped across his back.

'Answer your king,' barked one of the soldiers to Telamon.

'She's the last,' he replied, eyes downcast.

'Get with the others.' The soldier gestured to the Missing.

As Danae stumbled to her feet, an older man detached himself from the pack and stalked towards Hylas. His light-brown skin was spotted with age, and a gold band nestled on his greying hair. Yet despite this regalia, his navy robe and cloak were worn and trimmed with dirt. He lifted one of Heracles' emaciated arms, then let it drop against Hylas' snowy-white side, sounding a disparaging noise in the back of his throat. 'He looks dreadful. And no Kerberos.' The man glowered at Telamon and Atalanta as though this was their fault. 'How in Tartarus am I meant to reclaim my kingdom from that bastard Agamemnon now?'

This must be Eurystheus.

Danae stiffened as Hylas jerked away from him, two more soldiers grabbing hold of the horse's mane to restrain him. The deposed king backed away, but his eyes gleamed. 'Still, this creature may prove useful.'

Telamon glowered at Eurystheus. 'This is not what we agreed. We were to bring back Heracles, that is all. Let the others go.'

'I entrusted you with returning my hero, not this sack of bones and a rabble of the dead made flesh.'

'He said, let them go,' Danae repeated with force.

Eurystheus turned to look at Danae, his face tightening in disdain. 'You will kneel before your king.' Two men marched forward and forced her to her knees. 'I am the rightful ruler of Mycenae. You may have been released from Hades' kingdom, but you are in my service now.' He turned to address the Missing. 'You are all mine.'

'If you have lost your kingdom, then you are no longer a king.'

Eurystheus turned and struck Danae across the face, his rings biting into her jaw. She tasted blood.

He lifted her chin with a gnarled finger. 'A spirited one, eh?' He flicked the metal collar around her neck. 'Was this part of your punishment? Which realm did you come from?' Uncertainty bled through his imperious tone.

He is afraid, she realized. *Afraid of what he does not know.*

Danae looked up at Eurystheus and smiled. 'It is worse than you could ever imagine.'

The king faltered, and she seized the moment. Her legs screamed as she leapt up, slipping past Eurystheus and the soldiers beside her, who evidently had not expected her to run.

As though taking his cue from her, Hylas ripped his mane free of his sentries' hands, leaving strands of white hair wound around their fingers, and flicked out his wings, knocking down the soldiers either side of him. Danae sprinted to the horse and swung herself onto his back. Eurystheus' men surged forward, but Hylas launched into the air, out of their grasp.

Danae clung to Heracles and, as Hylas ascended, shouted at Telamon and Atalanta, 'An island that sounds like the healer!' Hoping they would understand her riddle.

A slew of arrows followed them as Hylas continued into the air. Danae's vision crackled from the effort of their escape, but she forced herself to hold on to the horse's mane with one hand, Heracles with the other. She could just about feel the hero's chest moving beneath her arms as he clung to life. She tried not to look at the Missing staring up at her, delivered from the realm of one tyrannical master into the clasp of another. As Atalanta had said, she could not save everyone. That didn't make it any easier.

Danae, Heracles and Hylas soared across the cerulean

ocean. As the cries behind them faded, Prometheus' parting words echoed in her mind.

Seek out Metis on Delos, she will help you.

Without the aid of the omphalos shard, she had nowhere else to go.

'Hylas,' she gasped, 'take us to Delos.'

She did not know who this Metis was, but they were her only hope of regaining her powers and saving Heracles.

As the sea and sky stretched out around them, the tightness in her chest finally began to ease. She had wasted enough time doubting the truths Prometheus had revealed, the reality that she had always known deep down yet could not accept.

Hades was dead, along with his wife, Persephone. The Twelve were now eleven. Danae's actions had led to the release of Typhon, the dragon, from its watery cage. She had set free the giants, Heracles and the Missing. She had destroyed Tartarus. All without her powers.

The world was a dark and terrible place, and she must fill it with light. She was the last daughter and finally she was ready to meet her destiny.

PART TWO

21. The Island

Danae hit the sea like a chisel cracking marble.

Her body responded before her mind had recovered from the fall. She struck out against the swell and broke the surface, gasping. Through stinging eyes, she watched Hylas collapse on the little beach, his white coat gleaming with sweat. Her chest ached at the invasion of salt in her wounds, but the wind was so strong and her arms so weak, she couldn't have held on to the horse a moment longer. And falling into the sea was preferable to smacking into hard earth.

She couldn't see Heracles. Heart thundering, she twisted about, then caught sight of a long shape drifting a yard or so behind her. She swam towards it. The gouges on her chest screamed, the collar growing heavier with each stroke, but she forced her limbs to keep slicing through the ocean.

When she reached Heracles, she flipped him onto his back and threaded his bony arm through hers, then kicked towards the shore.

The muscles beneath her collarbone felt like they were tearing as she dragged him through clouds of seaweed up onto the sand. He was so tall and thin it looked as though he'd been stretched, like the jealous sea had tried to keep hold of him.

As she gazed down at the hero, memory threatened to envelop her. Another beach, another body, a life swept away by the tide.

Not this time.

She let out a guttural moan as she heaved Heracles onto his side and thumped his back.

'Breathe, gods damn you.' She hit him again and again.

The hero coughed, and the memory of Alea was sent scurrying back to the depths of her mind as Heracles retched onto the sand. She rubbed his back, his bones sharp beneath her fingers. Her movements slowed as she traced the familiar scars, remembering a time when they lay together on a different shore; the strength of him then, his weight pressing into her, the power corded in his limbs. She held onto the sensation of being circled in his arms, feeling safe for the first time since fleeing Naxos.

'I'm sorry,' she whispered. 'I'm so sorry.' Her cheeks were damp. From the sea or sorrow, she could not tell.

Heracles' eyes were closed. His breath, a rattling rasp.

Danae sagged back on her heels and flopped down beside him, gazing up at the cloud-speckled sky through heavy lids. A lone gull hovered above her, buffeted by the wind. Every part of her ached. She knew she had to find help or they would both perish, but she could not move.

After escaping Lerna, they'd flown for hours. All the while Danae had clung to Heracles for fear of him falling. When Hylas eventually spotted Delos and dipped his wings, she almost cried with relief, before her limbs failed her and she slipped into the azure arms of the Aegean Sea.

If she did not know the winged horse so well, she would have thought he'd made a mistake in bringing them to this place. Delos was a small, stony island, with little to show for itself but craggy rocks, hardy shrubbery and tufts of yellowing grass. From the sky there appeared to be only one bay, shaped like a crescent moon. The rest of the coast was a saw of primordial cliffs and jagged boulders. There seemed to be no dwellings of any kind, no sign that the island was inhabited at all. But Hylas had never led her wrong before. The horse seemed to have an internal compass embedded in his skull, navigating the world as though following a trail on a map. She wondered if that was Hades' doing.

A shiver fluttered over her skin. With great effort, she sat up. The sun had dipped behind the island's rocky peak. In the shadow, the wind leached any warmth baked into the land. She looked at Heracles. His skin had prickled into gooseflesh.

She could curl up beside him, share her warmth for the night. But out here, exposed to the elements, her battered body might not be enough.

'Hylas! Come here.'

The horse whinnied, staggered to his feet, then walked towards her, his head low.

'Stay close and keep him warm. He must survive. Do you understand?'

Hylas wearily nuzzled her hand, then sank down beside Heracles and lifted a wing over the hero's shivering frame.

Danae brushed the grains from her palms and looked inland, shielding her eyes from the last blaze of light. She squinted, her gaze snagging on what looked like a whisper of smoke billowing from halfway up the rocky hill. She stared at the spot, wondering if she had been mistaken.

Then it came again, a dark tendril twisting into the sky before being erased by the wind.

'I'm going to get help.' She regarded the prone forms of Heracles and Hylas. 'Neither of you are allowed to die while I'm gone.'

Setting her jaw, she strode towards the stony hill. Between the swathes of tawny grass covering the land beyond the beach were splashes of colour; robust little flowers with thick stems and purple petals, mixed with yolk-bright blooms and even the occasional silken red poppy.

'Argh.' Danae glanced down at her calf, clawed by a nearby shrub of prickly spurge. Even the plants here were sharp.

The little vegetation there was thinned as she approached the hill. Only the spurge sprouted in spiky pillows between the granite boulders. Some of the rocks were a warm umber, some grey as a stormy sky, peppered with blotches of yellow lichen. Loose stones slowed her progress as she climbed, her once sure limbs weak and trembling.

The peak of the hill seemed to grow further away with each step she took. She glanced back at the beach. Heracles and Hylas were still nestled together on the shore. Fear curled tighter around her heart with each passing moment, as though she could sense death waiting for the last dregs of sunlight to vanish from the world. If she failed to find help, Heracles would not see another sunrise.

Soon she was forced to climb on all fours. Chest aching, she paused, clinging to a rock as the wind tore at her back.

Then she caught the scent of the smoke.

Finding a foothold between two boulders, she pushed herself up, but something tightened around her leg. She cried out and slipped backwards, landing painfully across the rocks.

Bracing against the sharp stones, she heaved herself up and tugged Telamon's knife from her belt. Her right ankle was caught in some kind of trap, the binding so tight it burned her skin. It looked to be concocted from thin but sturdy twine and twirled like a spider's web around her foot. It was secured to the surrounding rocks in at least ten places and had been completely invisible until she'd stepped on it.

'You're a funny-looking lizard.'

Danae twisted around, her knife in her fist.

A tiny woman stood on the lip of stone above her. She

was wiry with a delicate face, her deep-brown skin riveted by the sun. Danae could not place her age. Her long black hair, bound roughly in an old rag, bore no threads of silver, and she moved without the stiffness of advanced age, yet there was an ancient wildness about her that seemed to echo the rocks themselves. She was barefoot and wore the strangest clothes Danae had ever seen: a long-sleeved tunic of undyed wool and a skirt that was bound between her legs.

'Please,' Danae gasped, 'I need help, my friend is gravely ill.'

The woman cocked her head, staring at Danae. Her eyes were so dark they were almost black, like a bird's. 'You don't look so good yourself.' Her accent was broad and strange, her voice rough as though it were not often used.

'Are you Metis?'

The woman's nostrils flared, then she leapt down from the rocky ridge, landing on all fours beside Danae like a cat. Her beady eyes narrowed. Then she snatched Danae's knife, retreating to a safe distance to examine it, running a finger along its bronze length. Her gaze flicked back to Danae and settled on the iron collar.

'Why is that around your neck?' She gestured with the knife, staring at the collar like it was a viper.

Danae watched her, heart thumping a drumbeat in her chest. 'To keep me weak.' She tried to move her trapped foot. The more she strained the tighter the bonds became. 'My name is Danae. I've been told to seek out Metis on this island. But please, my friend is on the beach. He will perish before nightfall if I don't get him to shelter.'

'Who sent you?' The woman's eyes hardened, her expression all edges.

'Later. I will explain everything later, but we must go to my —' Danae stopped abruptly as the woman slashed through her bindings. She left the blade balanced on the rock between them.

'Leave by whatever means you came.' The woman turned and began to scurry back up the hillside.

Danae took up the knife and scrabbled to her feet. 'You have to help him. He'll die if you don't.'

The woman paused and glanced over her shoulder. 'I *have* to do nothing. You came here uninvited, trampled over my island and ruined a perfectly good lizard trap. Why should I help you?'

Danae opened her mouth, but words failed her. 'Please,' she repeated feebly.

The woman sniffed. 'Your friend is not of this island, he's not mine to heal.'

Rage flickered in Danae's aching chest. 'You won't even see him? You would just leave Heracles to die?'

At the hero's name something too quick to discern darted across the woman's face. 'Zeus' boy?'

In her urgency Danae did not dwell on the strange familiarity of the question.

'Yes.'

The woman seemed to wrestle with herself. Then she said, 'Take me to him.'

The woman navigated the steep rocky slope with the ease of a mountain goat, Danae struggling to match her speed. When they reached the beach, they broke into a run, pacing across the ribbons of sun-crisped seaweed strewn about the shore.

Hylas stood and flexed his wings as Danae fell to her knees and checked Heracles' pulse. Weak, but still there. Despite the heat of Hylas' body against him, he was as cold as stone. She rubbed his arms, his chest, vainly trying to encourage some warmth into his skin.

She glanced back to find the woman had stopped in her tracks, staring at the winged horse.

'Pegasus?' she breathed.

The horse trotted over and nuzzled the woman's hands with easy familiarity.

A prickle of jealousy furrowed Danae's brow. 'You know my horse? His name is Hylas.'

The woman's eyes flicked to her, mistrust sharpening the angles of her face.

'Did Poseidon think I would not recognize his steed? Did he put you up to this?'

'I don't know what —'

Heracles groaned.

The woman's gaze snapped from Danae to the hero. She stared at him for a moment, before pacing forward and squatting down beside him.

'By the Mother, he looks so like his father,' she murmured and gently brushed his sea-slicked curls away from his forehead.

'Can you help him?'

The woman loosed a deep, weary sigh. 'When did he last take his strength elixir?'

Danae opened her mouth to answer, then hesitated. 'How do you know about that?'

The woman waved an impatient hand at her. 'Answer the question.'

Danae recalled what Atalanta had told her in the Underworld. 'I think about six months ago.'

'Hm.'

'Can you help him?' Danae repeated.

'Don't know yet . . .' For a moment, the woman's eyes misted with that faraway look again. 'But I will try. We'll need to get him back to my hut. Help me lift him onto Pegasus.'

The unfamiliar name jarring through her, Danae moved around to Heracles' legs and helped the woman lift him. But her body had finally reached its limit. She dropped the hero's limbs with a groan and sank to her knees, ribbons of agony pulsing across her chest.

The woman laid Heracles' arms down and paced to her side. Without warning she tore the neckline of Danae's dress, ripping it open down to her sternum to reveal the marks gouged by the fury. The wet, dark fabric of her robe had concealed the blood.

The woman sucked the air through her teeth. 'Foolish girl, you should have said.'

The woman placed her hands either side of Danae's wounds, who gasped as warmth spread through her body. It felt as though liquid sunlight was pouring into her from the woman's fingertips. Then her pain began to melt away. She could feel her skin tightening, the muscles beneath knitting together. Tears pricked her eyes as she realized what was happening.

It was over so swiftly.

The woman sat back, rubbed her bloody hands on her tunic and pushed herself up.

'Come on, help me with him.'

Danae staggered to her feet.

'You . . . you have powers.'

The woman glared at Danae as she took hold of Heracles' arms. 'Course I have.'

'You *are* Metis, aren't you?'

The woman's eyes narrowed further. 'Last time I checked.'

A little burst of relief bloomed through Danae's freshly healed body. She had finally fulfilled Prometheus' last instruction.

'Grab his legs,' prompted Metis.

Danae hurried to do as she was bid, and between them

they heaved the hero onto Hylas' back. Danae clambered up beside him, her arms wrapped tight around his torso.

Metis pointed to the hill. 'See that boulder? Land the horse behind it. I'll meet you there.'

'One last push,' Danae whispered into Hylas' ear.

No, not Hylas. *Pegasus*, Metis had called him, Poseidon's horse. As he spread his snowy wings and launched into the air, Danae felt a jolt of unease. It grated over her skin like the wind. He did not have a voice with which he could have spoken his true name, yet he had accepted the moniker of Hylas without protest. Now, it felt as though the animal had been playing a part. Just as she had done aboard the *Argo*. Since the Caucasus Mountains it had been her and the horse against the world, his time as an Olympian steed erased by his choosing to be with her. But perhaps his past could not be so easily forgotten.

As they flew towards the hill, questions began to ripple like delayed shockwaves through Danae's mind. Why did Metis speak of Heracles' father as though he were an old friend? Why did she recognize Pegasus? Who was this woman?

Below them, the stony hillside began to reveal its secrets. Behind the rust-coloured boulder Metis had pointed to was a ledge of flat ground, and beyond that, the entrance to a tiny stone dwelling. It looked to be little more than a doorway in the rock-strewn hill, but the placement of the stones around it betrayed a human design. Rocks of a similar size had been stacked like bricks to form the outer walls, and those atop the dwelling slanted up to a peak like the roof of a hut. The smoke Danae had spied seeped from the shadowed entrance.

As the horse landed, Danae breathed in a lungful of relief at the sudden lull of the wind. She could see why Metis had chosen this sheltered spot, hidden from the beach with clear vantage over the entire western reach of the island.

As she eased Heracles down from Hylas' back, Metis appeared, and together they carried the hero's bony body into the stone dwelling.

'Wait here,' Danae said to Pegasus. The horse huffed and hoofed the ground but stayed where he was.

Inside, the hut was cool and strangely quiet given the wind whipping around the island. The internal walls were rough, as though the dwelling had been hollowed out of the mountainside by hand. Great cracks ran through the rock, and in the centre, nestled in a ring of stones, was a small fire. As they lay Heracles down beside this rudimentary hearth, Danae noticed a smell she recognized. She looked around and located the stench wafting from a woven basket and fishing spear leaning against the doorway. An eclectic collection of clay pots and bowls were piled around the edges of the walls, and the floor was strewn with dry leaves. Dried bunches of herbs hung from twigs prised between the cracks in the walls. There were lizards too, some as small as her thumb, some as long as her forearm, pinned to the stone with sharpened sticks. She was reminded of the trophies mounted on the wall of the Hunters Hall on Lemnos.

Danae's attention was drawn back to Heracles as Metis swaddled him in a navy woollen cloak trimmed with fur. It was strange to see such a piece of finery in a place like this.

Metis leant over Heracles, her ear to his chest. Then she sat back, closed her eyes and placed her hands upon his torso. Questions clustered in Danae's throat, fighting to be the first to pass her lips. But she did not dare disturb the healing. She sank to her knees and watched Metis work.

Finally, the woman let out a long breath, withdrew her hands and opened her eyes.

'I do not know if I have the skill to save him.'

Danae felt as though she were made of glass.

'If he survives the night, his chances will be better.' Metis pushed herself up with a sigh and walked towards a collection of chipped pottery piled against the wall. She moved slowly, as though each step cost her. Danae knew that feeling, the fatigue of expending life-threads. A primal longing ached through her.

Metis found what she was seeking, picked up a waterskin and gulped. She wiped her mouth, eyes never leaving Danae.

'Now, tell me what you're doing here.'

Danae's fingers curled around a loose rock by her thigh, ever aware of the collar around her neck. She knew her stone would be nothing against Metis' abilities, but it helped her to feel a little less powerless.

'I was sent to Delos to find you.'

'Given Pegasus and ordered by the Twelve to bring *him* here to be healed, were you?' She glanced at Heracles.

'I was not sent from Olympus.' Danae's pulse quickened.

Metis barked out a laugh. 'Don't test me girl. I'm in no mood for Zeus' games.'

'I promise you,' Danae said slowly, her mouth dry. 'I was not sent from Olympus.'

The sun had sunk beneath the waves on the far side of the island, and now the only light flickered from the last remnants of the fire. Shadows creased along Metis' scowl.

Sometimes, Danae's brother, Santos, had said when teaching her to play petteia, *you must sacrifice a stone or two in order to make the other player reveal their tactics. That's how you win the game.*

'Prometheus told me to seek you out.'

Surprise briefly smoothed Metis' face, before her brows thundered once more. 'Hm.' Another pause. 'That does not explain how you came by Pegasus.'

'I stole him after a fight with Hera atop the Caucasus Mountains.'

A flicker of something like amusement cracked Metis' scowl. 'I am to believe you not only spoke with Prometheus, but also bested Hera?'

'Yes.' Danae held her gaze. 'Prometheus told me you would help me.'

'I'm doing what I can for the boy,' Metis hissed.

'No, not that.' Danae slowly rose to her feet. 'He was never meant to be involved in this.' Her shallow breath raked over her cracked lips. The problem with the truth was, once you tugged at a single thread the whole tapestry unravelled. 'I am the one Prometheus prophesied would come. I am the last daughter.'

Metis stared at her, eyes shining in the firelight. She shook her head. 'I have lived in exile for almost a thousand years. I have never once left this island, yet still I am tested.' Danae flinched as Metis took a step towards her. 'Go back to Olympus and tell Zeus I did not fall for his trick.'

Danae stood her ground. 'I do not answer to the false gods.'

Metis' breath hitched in her throat.

'I know the truth.' Danae clenched her fists and repeated Prometheus' words, '*There are no gods. There were only ever mortals and those mortals chosen to become Titans.* I am the one that destroyed the oracle at Delphi. It was there that I heard the prophecy from a member of the Children of Prometheus.'

Metis barked out a laugh. 'So, the Children sent you? It has been centuries since they came here. I thought they had given up.'

'No, Prometheus himself told me to find you. Like him, I am a Titan.' She spoke with a confidence she did not feel. She still did not fully understand what it meant to be a Titan.

Metis stared at her, rage, confusion and disbelief all swirling like storm clouds across her face.

'Prove it.'

'I cannot.' Danae raised her hands to the collar. 'This cuts me off from my life-threads. If you free me, I will show you what I can do.'

Metis did not move. 'If you are really a Titan, Zeus must have given you an apple.'

'That monster gave me nothing.'

Metis' lips parted. 'You're brave, girl. I'll give you that.'

'It is not bravery when you don't have a choice.'

'We always have a choice.'

'Do we?' A beat fell between them. 'I think the fates would disagree.'

Metis continued to stare at her, then Heracles murmured, and they both looked at him. Metis sank down and once more laid her hands upon him.

'You can rest here until he is out of danger, or he dies. We'll know by sunrise. Either way, you will leave in the morning.'

The familiar crush of disappointment wrapped around Danae's heart. She felt as though she were once more standing before Prometheus, having travelled to the end of the world and risked everything, only to discover that she was on her own.

'That's it?' When Metis did not reply, she continued, 'Prometheus told me with his dying breath that you would help me. What a waste.'

Metis stiffened. She looked up at Danae. 'Prometheus is . . . ?'

'Slain by Hera. She tried to kill me too, but I escaped. I told you, that's how I came by Pegasus.'

Metis withdrew her hands, sat back on her heels and closed her eyes. When she opened them, they shone like the sea. 'The horse will need seeing to.' She wiped her cheeks, then pointed to a clay vase by the door. 'There's water in that hydria. You can use one of the bowls.' Then she turned back to Heracles.

Danae pressed her tongue against her teeth, a barrage of questions bubbling inside her. But she voiced none of them. She snatched up a large bowl with a faded owl painted on its belly, tilted the hydria with trembling hands and drowned the bird in its own little ocean.

22. Echoes

She was lying on a slab of marble. High above, polished obsidian walls stretched up to a ceiling shrouded in darkness. The air was close, the reek of decay permeating through the windless space. There were no windows. Nothing in this place had ever been warmed by the light of day.

The cold bit into her skin, but she could not move. She tried to scream, but it was like she was trapped inside a carcass laid out on a butcher's block. Even her eyes were fixed, forced to stare up at that never-ending ceiling.

Mist began to curl across the edges of her vision. Its cloudy breath prickled her flesh, raising the hairs on her arms. It drifted over her face, and for a moment she thought she had gone blind, then she saw shapes moving within it, looming over her through the fog.

'Were you made or were you born?' The words lingered, as though caught in the mist like flies in a spider's web.

Pressure began to build inside her, a cry that could not be released.

The figures leant closer. Two pairs of tusks pierced the fog.

'We have been made before and we shall be made again.'

Danae's ears thrummed with hissing as a tangle of snakes swam from the mist. Then the faces of the two gorgons pressed in, their rancid breath hot on her freezing cheeks. She could do nothing as they reached for her, their lips stretching back to reveal sharpened teeth. But just as their fingers were about to touch her skin, they vanished.

Her heart was thumping so fast, she was sure it would burst.

Then she felt something that stilled her pulse entirely.

Fingers creeping through her hair, tracing pathways across her scalp.

No, it could not be. She'd watched Typhon, the dragon, char him to the bone.

'Hello, little Titan.'

Danae woke, gasping. Pain spiked down her left arm, and she clutched it so tightly, her nails dug into her skin. The ache lingered, shooting down to her fingertips as she pushed herself up. She must have fallen asleep on the limb.

Pale moonlight spilled in through the doorway of Metis' hut, shadows pooling behind the stacks of pottery and burned-out fireplace. Metis herself was still hunched over Heracles, her hands laid upon his torso. She rocked gently as she worked, muttering under her breath.

Even as Danae watched her, she imagined the cold, thin light came not from the moon, but from the star crystals in the false sky of the Underworld. She became acutely aware of the stone wall of the dwelling, chill against her back. The cloying dampness of the earth and rocks swelled in her nostrils. Then her pulse quickened, her lungs expanding and contracting as though she were sprinting for her life. Reality bled away, and she became sure she was underground again, buried under all that soil and stone. Terror swallowed her whole. She had to get out, or she would suffocate.

Staggering to her feet, she lurched out of the hut. But even the dark expanse of sky and the biting chill of the wind could not free her from her cage of fear. She fell to her hands and knees, desperately sucking in air.

Pegasus, woken by her, trotted over from where he'd been sleeping and gently nudged her with his muzzle. His presence tethered her to reality, drawing her back to the island breath by breath. When her head had stopped spinning enough for her to move, she reached for him, dragging herself up to wrap her arms around his neck. Pegasus waited patiently as she sobbed into his coat, resting his head over her shoulder while her heartbeat slowly returned to normal.

'You all right, girl?'

Danae lifted her face from Pegasus' neck. Metis was standing in the stone doorway. She looked haggard.

'Yes,' Danae lied, wiping her cheeks and stepping away from the horse. 'How is Heracles?'

'He's alive. Just. The next few hours will be crucial.' Metis' eyes swept over her. 'You should eat something.' She disappeared back inside.

Danae gave Pegasus an encouraging pat. 'I'm well,' she whispered. 'I promise.'

The horse tossed his head as she walked back towards the dwelling, each step an effort. She was so exhausted she could no longer feel anything. In a way, she was glad. Numbness was preferable to fear.

She lingered before the doorway. The entrance seemed to gape at her like a great, toothless mouth. Summoning the last crumbs of her strength, she stepped inside.

Metis thrust a bowl and waterskin into Danae's hands before returning to her vigil at Heracles' side.

Danae drank then looked down at the contents of the bowl. It appeared to be filled with dried cicadas.

'Eat, you'll feel better.'

Danae tentatively crunched one between her teeth. It was surprisingly nutty. After a few mouthfuls she did start to feel more human.

'Which one of them put that on you?' asked Metis quietly, staring at the collar.

'Hades,' Danae murmured.

'Hm. You're lucky that's all he did.'

'He's dead,' Danae said sharply.

'And I suppose you killed him too, did you?'

'Not exactly. Charon, the ferryman, set free the dragon imprisoned in Tartarus, who burned him to ash.'

'That's quite a tale.'

'No stranger than a godlike being living in exile on a barren spit of land.'

Metis huffed a breath through her nose and checked Heracles' pulse.

'Why did Prometheus tell me to seek you out?'

For a while it seemed like Metis would not answer, then eventually she said, 'For the same reason the Children of Prometheus came to me. Because I opposed Zeus. A long time ago.'

Danae recalled what Phineus, Manto's father, the seer, had told her about Prometheus, that he had seen the downfall of the gods in the omphalos shard and along with his prophecy, had given the stone to mankind so they might rise up against the tyranny of the Twelve.

'You were on Prometheus' side? On the side of mortals?'

Metis shook her head. She reached across to a stack of bowls and slipped her hand between the third and fourth, pulling out an amulet. At first, Danae thought it was a twin of the one Dolos had carried, that bore Zeus's crest. But this was smaller, cast from bronze, its design more crudely carved.

Metis proffered it to her. Engraved at its heart was the tree.

'The tree of knowledge,' Danae breathed.

Metis barked out a laugh. 'The Children of Prometheus know only a fragment of the truth. The man of their order who came here gave this to me. He too wanted to know whose side I was on. Said to send that to him once I had decided. I told him his grandchildren would be dead before that pendant returned to Ithaca. People only choose a side if they're ready to go to war.'

Danae watched her, weighing her words. 'How did you oppose Zeus?'

Metis waved her question away. 'The hour is late, and I have the lad to tend to. Get some rest.'

Begrudgingly, Danae lay down on the leaf-strewn floor while Metis returned to her work.

After a while she murmured, 'I didn't think it was possible to heal others. I've only ever been able to heal myself with my powers.'

'It takes great patience and control,' Metis replied as she worked on the hero. 'And many years to master.'

More questions drifted through Danae's mind, but weariness overpowered her, and once more she slipped into sleep.

When Danae woke again, the hut was bright with the glow of morning. She sat up with a jolt when she realized that Metis wasn't there. Heracles lay wrapped in the cloak, still and grey. Scrambling across the floor, Danae pressed her fingers to his neck. The breath she held escaped at the faint pulse beneath her hand. She let the relief wash over her, then left the hut in search of Metis.

Pegasus was lying outside the dwelling, still asleep, his head tucked into his side. Danae stepped around him and walked out onto the hillside. From her vantage point she could see across the entire length of Delos to the cerulean sea lapping at its coast. Opposite the bay was another uninhabited island and a small spit of land where a smattering of white-winged gulls clustered. Further to the north were the green-flecked hills of a larger isle, and to the south, an expanse of ocean and the ghostly outline of another island hazed by the dawn mist.

Turning her attention back to the rocky reaches of Delos, she noticed a verdant area of land she hadn't spotted from the bay. A clutch of dark-green trees and bushes of reeds surrounded a small lake, a lone palm tree standing tall above the rest. Danae shielded her eyes against the rising sun. Through the foliage, she could make out a small figure crouched on the bank.

Picking her way down the stony peak of the hill, she noticed that patches of the spurge growing between the rocks were grey and dull. This was not strange in itself, but the dead sections of plant occurred at regular intervals; precise circles that never affected more than half the bush, as though the decay were following a pattern.

The stony hillside in her wake, Danae weaved her way between clumps of tawny grass, heading towards the lake. She found Metis bent over the water, filling the hydria.

'Heracles is alive,' said Danae. 'Thank you.'

Metis glanced over her shoulder. 'He's out of danger for now. But he's got a long road to recovery.'

Danae summoned the courage to ask the question she had been dreading to voice. 'Will he be able to fight again?'

Metis shook her head. 'His bones are frail and his muscles weakened. Nothing I can do about that. He'll have to live a quiet life for the rest of his days.'

Guilt sank through Danae like an anchor tumbling to the seabed. She thought of Heracles in all his glory, pictured him charging across the Doliones' shore with an army of Earthborn at his back. She remembered the depth of feeling in his ocean-blue eyes when he told her that all he had was his name, his legend.

He would never be the mighty Heracles again. Because of her.

Metis wiped her brow. 'Now you're here, you can give me a hand.'

Danae squatted beside her and helped Metis heave the full hydria from the lake.

The woman gestured to the large island to the south, lake water glistening on her wiry arms. 'That land is Myconus. They're peaceful, farming folk. Once Heracles wakes you can take him there to recover.'

Despite the rising heat of the day, a ripple of cold washed through Danae.

'You really won't help me fulfil my prophecy?'

'I've done what I can for the lad. It's best you both be on your way.'

Danae pressed her fingernails into the soft flesh of her palms. 'Prometheus trusted you. Whatever you were to him, he believed you would help me liberate mankind. Does that mean nothing to you?'

Metis loosed a sharp sigh. 'Even if you're telling the truth, and Prometheus really did send you to me, it's too late. I thought I could make a difference once, but the centuries went by, and I realized the only thing you can count on is that one day we will all be dust. When you have lived as long as I, you see how insignificant we really are.'

'I am not insignificant. I am the last daughter. Two of the false gods are dead because of me. Hera fled from me in battle. I survived the Underworld without the power of my life-threads. I set free the giants and I watched Typhon, the last dragon, burn Hades out of existence. I *will* fulfil Prometheus' prophecy.'

Metis stared at her. For a moment Danae thought she caught a flicker of belief in those dark eyes, before doubt narrowed them once more.

'The only way to become a Titan is to eat a Hesperides apple. Zeus guards that tree with his life. So, either he gave you one willingly or you tricked the most powerful being that has ever walked this earth.' Metis let out a mirthless laugh. 'You did well, however you convinced him. Zeus has not created a new Olympian in centuries. I was almost beginning to wonder if he no longer possesses the power . . . *Gold that grows bears no fruit.*' She shook her head. 'But then here you are.'

'You're wrong. I did not choose this. I would never choose this. To go on living while all those you love wither and die . . .' Danae's eyes stung. 'You want to know how I became like this? My sister drowned herself, and when I dragged her body from the water, a tree sprouted from her heart. A tree with golden apples. It was the worst moment of my life, the most terrible and beautiful thing I have ever seen, and I . . .' She fell silent at the expression on Metis' face.

'Her heart?' the woman whispered.

'Yes.'

Metis stared at her. 'If I discover you have lied about this . . .'

A wave of grief caught Danae like a riptide. Once more she was untethered, careering on a tempest of pain. She was so weary. Tired of fighting, tired of running, tired of carrying around the knowledge that she would never see Alea again. Tears swelled and tumbled down her cheeks. She made no attempt to stem them.

Then the hairs on her arms prickled. She grew very still as a warm breeze danced over her skin, soft as a butterfly's wing. The dissonant sounds of the island seemed to blend together into sweet harmonies of birdsong, murmuring leaves, whistling wind and the pulse of the tide that sounded like a heartbeat.

Metis' body shifted as though she sensed it too. Then the woman sank down beside the hydria and pressed her hands to the earth, murmuring, 'The tree of life, grown from the heart of the world.'

Just as swiftly as they had melded, the sounds fractured, and the wind reclaimed its bite.

When Metis raised her head, her eyes were bright with tears. 'She grew a tree . . . just for you.' She pressed her forehead to the ground. 'Mother forgive me, I thought you had forsaken us.'

Danae opened her mouth then closed it again as Metis rose to her feet. Something in her had shifted. There was a light in her face that had not been there before.

'I don't know how Prometheus expected me to help you,' said Metis. 'It's been almost a thousand years since I last set foot on Mount Olympus. But there is one thing I can do. I will teach you the ways of the Mother.'

Metis moved towards her, stretched out her earth-stained fingers and gripped the iron collar around Danae's neck. There was an intense surge of heat, then with a click the metal opened and fell to the ground.

Danae gasped, sobs erupting from her chest at the sudden rush of feeling her life force flowing through her body. It was like she'd been living in a dark, freezing cave, her senses smothered, and now she was stepping out into the sunlight for the very first time. The air was sweeter, the colours brighter, the sound of the wind the most beautiful thing she'd ever heard.

I am here, said the voice. *I never left.*

23. Divine Revelations

Hermes flew down the pillared corridor, screeching to a halt just in time to avoid crashing headlong into the megaron doors.

Two days earlier, he had left Hera in the north tower and flown back to Erebus to confront Hades once again, this time determined not to leave until his uncle gave him answers about the Underworld girl. He would never, in his wildest imagination, have expected the sight that greeted him.

Now, standing before the throne room, he longed to flee to the safety of Arachne's hut and never come out again. But he knew he could not. However devastating, his family must hear this news.

Heart thundering, he lifted a gauntleted hand and knocked. In the other he clutched a twisted piece of gold.

After a moment that felt like an eternity, the doors swung open.

Silence fell as he entered.

Nearly the entire royal family was in attendance. Enthroned at the feet of their marble statues were the twins, Apollo and Artemis, Poseidon, Hera, Athena, even Aphrodite. Hermes swallowed as she caught sight of him and sat up, her emerald eyes gleaming with expectation. The others were watching Ares, who had the floor. The God of War remained silent as, from the central throne, Zeus raised a hand.

Ares turned as the eyes of his family fell on his younger brother.

Hermes dropped to his knee. 'My lord father, my deepest apologies for the interruption, I have just flown from the Underworld –'

Ares whipped out a hand, and a rope of life-threads curled around Hermes' neck. The air pressed against him like an invisible fist squeezing his gullet. He dropped the piece of twisted metal he'd been carrying as he struggled for breath, instinctively clawing at the threads even though he knew his fingers would pass straight through them.

'How dare you interrupt my report, you insolent little –'

'Ares,' said Zeus softly.

Quiet rolled across the throne room.

Ares released Hermes and turned to his father. 'As I was saying, the Trojans are rallying their defences against the allied Greek army. Priam has secured aid from the Carians, Halizones, Lycians and Phrygians. This is shaping up to be the largest mortal war that has ever –'

'What is that?'

Ares fell silent as Zeus gestured to the lump of gold lying by Hermes' feet.

He retrieved the item with trembling hands. As he approached his father, Hermes could feel himself coming apart. He knew he must deliver his news soon or his mettle would fail him. Yet he must be careful; Zeus had forbidden him to reveal his mission to anyone, and like the sun burning his cheek, he could feel Aphrodite's eyes boring into him. He had not spoken to her since he visited her son and failed to convince the youth to leave Troy. That too he must keep secret. An ache began to pulse behind his eyes.

'I journeyed to Erebus to visit Hades.' This much he dared admit in front of his family. In reality, on Hera's suggestion, he had returned to question his uncle further on the Underworld girl's whereabouts. 'He wasn't in his palace, so

I searched the Asphodel Meadows and then Tartarus, where I found the giants set loose and the dragon's well empty –'

Gasps echoed around the megaron.

'Typhon is free?' asked Poseidon.

'Yes,' whispered Hermes, his ears ringing.

For a long moment, no one spoke.

'You have not answered my question.' Zeus' expression betrayed nothing, but his eyes blazed gold.

Hermes lay the piece of metal at his father's feet. 'This is all that is left of Hades.' He could barely force the unbelievable truth past his lips. 'The dragon burned him to cinders.'

There were more gasps, but Hermes could not tell who voiced them. His entire world had narrowed to his father's face. Zeus was staring at the melted gauntlet as though Hermes had just thrown Hades' body into their midst.

'What of Persephone?' asked Hera, gripping the armrests of her throne.

Hermes swallowed, dragging his gaze to his stepmother. 'She too has been slain.'

He felt as though he might faint. Hades and Persephone were dead. Gone, forever. He had lived as a mortal for fourteen years, yet now the concept of life ending seemed repellently unnatural. The Olympians were gods, they did not age then perish like the rest of nature. He knew the divine family could be hurt, he had borne enough beatings to prove that, but his wounds were always healed once he consumed another being's life-threads. A dark cloud settled around his heart, a fear that had not weighed on him since he took a bite of the golden apple all those years ago. His life might be finite after all.

His thoughts were broken by Artemis' gut-wrenching wail. The sound shattered the paralysing shock that had descended over the megaron. Artemis' twin, Apollo, ran to her side as she slid off her throne and sank to her knees. Poseidon leapt to his feet, shouting over and over, 'It cannot be!' while Ares and Athena began to bark questions at Hermes.

'Quiet.' At Zeus' command, his family fell silent. 'Everyone except Hermes and Poseidon, leave us.'

'This has gone on long enough.' Hera rose to her feet. 'You must tell the children the truth about the –'

'Silence!'

Hermes flinched as his father's voice resounded across the room. He stared at his stepmother, desperate to know what she had been about to say. What truth?

Hera's face was a devastating mask of ice. For a heart-pounding moment, it seemed as though she might defy Zeus, then she flicked the embroidered hem of her purple gown and stalked from the megaron. Artemis and Apollo ran after her, Ares close behind.

Athena alone stood her ground. 'Father . . .'

Something like compassion stirred in Zeus' face. A depth of feeling Hermes had never managed to rouse from their father.

'Not now, Bright Eyes,' he said softly. 'Go, be with your siblings.'

Athena lifted her chin, then sank into a bow and paced from the room.

The doors slammed shut, and Hermes was left alone with his father and uncle.

Poseidon had grown pale as the marble of his statue and looked at Zeus like a frightened child might look to their father. Then he crossed the mosaic floor and flung his arms around his elder brother. Zeus held him as sobs racked his powerful frame.

'He's gone . . . our little brother.'

'I know,' said Zeus, staring over Poseidon's shoulder, eyes

fixed on his son. Gently he pushed Poseidon away and bent to lift the melted gauntlet, turning it over as though it harboured a wealth of secrets.

'Did you see the girl?'

Hermes glanced at Poseidon.

'You can speak freely in front of your uncle.'

Hermes swallowed, then shook his head. 'I went to the Underworld because I thought, as the girl was created by Hades, she might return to him . . .'

'What else did you find?'

'Nothing,' Hermes breathed. 'Just the Underworld in disarray.' The part of Hermes' mind that wasn't still in shock marvelled at the grain of truth he seemed to have decided to keep hidden from his father. The object he had found amongst the chaos.

Keep it concealed, the voice had whispered. *Even from Zeus.*

'It was her, wasn't it?' Poseidon said to Zeus, his voice constricted with grief. 'She did this.'

Zeus ignored his brother, his gaze fixed on his son. 'The dragon, did you see it?'

Hermes shook his head once more. He clasped his hands behind his back to hide their tremors. 'I only saw the destruction it left, the scorch marks –'

'That is all? You are sure you found nothing else?'

'Nothing,' Hermes whispered, his heart threatening to break loose from his chest.

Zeus closed his eyes and released a long breath through his nose.

'Come here, my son.'

Hermes rose and walked towards the King of Heaven, pausing at the steps leading up to Zeus' throne. Poseidon was staring at Hades' long-neglected statue, fresh tears staining his cheeks.

'Closer.'

Hermes advanced until he stood on the final step.

'Sit.'

He obeyed.

'Remove your helm.'

Hermes' heart sank. He hated baring his boyish face in the presence of his family. If it were anyone else, he'd have refused. But no one defies the King of Heaven. With shaking hands, he lifted the golden helmet from his head.

Zeus smiled. 'Remind me how long it is that you've been searching for the Underworld creature.'

A familiar fear, cold and immobilizing, seeped through Hermes' limbs. 'A month,' he whispered.

Zeus' irises were almost entirely golden with life-threads, yet despite their glow they were colder than a winter wind. 'If you had caught her, Hades would still be alive.'

Hermes' stomach hollowed. He turned, looking to Poseidon for support, but his uncle's face was just as stony as his father's. Then Zeus grabbed his jaw in his gauntleted hand and turned Hermes' head to face his own.

'You will look at your king when he speaks.'

Hermes screamed.

His skin blistered beneath his father's metallic fingers. The smell of burning flesh filled his nostrils, white-hot pain searing through his face until it blinded him. Zeus released him, and he tumbled down the marble steps.

'Go.'

Hermes grabbed his helm from where it had rolled across the floor and fled from the megaron.

He ran down the corridor, barely able to breathe through the agony. Just as he turned the corner, a nymph came strolling towards him. The girl barely had time to open her mouth before Hermes had clamped his gauntleted hands around her neck and drained the life-threads from her body. But the pain in his jaw lingered, long after his skin had healed.

The palace blurred around him as he ran back to his chambers. The look in his father's eyes as he burned him had been one of such loathing; Hermes had truly believed that Zeus might kill him.

Even now, far from his father's gaze, that loathing burrowed into him, crawling beneath his skin. His father had trusted him, above all his siblings, and he was failing.

He must find the girl, before he ran out of chances.

24. The Way of the Mother

The day after Metis freed Danae of the collar, the woman led her across the sun-rusted earth, towards the northern reach of the island. As they clambered over the rocks Danae paused by a cushion of spiny spruce, a perfect grey circle marring the plant's centre.

'What happened to the spruce?'

Metis glanced over her shoulder. 'I used much of my ichor to save your friend's life. It needed replenishing.'

'Ichor?'

Metis tilted her head as though surprised Danae did not know the word. 'Life force. The threads of the tapestry that live within each of us.' Her lips quirked at the perplexed expression still lingering on Danae's face.

Danae gestured to the dead patch of bush. 'Surely it would be more effective to drain the entire plant? Or better still a tree.'

'Better for who? The spurge I've left living will grow again in time, and balance will be restored. If I drained the entire bush, the lives of all the creatures that rely on it would be threatened. Balance destroyed. See?'

Danae nodded slowly.

A lone gull soared overhead. Metis tilted her face to the sky, mimicking the bird's cry. The gull swooped low to land on her arm. Metis' caws softened to coos as she stroked its feathers and continued to walk.

'Why do you live alone on this island?' asked Danae, hurrying to keep up.

Metis looked at the gull. 'I am not alone.'

'Without other people.'

The woman launched the bird back into the sky, watching its flight against the wind.

'Punishment.'

Danae waited for the woman to elaborate. She did not.

Metis led them to the cliffs looking out towards Myconus. Lining the divide between earth and rock was a crop of flowers unlike the hardy little blooms scattered throughout the dry grass. Despite the baking land beneath, their leaves were a vibrant green, thick and strong like pointed fingers, their blooms the size of Danae's palm with pale feather-like petals the colour of a sun-bleached sky.

A line formed between Danae's brows. 'If Demeter does not command the seasons, then why does the earth cool and warm? Why do trees wither only to grow new leaves?'

Metis stared at her for a moment, then blinked. 'It is the cyclical nature of the tapestry of life. The old must die to make way for the new. It is the way of the Mother.'

'When are you going to tell me who the Mother is?'

'All in good time.' Metis squatted down beside the flowers.

'How am I meant to learn her ways if I don't even know who she is?'

Metis pressed one of the thick leaves between her thumb and forefinger. 'Collect a couple of handfuls of these. They'll aid Heracles' recovery.' She threw the bag she'd carried from the hut to Danae. It was woven from strands of dried seaweed.

'Where are you going?' Danae called as Metis walked away.

'To check the lizard traps,' the woman said without turning back.

Chewing the inside of her lip in frustration, Danae crouched beside the crop of flowers. Their leaves proved tough to harvest, and she was forced to use the knife Telamon had given her.

She'd collected ten of the leaves when she caught a dash of movement out of the corner of her eye. A little way off, in the crevice between two rocks, a speckled yellow lizard had become caught in one of Metis' traps. Danae opened her mouth to call for the woman, then paused. She watched the creature struggle, her fingertips tingling.

Take its life-threads, urged the voice. *Metis will be pleased at your skill.*

Like an avalanche, longing cascaded through her. She had not yet used her powers since being freed from the collar.

She recalled a time, back on Naxos, when her mother had shown her how to end a creature's life swiftly with minimal pain. Then she remembered the reptiles pinned to the wall of Metis' dwelling: the woman was evidently used to killing the creatures. She thought of the burst of ecstasy she knew waited for her.

She crept forward and reached into the trap.

It was over so quickly. One tiny wave of pleasure. She could barely feel the threads spreading through her body. Such a little life. It was not enough.

'What are you doing?'

She turned to see Metis standing behind her. The woman's dark eyes were wide with fury.

'Killing a lizard that was caught in your trap.'

'You took its ichor.'

'Yes.' Danae was unsure why she suddenly felt like a scolded child.

'That is not the way of the Mother.' Every word was laden with reproach.

Danae frowned, anger rallying to her defence. 'You kill them too – I saw the lizards in your hut.'

'I eat their flesh but I do not take their life-threads.' Her voice was low and dangerous.

'Why?'

'Because we are guardians not masters. Nature does not exist to serve us. Stealing a creature's life to feed your power is a crime against the Mother. However small that creature may be.' Metis bent down and grabbed the cut leaves, stuffing them into the seaweed bag. 'You have much to learn.'

'Then teach me.'

Metis stared at her, and Danae was unsettled to see something akin to fear flicker across the woman's gaze.

After a beat of hesitation she said, 'Did something tell you to take the lizard's ichor?'

Danae's lips parted in surprise. She felt as though Metis had suddenly laid her bare. The voice was such a secret part of her she'd never considered that anyone else might be aware of its existence. The shame she harboured over the lives she'd drained to feed her power rose like bile in her throat.

'Yes,' she breathed.

The line between Metis' brows deepened. 'Trees grow leaves that are shaken to earth by the wind, or wither and fall with the changing seasons. Imagine if one tree in the forest did not wilt as it should, but grew more leaves, and more and more, until it covered all the other trees and starved them of light. Soon the forest would contain only one tree and it would not be a forest at all. This is what the Olympians have done by hoarding their life-threads. They deny others life. Be careful, listening to that voice will do you no good.' Then she turned and began stalking back towards the hill.

'What is the voice?' Danae called after her. 'Where does it come from?'

Metis stopped, her shoulders hunched as though carrying a yoke. Then she glanced back. 'Bring the lizard.'

When they returned to the stone hut, Heracles was still asleep. After tossing the leaves into one of the clay bowls stacked against the wall, Metis took the lizard from Danae, then passed her the bowl.

'Grind these into a paste.' Metis proffered a large black stone that fitted perfectly in the palm of her hand, before pinning the lizard to a crack in the hut wall beside its kin.

Danae thought of the omphalos shard, lost in the depths of the Underworld. Her stomach hollowed, and she turned her attention to the leaves. The bowl, like the vessel that had become Pegasus' makeshift water trough, was decorated with pictures of owls, black against the red of the clay. The birds were beautifully detailed, each feather painstakingly defined. Such fine pottery belonged in the houses of nobility, not stacked in a rudimentary hut on an abandoned island.

'Where did you get all this?' Danae gestured to the bowls.

'My daughter used to visit. She always brought a gift.'

'Fond of owls, is she?'

Metis' eyes grew heavy. 'She was. She doesn't come any more.'

'Oh . . . I'm sorry.' Danae wondered how many years Metis had spent alone on this spit of rock. Perhaps her daughter had long ago taken her last steps upon the earth. Danae thought of her own family back on Naxos, her mind curling as she imagined her little nephews, Minos and Egan, passing through the seasons of life until they too returned to the soil. And she, through it all, would remain the same. Ageless. Trapped in an infinite cycle of endings.

Metis checked Heracles' pulse and lifted his eyelids, then stood.

'I must commune with the Mother. Make that paste and watch him.' She glanced back at Heracles and added, 'I'll be at the peak if you need me.'

'But . . .' Frustration flared through Danae's chest as Metis left the dwelling. She was tempted to set down the bowl and follow the woman, but she settled for slumping down beside Heracles and channelling her irritation into mashing the thick green leaves beneath the stone.

Metis was a clam she must prise open without shattering its shell. Patience had never come naturally to Danae, something her mother had often reminded her of, but she would have to learn. Like it or not, she needed Metis' help and she could not take it by force.

The plant was almost completely pulverized when Heracles murmured. Hastily, Danae set down the bowl and stone and crouched over him.

Heracles' eyes twitched beneath his lids, his cracked lips shaping the faint echo of words. She leapt up and searched for the waterskin, pouring a little water into her hand and tracing the moisture over his mouth.

'Heracles?' she said softly.

His lips moved again, and her heart lurched.

She curled her fingers around his bony hand. 'Can you hear me?'

His eyes remained closed, but finally sound croaked from his lips. 'Megara.'

The name pierced Danae's chest like an arrow.

Heracles' wife. The woman he had murdered, along with their children, when Hera drugged him and temporarily drove him mad.

She wanted to pull her hand away, but she did not. He would remember his wife was dead soon enough. She would not take this moment of merciful forgetting from him.

Squeezing his fingers, she leant in close. 'I'm here, my love. I'm here.'

The ghost of a smile parted his lips and his eyelids grew still. Danae waited until his breath had fallen back into the rhythm of deep sleep, then she slipped her hand from his.

It hurt, hearing him speak another woman's name, but not in the way it should. As she sat back on her heels, it was not heartache that burned through her chest, but shame.

She eased herself to her feet and stepped out of the hut, filling her lungs with fresh, salty air. She looked up towards the crest of the hill, but Metis was hidden from view.

When searching for Prometheus, Danae may have had a false idea of what the Titan would be like, but at least she'd heard of him. Metis was a mystery. Despite her time in the Underworld there was still so much Danae did not know: what it really meant to be a Titan, the truth of how the gods became the Olympian Twelve, the identity of the Mother.

You must learn Metis' secrets, said the voice.

'Yes,' Danae murmured.

A current of unease rippled through her as she thought of what Metis had said about the voice. 'You were wrong. Metis was not pleased.'

She guards her knowledge. She does not want to teach you.

Danae had worried as much herself. The way Metis had looked at her by the crop of flowers, it was almost as though the woman was afraid of her.

'Are you good?'

For a breath, the voice did not respond.

I want you to be strong.

Danae's pulse quickened. 'What if, to be strong, I must do terrible things?'

The voice did not answer.

Weariness crept into her bones. Turning back to the hut,

she caught sight of Pegasus soaring across the island, then out over the ocean. It was rare for her to see him in flight. Usually, when he was airborne, she was on his back. She marvelled at his grace and the great span of his gleaming white wings as they beat against the wind.

She did not worry as he chased the sun across the sky, growing smaller and smaller in the midst of all that blue. He always came back.

Metis did not return to the hut until long after the sun had fled the sky. The woman barely spoke to Danae when she finally crept back inside, pausing briefly to inspect the pulverized leaves, before smearing the paste on Heracles' lips. The hero had remained unconscious since he'd spoken his dead wife's name.

They ate their rations of cicadas in silence, Danae resolved to wait for Metis to reveal her secrets rather than trying to prise them from her.

As she lay in the dark, eyes wide against the gloom, Danae thought of Atalanta and Telamon and prayed to the fates that they would find their way swiftly to Delos.

The next morning, when dawn banished the shadows from the hut, Metis shook Danae awake and led her down the hillside towards the lake. They paused by a nondescript stretch of rocky earth, and Metis crouched, pointing to one of the little flowers protruding from the dried grass. It was a tiny lilac bloom, each petal barely the size of a baby's fingernail.

'See this?' Metis pointed. 'I want you to grow it a new leaf.'

Danae frowned, wrapping her arms around herself to stave off the chill from the wind. 'How?'

'Just give it a go.'

Danae crouched, tongue between her teeth, staring at the

little plant. She could feel Metis' gaze on her, drawing her attention like a gnat buzzing about her ear.

She looked up at the woman. 'I don't know how.'

Metis cocked her head, loose strands of dark hair whipping about her face. 'Try. I want to see what happens.'

Danae scowled and turned back to the flower.

She stretched out a hand. As her fingertip touched the wiry stem of the plant, she reached inside herself and seized a twirl of life-threads. She imagined the new petal she sought to create as she wrapped the glowing strands around the plant. Then she pushed.

The stem snapped, and a shower of lilac petals exploded into the air, immediately borne away by the wind.

Danae sighed sharply and slumped back on her heels.

'Hm.' Metis tilted her head and stared at the decapitated flower. 'Either you think the word "grow" means "destroy" or, as I feared, you have no control over your power.'

Danae scrambled to her feet.

'I have control. I vanquished the Stymphalian birds with seawater. I fought off Hera, the Queen of the Gods herself, with nothing but snow and ice!'

'Mm-hm.'

'You don't believe me?'

'Brute strength and luck are not control.'

The heat of Danae's pulse radiated through her skin. 'You don't know what you're talking about.'

A similar expression settled on Metis' face to the one she had worn when Danae killed the lizard. 'With Prometheus dead, I am the only one left who will help you understand your power. You'd do well to remember that, girl.' She cast about, then picked up a stick that had been wedged between two rocks. 'We'll start with something dead, seeing as you can't be trusted with anything that has an ichor.'

Danae's glare simmered.

'Now,' Metis handed her the stick, 'float this into the air. With *control*.'

Danae took the wood and held it across her palms. Channelling her life-threads into her hands, she sent several glowing strands into the stick and whipped them upwards. The twig shot into the air and was immediately hurled across the rocks by the wind.

She swore under her breath and ran to retrieve it.

Metis watched her, arms crossed, brow heavy.

'Try asking,' she said as Danae returned.

'Ask?'

'That stick might be dead, but when you fill it with your life-threads you are temporarily granting it an ichor. Even inanimate objects like to be asked.'

Danae flitted through memories of using her life-threads to conjure wind or rumble the earth.

'I've never had to ask before.'

'And how did you feel after?'

She considered for a moment. 'Tired. Exhausted if I've used a lot of threads.'

Metis nodded sagely. 'It takes much energy to impose your will on the world. If you learn to ask, you'll use far fewer threads.'

'But what if the stick doesn't do as I ask?'

Metis gave a slight smile. 'You must have faith. If your will is aligned with that of the Mother, it will do as you say.'

Faith.

The word tugged at an old wound. She'd had faith in the gods once. Faith that everything would be all right, and her family could weather any storm. That faith had died the day she dragged Alea's corpse from the sea.

It would have been a simpler task if Metis had asked her

to learn another tongue than entreat her to put her trust in something she did not understand and could not see. But, ever constant, the prophecy weighed heavy on her soul. She had to try.

Danae rubbed the sweat from her brow. 'If asking means I will use fewer life-threads, I won't have to replenish them as often...'

Metis nodded.

'In battle I could fight for longer.' She looked up at the woman. 'This is useful, thank you.'

Metis fixed her with one of her tilted stares. 'If you live for too long in anger, it becomes the colour of the world.'

'Some deeds should never be forgiven.'

Metis scratched the back of her neck. 'I should check on Heracles. Keep practising and let me know when you've done as I asked.'

Danae watched Metis trudge back up towards the hill. Then, steadying her breath, she felt once more for her life-threads and teased a twine of strands into the stick. But, unlike before, she did not hurl her will down the cord now connecting her to the wood. She stood still and closed her eyes, living in the sensation of the stick resting against her skin while her life force flowed into its length.

'Will you float?' she whispered, glad no one was there to witness her conversing with a stick.

She opened her eyes. The stick remained immobile in her hands.

'Will you float?' she asked again, a note of irritation straining her voice.

Before you could command the elements, now you cannot move a twig, said the voice.

'Be quiet,' she hissed.

She let out a sharp sigh, then drew in two steadying breaths. 'Please.'

The stick shivered. Then it lifted from her palms, slowly rising into the air. Danae did not dare breathe as she watched it ascend. Then a gust of wind knocked it from the sky. She swore as her life-threads snapped back into her body and the stick rolled away across the ground. She retrieved it from beneath a bush of spruce, swearing as the spines raked her hands.

The wind blustered, the sun blazed, and many hours later Danae still had not succeeded in levitating the stick from her palms and bringing it back with control. She glared at it, strands of hair stuck to her gleaming face. As time passed, it seemed to take on a life of its own, and now the swirl of its bark looked positively smug.

Her mouth was parched and her stomach twisted with hunger. She'd not yet eaten and the sun had already passed its peak in the cloudless sky. Clutching the stick like a knife, she set her sights on the hill and climbed towards the hut.

When she arrived, she was greeted by Pegasus chomping on a patch of grass outside the dwelling. But even the sight of her companion could not lift her gloomy spirits. She entered the stone hut in a cloud of defeat and sank to the floor, throwing the stick in front of her.

Metis was kneeling beside Heracles, dabbing his brow with a cloth woven from shredded palm fronds. She'd lit a fire, the flames filling the stone room with smoky warmth.

'Control is not something one learns in a day. It will take time.'

'I don't have time. I've wasted so much of it already.' Danae's chest tightened as she thought of the Underworld and her search for Alea. The chasm of despair began to open in her mind and, as though recoiling from a flame, she pushed the memories away. 'It would help if I understood where my powers came from. I've never known anyone else like me. Prometheus and I barely had a chance to exchange a few words. I've lived for so long trying to figure this all out on my own and I don't know if I can go on without knowing more. Why was I made a Titan? Who even are the Titans? And the Mother?'

Metis rose to her feet and handed Danae the flame-roasted carcass of a lizard on a skewer. 'Cooked 'em up earlier when you were practising. Saved this one for you.'

Despite her aching stomach, Danae did not eat.

'Please, tell me.'

Metis pressed her lips together, then sighed. 'It all happened so long ago, I . . . well, I suppose I was going to have to tell you sooner or later. I'd better start at the beginning.' She frowned. 'No, before that. I'll start with Chaos.'

25. The Earth and the Sky

Metis lowered herself down to sit cross-legged by the hearth, then began to speak.

'Before time, before the heavens, before life itself, there was the void of Chaos. The chasm stretched on forever with no start or end, no purpose but to exist. This was not enough for Chaos, who longed for meaning, and to understand the nature of all their disparate parts. So, in the darkness they fashioned a seed. A single, golden kernel shining in the formless mass. Then roots sprang forth, and a shoot forged its way through the kernel's glowing skin, branching into the void. This was the moment life began.

'As the tree grew, so did its seed, until it surpassed the tree itself and became a vast orb of earth. And this new world spun, suspended in the void of Chaos, with the top of that same tree protruding from its crust, while its trunk was rooted all the way to its heart. And Chaos named the earth Gaia, the first of their children. Then Chaos wrapped their breath around Gaia, protecting her skin from the wild nature of their elements. And this protector, this sky, they named Ouranos.

'From the moment of his conception, Ouranos loved Gaia. His affection burned so brightly it formed a blazing heart in the centre of his being. And so the sun was born. And Gaia was pleased, for its light teased forth life from her crust. More trees grew, bushes and flowers too, and soft downy grass. Encouraged by her pleasure, Ouranos forged another orb of silver and covered the darkest reaches of himself in stars, so that even the parts of her that were not touched by his sun would always have light. And although this too delighted Gaia, it was not enough. Ouranos desired to please her more. And so he painted himself in vibrant colours and formed soft clouds that sprinkled her with water when she became too hot. Soon great rivers ran like veins across Gaia's skin, feeding the life ripened by the sun. All manner of flora and fauna began to grow on her, until Gaia became luscious and verdant all over. And in this paradise creatures swam up from the depths of the rivers, some crawling from the water to make their homes on land. And through each new life ran the golden threads of energy that had all been contained in that first seed of creation, spreading from the origin tree rooted at Gaia's heart. The tapestry of life that flows through all living things.

'To Gaia, the children that lived on her skin were everything, and she poured all her motherly affection into nurturing them. Ouranos saw this and grew jealous. Instead of gentle rain he hurled down hail and thunder, instead of soft breezes he blew harsh gales that ripped whole trees from the earth, and instead of loving warmth his sun blazed so hot it scorched Gaia's skin. Many of her children suffered. Gaia wept for them all, and her tears pooled into several of the deserts burned by Ouranos' rage, forming great oceans of salt water. But despite the anguish she felt for her children, the Mother did not give in to Ouranos' demands of love.

'So, Ouranos sent dark clouds to cluster over the earth, their bellies swollen with water. He unleashed a torrent of rain that poured so hard and fast it formed a great flood, sweeping away entire forests and the creatures that had made their homes there. But Gaia whispered warnings to her children, sending as many as she could up to the mountain peaks, where they waited for the water to drain away. And when the flood receded, those that survived built new homes on the sodden ground and slowly repopulated the earth.

'Ouranos saw that once again his attempts to beat Gaia into submission had failed. And finally, he realized that he had been driven mad by desire. He was so ashamed, he sent his moon to block the sun and hide the light of his heart that now burned with guilt.

'From his dark kingdom, he watched all the creatures Gaia loved so dearly, especially the humans to whom she murmured her secrets. Then he looked at the rivers that threaded across her undulating skin and the forests that sent their roots deep into her being. Finally, his gaze settled upon the sacred mountain top and the single tree standing proud from its summit. The tree of life, whose roots ran deepest of all. And Ouranos knew then what he must do to win Gaia's love.

'He banished the moon back to the far side of the sky and unveiled his sun-heart just as it was setting in the west. He captured its golden glow, the Hesperides light, that ushers in the dawn and the eve, and poured it into the origin tree. Its branches shivered and its boughs sprouted clutches of golden apples, each one bright as a miniature sun.

'"Look what I have made," Ouranos cried. "A gift for your children. My eternal love shall grant eternal life. One bite of a Hesperides apple and they shall never grow old, never die, and they shall know the power of the tapestry of life."

'But Gaia looked on the tree with dismay. For with no death, there could be no new life. The cycle of the tapestry would be broken. Her body and her children would grow stagnant and decay. She saw what Ouranos could not, that the light of his love was poisoned by his desire to consume. To have all of her. Every single piece.

'Secretly, Gaia whispered to humankind, the cleverest of her children, "I will choose the twelve wisest amongst you to journey to the sacred mountain of the Hesperides tree. These brave few must each consume an apple, imbibing the might of the tapestry of life and the time-stilling power concealed in the fruit's flesh. These twelve must forsake the people they once were and guard the tree until I call on them to return their threads to the tapestry of life. Then another twelve will be chosen to shoulder the burden. Above all things let none but the chosen twelve approach the tree and pluck the golden fruit. They must save the rest of mankind from this poisoned gift."

'Then, hidden deep inside her, far from the watchful gaze of Ouranos, Gaia forged a stone. A rock of deepest obsidian, that granted glimpses of the future to all those who touched it. In secret, she gave this stone to her chosen protectors and bade them lay it between the roots of the Hesperides tree, saying, "I give you this eye that sees what yours cannot. This stone will show you those whom I have deemed worthy and those whose time has been served. It is your guide. Use it well, my Titans."'

The sun had sunk low in the darkening sky by the time Metis finished her story. Danae looked through the hut doorway at the golden light draped over the rough hillside beyond. The stars were eager tonight, already gazing down on the glistening sea. She felt like a child again, tugging at her mother's skirt, demanding to know the origin of those faraway lights. Then, her mind had been filled with wonder. Now, her thoughts floundered like lost souls in the darkness.

She had seen so much and knew so little.

She remembered the sound of Alea's chest cracking open with far more clarity than she ever had before, shuddering as she recalled the creak of the tree growing from her sister's heart, the crackle of its branches unfurling and the vibrations that had passed beyond sound itself when it lowered a golden apple into her palm.

After some time she said, 'The Titans' power . . . it's the same power you and I have. And the gods.'

Metis nodded again.

'Did Gaia make me a Titan too?'

'Yes,' Metis rasped, her voice hoarse after speaking for so long. 'Zeus and the Olympians were never meant to possess the apple's gifts. They were not chosen. Unlike me, and now you.'

'It was the Mother who grew the tree from my sister's chest,' Danae said quietly.

'Yes.'

'Why did it have to be *her* heart?' Each word was sharp, like a blade in her mouth.

'We are all part of the tapestry of life.'

It wasn't an answer.

'Why me?'

Metis' gaze flicked up to meet Danae's. 'I do not know.'

Danae pressed her eyes shut, still trying to make sense of what she'd just learned. 'The obsidian stone you spoke of – that's the omphalos stone that became the oracle at Delphi?'

'Yes.'

Danae wondered if Metis knew that a shard of the stone still remained. Now Hades was dead that one remaining piece would surely lie forgotten in the Underworld forever. She did not wish to admit her part in the loss of such a precious relic and invite yet more of Metis' scorn, so she asked another question.

'Were you one of the original Titans chosen by Gaia?'

'Not one of the first twelve, but like those who came before, I was called. I heard the Mother's song and made the journey to Mount Olympus to become a Titan and guard the Hesperides tree.'

'What of Zeus and the other Olympians? If they weren't chosen how did they come to eat the Hesperides fruit?'

The shadows deepened around Metis' eyes. 'That is enough for one day.'

Danae frowned. 'If Gaia really loves her children like the story says, why has she let Zeus reign with such cruelty for all these years?'

Metis' lips parted, then Heracles murmured in his sleep, and her head snapped to look at him. Her eyes lingered on the sharp angles of his face as he stilled, then she turned back to Danae.

'I've been asking the same question for nearly a thousand years.'

26. Stones for the Dead

The following days blurred together like a wet mural smudged by careless fingers.

Danae and Metis fell into a steady rhythm. They rose at dawn and lugged the hydria down to the lake to collect fresh water. As they walked, Danae kept an eye on the sea, waiting for a ship carrying Atalanta and Telamon to appear on the horizon, her disappointment mounting with each day they did not come.

After the water vase was replenished, she and Metis would walk the island, inspecting the lizard traps dotted between the rocks, and trawl the long grass for cicadas with a fine net fashioned from what Danae suspected was Metis' hair. She made sure that Pegasus' water bowl was refilled when it ran empty, and once the tasks were done, she continued her efforts to try and levitate the stick. While Danae trained, Metis tended to Heracles, who still had not fully regained consciousness.

As time crept on, Danae harboured a secret worry that Pegasus might abandon her. When he flew away each morning, the fear swelled in her gut, only to be dispelled when the horse returned just before nightfall. She was troubled by the idea that he would grow tired of traversing the same splash of sky and eating nothing but dry, brittle grass. Surely, he would wake one day and realize that the life she offered him was pitiful compared to the one provided by his old masters on Olympus.

On the fifth day she returned to the hut after another

frustrating afternoon with the stick to find Metis crouched over Heracles, her hands laid upon his chest. She approached slowly, then sank down beside them, captivated by the shimmering threads seeping from Metis' hands into Heracles' body.

The woman opened her eyes as though withdrawing from a trance and leant back with a soft sigh.

'Will you teach me?'

Metis flexed her fingers. 'It requires a great deal of control to heal a living thing, especially one as complex as a human. You are not simply extending your ichor into an empty object but guiding someone else's piece of the tapestry of life. To influence another's body into healing itself takes patience and diplomacy.' Her eyebrows arched on the last word.

Danae thought of the time she had tried to cure Heracles on Lemnos. She had hurled a clutch of her life-threads into him without any thought or direction, only to have them forcibly ejected.

'When I've mastered levitation, will you show me?'

'Once you can do as I asked on your first morning and convince a living plant to sprout a new leaf, you will have taken the first step towards learning how to heal others.'

Danae smiled. Her mind flew through possibilities. She thought of her family back on Naxos. She could cure the ache in her mother's back that lingered after birthing her children, her father's salt-cracked hands, her nephews' scrapes from playing in the yard. Then she imagined walking through the village and all those who had shunned her family falling to their knees, begging her to heal their ailing loved ones. And she would grant their wishes, despite how they had treated her kin.

You would be a benevolent god.

Her focus snapped back into the room. She glanced at

Metis, concerned that the voice might have somehow escaped her mind. But the woman's eyes were closed, her attention once more focused on Heracles.

By the sixth day, Danae had almost lost hope that Atalanta and Telamon were coming and realized that, once again, she must face going on alone.

She stood beneath the feathered shade of the lone palm tree beside the lake, the stick gripped between her fists. A moment before, she thought she'd finally cracked it. For five heartbeats the wood had hovered in the air on a cord of her life-threads, her plea chanted down the strands. Then as she asked it to return to her hand it fell, like it always did. A bead of sweat trickled between her shoulder blades. She knew why it hadn't worked, could feel the precise moment her question tipped into fear and the ebb and flow between her and the stick became a one-sided command.

You must have faith, Metis had said.

She looked around at the dusty earth, the wind-shivered water and the rustling trees. She held in her mind another time she had taken a leap of faith. When she'd stood before Manto's father, Phineus, on a faraway shore and, after months of lying about her identity, had revealed to the old seer who she truly was. But the courage that had flooded her veins then would not be summoned. Since the Underworld, she had taken too many steps into the unknown and been dashed on the truth that waited like jagged rocks beneath. Gaia may have chosen her to be a Titan, but that did not mean the Mother or anyone else would come to her aid. Creators were not always benevolent. Hades had taught her that.

You alone are enough, said the voice. *You are the coming of a new dawn.*

Danae bit the soft flesh of her lip so hard she broke the

skin. Blood staining her teeth, she dropped the stick and grasped a handful of the tall reeds swaying by the lake's edge. She gasped as their stalks snapped beneath her fingers and their life-threads surged into her, draining down from the tips of their leaves and up from their water-swollen roots.

She staggered back from the dead plants, revelling in the life coursing through her limbs. The ecstasy lasted longer than after the lizard, but still it was a pitiful drop compared to the ocean she knew she could bathe in.

A familiar surge of shame stung her throat as she looked at the dead reeds lying dull and broken next to their vibrant brethren. She glanced about the island, suddenly self-conscious. A flicker of movement caught her eye. Metis stood atop the island's rocky hill, silhouetted against the bright sky.

Anger chased away the guilt nesting in Danae's chest. Metis had promised to teach her, yet the woman had done nothing but instruct her to levitate a stick then left her alone to fend for herself.

The burning sun heating the bellows of her frustration, she stormed up the hillside. Each rock that slipped beneath her feet and spike of spruce that scratched her limbs only fed her rage, and by the time she arrived at the crest of the hill, she had amassed a barrage of accusations ready to fling at Metis.

Her tongue was stilled at the sight of the woman carefully piling stones upon one another, the largest at the base, the smallest at the top. There were several more of these mounds dotted about the hillcrest.

'What are you doing?'

Metis straightened up, the wind dragging strands of hair across her face. 'In my village we used to lay our dead upon the earth and bury them beneath stones. These,' she gestured to the mounds, 'help me remember.'

Danae pointed to the new mound. 'Is that for Prometheus?'

Metis blinked. In that moment she looked so small. A relic of an age gone by, standing still while time ravaged the earth around her.

'Did Gaia choose him too?'

Metis nodded.

'How long ago did you become a Titan?'

The woman gazed out across the island. You could see everything from their vantage point, the entire rusted patchwork of Delos and scattered spits of land floating in the cerulean sea beyond.

'I no longer mark the years, but it will have been at least a thousand.'

Danae sank down onto a boulder, the wind of her anger draining from her sails. Looking at Metis felt like gazing into a warped mirror of what was to come.

'What happened to you? Why aren't you still guarding the Hesperides tree?' When her question was met with yet more silence she whispered, 'What if the Twelve find me before I've mastered my powers?'

Metis lowered herself down onto a nearby rock.

'You must tell me what you know. Teach me how to fight.'

The woman ran a hand over her face. 'I am.'

'Levitating a stick is not going to help me defeat Zeus. I need to be able to match the Twelve's strength –'

'You can't.'

Metis shifted her weight to face Danae, one leg tucked beneath her. 'The Olympians have spent centuries hoarding life-threads and building weapons to amplify their power. That armour they wear isn't decorative, it allows them to harbour more of the tapestry of life than a single body could possibly hold. You will never beat them at their own game.

The only way you will win is by twinning your will with that of the Mother.'

Danae's stomach hollowed. She swallowed the fear thickening her throat, not daring to voice the question burning in her mind.

What if I can't do it?

As though reading her thoughts Metis said, 'Communing with the Mother is not like listening to the voice of your power. She doesn't speak in words. It is more like . . .' the woman held a fist against her gut, 'a feeling from deep in your core. A knowing of what is right, even if it is not the path you wish to take.'

Danae didn't have the heart to say that she had often prayed in the small hours to whatever divine presence had given her powers, but there was never a primordial goddess waiting to guide her, only the ghosts she carried.

She looked across the ocean, past the turquoise shallows to the wine-dark sea beyond. In the distance, the haze had burned off the water, and for the first time, she could see clearly the faraway island to the south of Delos. It was crowned with a wreath of clouds, and its hills looked strangely familiar.

'What is that land on the horizon?'

'Naxos.'

Home.

The word thudded through her, a longing greater than her thirst for life-threads tugging at her chest. During her life on Naxos, she'd never paid much heed to the islands surrounding her own. She had imagined them to be replicas of her home and therefore of little interest. Her thoughts had always flown further, to the mainland. She had no idea, when Prometheus instructed her to find Delos, that he would be sending her within reach of Naxos – like Lemnos, Metis' island was not marked on any map. They were so close; her ma and pa, Santos, his little boys, the familiar dusty path to her hut, the sharp tang of cheese cooking on the hearth muddled with the scent of her father's fishing nets, her mother's honey cakes, her secret cove. She could go to them now, envelop herself in everything she longed to return to.

She stood, her eyes stinging with salt as she scoured the land below for Pegasus. But even before the wind had stolen her tears, she knew she could not leave. Like the Titans before her, her life was no longer her own.

27. A Cold Hearth

The following dawn, Heracles woke.

Danae stretched on the cold ground and rolled over to find the hero sitting up. Metis was crouched beside him, helping him eat a bowl of leaf paste muddled with crushed cicadas. A gasp slipped from Danae's lips, and Heracles looked up, his bony fingers halting on the way to his mouth. Her heart thundered as she looked into his bloodshot eyes, shadowed by the bruised skin of their deep sockets. Before she could divine what feelings stirred in the depths of his gaze, Heracles lowered his head, set down the bowl and tugged the cloak over his torso, covering his emaciated chest. His finger joints were swollen, and every movement seemed to cost him.

Metis looked between them, as though she were judging a game of petteia, then stood up. 'I've got lizard traps that need tending.' And before Danae could protest, she darted out of the hut.

The stone dwelling felt small as a walnut shell and large as the Aegean all at once. Heracles shuffled back into the corner of the hut until his wasted face was draped in shadow. The familiar hand of guilt wrapped around Danae's throat. Was he afraid of her?

She swallowed, her mouth dry as a parched seabed. She edged toward the hydria and slopped water into one of the cracked bowls, gulping it down. The cool liquid sat painfully in her stomach, the clay trembling in her hand.

When the silence became too strained to bear, she held out the bowl, 'Do you want some?'

'No.' From the gloom, Heracles' eyes burned like the blue heart of a flame.

'How do you feel?'

'Like death.'

Silence slithered once more across the hut.

Finally, he rasped, 'Where am I?'

'An island called Delos. We – Telamon, Atalanta and I – rescued you from the Underworld. They ... there was a run-in with Eurystheus when we emerged at Lerna, so I had to leave them behind to get you to safety. Metis has been taking care of you. She saved your life.'

Heracles blinked.

'There is so much to explain. Much I still do not know myself ...' She trailed off, wondering how to begin.

'Why did you leave?'

Despite the light warming her back, Danae flushed cold. 'I left because I had to find the Titan Prometheus. That's why I came with you and the Argonauts to Colchis. He made a prophecy about me ... I wanted to tell you, believe me, there were so many times ... I thought we would find him together. I hoped –'

The angles of Heracles' face sharpened. 'Even now, you can't help but lie.'

'I'm not lying.'

Suddenly, Heracles leant forward, and Danae recoiled as his skull-like face twisted with hate.

'Then tell me, what happened to Dolos.'

Danae's lips parted, but no sound came. She was transported back to Colchis, to the icy quiet, snow creaking beneath her fur-wrapped feet as blood trickled between Dolos' sightless eyes.

'It took me a week to realize it was you,' Heracles continued, his teeth clenched in pain. 'Days of hunting for a trail through that freezing forest, thinking you'd been kidnapped by shades. Then it dawned on me – if Dolos and the shade were both killed in the clearing, how did the bag of medicine end up outside my tent. Who stole my lion hide?'

She felt sick, as though the world had turned to sand and she was slipping through it.

'It was you.'

Lies clustered to her aid: she could tell him that a group of shades had ambushed her and Dolos, she had tried to run back to camp and alert the Argonauts but only had time to drop the elixir by Heracles' tent before they overpowered her and stole his hide. But facing him now, those false answers turned to ash on her tongue.

'This is the truth: Dolos betrayed you. He spent his life manipulating you on the orders of your father. That medicine he fed you was an elixir from Zeus. That is the real source of your strength. It's why you grew weak when it ran out. That night outside Colchis, I followed Dolos and caught him meeting with a shade who'd brought him more of the potion from Olympus. When I discovered the truth and tried to force him to tell you, he stabbed me.' She drew a quivering breath. 'I killed him in self-defence.'

As she spoke, Heracles retreated further towards the back of the hut, curling his body away from the light pouring in from the rising sun.

When she was small, her mother had told her and her siblings the story of Atlas, a Titan, who, after his brethren's apparent defeat in the Titanomachy, was cast far to the west and condemned by Zeus to hold the weight of the sky on his back for all eternity. A tale Danae now knew to be a lie. But, in that moment, she felt as though the very heavens rested upon her shoulders. There was no going back now; Heracles too was a victim of his father. He deserved to know the truth.

'The Twelve have lied to us about everything.' Haltingly, she relayed the story Metis had told her: of Chaos, Gaia and Ouranos. She repeated the words of Prometheus' prophecy and finally she said, 'I was made a Titan by Gaia, in order to end the reign of the false gods of Mount Olympus.'

For a while neither of them spoke. Then Heracles rasped, 'This is . . . madness.'

Danae moved closer, the cold hearth a continent between them. 'It is the truth. Heracles, deep down you must know that the elixir was what made you strong.' Her eyes travelled across his atrophied limbs.

Heracles pulled the cloak up to his collarbones. 'Liar.' The rise and fall of his bony chest quickened with every breath.

Through the mire of guilt and shame, Danae found an anchor of logic and clung to it. 'You can ask Metis if you don't believe me.'

Heracles barked out a harsh laugh. 'Destroy the son, then kill the father. Was that your plan?' He looked wild, spittle flecking his cracked lips. 'Telamon and Atalanta would never abandon me. You killed them too, didn't you?'

'No! I would never . . . You aren't listening to me. I cared for you, I . . .'

She could not say it.

She had comforted herself with the belief that she could have meant little to a man like Heracles. He was a great hero, and she . . . she did not know what she was any more. The girl she used to be had loved the fantasy of the man who was unstoppable, the mighty Heracles who could stand by her side and take on the Olympians. Everything had changed that night in the snow-swathed clearing at the feet of the Caucasus Mountains. Dolos' revelation had torn Heracles from the lofty plinth she'd elevated him to before she'd ever set eyes on him. Now he sat before her, a man in all his complexity and pain, and she did not have the strength to fight for his affection. The storm had raged, and now all that remained of the intimacy they'd shared was flotsam floating on the tide of fate.

'I'm sorry,' she whispered.

His eyes flashed. 'Save your pity, Daeira.'

The breath caught in her throat. The name she had adopted while disguised as a seer. One last lie to crush.

'My name isn't Daeira. It's Danae.'

Heracles shook his head. 'I was a fool to think you ever needed saving.'

Tears bloomed in the corners of her eyes. She blinked them away.

'You told me once you wished you'd been born an ordinary man. Well, you were. You are. When you are well enough you can leave this island and do anything, be anyone.'

Heracles drew a deep, rattling breath. 'You would not speak this way if you were me, stripped of everything that made you worth anything.'

'I know how hard it is to feel powerless,' she said softly. 'My own powers were taken from me for a time. But, Heracles, you were never meant to be unnaturally strong. You are more than just your name.'

'I might as well be dead,' he murmured. 'There is no life for me in this body.' He squeezed his bony fingers into a fist. 'This weak, pathetic shell.'

'You don't mean that.'

Heracles' lip curled. 'You are just like my father. You used me, until I was no longer needed.'

Of all the arrows he had thrown, this found its mark. Heracles' face tightened as he watched her, as though her silence laid bare her heart.

'Get out.'

Tears fell, she could dam them no longer. 'Heracles, I'm sorry, I'm so . . .'

She reached across the gulf between them. He recoiled as though her touch would brand him.

'I said, get out.'

She stood and ran out onto the rocky hillside, the wind stinging her wet cheeks.

There was nothing left but hatred in Heracles' gaze. Eyes that had been so blue and bright, she'd once thought she could dive into their depths and swim in their waters until her final breath.

28. Allies

That night, Danae slept beneath Pegasus' wing in the shelter of the boulder outside the stone hut. Now that Heracles was awake, inside the dwelling felt too small, the air too thick.

As Pegasus snored beside her, she listened to the murmured tones of Metis and Heracles conversing until they fell silent. Even then, when there was no sound save the pulse of the horse's heartbeat, the rush of the sea and the ever-keening wind, sleep evaded her and she lay awake long into the night.

The following morning, she woke bleary-eyed to Metis standing in front of her, brandishing a basket and fishing spear. Danae took them gladly, grateful for anything that would keep her from the pain in Heracles' eyes.

When Danae reached the crescent bay, she sprinted across the seaweed-crisped sand and splashed into the shallows. The cool water lapping at her legs was a balm as she waded deeper, the basket slung over one shoulder, the spear clutched in her hand.

Since arriving on Delos she could not shake the feeling that she was failing. It didn't help that she occasionally caught Metis stealing glances at her, a wary ember burning in the woman's eye. Danae knew what it was that Metis saw. She stood in the light, yet her heart remained in shadow. Even now, as the sun bronzed her skin, it could not reach the darkness that had settled deep within her chest. Part of her was still buried in the Underworld, and she did not know if it would ever find its way out.

She breathed in the salty tang of the ocean and rooted her feet to the seabed, just as her father had taught her, then waited for the sand to settle.

If you're still for long enough, Danie, you'll become invisible.

When the gleam of a silver fin came weaving through the water, she let her spear fly. A pale cloud of sand rose around the buried shaft, but when it cleared, it revealed no fish impaled upon the wood.

Reclaiming her weapon with a murmur of frustration, she poised again.

Use your power, said the voice.

Danae squeezed her eyes shut, as if banishing her sight would quiet the voice.

'No,' she whispered. 'This is a part of me you cannot have.'

I am part of you too.

She grew still again and waited, breathing with the ebb and flow of the tide. Soon came another dart of silver. Swift as lightning cracking through the sky, her spear sliced the water and this time found its mark. Smiling, she tugged free the still writhing fish and tossed it into the basket. She waded in a little deeper and was about to still herself again when she caught sight of a dark shape atop the waves.

A rowing boat was heading towards the bay.

Her pulse quickened as the vessel drew close enough for her to make out Telamon's flame-red hair.

As she waded out to meet the boat, her heart constricted. She could not see Atalanta.

'Telamon!' she shouted, waving her arms. He glanced over his shoulder at her. He looked pale, his face drawn, the skin beneath his eyes puckered with shadows.

As the boat drew nearer she caught a gleam of silver armour by his legs and the edge of a body lying curled in the belly of the vessel.

'Atalanta! Is she all right?'

Telamon pulled in the oars and leapt out of the boat, grabbing the lip and dragging it towards the shore.

Danae splashed after him.

Once the boat was aground, Telamon drew his sword and spun around to face her. 'Where is he?'

'Heracles is alive, he's with Metis.' She gestured towards the hill.

'You should never have taken him from us.' Telamon's eyes simmered with a swell of rage that looked as though it had been brewing ever since she left them on the clifftop.

'If you'd told me Eurystheus was lying in wait, I wouldn't have had to improvise.'

'I had it under control.'

'Really? You were tied up.'

Telamon bared his teeth. 'You know nothing.'

'I know that Heracles would have died if I hadn't brought him here.'

She wanted to remind Telamon that she'd saved his brother, Peleus, back on the *Argo*, and if it weren't for her none of the Argonauts would have left the island of Lemnos alive. But no one knew what she'd done on that cursed shore, that she'd caused the fire that turned the tide of the battle against the murderous hunters of Artemis. She'd never let any of the Argonauts close enough to really know her. How could she expect them to trust her, when she had never trusted them?

Atalanta mumbled something inaudible. Telamon lowered his sword, and Danae rushed to the side of the boat. The warrior was slumped against the planks, her skin tinged with a green hue, her limbs slicked with sweat. Danae's eyes travelled down to the makeshift bandages she'd wrapped around Atalanta's legs back in the Underworld.

Even at this distance the smell told her the burns were infected.

'How long has she been feverish?'

'Two days.' Telamon glanced down at his companion, his voice tinged with worry. 'That clue you gave us was useless. We ended up sailing around the blasted Cyclades for days until we spotted that flying horse of yours and followed it here.'

'The island is called *Delos* – like *Dolos*. It was all I could think of in the moment.'

'*An island that sounds like the healer.*' Telamon glared at her. 'Your riddle was the man you killed. You have a twisted mind, you know that?'

'I told you, it wasn't like that.'

They glared at each other until Atalanta gave another pitiful groan. Telamon looked back at his companion, his anger fading.

'I don't know if she's going to make it.' In all the time they'd spent together, Danae had never heard him sound so afraid.

'She will,' Danae said firmly. 'The woman who saved Heracles will cure her.'

'A healer?'

'Of sorts . . . she's like me.'

Telamon frowned. 'She has –'

Before he could finish the sentence, he and Danae were hurled apart as a wall of sand erupted between them, the grains rapidly circling Telamon and the little boat in a glittering maelstrom. The metal of Telamon's sword flashed from within the tempest, but it was quickly thrown from his grasp as he tried to slice through the sand, the grains spinning so swiftly they ripped the weapon from his fingers. Danae scrabbled to her feet as Metis approached from the edge of the rocks. The woman's arms were outstretched, two streams of life-threads pouring into a swirling prison.

'Stop! They're my friends!' Danae shouted, but Metis either could not hear or would not heed her.

So, she drew her own life-threads into her hands and whipped a stream of wind towards Metis. It caught her in the chest, and she stumbled. The sandstorm wavered. Then Metis split her arms, strengthening the cage of gritty grains whirling around Telamon and Atalanta, while hoisting Danae into the air with another torrent of life-threads.

Danae gasped as the ropes of false wind tightened around her chest, arms and legs. She pressed her own life-threads against the binds but it was like trying to bend metal with bare hands. Metis looked as though she was barely expending any energy, her face serene while her dark hair whipped about her cheeks. Danae couldn't help but marvel at her control. She had two of them incapacitated without a single bead of sweat gleaming on her brow.

'You are not welcome here.' Metis' voice sliced through the wind.

'Metis,' Danae shouted. 'I can explain!'

'You foolish girl.' The woman's face twisted with rage. 'How many others have you told about me? The Olympians will come. Zeus has spies everywhere.'

'Only these two. Only they know!'

From his sandy gaol, Telamon called, 'We are Heracles' companions! We mean no harm. We've come to take him with us, that is all!'

Metis' eyes darted between him and Danae. Slowly, she lowered her arms, and Danae tumbled to the ground while the swirling grains slowed, then fell back to earth like fresh snow.

Danae winced as she pushed herself to standing. 'I'm

sorry,' she said to Metis, 'I should have warned you – I told them to come here, but I'd lost hope of them finding us. Telamon and Atalanta helped rescue Heracles and a group of the Missing from the Underworld. They're allies.'

Metis glowered at her, then flicked her gaze to Telamon, eyes raking over his fallen sword and battle-hardened limbs.

'You said two. Where's the other one?'

'Here,' Telamon gestured to the boat. His movements were slow and smooth as though Metis were a mountain lion he was trying not to provoke. 'She's gravely ill.'

Metis paced towards him and peered into the boat. She sniffed and wrinkled her nose, then lifted the edge of one of the makeshift bindings around Atalanta's legs. The warrior moaned, and Metis sucked a breath through her teeth.

'Her legs were burned by Typhon, the dragon,' Danae said as she hurried to Metis' side. 'Can you heal them?' Before the woman could reply she added, 'I know she's not of your island but please, I will do anything, I –'

Metis raised a hand, and Danae fell silent. The woman pressed her lips together.

'Forgive me,' Telamon said smoothly – now all courtly grace, though his eyes remained fixed on Metis. 'Due to the nature of our arrival I quite forgot my manners. May the Twelve see you and know you,' he bowed, and Metis' eyebrows crept up her forehead. 'I swear on the Styx, all we want is to collect Heracles and leave you in peace.'

The woman barked out a laugh. She glanced at Danae. 'You've not told these *friends* much, have you?'

'What is she talking about?' asked Telamon.

Danae bit the inside of her cheeks. They still did not know she was a Titan, or the truth about the false gods. But now was not the time for revelations.

'Please,' Danae looked to Metis, her voice low. 'I wouldn't be here without them.'

Metis considered her for a long, hard moment. Then she turned to Telamon. 'I accept your offer. But cross me, and that sword of yours will be of no help.'

Telamon inclined his head. 'I well believe it.'

Metis gave him a sharp nod, then began to strip away Atalanta's dressings, peeling off strips of pus-layered skin with them. Danae winced as Atalanta shuddered, a steady moan seeping between her cracked lips. She fought the urge to reach for the warrior's hand.

'Carry her to the sea. Those legs need to be washed.'

Telamon swooped down and lifted Atalanta in his arms. Danae followed behind as he walked to the shore and lowered the warrior into the swell, kneeling behind her to keep her head from slipping into the waves. As soon as the saltwater lapped at her legs, her whole body spasmed.

Metis waded into the ocean and crouched before Atalanta. Slowly, like she was bathing a child, she scooped handfuls of seawater and poured them over the warrior's legs until all the blackened skin was washed away. Atalanta let out guttural groans as the woman worked, slipping in and out of consciousness as pain broke through her fever.

Danae tasted metal and realized she'd bitten through the flesh of her bottom lip.

Then Metis splayed her hands over Atalanta's shins and closed her eyes. After a few moments, the warrior began to tremble violently, her eyes rolling back into her head.

'What are you doing?' hissed Telamon, as he gripped Atalanta's arms.

'She's healing her,' whispered Danae, watching the glowing threads flow from Metis' hands. Then Danae's lips parted as the skin of Atalanta's legs began to knit together and a patchwork of whirling scars appeared where before there had been raw flesh.

Metis' shoulders sagged and she sat back as the tension finally fled Atalanta's body. The warrior slumped against Telamon, her eyes closed.

Telamon stared in wonder at Atalanta's legs. Then his gaze sharpened as he glanced up at Danae. 'Can you do this?'

She shook her head. 'I hope to learn.'

'Atalanta?' Telamon gave her a gentle shake, but the warrior did not wake.

'She'll need rest,' said Metis, straightening up. 'Fighting a festering wound takes it out of a body.' She looked up at the sky. 'You'd best bring her up to the hut, while I hide that boat. Quickly, now.'

'Thank you,' said Danae, but Metis was already wading onto the shore.

Telamon hoisted Atalanta once more into his arms and carried her out of the water. The warrior's face was no longer taut with pain, and her skin had already lost some of its greenish tinge, as though her infection had been washed away by the tide.

Danae took up her discarded fishing tools and followed him.

As they began the climb towards the hut, Telamon asked, 'So she's a demi-god, like you?'

Danae blinked. Another of her lies returning to catch her unawares. To explain her powers to her crewmates aboard the *Argo* she had claimed to be the daughter of Poseidon, God of the Sea.

She glanced at him, then at Metis hauling the little boat across the sandy earth towards the lake. After a breath she replied, 'No. Back in the Underworld, remember I told you Heracles' strength didn't come from his father? Demi-gods don't inherit their parent's powers.'

Telamon cast her a sideways glance. 'Then what are you? What is Metis?'

'I will tell you, I promise. When Atalanta wakes, I will explain everything.'

Telamon said nothing, but his shoulders tightened. Danae suddenly felt intensely weary.

'What happened to the Missing after I left?'

'Atalanta and I broke free the night after you escaped from Eurystheus' camp. We led the Missing to the gates of the city of Argos, then found ourselves a boat and came here.' He shot her a glance. 'Like I said, we had it under control.'

Danae nodded, her heart a little lighter knowing the Missing who made it out of the Underworld were finally free. She hoped they would find a way to return to their families.

Wind-roughed and sweating from the climb, they found Heracles lingering at the entrance to the hut, leaning against the stone doorway. He had draped Metis' fine navy cloak around him like a shroud.

His haunted eyes widened at the sight of Atalanta in Telamon's arms.

'Is she . . . ?'

'Asleep.' Telamon stared at Heracles. Then he gently lay Atalanta on the ground and paced across the earth between them to throw his arms around the hero.

Danae remembered the first time she'd seen them together in that kapeleion in Corinth. Heracles had towered above his companions, dwarfing Telamon's tall, strong frame. Now the hero looked so fragile, like he might shatter in Telamon's arms.

Heracles let out a grunt of pain, and Telamon drew back.

'Sorry,' he muttered. Then he grinned. 'I'm so fucking glad you're alive.'

Heracles reciprocated a strained smile of his own. 'You came for me.'

'Of course, you'd have done the same for us.' Telamon looked at Danae, and she was struck by the genuine warmth shining through the anger and mistrust. 'Thank you.'

She inclined her head, her chest swelling, then made the mistake of glancing at Heracles. Her momentary joy vanished. There was no softness in the hero's gaze, not even a crack. He looked at her with all the vitriol of the last time they had spoken and, through it all, a twisted gleam of envy.

29. Tales and Truths

Atalanta woke calling for wine.

Danae rose from where she waited in self-imposed isolation between the boulder and the stone hut and rushed into the dwelling. Telamon and Heracles sat beside the warrior. Metis still had not returned from the lake.

'Need a drink,' croaked Atalanta, pushing herself onto her elbows.

Danae hastened to pour water from the hydria into a bowl and proffered it to her. The warrior knocked the vessel from her hand.

'Wine,' she demanded groggily.

'There's none on the island,' said Danae.

Atalanta stared at her, the warrior's gaze morphing from rage to despair. Then she looked down at her legs. Her lips parted, face softening in wonder as she smoothed her hands across the whirling scars.

Her dark eyes lifted to Danae. 'You healed me?'

'No.' Danae shook her head. 'It was Metis.'

Atalanta opened her mouth as though she would ask another question, then became aware of the two men crouched beside her.

'Heracles.' She grasped Telamon's shoulder and hauled herself up to sitting, staring at the hero. 'You look like I feel.'

Telamon laughed. Heracles did not.

'That's what withdrawing from a lifetime of taking strength elixir will do,' said Metis. 'Though you're free of it now.'

Danae turned around. The woman stood behind her, a clutch of dead lizards dangling from her fist.

'How are the legs?' she asked Atalanta as she moved past Danae into the hut.

'You're the one who healed me?'

Metis knelt and prodded Atalanta's shins before lifting and manipulating her lower legs. Then she placed a hand on the warrior's brow, which Atalanta knocked away. 'There may still be a trace of fever. You should rest.' She looked pointedly at Heracles. 'As should you.'

'Bollocks, I'm fighting fit.' Atalanta climbed unsteadily to her feet.

'Heracles, can you walk?' asked Telamon.

'Yes,' said the hero with as much defiance as he could muster.

'Well, then.' Telamon rose and bowed to Metis. 'We thank you for your hospitality and will take our leave as promised.'

The woman grunted and set about pinning the fresh lizards to the barbs wedged into the cracked stone.

Danae's heart lurched into her throat. 'Surely Heracles and Atalanta should build up their strength before they travel?' She gazed imploringly at Metis.

'I'm fine,' Heracles spat between clenched teeth, hauling himself up the stone wall for support.

Telamon moved towards Danae blocking the entrance. 'Daeira, move aside.'

She looked up into his freckled face and stood her ground. No longer would she play the part of dutiful servant of the gods, the seer willing to take orders from heroes. It was time to shed her old disguise once and for all.

'My name is Danae.'

Telamon made a disparaging sound in the back of his throat. 'All right, *Danae*, let us pass.'

Her skin was too tight, her blood racing.

'I can't do it on my own,' she whispered.

Metis paused halfway through skewering a lizard's tail and turned to look at her.

'What are you talking about?' asked Telamon.

Tears pricked her eyes. Of all the things she had done, all the terrors she'd faced, nothing had exposed her quite like this.

She needed them.

She had broken their trust, perhaps irrevocably. But she had to try and rebuild it. She stood before them, barefoot, draped in the torn dress Hades had given her in the Underworld, her shoulder-length hair barely contained in its unruly braid. All semblance of her old seer's disguise stripped away.

'Please, just listen to what I have to say. Then if you still want to leave, I won't stand in your way.'

'No one wants to hear it,' snarled Heracles.

'I do.'

Everyone looked at Atalanta. The warrior was scowling at Danae, arms crossed. 'I want to hear what she has to say.'

Metis slunk into the shadows of the hut, watching them all with bright eyes.

'You should sit,' said Danae. 'This might take a while.'

Telamon and Heracles looked at one another, but neither voiced their dissent as they lowered themselves down around the hearth. Danae moved into the hut and joined their circle.

'I was born on Naxos . . .' The first few sentences stuck in her throat like tar, but as she gained momentum they ran swift as a tumbling spring. She told them of her family, of the island she grew up on. When she spoke of what Zeus had done to Alea, of Arius' disappearance and Alea's death, silent tears fled down Atalanta's cheeks. Heracles would not look at her, his eyes hardening with every word.

Danae pressed on, describing how she had accidentally

destroyed the oracle at Delphi by shattering the omphalos stone with her powers, meaning the one remaining shard, now lost in the Underworld, was the only true source of prophecy left in existence. She told of Manto's revelation of Prometheus' prophecy and her fierce friend's heroic death at the talons of the harpies.

While she spoke, the sun's light faded from the hut, the sky blushing into twilight. After a while, Metis rose, quietly working around them to light a fire. Danae expected one of the group to interrupt and condemn her story or threaten to leave, but all remained silent. She continued to tell her tale until the only light came from the hearth, its glow flickering over her companions' drawn faces. She told them of why she had joined their group, and her quest to reach Prometheus at the end of the world. She repeated the truth of that fateful night with Dolos outside Colchis. She told them that she was a Titan, what that truly meant and all that Prometheus had revealed to her atop the Caucasus Mountains about the false gods. Finally, she spoke of the Underworld, of Orpheus' tragic death, the Missing and the terrible truth of the shades' origins.

Her voice had grown raw by the time she fell silent, the sky beyond the hut dark and star-cast. Her truth expelled, she felt empty, like a husk plundered of its soft insides.

No one spoke for some time. Danae felt so light she might laugh. There were no more lies left to weigh her down. They knew who she was, what she was, and what she must do.

'Gods, I wish we had wine,' Atalanta murmured.

'It is true. All she has said.' Metis stared at Danae, her dark eyes gleaming in the firelight. 'Prometheus, the Titans, the false gods. It is all true.'

'Why didn't you tell us before?' asked Telamon.

'Would you have believed me?' countered Danae.

Her question was met with silence.

'There were no dead in the Underworld . . .' croaked Heracles, still staring into the flames.

'The cleverest lie of them all,' said Metis.

'Where do they go?' pressed Heracles.

Danae stared at him. He believed her. Then she looked to Metis. She could not bring herself to repeat what Hades had told her.

Metis gazed around the circle. 'Back to the tapestry of life.'

'What does that even mean?' Atalanta's body was tight as a bowstring. 'Who are you? Why do you live alone on this island?'

Metis met the warrior's gaze with the weight of all her years. 'We've heard enough for one night. My story shall keep for another day. Besides, we could all do with rest.'

The fire crackled. No one moved.

Then Telamon murmured, 'What do we do now?'

'We fight,' said Danae, hope thrumming through her limbs. They had heard her truth and were still here. 'We end the tyranny of the false gods.'

'How?' Telamon breathed.

Danae lifted her chin, pressing her hands into the floor to prevent them betraying her fear. 'Once Metis has taught me how to fully master my powers, I'm going to storm Olympus and destroy Zeus.'

He blinked. 'I see.'

'You have a choice.' Danae willed her voice not to waver. 'You can join me or go back to your old life.'

'Fuck that.' Atalanta's chest heaved. 'Those bastards lied to us, to everyone. We sacrificed for them, we worshipped them, we loved them.' She fixed Danae with a glare hot as molten bronze. 'They all deserve to die.'

Metis tensed. Then the woman stood abruptly, saying, 'I'm going to see if Pegasus has returned.' She left the hut.

Danae looked after her for a moment, then turned to Telamon. 'And you?'

He was silent for a while, his brow heavy with thought.

'There are some truths you cannot come back from. I can't make sense of everything I have been taught being a lie. The origin of the world, the Titans being evil, the gods creating mankind . . . the three realms of the afterlife . . . It doesn't seem possible. But I know what I saw in the Underworld. And if that part of your story is true, then I suppose the rest of it must be . . .' He shook his head. 'We are heroes, and it wouldn't be very heroic if we ran from the greatest battle of our lives.' He braved a small smile. 'Think of the stories they'll tell.'

Atalanta nodded, her face grim.

All eyes slid to Heracles. No one voiced what they were all surely thinking. Even if Heracles wished to take up arms against his father and the Olympians, he could not fight as he was. In joining Danae, Telamon and Atalanta were treading a path Heracles could not follow.

Then Telamon gingerly slapped the hero on the back. 'What say you? Build up your strength then take revenge on your father?'

Danae bit the inside of her lip and glanced at Atalanta. The warrior was watching the two men under knitted brows. Danae could see her own thoughts mirrored in Atalanta's gaze.

A smile stretched the hero's wizened cheeks. Then he laughed, a pain-riddled sound that wheezed from him like a rattle. 'You cannot win.'

Danae pressed her fingers into her palms, nails biting through her skin. 'We can and we will. It is my destiny.'

Heracles blinked. 'Whether my father was once mortal or not, does not change what he has become – he is King of the Gods, the most powerful being on earth with the full might of Olympus at his disposal. We are but men.'

'I am not a man – I am a Titan. And fate is on my side.'

Danae could feel the others' attention shifting, their eyes turning to her like flowers stretching towards daylight. She remembered the first night she'd spent with Heracles' crew, huddled amongst the stones of an old ruin outside Corinth. A different girl had sat quivering before those heroes. A stranger who shared her blood, her bones and, though she had not known it, her power. They had travelled to the end of the world and back since then. So much had changed, and yet here they were, the remaining few together once more, ready to undertake the greatest challenge of them all.

But now instead of Heracles, they looked to her.

The following morning, Metis shook Danae awake. She looked around the stone hut, her heart swelling at the sight of Atalanta and Telamon asleep on the floor.

'Come,' said Metis.

Danae rubbed the sleep from her eyes, then followed the woman out into the saffron dawn.

'That was a brave thing you did,' Metis said as she picked her way down the hillside.

Danae swallowed. 'I know you want them gone, but I can't do it alone, I –'

'I know.' Metis sighed. 'They can stay.'

Danae stared at her, then beamed. 'Thank you.'

The other woman grunted. 'There is a reason there were always twelve Titans. Some burdens are not meant to be carried alone. Now, have you mastered your challenge?'

It took Danae a moment to remember the stick.

'Almost.'

'You will show me.'

A robust wind tore at their limbs as they climbed down the rocky hillside towards the lake. When they reached the vegetation, Metis foraged for a stick. Danae's eyes travelled to the clutches of reeds, her stomach lurching at the sight of the lifeless, cracked stalks she had drained two days prior.

Metis found what she was looking for and placed it across Danae's palm. Then she took a step back and clasped her hands behind her back.

'Go on.'

Danae closed her eyes, took several deep breaths, then concentrated on the stick. Gently, she extended a string of life-threads into the wood and asked it to float into the sky. As she had done before, she entreated not with words, but by sending her longing in the form of a question down the channel of life-threads. Slowly, the stick rose into the air.

As the wood climbed higher, her pulse quickened until a burst of excitement broke through her calm and sent the stick shooting into the air, before it tumbled back to the ground.

Metis raised an eyebrow. 'Do you know why I asked you to speak to Gaia?'

'Because of her charming wit.' Danae cast around for the stick.

'If you do not learn how to listen to the Mother, you will not be able to reach Gaiasight.'

Danae spied the stick and grabbed it.

'What's that?'

Metis watched the wind shiver across the lake. 'It is a state of pure communion with Gaia when the tapestry of life can be seen with the naked eye and your will is twinned with Hers.'

Danae thought of the bliss she had experienced when

draining the life-threads of other creatures, the glowing threads of energy she had seen surging through the living world, the pure unadulterated power.

'I think I have already felt it, when consuming life-threads.'

Metis was silent for a moment. 'Remember the story I told you of Gaia and Ouranos. The Hesperides apples are a poisoned gift. It is the burden of a Titan, to carry the desire and power to consume life yet not act upon it. It is true that at the moment of draining the ichor of another living being the tapestry is visible, but this is not Gaiasight.'

'If they feel similar then how do I know when I am in Gaiasight and when it's the desire to consume?'

'When you are in Gaiasight, you will know peace, not ecstasy. We walk in twilight, on the cusp of night and day, and sometimes it is hard to tell which way lies darkness and which path leads to the light.'

Danae chewed her lip.

Metis watched her for a moment, then continued, 'On the beach, when I apprehended Telamon and Atalanta, I was in Gaiasight.'

Danae raised her eyebrows. 'Is that why you could command such power without exhausting yourself?'

A smile twitched Metis' lips. She nodded.

'Teach me,' Danae said quickly. Heracles' words about his father's power and strength had lodged in her mind.

'What do you think I'm doing? It takes time to open your consciousness to the Mother. In the old days before the false gods, it would take some Titans years to achieve Gaiasight.' She paused. 'Think of life as a river, and your will is forever striding against the current of fate. That is all you have ever known. But it is not the only way to reach your destination. Imagine you cease your struggle and let the current take you – moving isn't so hard any more, eh?'

'But if I go with the flow of the river, I will not be guiding the direction. How will I reach where I need to go?'

'All rivers ultimately flow to the sea, do they not? Your destination is your destiny. Whichever path you take.'

Danae rubbed her brow, struggling to quell her frustration. She still did not understand, but she was willing to try. She closed her eyes as she fed her life-threads into the stick, silently asking it to float. As the wood left her palms, she held tight to the image of the river, and pictured wading through the rushing water she and her ma used to wash their clothes in on Naxos. In her mind, she turned and fell back, letting herself be washed downstream. As she relaxed, her thoughts tumbled like the current. She imagined her flesh melting from her bones and then her skeleton separating into beads of pearlescent water until she was a thousand separate teardrops and the entire body of water all at once.

The sensation of weight across her palms drew her back to reality. When she opened her eyes, the stick lay once more across her hands. Glowing threads of light crackled across her vision, flickering in and out of sight for a heartbeat before vanishing.

'Well,' said Metis, 'seems you aren't a hopeless case after all.'

'I . . . I did it.' Danae swayed, a little lightheaded. 'But I didn't see the tapestry, not fully.'

'That will come.' Metis' mouth curled into a smile. 'You did well.'

Danae stared at the stick, now lifeless in her hands. She still could not fathom that, only moments before, she had granted it a soul, and now it was empty once more.

'I can't believe this is it,' she murmured.

'Hm?' said Metis, wandering into the shade of the palm tree and plucking a fallen frond from the ground.

'Everything we are . . . all our memories, our wants, our dreams, just disappear when we die.'

Metis looked back at her.

'Who told you that?'

'Hades. With no afterlife in the Underworld, he said after death there is only oblivion.'

Metis shook her head.

Danae's heart tripped. 'It's not true?'

'Perhaps it is, perhaps it isn't.'

'What does that mean?' Her fingers tightened around the stick.

Metis cocked her head. 'It may be true – the souls of our dead do not wander the Asphodel Meadows. But as far as I know, Hades never died and somehow came back to life. How would he know what happens to the mind when the body perishes? No one does.'

'So, there might be an afterlife?' Danae stared at the woman, hope expanding in her chest.

Metis shrugged. 'I cannot say. It is better to live as the animals do. For them there is no death, only life until the end.'

In an instant Danae felt empty once more, as though she had expended a great deal of life-threads. She could not tread this path again. Without proof either way, the agony of not knowing if she would see her sister again would consume her. It had already nearly cost her life, her destiny. Alea was gone. Arius was gone. She must make peace with that.

When she looked up, she caught Metis watching her intently.

'I could tell you that those you love live on in your memories, and as long as you go on loving them they will never truly be gone. I believe that to be true, but I suspect that will bring you little comfort. So, I will tell you what I know for certain. Life-threads cannot be created or destroyed.' Metis crouched down and touched a withered blade of grass. A single glowing strand travelled from the woman's hand into the plant, flushing it from tawny yellow to vivid green. 'The ichor of those who have died is still part of Gaia. Their life-threads are merely dispersed, part of a tree, a fish, a bird, another mortal. From the earth we are born and to the earth we shall return.'

Voices wafted down from the hillside, carried by the wind.

Metis glanced up towards the hut. 'I best check on those companions of yours. Stay here and practise communing with the Mother.'

Danae nodded slowly as Metis scampered up the hillside.

She sighed and wandered for a while beside the lake, then through the bushes surrounding it, trailing her fingers through their rich, verdant leaves. She held on to the warmth she'd felt when Atalanta and Telamon agreed to help her. She was not alone.

Take their threads, whispered the voice. *You will need to be strong for what is to come.*

It sounded distant somehow, as though the voice was but an echo cast from far away. She paid it no heed.

Eventually, eyes heavy with the heat of the sun, she found the enclave of bushes and saplings where Metis had hidden Telamon and Atalanta's rowing boat. She sank down into its belly, stretching against its sun-warmed planks. Then she closed her lids and concentrated on the web of glowing threads circulating through her, but try as she might, without touching the omphalos shard she could not extend her consciousness to any part of the tapestry of life outside of her own body.

Her mind wandered as the heat-hazed air drifted over her skin, speckles of sunlight dappling her face through the leaves above.

Then she heard movement and opened her eyes.

Still soporific, she raised her head and peered over the lip of the boat through the foliage beyond. A pile of weapons lay on the bank of the lake, and beside them, a silver breastplate.

Danae's breath snagged in her throat as Atalanta's scarred legs stalked across her vision. Shifting ever so slowly, Danae moved her eye towards the gap in the foliage and stared through her leaf-framed window at the lake.

Atalanta stood on the bank, her naked body gleaming in the sunlight. Danae's eyes ached but she did not blink, did not dare draw breath as she watched the sweat trickle down the groove of the warrior's spine to the toned muscles beneath.

Something stirred in the base of her stomach as Atalanta waded into the lake, the water rippling across her rich brown skin. Then she submerged, and it felt like an age before she broke the surface, whipping back her braids to spray the air with glistening beads. The simmering within Danae became a drumbeat thumping through her chest, her gut, her thighs. She was transfixed by each pearly droplet trailing down the soft curves of Atalanta's breasts, and the rest of her taut, battle-hardened body.

Danae's pulse raced faster and faster, her lungs shrinking until she struggled to breathe. Longing transformed into nausea as a chill crept up her spine and her scalp prickled. Then the ghostly imprint of bony fingers scraped through her hair.

Gasping, she hurled herself out of the boat, crawling so fast she grazed her knees. Once clear of the trees, she broke into a run.

30. A Dance of Stone and Air

Another week passed, and Danae's world narrowed to the effort of honing her power. She rose with the dawn, practising all day until dusk stole the light. Her endeavours were not in vain. Soon, she was able to levitate the stick at whim, remaining in control while the wind snatched at the wood. Metis seemed content to let her neglect her tasks, instead recruiting Telamon and Atalanta to fetch water and forage for food.

Danae drew a deep, salty breath. She stood on the crest of the hill, the island of Delos sprawled beneath her.

A dash of red caught her eye. Telamon and Heracles were walking slowly along the sand of the crescent bay. The fishing basket was slung over Telamon's shoulder. Heracles clutched the spear, leaning on it like a staff. From this distance he looked like an old man. Despite remaining sceptical about their cause, he had not yet spoken of leaving. Danae supposed he had nowhere else to go. Atalanta and Telamon were the closest thing he had to family. Her chest ached at the thought that whether or not he came to believe they could defeat the false gods, soon they would be forced to part ways.

With a sigh she turned away and looked at a pile of Metis' remembrance stones. Her breath slow and calm, she reached out a hand, sending a single life-thread from each finger into each of the rocks. She closed her eyes and imagined herself melting into her river, the wind buffeting her transforming into the current carrying her downstream. As she breathed, she let go, releasing the shame gnawing at her chest, the fear scraping a hole in her gut, her longing, her joy, all of it she gave to the water. When she could no longer feel her body, she opened her eyes.

All around her, the island gleamed. A lattice of glowing threads lay over the land, ever moving, ever weaving as the tapestry of life thrummed around her. And she was a part of it, her own ichor singing in harmony with the island. There was no heady rush, no euphoria, like when she consumed the life of another being. Only calm. And a warm breeze whispering a familiar song. In this state of peace, she sent her silent request down the strands of her life-threads connected to the rocks, asking the stones to join the world of the living and celebrate by dancing in the sky.

And dance they did.

Each stone rose into the air, the smallest pebble first, down to the largest at the base. Danae watched them soar like a flock of gulls above her head before returning them gently to their home on the ground.

She suddenly became aware that she was not alone. The tapestry of life vanished from sight as she spun around.

Metis stood before her, arms behind her back.

'I'm sorry,' Danae said quickly. 'I meant no disrespect.'

Metis smiled and stretched out her hands. Nestled in the cup of her palms was one of the little violet blooms. It sat in its own clod of earth, its roots dangling between her fingers.

'Go on, show me what you've learned.'

Danae approached tentatively, stretching out a finger to touch the stem.

'Remember,' said Metis, her voice a chant on the wind. 'You are melding your life-threads with the ichor of the plant, not simply filling an empty object with your desire. The flower may need some convincing to grow if it is not ready.'

Tentatively, Danae sent one lone life-thread burrowing into the stem. She could feel the plant's ichor. Navigating the living kingdom within the little flower, she wound her life-thread up its stem towards the purple petals above. Chewing her lip, she sent a question down the thread, an invitation to create another bud.

She waited.

Then she felt the plant push back, as though it was trying to expel her will. She sent another thread as reinforcement.

'Charm, not force,' murmured Metis.

Sweat trickled down Danae's temple as she bit down harder on her lip and conjured images of Delos covered in an ocean of purple blooms. She poured the warmth of the sun into her vision, and the promise of prosperity.

A little green bump appeared on the stem where her finger made contact. Then it extended, unfurling into a tiny green branch and there at the end, a bud.

Excitement pounding in her chest, she poured more longing down the life-thread channel, and the flower began to bloom, blade-thin petals stretching out into the light.

You have forgotten your purpose. You are the reckoning, said the voice.

Danae clenched her jaw, and, as though struck by frost, the petals withered and fell to the earth. With a grunt of frustration, she paced away, roughly wiping her forehead.

'Have you been listening to the Mother?'

A beat fell between them.

'I've tried . . .' Danae squatted down and pressed her knuckles into the rocky ground. She drew a breath. Despite achieving brief moments of Gaiasight, she still could not hear the Mother. It was the final hurdle, sitting alone with her thoughts, waiting for divine inspiration. A hurdle she could not yet surmount.

'You must keep trying. It is imperative you grow your connection –'

Danae looked over her shoulder. 'It is imperative I learn how to defeat Zeus.'

Metis regarded her with heavy eyes. 'I ask you to listen to the Mother, because I know what else whispers in your ear. It will do you no good to heed that voice.'

Danae stiffened. 'It's kept me alive.'

'Of course it has,' Metis said sharply. 'You are a vessel for it to fill with its desire to consume.'

Danae stood. 'And what of the fate of Gaia's chosen Titans? When will you tell me the truth of what happened? How did the false gods take power from them?'

Metis cut across her. 'If you only listen to that voice, you will become . . .' she stopped herself.

A chill crept down Danae's spine. 'Say it.'

Metis' delicate face changed like the rippling sea, tugged by a snarl of emotions.

'You will become just like them.'

Danae squeezed her fist until a sweet burst of pain radiated through her palms where her nails dug into their old wounds. She turned away and paced down the rock-strewn hillside. Metis made no attempt to follow her.

Danae fell to her knees by the lake, splashing water onto her face.

She flinched as an arrow buried itself in the earth beside her. Atalanta stood in the shade of the trees, bow raised.

'You missed.'

'I never miss.' Atalanta stalked towards her, wrenched the arrow from the ground, loaded her bow and raised it to her cheek. The shaft sang through the air, perfectly weighted against the wind, and lodged itself in the trunk of the lone palm tree. The outline of a stag had been notched into the bark by the warrior's previous shots.

Atalanta lowered her bow. 'When do we leave?'

Danae sat back on her heels and sighed. 'When I'm ready.'

The warrior scowled. 'When will that be?'

'I don't know . . . soon.'

Atalanta huffed out a breath, fiddling with the knot at the end of her oxhide bowstring. 'Will Metis come with us?'

'I . . . don't know,' Danae repeated, suddenly feeling foolish. She had all but begged her former companions to follow her into battle against the false gods, yet she had not asked the woman training her if she too would take up arms. Danae did not want to admit the truth, even to herself: that she feared what the answer may be.

'What's the plan, then?' Atalanta slung her bow across her chest and crouched down beside Danae, cupping water into her hands and raising them to her lips.

'The plan?'

'To take Olympus. The gods are damn powerful and they have the advantage with the higher ground. But there must be a weakness – every fortress has one. What we need is a good old stakeout . . .' As the warrior spoke, Danae could not help but think of her without the shell of her armour, the lake water glistening on her bare skin.

She swallowed. 'Apart from the ability to heal themselves by consuming the life force of another living being, they are just as vulnerable as mortals.'

Atalanta's eyes raked over her. Then she said softly, 'It is strange to think they were all mortals once.'

'Zeus must still have access to the Hesperides tree, that's how he made the rest of his family Titans.'

Atalanta lowered herself to sit on the ground, and for a

fleeting moment her face flushed with a deep sadness. Danae joined her.

'I'm sorry about your sister.'

The current of rage that lived like magma beneath Danae's skin rose up to choke her. She could not speak.

'The child you mentioned,' continued Atalanta. 'Arius, is he . . . ?'

'Gone,' the word splintered in Danae's mouth.

Atalanta nodded. Then she reached out a hand and clasped Danae's in hers. 'Zeus will pay for what he has done. It is prophesied.'

As Danae looked at her, she recalled what the warrior had told her aboard the *Argo*, of the bond Atalanta and her fellow Arcadian hunters had had with Artemis. And how the goddess had betrayed them, abandoning them when they needed her most.

They held each other's gaze for a moment, Danae's hand softening beneath Atalanta's fingers.

Then the warrior asked, 'Do you know why he didn't give Heracles an apple, like his other children?'

Danae shook her head. She bit down on the insides of her cheeks. 'Atalanta . . . he can't come with us.'

The warrior sat back, withdrawing her hand from Danae's.

'He needs months more rest and care to be well.'

The truth tasted bitter on her tongue, but if no one else would voice it, she must. 'He would be a liability and most likely get himself killed.'

'We're not leaving him.'

'He hasn't even said he wants to take revenge on his father –'

'Of course he does.' Atalanta stood. 'We all want revenge for what those bastards did to us.'

Danae could feel the warrior withdrawing beneath her scowl. She was losing her. 'Will you show me?' She rose and gestured to Atalanta's bow.

The warrior's lip curled. 'What need has a Titan for the humble skill of archery?'

'When Hades put that collar on me . . .' Danae shivered. 'I never want to feel that helpless again.'

Atalanta's eyes lingered on her face for a moment, then she paced to the palm tree, retrieved the arrow and returned to Danae's side. She reached for Danae's hand and closed her fingers around the centre of the bow. The worn leather grip was warm beneath her touch.

'Hold it here.' Atalanta stepped behind Danae and placed her free hand around the string, hooking it with her thumb. 'Keep your weight balanced.' She gave Danae's back leg a kick. 'I said balanced. Now hold your front arm steady.' Together, they raised the bow, the weapon taut between Danae's arms. It was an effort to pool her concentration into her limbs with the warrior's lithe body pressed against hers. 'There's a strong westerly wind so aim to the left of the target. You won't hit it, but the shot will tell you how far you need to correct next time.' She stepped back and left Danae alone with the elements.

Danae drew a deep breath, then let the arrow fly. It shot far into the air to the right of the tree, to be whisked away by the wind and burrow into the crisp grass beyond the verdant plant life surrounding the lake.

Atalanta clasped her shoulder. 'You haven't fired a bow before, have you?'

Danae shrugged off the other woman's grip and paced towards the arrow.

When she returned, she reloaded the shaft and lifted the bow to her cheek. 'Again.'

Shot after shot was caught by the wind and hurled far from the target. After the ninth attempt, Danae emerged dripping from the lake, the sodden arrow clasped in her fist.

'Perhaps we should try a sword,' suggested Atalanta. 'A novice would never start learning in these conditions.'

'I can do it,' Danae grunted, fumbling the arrow back into position.

Let me help, murmured the voice.

Danae stared at the target, jaw clenched.

Don't you want to impress her?

She drew a breath. On the exhale, glowing threads wound from her palm to twist around the shaft. She let fly. It landed in the centre of the palm's trunk, between the stag's eyes.

She grinned. 'Not bad for a novice.'

Atalanta snatched back her bow. 'If you're not going to take this seriously, you can fuck off.'

Danae's chest constricted. 'How did you . . . could you see the threads?'

'You've clearly never held a bow in your life, yet you hit the target despite the wind. I'm no fool.'

'I'm sorry. I didn't mean to insult you.'

Atalanta scowled, then she looked down at the bow in her hands. 'When Artemis hunted with us in the forests of Arcadia, she would always use her power. It took me a decade to learn my skill, yet she was the better archer, though she never practised a day.'

'I understand,' Danae said swiftly.

The silence stretched between them, strained by the keening wind.

'I'm going to kill her,' said Atalanta, so softly Danae almost didn't hear. The warrior's brow darkened at Danae's expression. 'You don't think I could defeat her?'

Danae fought to hide the fear that suddenly chilled her

insides as she imagined Atalanta facing down the Goddess of the Hunt.

'You are the finest archer I have ever seen, but even you cannot match an Olympian.'

'I could take you.'

They stared at each other, then Danae's lips twitched into a smile. Atalanta's nostrils flared. She dropped her bow and punched her. Danae cried out as she staggered back.

Wiping her lip, she stared at the warrior in disbelief. 'You hit me!'

Atalanta's weight was perfectly balanced between her powerful legs. 'I'm not afraid of the gods. And I'm not afraid of you.'

'You should be.' Danae summoned a clutch of life-threads and, ignoring her training, whipped her will into a gust of wind strong enough to send Atalanta sprawling into the bushes surrounding the lake.

Danae advanced. 'Admit you cannot beat me.'

Atalanta ran her tongue over her teeth and leapt to her feet. She launched herself at Danae, and they slammed into the ground, rolling across the gritty earth. The warrior had the advantage of physical strength and pinned her. Danae engorged her arms with life-threads and was about to hurl Atalanta into the sky, when the warrior's scent stilled her.

Oak, salt and honeysuckle. A stolen moment on the *Argo* beneath the stars. Her skin prickled with heat.

'Giving up already?' Atalanta panted triumphantly.

Danae's retort died on her lips. She was acutely aware of the warrior's fingers curled around her arms, the weight of Atalanta's thighs pressing into her hips. She could toss her aside as easily as drawing breath, but she did not.

The air became thick as honey in the world between their faces. Perhaps it was the struggle, but Danae was sure

Atalanta's breathing had quickened. Neither of them moved. Danae's eyes were drawn to Atalanta's lips, the shape of which she had come to know better than her own hands.

Suddenly, Atalanta released her and staggered back.

'I should find Telamon,' she mumbled. She hastily retrieved her bow and arrow, then ran across the rust-coloured earth, leaving Danae with an ache in her chest and a fire in her belly.

Danae waited for her blood to cool before following Atalanta up the hillside. She slipped, cursing as a rock jarred against her ankle. A shadow passed overhead. Pegasus soared above her, his white wings bright against the cloud-bruised sky.

As she neared the hut, she heard Telamon's voice ring out against the wind.

'. . . she looks prepared to me. We can't keep going on like this.'

Picking up the pace, Danae scrambled up behind the boulder that guarded the stone hut. Pegasus was drinking from his bowl, while Heracles smoothed his flank. During their time on Delos, the hero had put on a little weight but was still painfully thin. Their eyes met briefly, before Danae ran into the hut.

Metis, Atalanta and Telamon stood around the blazing hearth, the skewered fish charring over the flames like drawn knives between them.

The flame-haired man rounded on Danae. 'When are we leaving?'

'When Metis tells me I'm ready.'

Telamon huffed a breath through his nose and slapped a hand on the cracked stone wall. 'When will that be? You asked us to go to war, not play at being farmers and fishermen on this hostile spit of land. We pledged to fight with you, but we still don't know how the false gods came to power.' He pointed at Metis. 'If she is really on our side why not tell us the reason she's living on this barren rock?'

Atalanta nodded, her arms folded over her battered silver breastplate. 'How are we meant to face an enemy we do not fully understand?'

Danae gazed at Metis. 'They have a point.'

The woman's eyes darted between them, the line of her lips hardening.

Then a voice from behind Danae said, 'I want to know about my father.'

She turned. Heracles stood in the doorway, his cerulean eyes like shards of ice within his wan face.

Metis met his gaze. 'You are not ready.'

'Fuck this.' Telamon picked up his sword from where it leant beside the fishing spear. 'I will not sit here waiting any longer. Heracles, Atalanta, Danae, are you coming?' Atalanta moved to his side.

'Wait.' Danae remembered the ease with which these people had existed together, the easy ebb and flow of conversation, how they had laughed and fought in the same breath, like a flock of birds in flight, of one mind, singing one song. Until she had come amongst them and shattered their harmony. She turned to face Metis. 'The Mother chose me. You say you are on our side, but if you do not tell us all you know then you are as good as aiding Zeus.' She drew herself up. 'I have reached Gaiasight. I know now what I must do to fight the false gods. I may not be ready, but if you do not tell us everything tonight, I will leave with them.'

Metis stared at her, a storm raging behind her eyes. Then to Danae's disbelief she said, 'The telling will be hard. As will the listening.'

'Try us,' said Telamon.

Metis looked at them each in turn. Her brow darkened,

then she moved to the rear of the hut, emerging from the shadows with a small clay pot.

'Sit.'

They did as she bade them and waited in silence as the woman handed round the roasted skewers of fish. 'You will need to eat first.'

Danae could barely swallow the sweet, smoky flesh as Metis set down the pot and reached out a hand to Heracles. 'Give me the cloak.'

Heracles' fists tightened around the navy garment as though he would deny her. Then, slowly, he relinquished it, wrapping his arms around his bare torso and edging nearer to the fire.

Metis set about covering the entrance of the hut with the cloak, pinning it with the sharp sticks used for spearing lizards, and weighing down the hem with rocks. Then she returned to the hearth and took up the clay pot.

'What I am about to tell you cannot be merely spoken. I will show you what I remember.'

She dipped her fist into the pot and threw a scatter of herbs onto the fire. Danae coughed as the smoke turned acrid and bitter. Her vision began to blur as hazy tendrils swirled about the hut. She felt as though she were underwater, her heartbeat pulsing in her ears.

Metis' voice echoed as though the woman stood far away. 'It began with a man who called himself Kronos . . .'

31. The Titans

He is late.

The Mother's song has long faded on the wind, the silence filled with the rustling of leaves and the whispers of golden fruit. I worry the folds of my cloak, glancing around the grassy plateau shadowed by a high ridge of stone at the crest of Mount Olympus. No one has ever been late before.

Themis, my fellow Titan, steps back from the trunk of the Hesperides tree into the circle of twelve standing below its branches. Her chest heaves. She should have returned her life-threads to the tapestry by now. She is breathing stolen time.

'What do we do?' her voice wavers across the mountain top.

'We wait,' says Prometheus.

'Perhaps some of us should search the mountain?' I offer. 'In case he has been injured.'

'No, Metis,' says Atlas. 'The Mother is never wrong. He will come.'

I am pulled taut, a bow string waiting to be released. Dread is slowly creeping through my veins, winding its way towards my heart. What if he never comes?

A breath later, he appears.

The clouds bleed behind him, stained crimson by the sun. He seems younger than in the vision shown to me by the omphalos stone. For a terrible moment, I worry I have made a mistake and misread Gaia's life-thread image. It was my first time reading the future in the eye of the world. Yet as I watch him, I decide it is undeniably the same face, the same bones. My pulse calms. The mountain has not been kind to this one. He has a wild look about him, his hands and tunic stained with dried blood. I wonder if he fell foul of a boar's tusks on his journey. It is no matter; his wounds will be healed soon enough.

He staggers to a halt and stares at us with eyes of sea and sky.

'I am Kronos. The Mother called to me in my sleep and showed me the face of creation.'

Themis watches him, her gaze full of stars. I wonder if she is afraid. If I will be afraid, when my time comes.

Prometheus looks at me, seeking clarity that this is the one we have been waiting for. I nod. He turns to the newcomer and asks, 'Are you ready, Kronos, to give your life to the Mother? To live and serve her as long as she commands?'

'I am,' he rasps.

His eyes meet mine and something stirs within my ichor. He is different, this Kronos. All who come to the sacred mountain carry the weight of the lives they've left behind, but there is something else he harbours. Something darker. I find I cannot look away.

'Then come, taste the fruit of life. Eat, and you shall know the power and blessing of the Hesperides light,' says Prometheus.

The man called Kronos walks forward. Phoebe begins to sing, and the rest of us twine our voices with hers, until all twelve of us raise our hymn to the heavens.

> Gaia, mother of all,
> we shall sing,
> the strong foundation, the oldest one.
> She feeds everything in the world.

Atlas unclasps Themis' woollen cloak as she lifts her arms towards the tree. Her hands tremble as she presses them against the bark. By her feet, the omphalos stone gleams from its nest of roots, its shining black eye ever watching.

> Whoever walks upon her sacred ground
> or moves through the sea
> or flies in the air, it is she
> who nourishes them from her treasure-store.

Tears stream down Themis' face as, behind her, Atlas fastens the cloak around Kronos' shoulders.

> Queen of Earth, through you
> beautiful children,
> beautiful harvests,
> come.

Atlas leads Kronos around the knotted trunk of the Hesperides tree, so he and Themis are like night and day on either side of it. Then Atlas retreats to take his place in the circle, and we clasp each other's hands, forming a ring about the tree.

> It is you who gives life to mortals
> and who take it away.
> Blessed is the one you honour with a willing heart.
> He who has this has everything.

Themis cries, the last sound she will ever make, and glowing life-threads stream between her fingers into the bark, igniting its cracks with golden light. Life pours from her, and the apples brighten until each shines like a miniature sun. It burns my eyes to look at them, but I do not turn away.

Themis slumps to the ground, her cold cheeks gleaming with tears. I press down the ache in my chest and lift my gaze to our new brother, Kronos.

He does not wait to be offered an apple but reaches like a child trying to catch the moon and snatches a golden orb from its branch. As he sinks his teeth into the fruit, I watch his limbs shake and his cerulean eyes blaze gold.

Glistening juice drips down his chin, flecks of flesh caught between his teeth.

He smiles and murmurs, 'He who has this has everything.'

My skin tightens as I wade into the chill water. My clothes are draped over the branch of one of the silver-barked trees that cluster the bank.

Above, the spring sprays from the rocks, feeding the marbled lagoon. I tread slowly, careful not to slip on the broad stones, until I am waist-deep. My back is already damp with sweat from the descent through the forest. We are only permitted to leave the Hesperides plateau once a moon cycle to bathe, and I intend to relish every moment. I run my fingers through the knots in my long, dark hair before submerging myself. The cold stings, but I remain below, the sound of the water another heartbeat in my ears.

When I emerge, I feel his eyes like the sun drying the beads on my back.

His lips part as I turn, his gaze ripening with lust. I make no effort to cover myself. It has been many years since I have been consumed by eyes that hungry. He watches me like a wolf, yet I do not feel like prey.

He begins to remove his clothes.

Now it is my turn to watch.

His limbs are lean and strong, the skin beneath his tunic ghostly pale. He has a collection of old scars and a couple of new ones. My cheeks flush as my gaze descends below the ridges of his abdomen. He smiles and lowers himself into the water, keeping his distance. I think of the unspoken rule that none of Gaia's chosen twelve may enjoy each other's flesh.

'You followed me.' My honesty catches me off guard.

His smile widens. 'I will leave if you wish it.'

I glance about the rocks. We are alone.

'You may stay, Kronos.'

He frowns. 'Do not call me that.'

'It is your name.'

'I would like you to call me Zeus.'

My mouth quirks. 'Shining one? Is that what you think of yourself?'

He slides below the water like an eel and swims towards me. I step back and slip on a moss-swathed stone. The lagoon swallows me, and I splash, fighting my way back to the surface.

He is waiting for me, closer but still out of reach.

'I did not mean to scare you.'

I blink the spring water from my eyes. 'Surprised, not scared.'

A beat falls between us.

'Where do you go at night?' I ask.

His eyebrow arches. 'You have been watching me.'

My heart flutters. I do not deny it.

'I feel at peace walking below the stars. Sometimes, I am still troubled by memories of who I was before.'

I understand and offer him a smile.

He looks down, his lashes beaded. 'I sense the others do not like me.'

I laugh at his strangeness. 'We are Titans, the chosen twelve. We are equally loved in the eyes of the Mother, so we equally love one another.'

'Equally,' he repeats, tasting the word as though savouring it. Mocking it.

I feel again that stirring deep within my core. I thought at first it might be fear, now I believe it to be something else.

Suddenly, his eyes swell with sadness. 'Do you ever feel like you're slipping away?'

'I do not understand.'

He trails his fingers across the surface of the lagoon. 'Can I tell you a secret?'

'Yes,' I whisper, drawing towards him.

'I came here with a purpose. I intended to consume the power of the Hesperides apple, then return to my village and cure someone very dear to me. My little sister, Hestia.'

My pulse quickens. I have never heard a Titan speak this way.

'But I did not go,' he continues. I cannot tell if his eyes are glistening with fresh water or salt. 'I remained here and let her die.'

'It is not your fault. If your sister has passed, it was her time.' I take his hands in mine. 'When we are called to serve the Mother, we must forsake our mortal lives. It is the greatest honour anyone can receive, but that does not mean it is easy.'

His fingers twist in mine like roots through the earth.

'Do you ever wonder what we could achieve if we left this mountain?'

I draw a sharp breath, but my hands stay twined with his. 'No. It is forbidden.'

I can feel the heat of him, the lagoon swirling between us.

'What if the Mother changed her mind?'

The hairs prickle on the back of my neck.

'You don't listen to it, do you? The worm that feeds on the apple.' Even now I can hear the voice in my head whispering its lies.

He closes the space between us, air and water pressed away as our skin touches.

'Never.'

Five seasons after Zeus joined us, I wake suddenly amongst the roots of the Hesperides tree. The sky is still inked with night. I am cold, Zeus' warmth no longer beside me. I think he has gone for another of his midnight climbs along the ridge, then I hear voices.

I roll over and see him standing between the tree and a man I have never seen before.

'You are early,' says Zeus.

The stranger's face is cast in shadow, his broad shoulders tense. 'Forgive me, the journey was swifter than expected.'

I push myself to standing. 'Zeus?'

He turns to look at me. Perhaps it is the darkness, but for a moment he seems afraid. Then his expression smooths. He smiles, and it warms every part of me.

'Wake the others. We must prepare for the ceremony. Another Titan has been chosen.'

'So soon?' I rub dust from my eyes.

As we speak, the other Titans stir from the roots of the tree.

'Who is this?' asks Prometheus, eyeing the stranger.

Zeus turns to face the rest of the twelve. The new arrival lingers behind him. It is strange; there seems to be a thread of tension between them as though they have met in another life.

'I was woken by a dream,' says Zeus. 'The Mother called to me and showed me the face of the next Titan.'

There are gasps.

'The Mother has only ever revealed her next chosen Titans through the omphalos stone,' says Phoebe.

Zeus nods slowly. 'I too doubted, so I consulted the stone. It confirmed my dream was indeed sent from the Mother. But that is not all it showed me. The world beyond Mount Olympus is changing, and we must change with it.'

'It is true.' The stranger steps closer. 'On my journey I saw great armies marching across the plains of Greece. Even in my humble village, we feel the grip of war upon the land. If nothing is done, the people will destroy themselves.'

The Titans murmur below the branches of the Hesperides tree, while the stranger eyes the golden apples glowing overhead.

'What is your name, friend?' asks Hyperion.

'Poseidon.'

There are many lone stalks amongst the twisted boughs of the Hesperides tree with no fruit dangling from their tips. I wonder if it is my imagination, or if there are fewer golden apples than there were before.

I begin to notice dead animals. A kestrel with broken wings lying by the lagoon. A wolf, its insides exposed and glistening, draped on the exposed rocks to the north of the Hesperides plateau. A boar in the forest below, bearing a wound that could only have been made by a blade. These deaths cannot be the work of a Titan. We do not kill for sport, only to feed ourselves. And we never, ever end another's life to consume its threads. Perhaps the evil Poseidon spoke of has already found its way to the sacred mountain.

I sicken a season after the night Poseidon arrived and Atlas returned his threads to the Hesperides tree. I think that whatever has twisted the minds of mortal men has poisoned me too. Then, one night, I feel the stirring of new strands of life inside me.

I tell no one, not even Zeus. I fear for what may become of me and my child if the other Titans discover the truth.

I wake to a knife at my throat.

Before I can react, the weapon is withdrawn.

'Not her,' whispers a familiar voice.

I shuffle back. The ground is warm and wet beneath my hands. I turn and see Phoebe, her throat slicked with blood, lips parted, eyes glazed.

I scream.

Prometheus, Crius, Iapetus, Tethys, Coeus, Hyperion and Poseidon wake. The others do not move from their root beds. I search the faces around me, alive and slain, but I cannot see Zeus.

Three shadowy figures emerge from behind the tree.

Assassins.

From their stature, they appear to be a man and two women dressed in homespun tunics. I catch a glimpse of the man's face under a dapple of moonlight. For a heart-stopping moment I think it is Zeus. But no, this man's face is sharper, his build slighter.

'Protect the tree!' Crius shouts.

Prometheus sends a stream of life-threads into the air and hurls the male assassin to the ground with a blast of wind. Crius, Tethys and Iapetus round on the two women, the Titans sending life-threads deep into the earth, summoning roots to bind the intruders' legs.

I think it will be over swiftly. They are mortals, and we are Titans.

Then the male assassin casts out a surge of life-threads of his own, battering back Prometheus' wind. My eyes stretch wide. How can this be?

I gape, unable to move, torn between my sacred duty and the life I feel growing inside me. I do not know how to wield my own life-threads and not touch the child's. I can barely breathe, blood is thundering in my ears. Then I see something that locks my breath entirely.

Poseidon moves about the remaining Titans like smoke while his brethren fight, a bronze blade in his hand.

Tethys falls.

I scramble back, screaming for Zeus, my eyes searching the plateau.

Then I see him.

Zeus stands a little way off, his back to the ridge, watching the bloodshed with golden fire in his eyes.

'Help them!' I scream.

He looks at me, and the glory in his gaze is the most terrifying thing I have ever seen.

Zeus raises his arms to the heavens. A channel of life-threads streams from his hands into the clouds, and the sky boils. Thunder rends the air, and lightning strikes the earth. Iapetus shrieks as a fork pierces his back. Next, Coeus is struck and collapses.

'I have done it!' cries Zeus to the raging sky. 'I have done as you bade me!'

It cannot be the Mother to whom he speaks. This cannot be Gaia's will.

Then there is a gut-wrenching crack, and my mouth stretches in silent horror as an arrow of lightning pierces the omphalos shard, shattering the eye of the world.

As the last of Gaia's chosen Titans fight a losing battle against our invaders, Prometheus, his body blackened and smoking, crawls towards Zeus. The man I love turns, his face as cold and cruel as moonlight, and lifts his hand.

A dam breaks in my chest. I push myself up and run faster than my legs have ever carried me before. I hurl myself at Zeus, hitting him only with the power of my fists, but it is enough to send him sprawling to the ground. The lightning ceases.

'Run!' I cry.

Prometheus pauses for a heartbeat, then with a roar he heaves himself up, grabs a single shard of the shattered omphalos stone in the hem of his cloak, and flees.

Zeus overpowers me and throws me to the scorched earth. This time, I know I am prey.

Tears burn my cheeks as he pins me down.

'My love,' he whispers, his eyes no longer full of sky but burning gold. 'You chose the wrong side.' His hand slips down to grip my neck.

'Please,' I whisper. 'I am with child.'

32. Mercy

Danae could not breathe.

The final vision from Metis' story swirled before her, the smoke from the burning herbs acrid on her tongue. Metis' words still echoed around the hut, pulling at the ghostly shapes like a puppet master. Danae shuffled away from the hearth until her back hit stone. She flailed through the hazed air and when her fingers finally connected with the cloak hanging over the entrance, she tugged.

Fresh salt wind billowed across her face as she crawled out onto the hillside, coughing. Startled, Pegasus brayed and launched into the air. Danae retched.

Inside she could hear the others speaking as the smoke cleared.

'The Titanomachy . . .' rasped Telamon. 'The war between the gods and Titans for dominion over the earth was no epic battle but an ambush.'

'Yes.' Metis' voice was hard and clear as a bell. 'A lie just like the one we chosen twelve were told of armies stalking the land. The only real threat was the viper in our nest. I learned after my fellow Titans were slain that Zeus was not the man called by Gaia, but his son, and he killed his father to take his place. Once he tasted the sacred fruit, Zeus found a way to send for his brother, Poseidon. Together, they stole apples to give to their other siblings, so they too would gain powers and be able to seize the Hesperides tree for themselves. The rest you have seen . . .'

'How long ago?' rasped Atalanta.

'A thousand years.'

'And Prometheus escaped . . .'

'He did. Prometheus went into hiding, where he divined his prophecy from the shard of omphalos stone he'd rescued and spread his vision throughout the tribes of men. When the news reached Zeus, he hunted Prometheus down, but never recovered the missing shard of stone. The rest of the eye was reformed and placed in Delphi.'

Danae's mouth dried as she listened, still crouched on all fours. Prometheus must have entrusted the shard to the first member of the Children of Prometheus, and it had been guarded by the order ever since, handed down through the years until Manto finally entrusted it to Danae. A wave of guilt swept through her at the thought of it lost in the Underworld.

She gazed down at Pegasus' empty water bowl by her hand. The owl painted on its inside seemed to shift, as though it was about to beat its dark wings and fly away into the night. She recalled Metis saying it was a gift from her daughter. Then Danae thought of another likeness of the bird, cast in bronze with little green gems for eyes, pinned to her sister's breast. The sacred animal of the Goddess of Wisdom and Warfare.

'Athena . . .' She pushed herself to standing and paced back into the hut. 'Your daughter is Athena.'

Metis rose slowly, lingering smoke tendrils clinging to her like dawn mist.

'Yes.'

The other three looked between them, eyes bloodshot.

'I remained on Mount Olympus for a year after her birth, while Zeus began his campaign to convince mankind that he was a god. But as soon as she could fend without her mother I was exiled here, to Delos.' Feeling swelled through the cracks of Metis' shell, like damp soil beneath sun-split earth. 'Zeus never forgave me for helping Prometheus escape.'

'When I first arrived, you said your daughter used to come here . . . she brought you gifts . . .' Danae's limbs twitched, a familiar thrumming vibrating through her body.

'Zeus allowed her to visit me while she was still mortal, but once she tasted the fruit of the Hesperides tree, became ageless and gained her powers, she came no more. That was centuries ago.'

'You lay with him,' Danae spat. 'You loved him.'

'When I saw what he truly was I stood against him. I attacked him, so Prometheus could escape.' Metis stepped towards her around the smoking remains of the fire. 'I know now what has guided him along this path. The same voice that whispers in your ear.'

Danae's nails bit through the flesh of her palms, but before she could hurl back a retort, Heracles spoke.

'Why did he do this to me?' They turned to look at him. The hero had heaved himself up to standing, leaning against the stone wall. 'Why didn't he give me an apple?'

Danae's heart ached at the rawness in his voice.

Metis gazed at him with eyes swollen with sadness. 'I cannot say. Zeus has not created any more Titans since Hermes' transformation centuries ago. I wonder if this is not of his choosing.'

'*Gold that grows bears no fruit,*' murmured Atalanta.

'Exactly,' said Metis. 'Perhaps the Mother has cut him off from the power of the Hesperides fruit.'

A bolt of realization seared across Danae's mind. 'You knew about Heracles' strength elixir. If Athena has not visited for centuries, then who told you? Who else has come to Delos in the last thirty years?'

Telamon and Atalanta rose to their feet.

Metis raised a hand. 'It's not what you think –'

'Zeus.' The name was venom on Danae's lips.

There was a pause before Metis whispered, 'Yes.'

Blood thumped in Danae's ears. 'When did he last set foot on this island?'

Metis looked as though she were crumbling. 'A decade, at least a decade.'

Danae thought of her sister, her mind racing with images, each more terrible than the last. Alea lying limp in their brothers' arms, her sea-bloated corpse, Zeus standing over her, his hands creeping over her flesh.

Metis had loved this man. This raping, murdering monster.

'You never wanted me to succeed.'

'That is not true.'

Telamon and Atalanta began to move towards their weapons.

'This is a trap.' The ache in Danae's chest burned into a furnace. 'You're keeping me here until he comes, aren't you?'

Metis' eyes shone with tears as she shook her head. 'I am on your side . . . all I ask is that you spare my daughter. She can change, I know she can. If I can only teach her like I have taught you, show her the way of the Mother . . .'

You know what you must do, said the voice. *To fulfil your destiny.*

A high-pitched keening rang in Danae's ears, her insides hardening to iron. 'They are all complicit! They all hoard life-threads and murder mortals.' Her own life-threads thrummed through her body, like a stampede. 'Your daughter has an ocean of blood on her hands. Every person her priestesses condemned, every family starving to pay her temple tithe, every mortal she drained to sustain her power.'

'I can bring her to the light,' Metis whispered. 'Please . . . have mercy.'

Her love obscures the truth, said the voice. *A mother would never let you harm her child.*

Persephone blazed into Danae's mind, twitching as the last of her life drained away. She could almost feel the goddess's blood lapping over her feet, washing over her limbs until it smothered her. Then the imprint of bony fingers raked across her scalp and the ghost of a memory whispered, *Hello, little Titan.*

The stone floor cracked. Dust and shards of rock fell from the ceiling, the hut shaking as life-threads pulsed from Danae into the ground.

'You preach the way of the Mother but all you care about is your own miserable life. How dare you hide on this barren rock rather than use your power to right the world you helped wrong. While you make little rock piles from the safety of your island, people are dying at the hands of the false gods.' Her hands shook as she stretched a finger towards Metis. 'You are a coward.'

'Control yourself!' shouted Metis.

But all Danae could see was burning gold.

'Out!' yelled Atalanta. 'Everyone out!'

Metis threw out a whorl of life-threads from each hand to twist like vines around Danae. She was thrown backwards through the entrance. Then Atalanta and Telamon burst from the hut, hauling Heracles between them.

Danae lay on the ground, Metis' power binding her own. There was no space for breath, for patience, for asking, as rage burned through her soul.

As she struggled, the violence in her body trickled away, leaving weariness in its wake. Then the pressure holding her evaporated.

There was a colossal crash, and Metis' hut imploded in a cloud of dust and grit.

Metis released her, and Danae pushed herself to her feet, facing the wreckage of the stone hut, now nothing but a pile of boulders. Telamon, Atalanta and Heracles stood together on the edge of the hillside, their faces smeared with dust.

'Look what you've done,' Metis spat, her forehead bloodied by a falling rock. 'I should have known, the day I caught you draining the ichor from that lizard –'

Danae barked out a bitter laugh. 'Not the damned lizard again.'

'It matters!' Metis' chest heaved. 'If you still don't understand that, then perhaps Gaia made a mistake.'

'Come now,' Telamon edged forward, his hands raised, 'let's not say things we'll regret . . .'

The hillside groaned, and they all staggered back as the remnants of the hut collapsed, belching ash and smoke into the air.

Night had come. A sliver of moon hung in the sky, a twin to the crescent bruises marking Danae's palms. The others were silent, the aftermath of the fight splattered across their faces like tar thrown at a fresco.

Metis regarded Danae with ice-cold fury. 'When dawn comes, you will all leave.'

Danae lifted her chin. 'Gladly.'

33. A Gilded Cage

Two weeks after Hermes brought news of Hades and Persephone's demise, Hera trod the mosaic path through the sprawling central garden, the heat of the stones radiating through her sandals. Around her, the walls of the palace of Olympus reared into the sky, a seamless monolith of shining marble balustrades and golden columns. She, Zeus, Poseidon, Hades and Demeter had dragged the stone from deep within the earth, sculpting it with the power of their life-threads. It had taken a decade to complete, and thousands of mortal slaves had been sacrificed, their ichor the Olympians' chisels.

She paused at the circular building standing in the centre of the garden, its pale pillars a ghostly infantry guarding the ancient treasure within.

'Gold that grows bears no fruit,' she murmured.

Since Zeus built the temple, she had never been inside. None but her husband were permitted to enter. Painted across the curving outer wall was a fresco of Zeus touching the head of a mortal with the tip of his gauntleted finger, supposedly sparking life into the first man moulded from river clay.

Remember the truth, said the voice.

She drew a sharp breath.

Zeus' word was law. The history of the gods that had been passed down to mortals was mirrored in every painting on Olympus, every carving, statue and mural. Even the divine family were forbidden to question their origins, as though

Zeus believed that one day they would simply forget what really happened.

'I do not forget,' she whispered.

Olympus was hers just as much as his. They had taken it together.

The air between two of the pillars rippled. Hera stepped back as a pair of crimson eyes blinked from the shadows between the marble.

Her pulse quickened. She turned abruptly and stalked away, striding past a row of pomegranate trees.

As she walked, an old bitterness twisted through her. Zeus and Poseidon should be the ones to deliver the news of Hades and Persephone's demise, but since Hermes' revelations they were too absorbed with their secret councils.

As high up as the palace was, the heat was stifling, with no clouds to temper the sun and the wind kept at bay by the high walls. A bead of sweat trickled down her temple. She chose the path with the most shade through a grove of laurel trees. Dappled light teased through the dense foliage above her, which provided momentary relief from the glaring sun.

'We are closer to the celestial bodies than those creatures that expire in the dirt,' Zeus had said in the infancy of their reign.

Back when their palace on Mount Olympus was newly constructed, she would stand on her balcony and force herself to stare at the sun. 'We are the same,' she would whisper through tears drawn out by the terrible brightness. 'We will shine together for all eternity.' But the sun beat down on her here just as it had done when she was a girl, running across the dusty earth with scabs on her knees. Despite the long years they had endured together, it still drew sweat from her skin and blinded her if she dared meet its eye.

The trees fell away to be replaced with a patchwork of

flowers, swirling rainbows of orchids, crocuses, hyacinths and peonies. Nymphs darted between the beds, misting the greedy leaves with watering cans. Hera set her sights on a crop of yellow blooms and strode towards them.

She slowed as she approached the woman sitting on the stone walkway between two crops of narcissi. Beyond stood three nymphs in blue tunics, their hands clasped behind their backs. The woman's unkempt raven hair trailed on the floor. Wispy tendrils, curled by the heat, were stuck to her face. She didn't look up as Hera approached, continuing to stroke the trumpet of a nearby flower.

Hera lowered herself onto the edge of the flowerbed, careful not to drape her purple dress in the soil.

'Hello, Demeter.'

Slowly, the woman wrenched her gaze from the narcissus and looked bleary-eyed at Hera.

'I know you.'

'Yes, darling, it's Hera.'

'Oh.'

Demeter returned to the bloom. The structure of her face was so like her brother's, but there was nothing of Zeus' metal in her eyes. Each twitch of his mouth was like the slice of a blade, but Demeter's features moved like clouds nudged by a benevolent breeze. Whatever edges she'd had had been eroded a long time ago.

'That's a pretty flower.'

'Mmm.' Demeter smiled absentmindedly. 'They're Persephone's favourite.'

Hera felt a twinge of pity. Demeter still spoke of her daughter, after all these centuries. Hera remembered Zeus' promise, that Persephone would always see the sparkling sky, the light of the sun, the fishes in the sea. He had spoken those words, yet he knew his brother's nature. If it had been up to Hera, Hades would have been executed for what he'd done to Persephone, his own niece, whom he had forced to become his wife. But he was Zeus' blood, and that meant never leaving the Underworld had been his punishment. A barb of satisfaction shot through Hera's chest. Until the dragon had done its work.

Hera reached out to clasp a stem between her fingers. 'May I?'

Demeter sucked in breath like she'd been scalded and furiously shook her head. The nymphs in blue stepped forward.

'It's all right.' Hera glanced at them. Then she smiled at her sister and withdrew her hand.

The Goddess of the Harvest giggled and cupped a trumpet in her fingers.

'I have something to tell you –'

Demeter stroked the flower. 'The bees have come.'

A faint crease formed between Hera's brows. 'It's about Hades.'

Demeter's eyes snapped up, and Hera thought she glimpsed a shard of clarity before the fog settled back across the other woman's gaze.

'I have a brother by that name. He's strange.'

'Darling, he's dead.'

Hera held her breath as Demeter's alabaster forehead crinkled into a frown. Then she laughed. 'No, silly, he is their king.'

Hera had admired Demeter once. The woman had been an extraordinarily talented botanist. Once, there wouldn't have been a plant in all of Greece that Demeter couldn't name or recite the properties of. Now, she lived in a world of misted dreams, all the sharp lines of reality blurred by the lotus-flower concoction Hera had been making for her since Persephone was abducted.

What a waste of a mind. Of all that potential.

Hera briefly closed her eyes and summoned the courage for what she must do next.

'Persephone too no longer walks with the living.' As she spoke, she noticed the nymphs behind Demeter tense, ready to spring forward and restrain her if needed.

Hera held her breath, watching the shifting terrain of Demeter's face, a strange land with unpredictable storms. She waited for the inevitable tide of grief, but it did not come.

Instead, Demeter reached out and petted Hera's hand.

'I know.' She paused. 'The Mother whispered to me in my dreams. My Kore is with Gaia now.'

Hera stared at her, then sharply drew back her hand and rose to her feet. She nodded to the nymphs in blue and hurried away down the path, her sandals slapping on the stones.

As she reached the shade of the laurel trees, she hastily wiped her cheeks dry.

Then a nymph came hurrying towards her.

The girl bowed. 'My queen, your son requests your presence in the War Room.'

Hera sighed and flicked her hand. The nymph scurried away.

The War Room was Ares' domain; a large chamber nestled deep in the belly of the palace. No pillars or statues filled the space, no mosaics adorned the stone floors, and no chandeliers hung from the ceilings. Bronze braziers, thick as branches, flamed from holders nailed to the walls illuminating a vast mural spanning all four walls, painted over the grain of the rock.

The greatest war of all: the Titanomachy. Or at least the version that Zeus had decreed truth. The depiction of the Titans was grotesque; Gaia's chosen twelve cast in the image of the primordial giants that walked the earth when the world was young. Their naked bodies were corded with strength as they battled the golden-clad Olympians, mounted on sky-borne chariots drawn by a fleet of winged horses. The ground beneath the Titans' feet bled, rivers of molten rock spewing from the cracks their huge fists wrought upon the earth. Some held boulders in their hands, some trees and some entire mountaintops, all turned as weapons against the gods. Zeus led the Olympian charge against these beasts, his eyes gleaming like the sun, a bolt of lightning poised in his hand.

Hera's lip curled as she gazed at the fresco. The scene was intended to be imposing, yet it seemed almost comical to her now. The real fight for Olympus had been a cowardly ambush. She, Zeus, Poseidon, Demeter and Hades had moved like wolves amongst a flock of sheep, slaughtering the Titans before the sun crested the sea. It had almost been too easy.

She'd believed her future set when Zeus gave her a bite of ripe golden fruit. She could still remember the blinding brilliance of that apple, so bright it hid the rot within. For decades she lived in a daze, consumed by love and power. Until the voice that had awoken with her divinity whispered, *Your husband's appetites are insatiable.*

She didn't want to believe it, but one night she'd followed Zeus to her temple in Argos and found him fucking one of her priestesses, Io, at the stone feet of her statue. A lesser woman might have revealed herself. Not Hera. She lingered in the shadows, watching until the deed was done and her husband flew back to Olympus. Then she burned Io alive on her own altar, like a sacrificial heifer.

Hera brushed the memory away as she approached a giant map of Greece and the surrounding territories chiselled into the marble floor, the grooves filled with black paint. Upon it, a piece of land had been elevated. A larger replica of the Trojan Bay stood like a banquet table with its stone legs planted in Phrygia and the Aegean Sea. A cluster of carved ivory ships had been placed along the shore opposite the fortress city, and a series of miniature tents fashioned from silk were scattered across the land beside them.

Her son, Ares, leant over the enlarged section of Troy, his hands splayed on the stone. The twins, Artemis and Apollo, lounged against the chamber wall, their foreheads touching as they whispered together. Hera's lips tightened as Aphrodite walked over to the map to gaze at the little city, and Ares slipped an arm around her waist. Hera's younger son, Hephaestus, lurked on the far side of the room to his wife. He was covered in soot, still draped in his leather apron. He must have come straight from his forge.

It seemed that Ares had summoned everyone.

The Goddess of Love was putting on an excellent performance of vulnerability, her emerald eyes shining with just a hint of moisture, her bottom lip reddened as she worried it between her teeth. Even Poseidon had been drawn in, flanking her other side, glancing at her like he really was a concerned uncle.

Ah yes, Hera recalled that Aphrodite still had a bastard child living in Troy.

'Do not underestimate Priam's defences,' said Ares. 'Even with their numbers, the Greeks cannot hope to fully surround the city. They will never starve Troy to its knees.'

Athena faced him across the table, gesturing to the miniature vessels. 'Over a thousand ships have already congregated. Sea-trade to the Troad has been eradicated. Priam's city will not survive on squirrelling supplies through Phrygia alone. Besides, the Trojans have only one great tactical general, Hector, whereas the Greeks are blessed with several strategists. Odysseus of Ithaca, in particular, is the most skilled —'

'Odysseus,' Ares drawled. 'Your favourite pales in combat next to Hector. Now that Achilles has abandoned the war, you will see the mighty Greek army crumble against the power of Troy.'

Athena's eyes flashed. 'It does you little credit to dismiss the King of Ithaca. He has a brilliant mind.'

'That won't save him on the battlefield.' Ares spread his arms and took in the room. 'You will all bear witness.'

Apollo sighed. 'Brother, I told you the last time you dragged us here, I won't go to Troy unless Achilles fights. My priestesses say he's the greatest mortal warrior that has ever lived. The others aren't worth my time. Get him back, then I'll come.'

'Agreed,' said Artemis.

Before Ares could rage against his siblings, Athena interjected, 'It is already done.' She met Ares' stare with a soft smile. 'And when Odysseus brings Achilles back to Troy, you will be forced to admit he is the greatest mortal mind of his generation.'

Tired of their bickering, Hera cleared her throat.

'Mother.' Ares' disposition brightened as he paced to her side and guided her to the table. 'Look at this.' He gestured across the map. 'Under the counsel of my priestesses, Agamemnon of Mycenae has amassed the greatest Greek allied army the world has ever seen. Won't Father be pleased?'

'I'm sure he will.' Hera massaged the back of Ares' neck.

From the shadows, Hephaestus barked out a laugh.

At that moment the doors were thrown open, and Zeus entered, followed by a quivering Hermes.

The King of the Gods paused at the edge of the map and took in each member of his family. Then his gaze fell on the raised segment of Troy. He advanced, eyes consuming every detail.

'Father.' Ares drew himself up to his full height. 'The entire Greek force is now camped at Troy. I was just telling Mother, Agamemnon has –'

In one swift motion, Zeus gripped the underside of the marble and hurled it into the air. The Olympians scattered as the great slab came crashing down, chunks of glittering stone shattering across the room. Hera grasped Ares' arm.

'Typhon, the dragon, has been sighted above ground.' Zeus spoke softly, yet his words rolled over them like a great wave.

'No . . .' said Aphrodite, her voice quivering.

'Who set the dragon free?' asked Apollo, clinging to Artemis' hand. 'Hades would never . . .' he trailed off, the name of the dead heavy on the air.

'This was *her* doing, wasn't it?' asked Athena. 'The creature who looks like a mortal girl. Father . . .' she approached Zeus, 'I do not believe Hades created her. When I faced her over a year ago, her power was so like our own . . .'

Zeus stood still as a pillar of salt. Hera's chest tightened. Without realizing, Athena had laid bare the truth.

The King of the Gods turned his golden gaze on his daughter, and Hera watched his rage burn into pride.

'My Bright Eyes, always the cleverest of my children.'

Beside her, Ares stiffened. Hera felt the barb like it was her own wound.

'The creature I tasked you with destroying is a Titan.' Zeus' words rippled through the divine family like shockwaves, their eyes flicking to the fresco towering around them. Before anyone could speak, he continued, more lies pouring from his lips, 'She *was* Hades' creation, her beastly flesh altered to appear mortal. He hoped to use her as a weapon against me to claim the throne of Heaven. Hubris led Hades down this path, and his own invention ultimately became his downfall. Like all Titans she is treacherous. She murdered him and Persephone and unleashed the dragon.' Zeus looked down at the ruined floor before him. 'Let this be a reminder, she will not stop until she has destroyed everything we have built. Everything you care about, your cities, temples, wars, worshippers, none of it will exist if she reaches Olympus. From this moment on, all you will think of is killing her. Nothing else matters.'

Hera watched the faces of her family change, shifting with tides of anger, confusion and fear.

'But Troy . . .' Ares stared at the crumbled remains of his map. 'I must be there when it begins. All those sacrifices, all those mortals praying to me, all the bloodshed in my name –'

'Nothing. Else. Matters,' repeated Zeus, each word a shard of ice.

Ares did not question him again.

'What will we do about the dragon?' asked Artemis. 'It will surely come here seeking revenge.'

'Concern yourself only with the girl. I will deal with Typhon, just as I did before.'

Zeus cast one last sweeping look at his family, then paced out the chamber. Swiftly following, Hermes flew from the room, having refused to make eye contact with anyone.

'Hermes,' Hephaestus called as he hurried after his brother. 'Pip, wait!'

The others lingered, staring at each other.

'I will not let this ruin my war,' Ares muttered, his hands squeezed into shaking fists.

Athena remained very still, staring at the miniature Greek camp. 'We do not have a choice.'

'I will have my fucking battle!' Ares shouted.

'Did you not hear what Father said?' said Apollo. 'Olympus is under threat!'

Aphrodite began to weep.

'Poseidon.' Hera gestured for him to follow her and swept from the room. The children's voices clashed behind them as they paced down the pillared corridor. When Hera was sure they were alone, she drew him into a shadowed alcove.

Poseidon appraised her, his expression grim. 'What do you want, Hera? The last time I granted you aid, it cost me my best horse.'

'I regret the loss of Pegasus, but heed me; with Hades dead and Demeter's mind lost, besides Zeus, you and I alone know who the girl really is,' her voice grew quieter, 'what Prometheus prophesied she would do. You also know there is another of the original Titans left in the world. One she might go to for help.'

Poseidon's brow creased. 'You cannot mean . . .'

'Think on it,' Hera glanced over his shoulder, eyes straining to catch the tell-tale shimmer of a shade.

'No one besides us, Zeus and Demeter know Metis exists.'

'That's not true. The girl spoke with Prometheus – he may have told her that Metis saved his life during the fight for Olympus. He knew of her exile to Delos – Zeus taunted him with it after his own capture.'

'No.' Poseidon ran a hand over his beard. 'Metis has been brought to heel.'

'Trust is a luxury we cannot afford,' hissed Hera. 'My husband is blind when it comes to that woman. But she stood against him once, she could do it again.'

'She would never endanger Athena.'

'Are you sure?' She placed a hand on Poseidon's chest, above his heart. 'Would you stake your life on it?'

He flinched from her touch, backing into the curved

wall behind him. Hera stepped forward, bridging the space between them, her lips almost brushing his ear.

'Once, Metis forsook her mortal family to become a Titan. Perhaps she still serves the Mother above all else.'

'We must not speak of these things . . .' Poseidon rasped.

Triumph thundered in Hera's chest. She could see the resolve crumbling in his eyes.

'Go, now, while Zeus searches for the dragon. Metis will heed you better than me. Make sure she remains loyal to us.'

Poseidon blinked, his eyes darting about the hallway. 'If my brother discovers what we have discussed, where I have gone –'

'He won't.' Hera took the hand that had touched his chest and placed it above her own heart. 'I swear on the blood of my children.'

Just as she had hoped, the final threads of his resistance snapped.

'Fine. I will go to Delos.'

34. The Sea's Revenge

Danae woke, damp and shivering. Rosy-fingered dawn daubed the sky with the first blush of morning. She lay on the bank beside the lake, chill wind scraping her skin. Heracles, Atalanta and Telamon were curled in the shelter of the upended boat, their limbs folded over one another like children. But instead of dolls, their fists clutched weapons.

They had all retreated to the lake after Danae destroyed the stone hut. Metis alone had remained on the hilltop to sleep beside the wreckage of her home.

Danae missed the protective warmth of Pegasus' wings all those nights they'd huddled together in forests, caves and abandoned dwellings while seeking the entrance to the Underworld. An ache of worry shivered through her. The horse had flown away and not returned to the island since she'd lost control and obliterated the hut the previous night.

She crawled to the water, splashed her face, drank, then eased herself to her feet and rubbed her arms. Her head pounded as though she'd consumed a whole amphora of unmixed wine. Sighing, she cast her gaze towards the hill.

In the aftermath of her rage, she could not recall the detail of all that had been spoken outside the collapsed hut. But one sentence was branded across her memory. *Perhaps Gaia made a mistake.*

Danae set her jaw. 'You're wrong,' she muttered and strode towards the hill. She was loath to face Metis, but the crest would give her the best view across all sides of the Aegean and surrounding land. The sooner she could find Pegasus and they could leave this cursed isle, the better.

She avoided the usual route towards Metis' hut, clambering over lichen-stained boulders and picking her way between prickly cushions of spruce, the peach-gold light brightening as she climbed.

She was halfway to the peak when a flurry of loose stones tumbled down to her right, swiftly followed by Metis hurtling towards the bay. Danae caught a flash of sunlight glinting on metal. Something bronze was clutched in the woman's outstretched hand.

Anger once again licked its heat across Danae's skin. She turned and scrambled after the woman, sprinting as soon as she reached the ground. Ahead of her, once Metis reached the bay, she called to the gulls nesting on the earthen rock opposite the beach. As one they rose, buffeted by the wind as they soared to her. One landed on her outstretched arm and finally, Danae saw what the woman had been holding: the medallion Metis had shown her when she first arrived on Delos.

Metis slipped the amulet around the bird's neck, cooing as she stroked its wings, before launching it into the sky. The gull did not return to soar with its brethren, but climbed up towards the sun, before careering east.

'Metis!' Danae doubled over, sucking the sharp air into her lungs. 'What are you doing?'

'What I should have done a long time ago.' Metis strode towards Danae and grasped her arm, attempting to drag her off the sand. 'You must hide, quickly.'

Danae did not move. In the distance, a dark shape floated atop the glinting sapphire waves. It was the strangest vessel she'd ever seen, the size of a great warship, yet the oars looked thick as tree trunks, the helm bulbous rather than tapering to a sleek point. She could see no crew moving aboard the boat, but in the centre stood a figure who appeared to be cast from gold. Then the curved end of the stern flexed, and her entire body ran cold.

It was no ship. It was alive.

'Poseidon has come,' hissed Metis, redoubling her efforts to drag Danae from the shore.

She wrenched her arm from the woman's grip. 'You summoned him here!'

'No.' Metis looked worn through. 'I swear on Athena's life, on the Mother herself. Go, find the others, hide by the lake until I come to fetch you. Now, before he sees you!'

Despite all that had passed between them, Danae believed her. She had never seen Metis look so afraid.

'I can fight. I'm ready.'

'No, you are not.'

'I faced Hera, I sent her flying back to Olympus!'

'Poseidon is something else.' Metis took her by the shoulders. 'If you fight him now, you will die, and so will your friends.'

The clarity in the woman's eyes stilled her. Just for a moment, Danae saw a flicker of her mother.

She hesitated for a heartbeat, then turned and ran.

'Poseidon is here!' Danae yelled as she thundered towards the lake.

Telamon and Atalanta leapt to their feet, then Heracles' gaunt face appeared behind the upturned rowing boat.

'My uncle?' he croaked.

Danae's lungs ached as she gasped, 'And a fucking great sea-monster. We have to hide, now!'

Telamon and Atalanta looked at one another, sword and bow clutched in their hands.

'We hide from no one,' said the warrior.

Danae slicked back the flyaway hairs plastered to her brow. 'Metis says he is too strong.' She clenched her teeth, casting her mind back to the Underworld. 'And she's right. If Poseidon's power is anything like Hades' we are not ready to fight him. Not as we are.' Her eyes flicked to Heracles. 'We must conceal ourselves.' Then she added, 'That's an order.'

She waited, the breath locked in her chest, convinced Telamon or at least Atalanta would rail against her. But to her astonishment, Atalanta slung her bow over her shoulder and grasped the side of the boat, tipping it onto its belly. A heartbeat later, Telamon sheathed his sword and helped her drag the vessel into the undergrowth.

Heracles remained. For the first time since arriving on Delos, Danae did not flinch at the loathing in his gaze.

'You will never replace me,' he whispered.

'I don't want to,' she said softly.

She felt the urge to move towards him. 'Heracles, please, you must hide . . .' her fingers brushed his.

He recoiled from her touch and stalked after his companions into the trees. Danae clenched her fist, then crouched down, concealing herself in the bushes.

Before long, voices could be heard, carried on the wind.

'It's good of you to visit after all these years. As you can see, I am rather starved of company.'

'You have the gulls.' A male voice, deep and cold as a winter sea.

'True, although they have a terrible sense of humour.'

'You haven't changed.'

'Neither have you. Apart from the beard. Congratulations, you finally look older than Zeus.'

Poseidon laughed.

Danae's skin prickled. They spoke like old friends. Like family.

A mocking lilt crept into Metis' tone. 'I wish I could offer you hospitality, but I have nothing worthy of the God of the Sea.'

'A drink from the sweet water of your lake will suffice.'

Danae's breath hitched in her throat. She peered between the leaves.

A figure clad in golden armour strode over the dusty earth. He was tall and powerfully built, a trident clutched in one hand, his helm in the other. He had always appeared sturdy and wild in his statues, with a great curling beard and long, shaggy hair. In the flesh, his skin was the colour of ripe grain, his hair the rich hue of an oak tree. He was cast in a rougher mould than Zeus and Hades, possessing none of the beauty his brother had passed onto Heracles, but there was a whisper of their shared blood in the lilt of his jaw and the furrow of his brow.

Metis hurried to place herself between the god and lake. 'Spare me the niceties, Poseidon. Why are you here?'

Danae longed to check that the others were well concealed, but she dared not move.

Poseidon drove the end of his trident into the earth. 'Hades and Persephone are dead.'

To her credit, Metis stiffened as though the news were a shock.

'Slain by the very girl Prometheus prophesied would end Zeus' reign. In a bitter twist of fate, the Titan too was killed by her hand.'

Danae's mouth dried at the lie. She wanted to scream, to hurl herself from the undergrowth and savage him, but she willed herself to remain immobile as stone.

'How can this be?' breathed Metis.

'She is a creature of pure malice that will stop at nothing until she has destroyed all Titans, Gaia's chosen and Olympians alike. Prometheus was mistaken. The champion of mankind will be the end of us all.'

'Why are you telling me this?'

'I believe she might come here, seeking your help.' He drew out a golden medallion from the pouch at his waist. 'If she does, keep her here and send for me, then . . .'

Poseidon trailed off and tilted his face skyward.

Danae strained to see what was happening. Then she heard the beating of wings.

Pegasus landed before his old master and nuzzled Poseidon's hand.

Metis forced out a laugh. 'A little much isn't it, to arrive on the back of Skolopendra *and* bring your favourite winged horse.'

Poseidon wrenched his trident from the earth. 'My steed was last spotted in the company of the girl. Where is she?'

Metis took a step back. 'Not here.'

Poseidon's azure-grey eyes turned to scour the greenery around the lake.

'Poseidon, I swear –'

As though swinging an axe, the God of the Sea raked his trident through the air and a surge of life-threads shot from its treble prongs to wrap around Metis.

Danae waited, limbs bound with tension, expecting Metis to throw him off. But it seemed she could not. Her face reddened, her body twisting until there was a sickening crack and one of her arms folded inwards at an unnatural angle.

Metis screamed.

He was going to kill her.

You can do this, said the voice.

'Please, Gaia, help me,' Danae mouthed. She imagined

everything bleeding away, all the noise, wind and fury, and pictured herself melting into her river. Lines of gold began to crackle across her vision as the tapestry of life faded in and out of sight. She tried to hold onto the feeling of calm, but her connection to Gaiasight was weak.

It would have to do.

Summoning her life-threads into her hands, she emerged from the bushes. In that moment, all the resentment she'd harboured burned away. She was risking everything, but even after discovering the past Metis had concealed, she couldn't let the woman die. Gaia's last true Titan. The only person left who truly understood what it felt like to be a protector of mankind, and how much it cost.

Poseidon looked towards her, Metis still caught in his rope of threads. His gaze swept over Danae and his lip curled.

'Finally, in the flesh.'

Her breath steady, Danae hurled two cords of gleaming strands at him. But the God of the Sea was swifter.

The power of his trident still binding Metis, Poseidon blasted Danae's threads away with a coil of wind and hoisted her off the ground. She struggled in the air, her limbs bound like a bird trapped beneath a lion's paw. As the breath was squeezed from her lungs, panic consumed her, and the tapestry of life vanished from sight. She no longer asked the wind to come to her aid, but internally screamed at it, hurling her life-threads against Poseidon's barrier of air. The pressure around her chest only tightened and from the ground, the false god laughed.

'How my brother will reward me, when I return to Olympus with your head.'

The next thing Danae knew, she was slamming into the ground, suddenly free. Dazed, she staggered to her feet. Atalanta was hanging about Poseidon's neck, trying to find an opening in his armour to drive her knife through to the soft flesh beneath.

Lying a stone's throw from Danae, Metis groaned. The woman flung out her good arm, her life-threads snaking away into the earth.

Poseidon ripped Atalanta from his back, smashing her into the bank. He raised his trident, but before he could strike, he stumbled, the ground cracking beneath his feet. For an agonizing heartbeat, the God of the Sea flailed. Then he fell, and with hungry earthen lips, the island swallowed him whole.

'Go!' shouted Metis.

Danae ran to her side, but Metis pushed her away.

'I can't hold him for long,' she gasped. 'You must go.'

Before Danae could protest, Atalanta grabbed her arm and pulled her towards Telamon and Heracles, who had heaved the little boat from the undergrowth and were dragging it towards the shore.

Danae grabbed onto the side of the vessel, her sweat-slicked fingers slipping across the oiled wood as she fought the urge to look back. They hauled the boat through the sun-crisped grass until their feet sank into sand. But before they reached the shallows, all four of them froze.

Emerging from the sea was Skolopendra, the creature Poseidon had arrived on. Water sluiced from its mottled navy shell as it loomed over the bay, supported by at least fifty legs, its crayfish tail beating the water. It looked like something from the dawn of time, a giant, primordial crustacean that had crawled from the deepest crevice of the sea. Even after meeting the beings that dwelt in the Underworld, Danae quaked at the sight of its crab-like head; eyeballs the size of human skulls bulging on stalks, tentacle-thick hairs trailing from its nostrils, and its bone jaws clicking like two saws as it stormed towards them.

For a moment, they all stood dumbstruck. Then, with a guttural roar, Heracles grabbed Telamon's sword, his limbs shaking with the effort, as he ran doggedly towards the beast.

'Heracles, no!' Danae sprinted after him, tackling him round the waist and bringing them both crashing to the sand. 'Stay back!' she barked as she leapt up in front of him, casting two ropes of life-threads into the sand. As the sea-monster reared, she was transported back to fighting Kerberos on the midnight bank of the Styx. She whipped her life-threads and threw two clouds of sand up towards its eyes, piercing its giant eyeballs with thousands of razor-sharp grains. Dark blue liquid sprayed down as the beast screeched.

Then Telamon and Atalanta came sprinting from behind her and Heracles. Telamon stooped to retrieve his sword mid-run and, like ants climbing the roots of a tree, they scurried up the creature's spiny legs.

Danae cast her threads wide this time, creating a shimmering web through the air, as she willed the wind to form a net and drag the sea-monster to the earth. It was a colossal effort to keep it restrained, every part of her aching. She knew she should try again to achieve Gaiasight, but there was no time.

Atop the beast, Atalanta and Telamon clung on, driving their blades beneath the rim of its shell.

Then a blast of rocks smacked into Danae's back. She staggered, losing her control of the life-thread net.

By the lake, Poseidon had freed himself from his earth prison, and he and Metis faced each other across the water, hurling trees and chunks of the island at each other, scattering stones and earth through the air.

Freed and furious, Skolopendra tossed Atalanta and Telamon from its back. It rose up on its many legs, then thudded its body into the shallows, causing a quake that sent them all tumbling to the ground.

Danae furiously rubbed the sand from her eyes and squinted through her tears as the beast lowered its grotesque head towards the prone form of Atalanta lying on a bed of sun-crisped seaweed.

It might have been blinded, but it could still smell.

'No!' Danae screamed as its bone jaws closed around the warrior.

Without pausing to attempt Gaiasight, Danae summoned her life-threads and drilled a concentrated blast of air towards the belly of the beast, trying to break through its shell. Skolopendra roared, then flung Danae aside with a flick of one of its tree-length legs. Telamon was valiantly still trying to scale another of the monster's limbs, using his sword to drag himself up between the ridges of shell. Heracles had mercifully retreated to crouch behind the boat, watching his friends battle with wide, haunted eyes.

The sea-monster swung its head towards Danae as she gathered her threads for another attack, then it launched itself at her. She braced for impact. But mid-strike, it stopped and began swaying. Telamon, who had been tossed into the shallows, splashed away as Skolopendra jerked wildly, then let out a deep, bone-rattling shriek and crashed down onto the sand. It lay for a moment, legs twitching, then grew still.

Six agonizing heartbeats later, the bone jaws shuddered apart. Atalanta emerged, sword drawn, the blade drenched in blue blood.

Telamon sagged back in the water. 'Thank the gods –' He caught himself. 'You know what I mean.'

Danae sprinted towards the warrior, throwing her arms around her. She could feel Atalanta's pulse beating through her silver breastplate.

They pulled apart, and somehow the words Danae wished to say became: 'You stink.'

Atalanta wiped her face. 'I know.'

There was another earth-rumbling crash, and Danae looked back towards the lake, where Metis and Poseidon were ripping the island apart.

'The power's in his trident,' Danae murmured. She looked back at Atalanta. 'I think I know how to beat him.'

The warrior's lip curled, the heat of battle blazing in her eyes. 'Let's go slay a god.'

Danae, Telamon and Atalanta left Heracles by the boat and sprinted inland. Metis and Poseidon's battle had moved away from the lake, towards the cliffs on the far side of the island. Metis staggered on the wave-sprayed rocks as the sea crashed below, her broken arm hanging at her side. She'd had no time to heal herself. Poseidon whipped a tempest around the prongs of his trident and hurled it at her, until she became nothing but a dark blur in the centre of the maelstrom.

Danae's eyes stretched wide in horror; Metis was going to die if she didn't intervene. But she was weakening. It was one thing achieving the calm of Gaiasight in solitude, but in battle her pounding heart and racing blood too often betrayed her. She delved deep inside herself, trying to imagine the flow of her river.

Beside her, Atalanta slung the bow from across her back and nocked a blood-soaked arrow. The shot pierced Poseidon through the cheek, and he roared, turning on them with eyes of molten fury. The tempest around Metis dissipated, and she gasped, struggling to heave her bruised body off the rocks.

Danae ran, launching herself towards Poseidon, with Telamon and Atalanta beside her. The Olympian ripped the arrow from his face and flicked his trident. A hard wall of air slammed into Danae, and she hit the ground, gasping.

Lights bursting across her vision, she pushed herself to her feet, as a dank mist billowed across the island. It was Metis: battered and bloody, her good arm raised as she summoned the fog from the sea. It swallowed them all in a cocoon of damp grey air, robbing their sight.

Arms outstretched, Danae stumbled forward, then her foot caught on something.

She crouched down and felt a mound of stones.

Through the cries of battle and clash of metal and rock, she heard something else. A melody sung by the wind, cawed by the gulls and echoed in the earth.

She drew a long, deep breath, then let go. For a moment, she was terrified. Then everything seeped away. She was the river, her blood its racing current; she was the sea; she was every body of ocean pooled across the earth.

She was all of creation.

Through the mist glowed the tapestry of life. She could see the shining form of Metis, and the swirl of her life-threads pouring into the air. She could see Atalanta and Telamon, the shimmering shape of their lives in harmony with the blades of grass beneath their feet. She could see Poseidon, his body glowing brighter than the rest, and another light that eclipsed all others: his trident. It burned like a white-hot flame, and Danae now understood why it held so much power.

Hundreds, maybe thousands of ichors surged through the gold, ripped from their hosts over the centuries and trapped in this cold shaft of metal.

Her body was no longer her own as she walked forward. Poseidon swung his trident wildly through the air, cleaving scars of clarity through the fog, just as she had done on the Doliones shore.

He only saw Danae when she was barely an arm's length away. His ravaged face stretched into a terrible grin. He brought his trident down as though he would split her in half. She reached up, her entire being singing with energy, and the shaft crashed into her outstretched palm.

It was as though she had been struck by lightning. Power reverberated through her, rattling her teeth.

Take them, urged the voice. *Consume the life-threads.*

She could hear no other sound, save the ringing in her ears.

Metis had told her that life-threads could not be created or destroyed. She did not know if the strands trapped in the trident held the memories of those they had animated, but they had once been people. And that was enough. She would not be like the gods.

Screaming in pain, she wrenched the weapon from Poseidon's grip and smashed it into the rocky earth, channelling the power of the tapestry of life into the blow.

The trident shattered.

Danae gasped, her vision returning to normal as the trapped life-threads dispersed from the shards of gold, fleeing back into the air and the earth. Back into the tapestry where they belonged.

Poseidon roared and grabbed Danae, hurling them both into the ground. He clamped his gauntleted fists around her neck, pinning her beneath his weight, blood dripping onto her face from his wounded cheek. Power vibrated through her, radiating from his armour: it too was engorged with life-threads and somehow amplified his strength. Then Metis appeared through the dissipating mist, her arm healed. She ran at Poseidon, propelling him off Danae, but the God of the Sea was swiftly on his feet. He grabbed Metis by the neck. She gasped as he lifted her like a rag doll and hurled her across the cliff. She hit a crop of rocks with a sickening crack, rolled to the earth below and remained still.

Telamon and Atalanta came sprinting towards Poseidon,

but he flicked them aside like leaves blown by the wind. He advanced on Danae. She struggled to push herself to her feet, but Poseidon sent a cord of glowing strands to pin her down once more.

He stood over Danae and again gripped her neck. Baring his teeth, he began to drain her.

She shuddered, her vision darkening, limbs twitching as the warmth was leached from her body. Then her fingertips brushed an edge of cold, hard metal. She stretched, her hand curling around a sliver of broken trident. With a grunt that expelled the last of her strength, she thrust the shard into Poseidon's neck.

The God of the Sea crashed to his knees, mouth stretching wide as blood filled his lungs. Danae stared as he choked, his face reddening, the air ripening with the earthy stench of human waste. It seemed to take an age for him to sink to the ground.

Take his threads! commanded the voice.

But Danae did not move. Something beyond the raging desire for life-threads was alive within her. A calming presence, strengthening with each breath. An innate knowledge of what was right. She must give Poseidon's life force back to the Mother.

She did not dare look away until the light faded from his eyes and the last of his threads returned to the soil. Glancing up, she saw Telamon helping Atalanta to her feet. Pushing herself to standing, Danae turned and ran towards the crop of rocks.

When she reached Metis, the woman lay very still, blood trickling from the corners of her lips. Telamon and Atalanta crouched beside Danae while Heracles stood a little way off, like a ghost watching from another world.

'Poseidon is dead,' said Danae, squeezing Metis' hand.

Metis' eyes traced the sky to meet Danae's. She tried to speak, but her words were so faint Danae had to lean in close. The other woman's breath fluttered like a butterfly's wing against her cheek.

'Have faith.'

For a moment the wind lulled, and the air was filled with the caws of gulls, the whisper of the sea and the murmur of petals turning towards the sun, as Metis' ichor returned to the Mother.

35. Ghosts of the Living

Danae, Atalanta and Telamon stood on the peak of the hill. The wind moaned, and the white-crested waves beat against the battle-ravaged island. Before them lay a fresh mound of stones. Metis' body was buried beneath, wrapped in the fur-trimmed cloak Danae had pulled from the wreckage of her hut. In its folds, she'd tucked sprigs of the little purple flowers, as though they had grown from the cracks of Metis' funeral shroud. It felt strange not to place coins on the woman's eyes, even though she now knew that Metis would have no need of them.

Below, keeping vigil beside the lake, were Heracles and Pegasus, the horse's wings tucked into its sides.

Once Danae had revived her ichor on several bushes of spruce, she'd stripped Poseidon's body of its golden armour, weighted down his corpse with rocks and tossed it into the lake. It had struck her that, when free of his armour, the God of the Sea could have been anyone. A fisherman washed ashore after losing a battle with the ocean.

Heracles had said nothing while they worked to drown Poseidon's body, but he remained by the water when the others left the bank and trudged towards the hill.

'Aren't you coming?' Atalanta had asked.

'He was family. I should pay my respects,' was all the hero had replied. Pegasus too lingered by the lake, having returned to the island after flying away during the fight. With a bitter tang in her throat, Danae wondered if the horse too was in mourning.

'We should say something,' said Telamon.

Danae blinked, her thoughts returning to the hillside.

Atalanta and Telamon were gazing at her, waiting. The expectation in their weary eyes settled across her shoulders like a yoke.

Since learning she was the last daughter, she had sought out the people she believed would help her evolve into the warrior she must become. First Phineus and Prometheus, then Metis. Now there was no one left to teach her, no wise counsel to turn to. She had assumed that one day she would feel ready, that once she had mastered her powers she would unlock the secret of how to defeat Zeus. But now she knew that day would never come.

She would never stop being afraid, never stop feeling like she wasn't prepared. But despite that, she had killed a god. Perhaps she was enough, broken and unskilled as she was.

She drew a breath. 'From the earth we are born and to the earth we shall return. Gaia, take care of Metis' ichor as she returns to the tapestry.' She lowered the final stone cradled in her hand and placed it upon the burial mound.

The rusted grass shimmered about the island as it moved with the wind. Danae wondered if the woman's life force was now woven into its blades. It seemed fitting that Metis' threads should become part of the island she'd cared for.

'We can't stay here,' Danae said. 'The Olympians will send someone after Poseidon soon enough.'

'Agreed,' said Atalanta.

Danae's eyes travelled again to Heracles. 'You saw what happened with the sea-monster . . .' She turned back to her companions. 'He cannot come with us to face the false gods.'

Atalanta's gaze sharpened. 'We will not leave him behind. He has improved much these past weeks.'

Danae ran a hand over her face. 'If he comes to Olympus, he will be killed.'

Telamon folded his arms, his jaw set. 'If you want our help, Heracles is non-negotiable.'

You do not need them, whispered the voice. *You alone are the reckoning.*

But deep in her core, Danae knew that wasn't true. She would not have survived Poseidon if it weren't for Telamon and Atalanta. If it weren't for Metis. She could not do this alone.

She fought the ache that rose in her chest at the thought of the sacrifice made by the woman now cold as the stones upon her skin.

She sighed. 'Fine.'

They picked their way down the hillside to join Heracles and Pegasus beside the lake. The hero looked up as they approached, his eyes deep as the wine-dark sea.

'What now?' he rasped.

'You three sail in the boat. I'll follow above on Pegasus.' Danae gazed towards the land beyond Delos. 'We'll head to Myconos first. Regroup, gather supplies, then on to Olympus.'

'What are you going to do with Poseidon's armour?' asked Atalanta.

It lay in a golden pile beside the lake, along with the shattered remains of the trident, flecks of dried blood staining the metal like rust.

Danae had been wondering this herself. It's power-amplifying properties could be useful. At first, she thought she might wear it, but it was far too large, designed for a man at least a head taller than her.

'We take it. It could be of use, even if only as a disguise

once we reach Olympus. A way to gain entry to the palace.' She looked at Telamon. 'I was thinking perhaps . . .'

His pale eyes widened. 'You want me to dress up as the God of the Sea?'

'You're a similar build to Poseidon.'

'We can't just *sneak* into the palace of the gods – and even if we could, they would surely kill me once they discovered the deception.'

'I think it's a good plan,' said Atalanta.

'You put the armour on, then!'

The warrior glared at him. 'When did you become such a coward?'

'When I learnt there's no fucking afterlife!'

While they spoke, Heracles bent down and pulled on a gauntlet, wincing as the metal slid over his swollen joints. With effort, he straightened up. 'I will wear the armour.'

Danae looked between Telamon and Atalanta. They remained silent, avoiding her gaze.

She clenched her jaw and turned back to Heracles. 'It cannot be you.'

He turned to face her, chin held high. 'I have led armies, slain hundreds of men on a single battlefield. I am the one who should wear it.'

Danae's pulse quickened. 'The Olympians will know you are not one of them.'

The hero's gaze narrowed. 'Why?'

'Because . . . look at you!'

Atalanta inhaled a sharp breath as the gauntlet slipped from Heracles' hand to clatter against the earth.

'Heracles . . .' Danae called as the hero turned and stalked away towards the cliffs. Pegasus snorted, flexed his wings, then trotted after him.

Telamon shot a barbed look at Danae. 'I'll go.'

As he walked away Danae sighed. 'I don't know how to do this.'

'You could have been softer with him. But you weren't wrong.'

Danae glanced at Atalanta. The warrior was staring after the men, thoughts blustering across her face like wind-chased clouds. Then she looked at Danae, 'You're doing better than you think.'

Danae's heart swelled. She looked down at the battle-churned soil. 'Thank you.'

Atalanta grunted. They stood in silence for a moment.

'Poseidon would have killed me if you hadn't been there,' said Danae.

'I only did what I had to.'

The corners of Danae's mouth twitched. Atalanta was not half the liar she was.

'Come on, let's get the boat down to the shore.'

They walked over to the little rowing boat and began dragging it across the earth. Danae coughed as the wind gusted the scent of the sea-monster's dried blood caked on Atalanta's limbs.

'You smell like the inside of my father's fishing boat.'

Atalanta raised an eyebrow, then lifted her arm and sniffed her skin. She wrinkled her nose. 'You've got a point.'

Once they reached the sand, Atalanta dropped her end of the vessel and sprinted towards the glistening water, Skolopendra's corpse looming over her. She ran like a gazelle, sure-footed, swift and graceful. As she splashed into the shallows and dived beneath the waves, Danae felt an ache deep in her core. She imagined running after the warrior, letting the sea envelop her, the water sweeping around them both, drawing them close. Her cheeks reddened. Then something caught her eye. A shard of pottery, nestled in a crisp nest of seaweed. Danae glanced up towards the hillside. It must have tumbled down, propelled by the force of the collapsing hut when she rumbled the earth the previous night.

She bent down and picked it up. The edge of an owl's wing was visible on the clay. Her hands trembled as she traced the outline of the painted feathers, pressure building in her chest.

By the time Atalanta emerged from the water, Danae was undone.

'Danae?'

She knelt on the shore, mouth stretched wide, tears splashing onto her thighs, the shard of pottery digging into her palms.

Atalanta crouched beside her.

Danae's face ached, her cheeks stinging with salt. For a while she could not bring herself to speak. When she was able, she murmured, 'I called her a coward.'

'You can't dwell on that. Metis knew those words were said in the heat of anger.'

Danae looked up at the warrior through swollen eyes. 'Do you think she was right? Am I like the Olympians?'

Atalanta sat back on her heels.

'You are and you aren't.'

Danae's heart plummeted. That was not the answer she'd hoped for.

'It's not a bad thing. You killed another false god today. No mortal has ever done that. Perhaps being like them is what it takes to be the champion of mankind.'

Danae tried to find comfort in the warrior's words but she could not. Then her mind settled on the last part of what Atalanta had said. 'You believe I'm the champion of mankind?'

'That's what the prophecy says, doesn't it?'

As she held the warrior's gaze, light sparked in the hollow cavern of her chest.

Then the pound of footsteps sounded behind them.

Danae turned to see Telamon sprinting through the tawny grass, a bloody gash across his forehead.

'Heracles has gone,' he gasped.

Danae hurriedly wiped her face as she and Atalanta leapt to their feet.

'What?'

'He hit me,' Telamon pointed to his head. 'Came at me with a rock. By the time I was on my feet he was on the back of that horse, flying away.'

Icy dread seeped through Danae's body. 'Pegasus . . .' She tilted her face to the sky. There was nothing, just endless blue. No white wisps of cloud or airborne steeds. She wondered if this was how Heracles had felt, when he discovered she'd abandoned him. Perhaps this was his revenge. But Pegasus . . . the horse's betrayal cut like a silent blade. She had felt their bond weakening ever since she learnt his true name, but when the moment came, she'd hoped he would choose her.

'No.' Atalanta's voice was deep and hollow. 'He would never . . .'

'He's gone, Atalanta!'

'What did you say to him?' The warrior rounded on Telamon, pushing him in the chest.

'Nothing, he . . . oh gods.' Telamon ran a hand through his flame-red hair.

'What?'

'He said he couldn't go on like this.'

Atalanta paled. 'If he felt that way why would he take the horse?'

A terrible thought unfurled in Danae's mind. 'What if he tries to get more strength elixir from his father?'

'He wouldn't betray us,' said Atalanta quickly.

Telamon sank down into a squat, cupping his head in his hands.

Blood pounded in Danae's ears. How could she have been so careless? Heracles had worn his misery like an open wound, and she had just twisted the knife in deeper.

'He would never go to his father . . . not after everything Zeus has done to him.' Telamon shook his head, his eyes gleaming like polished bronze. 'He must have realized he couldn't come with us, not as he is. He's a proud man. He'd never have been able to admit that to us.'

Atalanta's limbs trembled. 'I'm going to kill him. If I ever see him again . . . I'm going to fucking kill him.' She stormed away across the shore.

Danae was about to follow the warrior when a strong hand stilled her.

'Leave her be. She'll come back in her own time.'

Danae watched her for a moment, then stepped back, freeing herself from Telamon's grasp.

'There is something I must do.'

She stalked the shore, collecting loose stones in the hem of her dress. Then she walked across the sand onto the dusty earth and paused by a scattered crop of yellow, violet and red blooms. She crouched, unfurling her bounty, and began to build a mound of rocks, the largest at the bottom, the smallest at the top.

When she was done, she knelt on the ground.

She had put finding Alea's ghost before her destiny, and it had almost cost her everything. Metis had told her the original Titans sacrificed all they were to become Gaia's champions. Now she must do the same. When she left Delos there could be no more distractions; her life was no longer her own.

'Wherever you are, I will never stop loving you and I will

never forget . . .' fresh tears streamed down her cheeks, 'but I cannot keep carrying you.'

Then she rose and walked back towards the sea.

Danae found Telamon sitting by the boat. Nestled in its belly was a bundle of Poseidon's armour, the shards of his trident and the collar that had subdued her powers, all wrapped in an old cloth salvaged from the wreckage of Metis' hut.

'You brought the trident and the collar.'

'I thought you might want them,' replied Telamon.

She frowned as she considered the jumble of metal. She did not know what she would do with them, but a spark of intuition told her they had not yet served their purpose.

'Good thinking.' She glanced about. 'No Atalanta?'

He shook his head.

'Should we go after her?'

'No. She'll come back when she's cooled down. Trust me.'

Danae lowered herself down beside him, and they both gazed out towards the ocean.

'I take it we're still sailing for Olympus?'

Danae nodded, then briefly closed her aching eyelids. 'Tell me a joke.'

Telamon looked thoughtful for a moment. 'A money lender from Mycenae died. When his family read the will, they discovered he'd named himself as heir.'

'I don't get it.'

He clicked his tongue. 'Everyone knows Mycenaean money lenders are the most miserly men in all of Greece.'

'Not everyone.'

Telamon glanced at her, his lip curled. 'Anyone who didn't grow up on a backward rock in the middle of the Aegean.'

Danae snorted. 'Where were you born that is so superior to Naxos?'

'Aegina. But I spent many years on Salamis.' He let out a long, wistful breath. 'Now *that* is an island. Finest olive groves in Greece, and the women, ah the women . . .' a dreamy expression softened his face. 'Hips like ripe figs and skin so soft when they wrap their thighs around you –'

'I get it.'

Telamon glanced at her. 'Although perhaps not quite to your taste. I suspect you enjoy a tougher variety of fruit.'

Danae swallowed. He was steering the conversation into waters she did not wish to sail. 'Aboard the *Argo*, Peleus told me about your younger brother Phocus' accident. It wasn't your fault the discus hit him, you know that?'

Telamon stiffened. 'Ah.' He paused. 'Be that as it may, mine was the hand that threw it.'

'Is that why you went to Salamis?'

He nodded. 'A blood crime like fratricide requires cleansing by an anointed king. Luckily, Cychreus of Salamis was happy to do the honours.' He barked out a laugh that didn't ease the weight behind his eyes. 'I was lucky, where Heracles was sent on death-defying labours by Eurystheus, as penance for the death of his family, I was given Cychreus' blessing to marry his lovely daughter, Periboea.'

'You have a wife?' Danae did not know why she found this surprising. Many men left their spouses at home to seek glory in battle and pleasure in strangers' beds, but Telamon had always struck her as incapable of any serious attachment. Despite the crinkling lines at the corners of his eyes, she'd always thought of him as boyish. But looking at him now, she realized he must be a similar age to Heracles; perhaps a few summers past his thirtieth year.

Telamon gazed out across the bay. He looked the most sombre she'd ever seen him.

'Oh yes, and a child. We were children ourselves, both

barely sixteen when we married. To have a wife at that age was one thing, but a baby.' The sea shimmered in his eyes. 'I fled a month after my son was born. You see, I have always been a coward.'

'I would never call you that.'

Telamon smiled ruefully. 'Fighting's easy, but taking responsibility for others . . . that requires real bravery.'

There was a crunch behind them. Danae turned to see Atalanta striding across the beach. She and Telamon rose to their feet.

'If you two have finished gossiping, shall we get a move on?'

Danae's mouth twitched into a smile.

They dragged the boat into the shallows and clambered in. Telamon took up the oars and rowed them out of the crescent bay, past the rock where the silver-winged gulls nested, onto the open sea.

Danae gazed back one last time towards Delos, and the tiny mound of rocks just visible on its peak, then down at its smaller twin at the edge of the sea.

'Goodbye,' she whispered, the wind stealing the word the moment it left her lips.

PART THREE

36. The Fury of Fire

Typhon, the dragon, soared through the crisp air, his emerald scales gleaming in the sunlight. Far below, hazed through layers of cloud, the sparkling sea winked. Goading him.

Freedom ignited the furnace of his lungs. The clouds sizzled over his burning belly, his vast wings churning their misted bodies like a riptide. His limbs still ached from centuries of confinement, but the agony of his grating bones in flight was ecstasy after being cramped in the watery depths of Tartarus.

Typhon thought of the smouldering bones of his captor and felt joy.

The dragon beat his wings and surged higher, up to where the air was thin and frost cold. Never again would he succumb to a body of water. Never again.

The world had sickened since his imprisonment centuries earlier. He had sensed it as he flew through the cavernous space beneath the earth. Even in the deep, so far from Gaia's skin, he had felt her pain echoing up to the silver stars.

Typhon looked to the west, where the men that called themselves gods had built their palace of stone.

A rumble rippled through his gut. It had been too long since his last meal. If he did not eat soon, he would perish. And perish he must not, for he was the last of his kind. He felt the truth of it in his bones, in the heat of his molten marrow.

He was the last dragon.

Typhon understood now why the Mother doted so on her

undeserving children. To give life, to see oneself reflected, even in a shattered mirror, was better than not being able to perceive oneself at all.

He sniffed the air and followed the verdant scent of a forest, diving down below the cloud line. The earth was bathed in gold, the sun ripening before relinquishing its watch to the pale moon.

Then a dash of movement caught his eye. He dipped lower, salivating at the thought of more fresh meat after centuries of mouldering scraps.

Yet he paused before unleashing his flames. He knew that scent. It had been his constant companion during his imprisonment.

Below, lumbering towards the trees, were three giants who, like Typhon, had found their way above ground.

Ravenous as he was, he could not bring himself to feast upon his ancient companions. They were united in suffering at the hands of the gilded men.

The dragon flew on, until another scent snared his attention: a herd of cattle, burnished bronze in the Hesperides light.

He swooped.

The delectable scent of charred flesh filled the air as he unleashed a bellow of fire across the field. A few cows escaped the blaze, lowing as they cantered away from his flame's reach.

He growled in frustration. Despite weeks in the open air, his heat was dulled from his imprisonment, his body still riddled with the murky waters of the Underworld. He must be patient. Sure as the tide of life ebbs and flows, he would regain his strength. And take his revenge.

His thoughts were drawn to more pleasurable musings as he devoured the smoking cattle caught by his blaze. As the flavours burst over his tongue, he dug his claws into the earth and exalted in the tingle of the tapestry of life working through him. He had been drowned for so long, there were so many joys he was only just remembering.

Newly revived, Typhon launched into the air, sending a plume of fire to clear the clouds in his path. But his victory cry turned to a roar as pain lanced through his right wing. He turned his head to see a bolt of lightning sizzle through his scales like a glowing thorn.

The sky was no longer his.

A golden figure rode across the clouds on the back of a winged ebony steed. Recognition sparked in Typhon's mind as he recalled a man with eyes of sun-drenched sea casting him down, down, down into the depths of the earth.

He twisted, soaring towards the little godling with a burst of fire. But the man anticipated his movement, darting up into the treacherous clouds that swallowed him from view. The dragon pursued him, rage blunting his progress as the man flitted through the sky on his horse like a golden insect. He would end in smouldering ashes just like his kin.

Typhon filled his lungs once more, blasting flame across the dusky sky. It was only when a great body of ocean opened up beneath him that he realized his mistake. His fire was all but spent, and now there was no earth to hold him if he tired, only inked sky and sea. Twin conspirators with the golden man.

But the dragon had a few tricks of his own.

Typhon let his wings sag and tumbled towards the ocean, as though he were exhausted enough to let it swallow him whole. The little god left the cover of the clouds and flew after him, no doubt eager to watch the dragon be claimed by the watery depths.

At the last moment, Typhon twisted, the chill of the sea almost at his wings, and sent a blast of boiling air shooting towards his attacker. It caught the wing of the godling's steed, and the animal screeched, careering through the air as its rider fought to say astride.

The dragon surged upwards, snatching the golden man from his wounded horse. Typhon flew towards a landmass on the horizon, crushing the man's metal shell beneath his claws. The creature squirmed in his grip, forcing his stolen life force against the might of Typhon's talons. But the dragon had centuries of vengeance in his veins, and he met the man's power with his own.

He landed on the peak of a snow-swathed mountain and held his foe out before him.

'You have lost your way since last we met.' Typhon's cavernous voice rumbled across the land, sending plains of ice sluicing down the mountainside. 'You have grown weak, Titan.'

The golden man smiled, baring each of his minuscule teeth.

'You are mistaken, dragon. You may have wings, but I am master of the sky.'

Rage ensnared Typhon and, despite his dreams of an exquisitely lengthy revenge, he opened his jaws to deliver the man a swift end.

The dragon hesitated at a sudden crackling sound above his head. His jaws snapped shut, and he looked up to see a storm roiling above him. Thunder rolled across the heavens. Then came the lightning.

Rods of agony shot through him as he was stabbed again and again by searing bolts, slicing through his armoured scales as if they were soft clay. Typhon loosened his grip, and the golden man burst from the dragon's claws, glowing life-threads crackling around him as he rose into the air on nothing but the wind itself.

'I am Zeus, the Lord of Thunder, and I will send you back to the darkness from which you came.'

The dragon tried to draw air into the furnace of his lungs, but the barbs of lightning robbed his breath.

Then the earth groaned. The snow-encrusted crag split open and swallowed Typhon whole.

37. The Many-Faced Man

'Row faster!' Atalanta crouched at the prow of the little sailing vessel, elbows resting on her scarred knees, the ruby glow of dusk pooling in the rivets of her silver breastplate.

'Still your tongue, woman,' Telamon grumbled as he heaved the oars. He glanced over his shoulder at Danae, 'Can't you do something with those Titan powers of yours? Conjure us a breath of wind?'

Danae shook her head. 'I need to conserve my strength.'

The island of Myconos had looked so close from the shore of Delos, yet now it seemed to grow further away with each stroke of the oars.

Atalanta scowled. 'This next island better have wine.'

Danae closed her eyes and took comfort in the familiar rocking of the boat. When she cast her mind too far ahead, her chest tightened and breathing became difficult, so she focused on what would happen next. They would land at Myconos and find shelter for the night. Tomorrow was a problem she would face with the dawn.

'We've got company.'

Danae's eyes snapped open. She looked to where Atalanta pointed, and her heart tripped.

A sleek black penteconter with a billowing white sail was heading towards them.

Had the Olympians already sent reinforcements after Poseidon?

Telamon stilled the oars, his hand travelling to the sword lying beside him on the bench. 'Looks like it's heading to Delos.'

The ship was a little larger than the *Argo*, with space for around fifty rowers. No figurehead presided over its prow, but the all-seeing eye of the Twelve was painted on either hull, and a row of bronze shields lined its sides. The benches only seemed to be half full, but from their armour, the occupants appeared to be soldiers.

'The shields,' whispered Atalanta, 'they're Ithacan.'

Danae knew little of Ithaca, only that it was an island far from Naxos, located on the other side of mainland Greece in the Ionian Sea.

'Danae . . .' said Telamon in a low voice, his green eyes fixed on the penteconter.

'I've got enough strength to use my powers if I must.' She set her jaw, gathering her life-threads into her hands.

Telamon kept his sword hidden below the lip of their boat, likewise Atalanta readied her bow out of sight. They were at a disadvantage to the larger vessel, but if it came to it, Danae was sure she could hold the men off long enough for her comrades to climb aboard and subdue the crew. That is, if there wasn't an Olympian on board.

Their little tub bobbed violently in the swell as the ship drew closer. The penteconter's rowers hauled in their oars as they approached, several men clustering to the starboard side of the deck.

'You there!' called a plain-clothed man in a teal tunic and grey cloak, as he gestured towards Delos. 'Have you come from that land, yonder?' He was of medium build, and his features were ordinary, forgettable even. He was neither tall nor short, and looked to be around his fortieth year. His wavy hair was the hue of a walnut, his weather-creased skin richly tanned as though he spent much of his days outdoors. He didn't look threatening, yet Danae had survived too much strife to take anything at face value.

'Who's asking?' replied Atalanta, her nonchalant tone at odds with the concealed arrow that could pierce the man's jugular in the space of two breaths.

As she spoke another man appeared beside the first. He too wore a plain tunic, rather than armour, but Danae assumed he must also be a soldier. He leant upon a wooden crutch, his arms covered in prominent scars, his face partially obscured by long chestnut curls buffeted by the breeze.

At the sight of them, the second man stiffened. Then he whispered into the first man's ear. As she watched the fervent exchange, Danae's skin prickled like an animal sensing rain before the first drop has fallen. The man who had called to them grew very still, focusing on Danae as though she had suddenly swallowed the sun.

Pulse thumping, she realized she barely had moments to act. If this man knew who she was, and what she could do, they had lost the crucial element of surprise.

She flung her arms out, throwing her shimmering lifethreads into the sea. Taking her cue, Atalanta rose to standing, an arrow drawn at her cheek. But before either of them could attack, Telamon sprang to his feet, tipping their boat into a violent sway.

'By the fates!'

'What?' Danae hissed, threads snapping back inside her as she stumbled.

Telamon ignored her, lowering his sword as he stared in slack-jawed amazement at the scarred man.

Danae's eyes snapped to the stranger. His gaze met hers. Familiarity blossomed at the corners of her mind. They looked at each other for a breath, then her heart imploded. It felt as though she'd been punched backwards through time, falling into an endless cascade of memory.

A ghost. A friend who had fought by her side, who had tried to kiss her then saved her life before he was ripped from the deck of the *Argo* by an Earthborn's vicious claws. A companion whose death she'd imagined over and over again. The man whose name she had given to her winged steed.

But she had imagined a fate that had never come to pass.

Atalanta's bow clattered to the floor of their little boat. 'Hylas!'

Danae could not move, heart thundering against her ribs as a swell of emotion coursed through her. She was afraid to blink, as though at any moment the mirage of her friend would disappear.

'It seems the fates have indeed been weaving their webs,' said the man in the teal tunic, watching the exchange with an air of controlled calm. 'Come aboard, friends of Hylas.'

No one moved.

'Who are these men?' Telamon called to Hylas.

Without waiting for him to reply, the first man smiled, the dying light gleaming in his eyes. 'I am Odysseus, King of Ithaca.'

Danae barely registered his words. She felt as though she were wading through a dream, the air thick and blurred with sleep. Atalanta's and Telamon's eyes flicked between her and Hylas. It took her a moment to realize that they were waiting for her instruction.

Something about this Odysseus filled her with unease. He was impossible to read, like sand washed clean of footprints. She could not tell if he was friend or foe. But Hylas was with him. That had to count for something.

Hylas was alive.

'We go aboard,' she said thickly.

They secured their rowing boat with rope thrown down by Odysseus' men to one of the ladder pegs bolted to the starboard side of the ship, then climbed up. Danae carried the bundle of Poseidon's armour, shattered trident and the collar slung over her shoulder. It was cumbersome, but too precious to be left unattended in the little tub.

The soldiers moved away from them, retreating to the benches as the three pulled themselves up onto the stern deck. There was something strange about the way the soldiers looked at Danae and only her, their faces flushed not only with the last vestiges of light, but something else. Something like wonder.

A breath slipped between her lips as Odysseus and Hylas clambered up to the deck to meet them. Her old friend was much changed. In addition to the scars on his limbs, Hylas' left cheek bore the deep gouges of an Earthborn's claws, and his left leg ended just below the knee, a false limb with a moving ankle joint fashioned from oiled wood attached via leather straps.

Odysseus took a couple of measured steps towards them. His features might be ordinary, but his eyes were sharp and flecked with amber, like a wolf's.

Suddenly, she remembered that these men were not privy to the secrets she and her companions had learnt on Delos and swiftly intoned the sacred greeting, 'May the Twelve see you and know you.'

Odysseus did not raise his hand to his forehead in response. He watched her carefully. Then his face cracked into a smile.

'My lord,' said Hylas, 'these are my old companions from my days travelling with Heracles – Telamon, Atalanta and . . . Daeira.' He spoke her name as though it were a gem freshly pared from the earth: precious with edges that could slice skin.

Danae stared at him, trying to fit her memory to the man stood before her. It was not just his appearance that had changed – there was a coldness to his demeanour that had not been there before.

Then Telamon cut in, striding forward and scooping Hylas into an embrace. 'How in Tartarus are you alive?'

Hylas blinked as the flame-haired man released him, his cheeks flushing. 'Because the fates wished it.'

'Indeed . . .' said Odysseus, his eyes raking over the strangers to his ship. 'Nothing has been seen or heard of the hero, Heracles, since the usurped Eurystheus sent him to the Underworld. Where is your leader?'

Danae could feel Atalanta and Telamon tense beside her. 'We don't know,' she said quietly.

A shadow of worry flickered across Hylas' face.

'A pity,' said Odysseus, his amber eyes betraying nothing.

Danae wished a cloud would swallow the low sun, everything was so bright, the reflected light piercing her eyes from every shining blade and curve of armour.

It was then she noticed the gold pin at the gather of Odysseus' cloak, the image of an apple tree stamped upon it. Hylas too wore a similar brooch attached to the left shoulder of his tunic.

Pulse quickening, she asked, 'What is your business in this part of the Aegean?'

Odysseus smiled, his expression a veneer of courtly grace. 'I was summoned to Delos. Fortunately, my ship happened to be nearby when I received the call.' He prised his fingers beneath the collar of his tunic and pulled out a chain. Dangling from it was Metis' bronze medallion, engraved with the Hesperides tree.

'This amulet is infused with the blood of my ancestors. Prometheus fashioned it forty generations ago and gave it to the first of his followers. It acts as a compass, guiding a bird towards the nearest person who shares kin blood. Which, as my father is back in Ithaca, was me.' This was who Metis had called upon when Poseidon came. Guilt hollowed

Danae's chest. Even as she had accused Metis of summoning the gods, the woman had already chosen to fight on their side. Perhaps she had even known she would not survive the encounter with the God of the Sea.

Odysseus slipped the pendant back inside his tunic. 'I believe the false gods use similar medallions to commune with their priestesses.'

'False gods . . .' she repeated.

Odysseus' lips twitched.

'What are you, besides your royal title?'

'I think you know,' he said softly.

'Say it.'

Odysseus inclined his head. 'I am a loyal member of the Children of Prometheus.'

Danae's heart thundered so fast she could barely hear him. The secret organization of mortals who kept Prometheus' prophecy alive so that she, the last daughter, might one day overthrow the gods. Manto, the brave person who had first revealed the prophecy to Danae, and their father, the exiled seer Phineus, had both been members. As she thought of them, the recollection of something Manto had said darted across her mind. 'A member of the Children would never reveal themselves.'

Odysseus' smile broadened to a grin. 'Oh, but they would . . . to the last daughter.'

Danae took a step back, the metal bundled in her hands clinking as she moved.

Odysseus fell to his knee, all studious calm stripped away. His men followed, sinking in a ripple across the ship. She looked at Hylas, seeking the reassurance she often used to find in his face, but was met only with a cold stare, then a flash of irritation as he leant on his crutch and slowly lowered himself to the ground, his wooden leg bending beneath him on its ankle joint.

Danae glanced at Telamon and Atalanta. They were the only two left standing.

The warrior curled her lip. 'I'm not fucking kneeling.'

'Get up.' Danae's face burned.

Odysseus and Hylas obliged, but the crew remained in reverence.

'What makes you think I'm the person you seek?'

'I'd heard whispers from my contacts in Delphi that the last daughter had come and destroyed the oracle – *when the prophet falls*. Then I crossed paths with Hylas, and he told me of your abilities.' Odysseus' eyes gleamed. 'I knew you must be the one from Prometheus' prophecy.'

Danae's brow creased. She was sure that when Manto rescued her from the prison beneath Apollo's sanctuary, they had told her that they were the only person who knew the last daughter had come. Perhaps they had been mistaken.

'We are, all of us here, members of the Children of Prometheus,' Odysseus continued, gesturing about the ship. 'Every man here is your humble servant, honoured to lay down his life for the cause.'

Danae stared at him, each beat of her heart driving a wave of relief through her chest. Part of her still couldn't believe this was real. Hylas' return from the dead had stripped away all her cunning.

'Tell me,' pressed Odysseus, 'why has Metis summoned me? My father passed down the knowledge from my ancestors that she will not stand against the Olympians. Perhaps your coming has changed her mind?'

The sun had been swallowed by the sea, the chill of the

night creeping over the ship. Danae shivered, her throat thickening as she thought of Metis' body lying cold and lifeless upon the earth.

'She sent for you because Poseidon came to the island.'

Odysseus' eyebrows rose. 'What became of that encounter?'

Danae hesitated for a moment, then untied the bundled fabric in her hands.

'He is dead.'

Gold clanged onto the deck, a shard of trident skidding to a halt at Hylas' sandal. He gazed down at the pieces of metal, then his eyes flicked up to meet Danae's. Something flashed through his gaze, like a star shooting across the darkness. It happened so quickly she could not divine what it was.

Odysseus laughed, a full belly rumble. He turned to his men. 'The last daughter has already begun to deliver us from the tyranny of the Olympians, who are no longer twelve, but eleven!'

'Ten,' corrected Atalanta.

Odysseus spun to face her.

The warrior squared her shoulders. 'Hades too is slain.'

Light danced in Odysseus' eyes. He looked down at the scattered fragments of armour and trident as though they were a puzzle he must piece together.

'And what of Metis? Does she await us on Delos?'

'She died fighting Poseidon,' Danae said quietly.

The joyous spark died in Odysseus' eyes.

'That is a great loss. For all of us. My father raised me on stories of Metis and Prometheus, true Titans who stood against Zeus' tyranny. I never believed she would call for my bloodline in my lifetime, but I hoped, and when that gull flew to my ship, the medallion around its neck . . .'

'Prometheus too is gone.'

Odysseus' gaze sharpened.

'I spoke with him atop the Caucasus Mountains, before Hera attacked, slaying him.'

'What did he tell you?' breathed Odysseus.

'Things I suspect you already know.' She wondered how much of the truth he, Hylas and the rest of his men knew. Manto had only been privy to a fraction of the twisted history of the gods, yet Odysseus did not seem surprised by Danae's words.

He regarded her for a moment, then said, 'You and your companions must come with me, Daeira.'

She winced at the use of her false, Argonaut name. 'My name is Danae.'

Again, she caught a flicker of feeling dart across Hylas' face. This time he did not hide it so well. It looked an awful lot like anger.

'We have a long journey back to Troy,' continued Odysseus. 'And much to discuss on our way.'

'We're not going to Troy.'

Odysseus blinked. 'Where, might I ask, are you going?'

Danae shifted her feet on the oiled deck, widening her stance. 'If you know who I am, then you know what I am destined to do. Where I must go.'

'Surely you do not mean to sail for Olympus in *that*.' He glanced down at the rowing boat.

'We will change vessels at Myconos.'

Odysseus' eyes swept over Telamon and Atalanta. 'Your army is currently rather small.'

'Size isn't everything,' quipped Atalanta.

Odysseus' lip curled. 'Do you really believe the three of you will successfully storm Mount Olympus and defeat the most powerful god in the Pantheon? And what of the rest of them? Prometheus' prophecy foretells that you will end Zeus' reign. It says nothing of the other Olympians. If you are not careful, you might kill Zeus only for a new King or Queen of Heaven to be crowned in his stead.'

There was a pause before Telamon murmured, 'He has a point.'

'All of us here have spent our lives in the service of the Children of Prometheus, at great personal risk, all in aid of ensuring your victory against the false gods,' Odysseus pressed, an idea igniting behind his eyes. 'I know for certain several of the younger gods plan to watch the coming battle for Troy. With my men at your side, we could kill them. Thin the herd, clearing your path to take Olympus.'

Danae looked at the crew. They were still kneeling between the benches, gazing at her like she was salvation incarnate.

Odysseus drew close enough to whisper in her ear, 'I too know the extent of the gods' lies. I have been to the Underworld. I have seen that the dead do not live beneath the earth.'

A chill shuddered through her limbs. Her scalp prickled, as though bony fingers were tracing through her hair.

She glanced once more at the men on the mid-deck. 'You only have around forty soldiers here.'

'There are a hundred more loyal Children of Prometheus men waiting at Troy,' Odysseus said swiftly. 'Your very own army.'

'Come with us, Danae,' said Hylas.

For a moment she allowed herself to imagine what it would feel like to have an army beside her, her old companions reunited. No more lies souring the bond between them.

'My lord,' called one of the soldiers from the mid-deck. 'The sun has set – would you have us land at Delos for the night?'

'No.' Odysseus tilted his head to the west. 'Sail for

Myconos.' He looked back at Danae. 'We can at least bear you that far?'

She took them all in; the strangers who looked at her with wonder, her companions, the friend she thought had left this world. Hope was the cruellest blade of all. Hers had been dashed too many times; she did not know if she had the strength to let it live within her again.

Her gaze returned to Hylas, the man who had twice sacrificed his life to save her. So much time had passed, and so much had changed. But perhaps the person he had been was still there. The man she knew. The man she could trust. The man who had loved her.

'We will come with you as far as Myconos, and I will think on what you have said.'

Odysseus flashed her a gleaming smile. 'As you wish.'

38. A Seer's Choice

Odysseus' ship docked at Myconos harbour under a pathway of stars. A scatter of mud-brick buildings clustered around the bay and across the surrounding hillside, their windows glowing with firelight.

Danae, Telamon and Atalanta joined Odysseus, Hylas and four of the Ithacan soldiers in going ashore, while the rest of the men remained on the ship. Danae carried her bundle of Poseidon's armour, the trident and the collar slung over her shoulder. The bounty was too precious to be left on board. Two of the soldiers ran ahead, the other pair lingering a pace behind Danae.

By the time they entered the heart of the little town, the first soldiers returned, a set of rooms procured. As they headed towards the lodgings, the smell of roasted meat wafted down the narrow street, driven by the wind that had chased them all the way from Delos. A kapeleion stood on the corner, voices and hearth-smoke curling from the windows and doorway.

'I'll see you at dawn,' said Atalanta.

Before Danae could reply, the warrior darted down the street and disappeared into the kapeleion.

'Don't mind if I do,' said Telamon, striding after her. When he reached the doorway he glanced over his shoulder. 'Danae, Hylas, you coming?'

Danae lingered. She would love nothing more than to join her companions and drown the night in wine. But she knew she must keep a clear head. She had a decision to make.

'I need rest. I'll see you tomorrow.'

Telamon looked expectantly at Hylas, who glanced at Odysseus, then said, 'Not tonight.'

The flame-haired man shrugged. 'Please yourself. But don't think you've escaped recounting your tale.'

Hylas' face broke into a half-smile, and for a moment his coldness thawed, and he looked like himself again. 'I know you'll get it out of me whether I want to tell it or not.'

Telamon grinned then followed Atalanta into the depths of the kapeleion.

'The rooms are this way, my lord.' One of the soldiers gestured further down the street.

The weight of Poseidon's armour dragged down her back as Danae followed Odysseus and Hylas to the end of the row of buildings, the soldiers ghosting her steps.

One of Odysseus' men pushed open the door of a modest single-room hut. A lone candle glowed from within. The furniture was sparse. A faded rug stretched over the floor, and a pallet rested against the far wall with a single table and stool to its left.

'I will have my men bring you food while I attend to a small matter of business.' Odysseus shared a look with Hylas. 'I'm sure you two have much to catch up on.'

Danae set down her bundle at the foot of the pallet. Hylas lingered in the doorway, leaning on his crutch.

'You can come in.'

He did so and closed the door behind him, leaving the soldiers to stand guard.

Even as she watched him walk over to the stool and lower himself down, she still could not quite believe he was real. She was afraid that, like a dream in which the dead once more walk the earth, she would blink and find that he was not really Hylas at all, but a stranger whom grief had painted in the likeness of her friend.

But ghosts did not bear scars of the flesh. Those wounds were her doing. She might as well have gouged them herself.

'I thought you were dead.'

Hylas ran a hand through his curls. The longer hair suited him. He looked leaner, sharper, older than the youth she had known. She wondered if she too appeared as changed as she felt within. Then she remembered: her features were frozen in time. She pressed the thought away as she sank down onto the pallet.

Hylas watched her. 'For a while, so did I.'

'How did you survive?'

'The Earthborn that snatched me took me back to its nest – a cave in the mountain. Then a fight broke out. I think over which would eat me . . .' He paused at the horror blooming across Danae's face. 'In the chaos, I hid. I waited for two days until all of them had left the cave. Then I seized my chance and escaped.'

She could tell he was trying to spare her the worst of it.

'You didn't see Heracles?' During the battle with the Earthborn, the hero had dived from the deck of the fleeing *Argo* and returned to the Doliones shore in an attempt to save Hylas from the six-armed beasts.

Hylas shook his head, his brow furrowed.

'He went back for you . . .'

Hylas' eyes widened. Then he winced, stretching out his false leg. He undid the leather straps and removed it, then massaged the end of his limb.

Danae stared at the wooden leg, marvelling at how something carved from a tree could move like a limb of flesh and bone. She had never seen anything like it.

'Brilliant, isn't it?' Hylas flexed the leg, the ankle joint rolling. Danae caught a couple of glints of bronze as it moved, the pins that must hold the contraption together. 'The inventor, Daedalus, made it. He's incredible – you'll meet him when we reach Troy – if you come with us,' he added swiftly. 'There's nothing that man can't create.'

'How did it happen?'

Hylas was silent a moment. 'The Earthborn like to play with their food.'

Danae swallowed. 'And then . . . once you escaped? How did you come to travel with Odysseus? Have you always known about the Children of Prometheus?'

Hylas shifted his weight forward, leaning on his crutch. 'I made it back to the beach. The Doliones took pity on me, treated my injuries as best they could. I lived with them for a few weeks, until Odysseus came,' his eyes settled on Danae, 'looking for you.'

Another bare bone of an answer.

'How did he know I'd been there?'

'He knows many things. And before you ask, I did not know of the Children of Prometheus before I met Odysseus. He told me who you really are.' An edge had crept back into his voice. 'His vision for the future is unlike anything I've ever heard before. A world without gods, without priestesses, each person in command of their own destiny . . .' Her doubt must have been written on her face, as he added, 'You can trust him.'

His words hung in the air between them.

'How much did he tell you?'

Hylas watched her. 'I know the truth of what lies in the Underworld, if that's what you mean.'

She drew a breath. 'How did you know you could believe Odysseus when he told you?'

'Because when he spoke of the last daughter, I knew in my bones it was you. I have faith in him, Danae. I believe he can help you win this war.'

Faith. There it was again, that word that held mountains. She wondered how he could offer his so easily, when she found it so terribly hard.

'Hylas . . .' Words failed her. She remembered the last moment they'd shared together before they charged into battle with the Earthborn. The two of them squeezed together on the viewing platform inside the Doliones' cave. He had tried to kiss her. And in return she'd left him to be savaged by those six-armed beasts. Another casualty of her destiny.

As though he could divine her thoughts, Hylas murmured, 'It's all right, Danae.'

'No, it's not.' Tears stung her eyes and spilled down her cheeks. 'I left you. I just stood there and let that thing take you. I could have used my powers, I could have jumped into the sea and swum back to you —'

'You couldn't have done any of those things. I carried you to the ship, remember? You couldn't stand, let alone save me.'

'Don't. Stop making it easy for me.'

He huffed a sharp breath. 'What do you want me to say? That I hate you?'

'Yes.'

'I don't.'

'You should. I lied to you about who I was, I concealed my true mission. I only joined Heracles' crew because I overheard you were joining Jason's expedition sailing for the end of the world, and that's where I needed to go to find Prometheus.' She paused. 'I chose following my destiny over your life.'

Something raw flickered in the depths of Hylas' eyes. 'You

did what you had to do. You are the hope of mankind.' His voice was hollow, as though repeating something he had learnt.

Danae stood, her blood racing. 'I lied to you! I left you to die. Don't you care?'

A muscle pulsed in Hylas' jaw.

'All right,' he said quietly. 'I didn't just hide in the Earthborn's nest, then escape. I slit the belly of a dead one with its own claws and climbed inside. I lay there, in that stinking carcass, for two days until finally, when the others were out hunting, an opportunity came to crawl out of the cave. Yes crawl, because my leg had all but been chewed off. I dragged myself down the mountain, and the pain was so excruciating that when I reached the cliff I threw myself over the edge. But the fall didn't kill me, so I lay there, on that gods-forsaken shore amongst the rotting corpses, praying for death. But the Doliones found me instead. They cut my damaged leg off then and there. I can still feel it. The limb has gone but the pain wakes me in the night. Gnaws at me every godsdamned day.'

She stared at him, eyes stinging with salt. 'I'm sorry,' she whispered, the word a drop in the well of her remorse.

Hylas shook his head, lips pressed together. 'I care. I didn't realize how much until I saw you.' He drew a breath. 'Still, you are here now and two of the Twelve are dead. Every man in Odysseus' army would do what I did for you on the Doliones shore, because they believe like I do, like Odysseus does. Don't let your pride stand in the way of your destiny.'

Danae wiped her face. His belief burned so bright she could not look at him.

Have faith.

She forced herself to meet her friend's gaze. 'We will

come with you to Troy. We will face whatever awaits us there together.'

Hylas blinked as though he hadn't expected her to give in so easily.

A knock sounded at the door.

'That will be the food,' said Hylas.

'Come in,' called Danae.

The door swung open to reveal Odysseus. For a moment, Danae wondered if he'd been outside the entire time, listening to their conversation. But there was a swathe of black fabric in his arms.

'I thought, if you did decide to join us, it would be prudent for you to take on a disguise.' From beneath the fabric, he produced a blade. 'I believe you are familiar with the duties of a seer.'

Danae's heart sank. She glanced between the two men. It looked as though Hylas was holding his breath.

'All right. I will come with you.'

Odysseus' weathered face broke into a grin. 'Excellent.' He slipped across the room and lay the clothing down on the pallet, alongside the knife. 'We shall leave you to it.'

For a moment, Danae expected Hylas to offer to cut her hair, like he'd once done aboard the *Argo,* as seers were expected to wear their hair cropped. But he rose and followed Odysseus out into the street, leaving her alone with the shadow of her lies draped across the pallet, a skin she must don once more.

39. Lure of the Sea

Danae emerged from her lodgings, dressed in the obsidian seer's robe and matching cloak. The yellow light of dawn spilled through the narrow streets like pressed oil. Odysseus' guards were waiting for her outside. Silently, they escorted her back to the ship, snatching sideways glances at her as they walked.

Once aboard, she tucked her bundle of broken armour, trident and collar behind a barrel in the prow cabin. A strong northerly wind whipped her crop of hair as she emerged onto the mid-deck. She ran a hand through her short curls, and a smile tugged at her lips. Reluctant as she'd been when Odysseus first suggested she slip into her old role, it was strangely comforting to be back in the familiar disguise.

As she climbed up to the prow deck, Telamon's voice boomed across the ship, regaling Hylas, Odysseus and Atalanta with last night's antics.

'. . . by the time Hylas joined us, the man was four drachmas down and ready to throw his eldest daughter into the bargain.'

Hylas laughed. 'You lost a round later, as I recall.'

Danae was pricked with jealousy. Hylas had evidently joined Telamon and Atalanta in the kapeleion after leaving her room. They'd all been together, without her.

'The game was rigged,' grumbled Telamon.

'Can't rig petteia.' Atalanta leant on the prow rail. 'You lost because you're an arrogant arse who doesn't know when to take his coin and leave.'

'You can talk,' Telamon began, then noticed Danae. 'Ah! You look like Daeira, the Seer, again.'

'Yes, we must think of a new name for you,' said Odysseus. 'It cannot be the one known by the Argonauts.'

'What of Danae?' asked Hylas.

'No,' she said sharply. She had so little of the Danae from Naxos left, she did not want to pollute her true name with another false identity. Besides, Heracles now knew her by that name. She had no idea where the hero had gone, who he might have spoken to . . .

A hand brushed her arm. 'You all right?' Atalanta had moved to her side, dark eyes searching Danae's face. The warrior's lids were heavy, her breath laced with yesterday's wine.

'I'm fine,' Danae replied, with more of a barb than she intended.

Atalanta folded her arms, raising an eyebrow. 'Doris.'

Danae glared at her. 'No.'

'Dione?' offered Odysseus. 'A strong seer's name.'

She considered it. 'Dione it is.'

As the ship left Myconos harbour, its sail spread wide like the wings of a swan, she glanced behind her at the Ithacan soldiers sitting idle on the rowing benches. They were doing an admirable job of pretending they hadn't been watching her.

'You're sure you trust these men?' she asked Odysseus.

'With my life. Like me they've been taught the ways of the Children of Prometheus from their parents and their parents' parents by their forebears before that.'

'We are all here to help you,' added Hylas.

Danae wondered how he'd gone from being a wounded Argonaut rescued by Odysseus from the Doliones shore to a trusted member of the King of Ithaca's inner circle. Hylas was brave and loyal, but Danae sensed these were not the qualities that had convinced Odysseus to keep him close.

She walked to the ship's rail and looked out over the turquoise ocean, the sea darkening as they entered the open waters of the Aegean. For a while the wind drove them onwards, until the sea's breath lulled and the men were forced to row.

There were footsteps on the deck behind her, then Odysseus appeared at Danae's side.

'Tell me, in Delphi, were you given a shard of the omphalos stone?'

Danae's insides twisted. 'Yes . . . I was given it by Manto, a member of the Children and one of the bravest, fiercest and most brilliant people I've ever met.' She swallowed. 'But it is lost now.'

Odysseus' hands tightened on the ship's rail. 'Lost? If that shard falls into the hands of the Olympians –'

'Hades took it from me in the Underworld and he is now dead. He concealed my presence from the other gods and wished to use me as a weapon to overthrow his brother, Zeus. I doubt he would have told Olympus that he had the stone.'

Odysseus considered her. After a pause he asked, 'Tell me, how did he die?'

Danae drew a lungful of fresh, salty air. 'The ferryman, Charon, set free the dragon, Typhon, who was imprisoned in the Underworld. It burned Hades' flesh from his bones.'

'I'd heard tales,' breathed Odysseus, 'but it is true, the dragon exists. One would hope the creature is now bent on revenge . . .' For a moment he seemed lost to his thoughts, then the sharpness returned to his gaze, and he turned, calling Hylas, Telamon and Atalanta to him, guiding them close to Danae. 'I must ask that you tell no one beyond this deck the truth of the Underworld.'

Danae glanced at the men on the rowing benches. 'Your men do not know?'

Odysseus shook his head. 'I believe we are the only mortals who know the reality of what lies beneath. It's a kindness to keep that particular piece of knowledge from the men. Especially given what they must face. Wouldn't you agree?'

Danae looked into those amber-flecked eyes. A kindness? Or a calculation that they would not fight if they knew the truth of what waited for them when their bones returned to the earth. But whatever his reason, Odysseus had a point. She must emerge victorious against the false gods, and for that, she needed an army.

'Fine.' As she spoke, weariness stole over her. She took hold of the side of the ship once more and closed her eyes, focusing on the motion of the boat swaying beneath her feet. Far in the deepest reaches of her mind echoed a melody, a song she could not quite place.

'When we reach Troy, I will introduce you as my seer,' said Odysseus. 'There are several royal generals in command of their own armies, but all answer to Agamemnon, the King of Men. It is the wife of his brother, Menelaus, who was kidnapped, or ran away – depending on who you ask – with Prince Paris of Troy. We will have to report to Agamemnon once we arrive.'

Danae opened her eyes and gazed down into the wine-dark water. What she would give to dive into those waves, be rocked by the sea and serenaded by the sweet voices still singing in her mind.

'As soon as we reach Troy you must be Dione the Seer. It is imperative no one but the Children of Prometheus knows your true identity,' continued Odysseus. Then he grew silent, frowning as though listening to something.

Hylas and Telamon had drifted to lean over the starboard rail. The singing had grown louder. Danae thought it was in her mind, but now the melody echoed around the ship as though rising from the sea itself.

There was a splash.

'Man overboard!'

Danae's head snapped around. The soldiers had abandoned their benches and clustered to the port side of the ship. She ran to the rail and leant over. The water churned, white froth stained crimson.

'He just jumped!' one of the soldiers called from the middeck. 'He . . .' the man's face fell slack and slowly he turned towards the waves. 'Can you hear that?'

'Get back from the side!'

Danae spun round as Odysseus slammed his hands over his ears and shouted, 'Block your ears! Tie yourselves to the ship!'

Her hands began to rise to her head, then she paused. Part of her was screaming to bind herself to the benches like the men were now doing. But with each breath her limbs filled with an eerie calm. She lowered her arms and gazed over the rail, watching the marbled waves crest against the hull. The tune filling her ears was so beautiful, even more harmonious than one of Orpheus' songs. It must be a melody sung by the nymphs of the sea. Tears blossomed in her eyes and tumbled down her cheeks. She had thought they too might be fiction after she learnt the truth about the gods, but this singing was proof of their existence.

She gasped as silvery bodies came into focus swimming beneath the waves. Their flowing hair streamed out behind them in ribbons of raven, gold and copper, and shimmering rainbow fins protruded from their backs like wings.

Danae reached down, the wooden rail digging into her chest as she stretched her hand towards the waves. A sudden clarity burned through her. If she followed the nymphs, all would be well. There would be no more pain. The ache of all she had seen and all the agony to come would wash away. There was no space for anything but peace beneath the water, the waves would protect her from the world, and the sea nymphs' song would fill every part of her with joy.

Desire burned through her, so hot and scalding only the sea could quench it.

A hand reached out of the waves to meet her fingers. Their tips touched, and she was shocked at how cold they were. Then a face followed. A face that had looked so beautiful beneath the water, now twisted and bestial. And out of a mouth full of blood-flecked teeth, that sweet, harmonious sound grated into a shriek.

Suddenly, she was yanked back from the water and slammed into the deck. Odysseus sat on top of her, pinning her arms and legs. Two pieces of sail rag were stuffed into his ears. Even after the horror of what she'd seen in the water, Danae's mind began to twist. She recalled not a terrible face, but a beautiful one, a woman reaching to her, soft-cheeked and lovely, longing for her embrace.

'Please,' she gasped, 'let me go to her.'

Odysseus would not release her, and Danae delved within, calling her life-threads in order to repel the king. As though sensing what she was about to do, Odysseus shouted, 'This is for your own good!' and delivered a blow to Danae's temple that knocked her unconscious.

Danae came to with a vicious throbbing across the left side of her skull. She lay propped against the side of the prow deck, the sun prising itself between her heavy lids. She blinked, and pain shot through her left eye. It wouldn't open all the way. Tentatively, she prodded the swollen skin. If it felt this bad, gods know how it looked.

'Welcome back.'

She was afforded a brief respite from the sun's glare as a pair of scarred, muscular legs planted themselves in front of her.

Wincing, she squinted up at Atalanta. 'What were those . . .'

'Sirens. They lure sailors to their deaths.'

Danae's heart lurched. She'd heard tales of the perilous siren song from merchants and fishermen back on Naxos.

'Telamon, Hylas?'

'They're fine.' Atalanta lowered herself down beside Danae. 'Most of the crew managed to tie themselves to a bench or the mast before the song took hold.' The warrior glanced at her. 'Not all succumbed as quickly as you. Although, two more of those Ithacan soldiers jumped overboard. Telamon and Hylas have had to take their place on the benches.'

The wind had lulled, and the ship now sliced through the waves on the power of the men's limbs.

Three lives lost. Danae wondered how many more of these soldiers would die once they reached Troy.

Her eyes flicked to Odysseus and the navigator conversing on the stern deck, then travelled to where Hylas and Telamon now shared a rowing bench. A surge of warm familiarity swelled through her. For a moment she allowed herself to imagine they were back on the *Argo*, one united crew, heading towards Colchis. Back then the prophecy had felt like a mountain resting on her shoulders. Now she longed for that simpler time, before she'd learned that gaining Titan powers meant she was doomed to watch those she loved grow old and perish while she remained fixed in time, before her belief in the afterlife had been shattered, before the Underworld had beaten her spirit beyond recognition.

'Odysseus didn't have to knock me out.'

'Yes, he did.' The warrior flicked her braids over her shoulder. 'Otherwise you'd have thrown him off with your powers and dived into the arms of that siren.'

The colour in Danae's cheeks ripened. They sat in silence for a moment, the waves raking against the ship.

'It suits you,' said Atalanta.

Danae arched an eyebrow. 'The black eye?'

'The hair.' The warrior paused. 'I've always liked it short.'

Danae was very aware of the sliver of air between their arms, the notes of oak, salt and honeysuckle woven into the other woman's scent. She stole a glance at Atalanta and found the warrior watching her.

'Back on Delos, did you like what you saw?' Atalanta's words were so softly voiced they were almost lost to the wind.

Danae's lips parted. She thought of the lake, of the warrior's discarded silver armour glinting in the sunlight, Atalanta's lean body being lowered into the water's embrace and the shining trails the droplets had trickled across her skin.

'Yes,' she breathed.

They stared at each other, heat rising in the pit of Danae's stomach. There was something sharp and raw in the depths of those fierce, dark eyes. Something dampened by years of drinking, fighting and fucking.

'I never meant to hurt you,' Danae whispered, curling her fingers around Atalanta's hand.

The warrior drew back as though a blade had been drawn between them. Her lip curled.

'Don't flatter yourself.'

'Atalanta . . .'

Her eyes cold as starlight, the warrior leant close and whispered, 'I'm no fool. If Heracles had his strength back and was here on this ship you would be fawning over him like a lovesick girl.'

The longing ache in Danae's throat turned bitter. She rose, her head throbbing with the sudden movement.

'If you really believe that, then you *are* a fool.'

She stalked away across the prow deck and had almost reached the rowing benches when the navigator shouted, 'Land ahead!'

She spun on her heel. The green and gold hills of a verdant island stood proud against the sky.

Marching through the benches, she called to Odysseus, 'That is not Troy!'

'Indeed.' He greeted her with an infuriating smile as she climbed up to the stern deck. 'That is the island of Skyros.'

Rage bubbled inside her, life-threads automatically surging into her hands. 'If you have tricked me, King of Ithaca, I will strike you down where you stand.'

Odysseus did not so much as blink. 'We are on our way to Troy, be assured of that. But we have an important person to collect first. I was sailing to this island when Metis' gull found me.'

Danae's eyes narrowed. 'Who is this person?'

'The best of the Greeks. A young warrior named Achilles.'

40. The Best of the Greeks

Recollection sparked in Danae's mind. Telamon's brother, Peleus, had spoken of a son, Achilles, aboard the *Argo*.

'He's your nephew?'

Telamon nodded, his brow furrowed.

'Is that so?' Odysseus gestured for Telamon to join them on the prow deck. 'The fates have indeed placed you in our path. I predict Achilles will not come with us willingly. He may need some encouragement to join the Greek army.'

'Why?' asked Danae.

'He had . . . a disagreement with King Agamemnon.'

'Go on.'

Odysseus sighed. 'The Greek army congregated at Aulis before sailing for Troy. Plague broke out, and Calchas, Agamemnon's seer, told him that the gods demanded a pure sacrifice of royal blood or the entire Greek force would be decimated by disease. Agamemnon sent for his daughter, Iphigenia, under the false claim he wished to give her in marriage to Achilles. Instead, she was killed as an offering.'

Danae's heart grew hard and heavy as stone.

You will destroy them all, whispered the voice. She knew she should no longer heed its advice, but still it gave her mettle.

'Achilles did not bear the duplicity well,' continued Odysseus. 'He left the Greek army, taking his warriors with him.'

'Why does it matter if he fights?' Danae pressed. 'Is he a member of the Children of Prometheus?'

The king shook his head. 'It is important because he is the best mortal Greek soldier alive. We need him to make the fight for Troy worthy of luring the gods down to the battle.' Odysseus leant upon the ship's rail, his eyes bright. 'They care deeply about the coming war. Several of the Twelve have already proclaimed their favourites. I believe that, at the very least, Ares, Athena and Apollo will come to the battle. But we must draw as many Olympians as we can. As I said yesterday, this is our chance to clear the way for you to take Olympus.'

'How do you know all this?' asked Danae.

His lips twitched into a small smile. 'Trust me.'

'Trust must be earned.' She held his gaze. 'Who are your sources?'

Odysseus spread his hands. 'A few carefully chosen priestesses I've managed to turn to our cause.'

His face was calm as a placid sea. But like the ocean, who knew what secrets lay concealed beneath his depths. She did not know if she believed his answer, but even if he spoke the truth, it had taken a dragon to best Hades, two Titans and two warriors to defeat Poseidon. She may have gained a small army, but they were only men. She would need to work on strengthening her connection to Gaiasight before facing any more of the false gods in battle.

'The Olympians are incredibly powerful . . .'

Odysseus straightened up and placed a hand on her shoulder, like a father might do. 'You are the last daughter, and have already slain two of the false gods. You can do this.'

'What of Artemis?' Atalanta interrupted. 'Will she come to Troy?' Her knuckles strained through her skin as she clutched the side of the ship.

'My sources did not say.'

Danae drew a breath, about to press him further, when Telamon interjected, 'I haven't seen Achilles since he was a babe, I doubt he'll remember me.'

Odysseus beamed, throwing an arm around his shoulders. 'Come now, your nephew will surely be delighted to see his heroic uncle who fought alongside the famous Heracles.'

Telamon's spine straightened.

'How did Achilles become the best of the Greeks?' Atalanta asked.

Danae wondered if the warrior was thinking of Heracles' strength elixir and whether the gods had meddled in the life of this young man too.

'Some say his mother, Thetis, is divine.'

Telamon laughed. 'She is no such thing! A rumour started by the woman herself no doubt.' He shook his head. 'I told Peleus she would be trouble. A wife that ambitious and proud . . . a dangerous combination.'

Their conversation halted as the ship glided through turquoise shallows to a stretch of beach. The creamy sand was crowded by a small fleet of penteconters. Like their own vessel, the ships were sleek, painted black and designed for speed.

Sweat rolled down the navigator's back, dripping onto the deck as he steered them into a space between the ships. Once their vessel was hauled ashore, Odysseus ordered several of the men to stay with their penteconter, whilst he and the others went to secure an audience with the King of Skyros, Lycomedes.

'It would be an offence not to formally introduce myself,' said Odysseus as they paced across the sand. 'We will likely need Lycomedes on our side if we are to convince Achilles to leave with us.'

As on Myconos, a pair of soldiers lingered behind Danae. She bit back the desire to tell them she didn't need guarding.

Ahead of them, stone steps had been carved into the cliff, meandering up to a rocky peak. Nestling beside the uppermost crag was a modest palace, constructed from a blend of wood and the same white stone as the rocks. Music drifted down, the bright strings of harps and lyres twining with a symphony of voices and drumming feet.

'Sounds like we've stumbled on a celebration,' Odysseus called back as they climbed the steps.

Danae watched Hylas ahead of her, marvelling at the movement of his wooden limb as it gleamed in the sunlight.

Wild goats ran freely across the rocky hillside, and gulls called to each other as they careered through the sun-bleached sky. Perhaps it was the climb from the beach, but it seemed as though time itself had melted into the warm stones. Skyros reminded her a little of home.

All of them were breathing heavily, their brows stung with sweat by the time they reached the palace plateau. As she leant on her knees to catch her breath, Danae noticed Hylas' mouth was pressed into a hard line, his knuckles white against the dark grain of his crutch. She sorely wished she'd had more time on Delos to learn how to heal others and could do something to ease his pain. If she had, perhaps she'd have been able to save Metis.

Odysseus approached the great wooden doors and rapped upon them. Several moments later the left-hand panel creaked open, and a guard's face appeared in the gap. The noise of revelry grew louder.

'Who are you?'

'The Twelve see you and know you. I am Odysseus, King of Ithaca. We were beset by ill winds on our journey, but I am relieved that, by the sounds of it, I have not missed the celebration.' He flashed the man a winning smile.

The guard's eyes narrowed. 'You are not one of the invited guests.'

Odysseus did not miss a beat. 'Of course I am, why else would I be here?' When the guard did not answer,

Odysseus' brow darkened. 'I'm sure King Lycomedes would be aggrieved to hear that one of his men flouted xenia, Zeus' sacred rule of hospitality. Especially when he learns the offended is the King of Men's most trusted general.'

Danae scoured Odysseus' face. She could not tell if this was information he had previously withheld or a honeyed lie.

The guard paled. A moment later the door was heaved open.

'Gifts for the royal couple can be left in the southern chamber,' said the guard, ushering them through.

'Must be one of the king's daughters getting married,' whispered Telamon.

Their group stepped into a pillared entrance hall bustling with people. Women in brightly dyed dresses wafted past, jewels glinting at their necks and wrists, goblets of wine clasped in their hands. Many of the men were just as richly clothed, but Danae noticed there were several dressed in fortified leather armour. Guards too were stationed at the doorways, bronze-tipped spears clutched in their fists. All the guests wore elegant masks over the upper half of their faces. Some were fashioned in the likeness of animals, some adorned with a rainbow of feathers, and some sported twisted horns like the mask worn by the Hades-priestess at the Thesmophoria on Naxos.

'Please choose a mask.' The guard gestured to a basket piled high with various face-coverings. 'It is customary.'

Atalanta chose one woven with threads so bright they resembled flames. Odysseus chose an eagle, Telamon a boar, Hylas one painted with leaves, and Danae a mask of plain black leather.

'This way.' Their guard ushered them out into a large, sun-drenched courtyard.

A vast wooden pergola wound with vines dominated the space. Streams of cloth dyed indigo, crimson and saffron billowed above the heads of a sea of revellers, dancing to the music plucked by a clutch of musicians stationed under an awning. Beyond the pergola, at the end of the courtyard, was a dais flanked by potted olive trees. Cushion-strewn couches sat upon it, and reclining on them was an elderly man with a lacquered grey beard surrounded by several sumptuously dressed young women. The man nodded his head in time to the music, a contented smile about his wizened lips.

As the rest of them took in the scene, Atalanta slunk towards a table in the shadow of the pergola and swiftly filled a cup with mixed wine from a bronze dish.

'I take it *that* is King Lycomedes?' whispered Hylas, staring at the older man upon the dais.

'It appears so,' said Odysseus, scanning the crowd.

'Where is Achilles?' asked Telamon.

Odysseus' lips tightened. 'I cannot tell.' As Atalanta returned to their side, wine in hand, he continued, 'But we will find him. Those leather-clad soldiers are his elite warriors, the Myrmidons. He can't be far. Mingle with the guests, discover what you can.'

With that, Odysseus slipped into the swirl of dancing bodies flowing in time to the music. Atalanta and Telamon followed him.

Hylas looked at Danae. 'I've got a wooden leg, what's your excuse?'

'I dance like a bear.'

The corners of his mouth twitched, and her heart lifted. For a beat, it was as easy as it used to be between them.

She looked back at the crowd. Her eyes settled on a woman towards the centre of the revellers. The girl's long copper hair streamed in molten waves over the back of her sky-blue dress, the bracelets at her wrists and ankles jangling as she twisted like a ribbon blown by the breeze. Her limbs were long, lithe and strong. She moved as though the music were her heartbeat. Danae was reminded of a mountain brook, a wild deer and the undulating might of the sea. The little she could see of the woman's face was delicate and angular, her skin as pale as the moon. The mask she wore was that of a golden ram, horns twisting to the sky.

Danae's focus was snared by the sight of Atalanta twirling a pretty blonde woman, the skirt of her dawn-bright dress sweeping around the warrior's scarred legs. Danae's chest tightened.

A moment later, as she weaved into the dancing crowd, Telamon brushed past her, whispering, 'One of the guests just told me, it's Achilles' wedding! Looks like he got to marry a princess after all . . .'

As the flame-haired man made his way towards Odysseus, she stared about, but beneath all the masks it was not clear which of these people were the married couple.

A man turned into her path, his limbs stiffening at the sight of her black clothing. He touched his finger to his forehead. Meanwhile, Telamon had located Odysseus and whispered his news in the king's ear. Odysseus detached himself from the crowd and sank to one knee before the dais. King Lycomedes gazed down at him, brow furrowing.

'May the Twelve see you and know you.' Odysseus slipped off his mask as he stood. 'I am Odysseus, King of Ithaca.'

The music halted abruptly. All heads turned to the dais.

'I have come to humbly pay my respects to your radiant daughter, Deidamia, and her new husband, Achilles.' He glanced about the guests. 'I am glad for you, Achilles, that in the year since we parted at Aulis you have found yourself another bride.'

A woman with raven curls and a sea-green mask stepped out from the heart of the crowd. 'I know what you want, and you cannot have him!'

Danae presumed this must be Deidamia.

Lycomedes' mouth curled. 'I too have heard of you, King of Ithaca. Do not insult me with silver-tongued talk. Tell me why you are really here.'

The guards who had before shadowed the walls edged forward, their bronze armour gleaming in the sunlight.

Odysseus inclined his head. 'I should have known you would see through my ruse, wise Lycomedes.'

The king's eyes narrowed. 'I believe Achilles made it clear to you and your master in Aulis that he will not be a part of your war over another man's wife. Nor will I. Skyros has no quarrel with Troy.'

Odysseus' expression remained placid. 'As is your prerogative, my lord. I would, however, think to the future. Once the allied army has vanquished Troy, Agamemnon, the King of Men, will remember those who fought at his side.'

Lycomedes bristled. 'If you are so sure you will win, then why travel all this way to entreat my new son-in-law?'

Odysseus smiled. 'He is the best of the Greeks.' He looked about. 'Speaking of your son-in-law, where is Achilles?'

Lycomedes sat back and folded his arms.

'I see,' said Odysseus.

There was a long pause. Then Odysseus drew a dagger from his belt and threw it at Deidamia. It all happened so fast, the princess did not even have to scream. But before the blade pierced her flesh the figure Danae had spotted in the blue dress and golden ram mask threw herself forward, her body cascading like liquid sunlight as she rolled effortlessly across the dusty ground.

A cacophony of gasps echoed around the courtyard as the woman straightened up, the blade clenched in her fist, Deidamia unharmed.

In two heartbeats the guards had ruptured the crowd, surrounding Odysseus with a ring of bronze spears. They looked to their king for further instruction, who seemed frozen in shock, his hand clutched at his chest, the colour drained from his face.

'Greetings, Achilles,' said Odysseus to the person in blue.

Danae gaped. She had been mistaken.

Achilles ripped the golden mask from his face. She was stunned at how young he was – no older than sixteen. He was as beautiful and slender as a maiden, yet powerful as a bull.

'How dare you.' The youth's voice was light and soft, like a hazy summer morning, but his pale-blue eyes were cold with fury.

'You had only to reveal yourself . . .' Odysseus opened his palms. He winked at the raven-haired girl, who glared at him in return. 'I meant you no harm, princess. It was merely a test.'

'Go back to that pig, Agamemnon,' Achilles spat, 'and tell him there is nothing in this world or the next that could ever convince me to rejoin his rabble.'

Telamon emerged from the crowd. He removed his mask and bowed to Lycomedes before turning to Achilles with a winning smile. 'It is I, your uncle Telamon. I sail with Odysseus and his companions.'

Achilles stared at him blankly.

Telamon's grin faltered. 'Your father's brother.'

'Oh.' Achilles twisted a strand of copper hair between his

fingers. 'I don't remember you. And I think little of the company you keep.' He glowered at Odysseus.

'Told you,' hissed Telamon to the king.

Odysseus sighed. He looked to Lycomedes. 'It seems I have journeyed here in vain. I shall sail for Troy tomorrow, but tonight I beg beds, a meal and safe passage for me and my men.'

As he spoke, the raven-haired girl wrapped her hand around Achilles' arm. He did not push her away, but his body tensed as though he did not welcome the touch.

Lycomedes regained his senses, trembling as he pointed at Odysseus. 'You dare come here and threaten my daughter on her wedding day! Guards, take him away!'

Danae readied herself to move to Odysseus' defence as the guards closed in, but he raised a hand. 'Please, let me speak.' The guards looked to Lycomedes. The king nodded.

'I meant no ill-will. I knew, with Achilles nearby, your fair daughter was never in any real danger. As I reminded your gatekeeper, the King of Heaven teaches us to look kindly on strangers seeking respite. I ask you, in Zeus' name, to grant myself and my men xenia.'

Danae knew her cue. She stepped forward, threading herself between the guests to stand before Lycomedes.

'I am Dione, seer to King Odysseus and humble servant of the gods. With your permission, I will sacrifice to the Twelve at dusk to honour your daughter's marriage.'

Lycomedes stared at her, then nodded slowly, the colour returning to his cheeks.

'If it is the gods' will, so be it.'

41. Love and Duty

Danae stood before a stone altar overlooking the sea. The sky was a ripening bruise, the bright carcass of the sun half sunk beneath the waves. Behind her, the wedding guests were silent as the dusk chorus of Skyros serenaded the dying day.

In one hand, Danae raised a knife; the other held firm to the rope collar of a bound goat. She brought down the blade. As the animal's blood trickled into the rivets carved into the altar stone, her mind ran with it, sinking deep into the soil.

She recalled a chamber in the depths of the earth, another's blood spilt by her hand. In Danae's memory, Persephone's lips parted, rasping her last, guttering breath.

Take its threads, hissed the voice, dragging her back to the world of the living.

Her limbs ached as the goat's life-threads seeped away into the ground, but she held firm. She would be ruled by the voice no longer.

Filling her lungs, she lifted her bloody hands to the sky.

'Goddess of Love, Aphrodite, hear my prayer. Bless the union of Achilles and Deidamia, hold them forever in your grace. May their love endure, like the deathless gods of Olympus.'

She turned to the young couple kneeling behind her. Deidamia's eyes shimmered as she clutched her new husband's hand. Achilles stared out over the waves, as though he wished he were somewhere far away.

'Go with the blessing of the Twelve,' Danae murmured, daubing a fingerprint of blood on each of their foreheads.

Once the ceremony was complete, the guests removed their masks and gathered in the feast hall. Despite Lycomedes' previous hostility, as was fitting, he respected Odysseus' rank by inviting his fellow king, Danae, Telamon, Atalanta and Hylas to join him and his family at the head table, while the Ithacan soldiers sat with his courtiers at long wooden tables spread across the rest of the hall.

Despite the pomp of the wedding festivities, there was a shabbiness to the palace at Skyros Danae found comforting. The painted frescos along the walls depicting harmonious scenes of farming and hunting were peeling in places, their rich colours faded. Several of the stone pillars were chipped around their joins, and a few wooden joists were in need of replacing. Another reason, perhaps, why Lycomedes was reluctant to lend his support to the allied Greek army. War was an expensive endeavour.

The king eased himself to his feet and lifted his cup to the ceiling.

'The first drink I give to Zeus, King of the Heavens and Lord of Hospitality. I honour these guests with all my home has to offer in your name.' He flicked his wrist, and a splash of wine splattered the stone floor.

Around the room, the people of Skyros raised their fingers to their foreheads. Danae swiftly followed the gesture.

'Now,' proclaimed Lycomedes, 'eat!'

They fell upon the food. Danae licked her fingers clean of honey, fruit juice and boar grease, each bite more delicious than the last. She was halfway through a mouthful of bread soaked in olive oil when Atalanta abandoned her seat to slip in beside the woman she'd danced with earlier. A pretty girl, one of Lycomedes' daughters, her silken hair plaited like ears of sun-ripened wheat. The warrior had been making her way through Lycomedes' wine store since they arrived and was now loose-limbed and heavy-lidded. She leant towards the blonde woman, whispering something Danae could not hear. In response the woman laughed, peering at the warrior from beneath her lashes.

Danae swiftly lost her appetite. She signalled to a servant hovering behind their table with an amphora and, once her cup was brimming with wine, drained the vessel. At the prickle of eyes on her, she turned to Hylas, who sat beside her.

He glanced away.

'What?'

Hylas toyed with a bunch of indigo grapes. 'It is strange, for someone who so skilfully hid their truth while aboard the *Argo*, you wear your desire for all to see.'

Her lips parted. She stole another look at Atalanta then scowled at Hylas. 'Whatever you're thinking, it's wrong.'

Her gaze flicked once more to the warrior. Atalanta was now feeding the Princess of Skyros a honey cake. Her stomach twisted.

'It is no easy thing,' Hylas murmured, 'caring for someone who carries the fate of humanity on their shoulders.'

Danae's head snapped towards him. 'If she cared for me, she would not . . .' She fell silent at the anguish writ plain on Hylas' face. In a heartbeat it vanished, like smoke, leaving her questioning if it had really been there at all.

'Achilles,' called Odysseus from across the table. 'Tell me, how did you come to settle on Skyros?'

The youth picked languidly at his plate.

When he did not reply, King Lycomedes answered for him, 'Achilles' mother, Thetis, sent her son on a prolonged visit to my kingdom. I was delighted, of course, to entertain such a renowned warrior, but when my daughter expressed a fondness for our guest and the opportunity to unite the kingdoms of Phthia and Skyros presented itself ... well, how could I not bless such a marriage?'

At her father's words, Deidamia beamed at Achilles. At the same time, the Myrmidon beside him stiffened. The soldier looked not much older than his captain, perhaps only sixteen or seventeen. He was similarly tall and lithe, with tawny-brown skin and dark, tightly curled hair. Achilles never looked at him, but moved his hand ever so slightly, so his little finger brushed against the Myrmidon's clenched fist.

'What a happy arrangement,' said Odysseus, his eyes drinking in the exchange. Danae was sure he had missed none of what just passed between the three young people. 'But surely your Myrmidons must be growing bored with only serving girls and goats to entertain them.'

Telamon laughed. Lycomedes' lips pursed, and Achilles' spine straightened, like a snake jabbed with a stick.

'My men go where I go. If I am happy, they are happy.'

The Myrmidon next to Achilles glared at Odysseus.

The King of Ithaca laughed easily. 'You are blessed, Achilles, best of the Greeks. I wish I could say the same for my men.'

Achilles did not return his warmth. 'I meant what I said. I will not come with you to Troy.'

Odysseus nodded. 'Remind me again what it is exactly you took offence to in Aulis?'

Achilles' cheeks flushed. 'You know damned well – he used my name! He lured that poor girl to her death with my name as bait.'

'It was a tragedy the girl had to die, but it was the will of the gods.' Odysseus' voice rang out for all to hear. 'Surely you do not mean to criticize the Twelve?'

The colour in Achilles' face deepened. 'Never. It is not the sacrifice that angers me, but the use of my name. I am Achilles, the greatest mortal soldier Greece has ever seen. My name is worth more than gold, and I will not have it used by a duplicitous king for his own ends.'

Danae stared at him: this boy who was so sure of himself. The youth who commanded his own army. The man who cared not for the life taken, but only his reputation. She was flooded with the desire to fling him to the floor and watch that beautiful face twist in pain as she buried her fists in his ribs. But she knew the hollowing in her chest had been carved before this night, by another hero who valued his name above all else.

'I see,' said Odysseus, 'thank you for indulging my curiosity. I shall speak no more upon this matter.'

When the platters had been picked clean and the wine jugs drained, Lycomedes proclaimed the feasting at an end and retired to his bedchamber. The courtiers drifted back to their homes, and Odysseus' men were shown to rooms in the servants' quarters. Telamon had already retired to his chamber, and Atalanta disappeared with the blonde princess. Danae tried not to think about it. Imagining them together felt like swallowing hot ashes.

Finally Danae, Odysseus and Hylas were left alone with two of the Ithacan soldiers and several Skyros guards. As they rose from the feast table, Odysseus said to Hylas, 'You should get some rest. We leave at first light.'

Hylas' gaze flicked between the king and Danae, and for a moment it seemed like he would dissent. Then he turned, leaning on his crutch, and walked away across the stone floor.

'What's your plan?' Danae whispered, both sets of guards

following them as they stepped out into the pillared corridor. 'Achilles is married – surely it will now be impossible to persuade him to leave.'

'It is not I but you who must convince him,' Odysseus murmured.

'Me?'

'Remember, you are a seer, *Dione*. As we learned at dinner, Achilles is both proud and pious. So,' he glanced behind them, 'you will go to his chamber tonight, and tell him that the gods demand his presence in Troy. You will say that if he does not fight for the Greek allied army, the Twelve will be incandescent with rage.'

'You want me to lie?'

Odysseus regarded her for a moment. 'I know you do not trust me. I don't blame you – we've only known each other a short while. But we are on the same side. Everything I do is in your service, to clear a path for you to fulfil your destiny.' He paused. 'I can see it is a burden for you to deceive –'

'You do not know me.'

'No, but Hylas does. I admit, I took him with me when I left the Doliones' shore because he knew you, and I have been searching for you ever since you destroyed the oracle at Delphi.' Danae opened her mouth to ask how he knew, but Odysseus continued, his voice a fervent whisper, 'Since then, Hylas has become a most valued advisor, and a friend. I hope in time you can learn to trust me as he does.'

An old desire ached in her like a long-healed wound on a cold winter night. A memory of how it had felt when she'd believed Heracles was destined to help her find Prometheus, and she would have the might of a demi-god beside her against the formidable force of the gods. Odysseus was offering her an army, a plan, and she sorely wanted to trust he would deliver. She wondered now how she ever thought she could storm Olympus with only Telamon and Atalanta by her side. Even if she could learn to master Gaiasight, the more she dwelt on the coming fight, the more facing the Olympians in battle seemed an insurmountable task. But, as Metis would say, she must have faith.

'Fine,' she said quietly, 'I will do it.'

Danae lingered in her chamber, waiting for the rest of the palace to slip into sleep. As she paced back and forth across the stone floor, Odysseus' words chased each other through her mind: . . . *he is the best mortal Greek soldier alive. We need him to make the fight for Troy worthy of luring the gods down to the battle.*

She clenched and unclenched her fists. She could do this, she must.

Finally, when she could wait no longer, she eased open the door. Odysseus' Ithacan soldiers stood like sentries outside the room. She lifted a finger to her lips as she emerged. They remained silent but moved to follow her as she stepped out into the corridor.

She shook her head and whispered, 'You must stay here.'

The man on the left inclined his head. 'Begging your pardon, my lady, but you are the last daughter. We go where you go.'

Wrapped in the shadows of the pillared passage, for the first time she saw them not as Odysseus' servants, or Ithacan soldiers, but men who would lay down their lives for her destiny. Just like Manto had done.

'What are your names?'

The guard who had spoken replied, 'Sinon, my lady, and this is Evenor.'

Danae nodded. 'I thank you for your service, Sinon and

Evenor, but I order you to remain here. If the palace guards pass by, they must think I am abed like the rest of the household. I'm sure you have your instructions from Odysseus, but no harm will come to me, I swear it.'

They glanced at one another, conflict raging between them, then both bowed their heads.

'As you command,' said Sinon, and the pair stepped back to flank her chamber door.

Danae's feet whispered along the corridor that led to Achilles' chamber. Darkness stretched between the brazier lights spilling across the faded frescos. Earlier, Odysseus had told her which room belonged to the best of the Greeks. How he had come by that information she did not know.

At the sound of footsteps, she flattened herself to the wall, sinking into the darkness behind a pillar. The last thing she wanted was for Lycomedes to suspect foul play.

A moment later, two guards walked by, spears in their hands. Only when they turned the corner did breath return to her lungs.

When she reached Achilles' chamber she paused before knocking softly on the wood.

After a few moments, it opened to reveal the Myrmidon who'd sat next to Achilles at the feast. He stood barefoot, wrapped in nothing but a leather kilt, his skin gleaming with sweat.

His eyes swept over her with barely veiled disdain. 'What do you want, Seer?'

'Who is it, Patroclus?' Achilles' voice sounded from inside.

Patroclus' jaw tightened. 'Odysseus' seer.'

She glanced down the corridor, pulse quickening as she waited for a glint of bronze to appear.

'Let her in,' called Achilles.

For a moment, it seemed as though Patroclus would disobey his captain. Then he stepped back, and Danae swiftly slipped into the room.

The air was sweet with the scent of fresh flowers and brazier smoke. A great bundle of blooms was arranged in a painted vase on a low table in the centre of the chamber, and a grand bed carved from dark wood dominated the far wall. Achilles lounged upon it, naked but for a cloth draped over himself.

'Leave us,' Danae said to Patroclus.

He did not move.

Achilles nodded his consent, but Patroclus lingered. The best of the Greeks rolled his eyes.

'Go.'

Patroclus' brow darkened, his eyes raking over Danae as if scanning her for a hidden weapon. Then he bowed to his captain and left them alone, shutting the door behind him.

'You must forgive Patroclus. He's very protective.' Achilles propped himself on his elbow.

'Where's your wife?'

Achilles blinked. 'Asleep in her chamber. Not that it's any of your concern, seer.'

'Why marry her, if you would rather spend your wedding night with one of your soldiers?'

'I am the son of a prince. There are expectations . . .' He frowned. 'What happened to your eye?'

Involuntarily, Danae twitched a hand to the tender skin around the left socket, where Odysseus had struck her. The swelling had gone down, but she imagined she had an eye the colour of a ripe fig.

'You should see the other man.'

Achilles' lips quirked. He stretched like a lynx. 'Go on, then, what have you to tell me?'

Danae lifted her chin. 'The omens have spoken. You must come with us to Troy.'

Achilles flopped back on the bed and sighed. 'Did wily old Odysseus put you up to this?'

'You dare defy the gods?' The old threat tasted bitter in her mouth.

He sat up. 'Never.'

'Odysseus may be my king, but a seer answers to no mortal master.'

The best of the Greeks, mocked the voice. *You are a Titan. He should be worshipping at your feet.*

She advanced. 'You should show a mouthpiece of the Twelve more respect. It is not just their words that flow through me.' She placed a hand on the bed frame and sent a bolt of life-threads into the wood. The frame cracked, splintering beneath her touch.

Achilles sprung from the bed, landing crouched ready to spring, like a cat. He looked at the bed then back at Danae. Slowly, he rose to stand naked before her, staring as though seeing her through fresh eyes.

'Very well, Seer. I should have known my mother's plan to cheat the fates was foolish and my destiny would come for me sooner or later.' He clenched his fists. 'I am not afraid.'

Danae frowned. 'What destiny –'

At that moment the door flung open, and Patroclus ran into the room.

'I heard . . .' he trailed off at the sight of the broken bed frame and Achilles standing bare before Danae.

The tension fled Achilles' limbs. He moved to pluck a cloak from a nearby chair and swept it around his shoulders.

'Come, Patroclus.' He strolled towards his Myrmidon, his gait almost convincingly nonchalant. 'I have a sudden urge to swim.'

Patroclus eyed Danae as though she were a viper. Then he followed Achilles towards the door.

'We leave at dawn,' said Danae.

Patroclus turned sharply to Achilles. The best of the Greeks lingered, his face half turned in shadow, then he nodded.

42. The Camp

Odysseus' penteconter charged through the Aegean Sea, the Myrmidon ships following like a flock of midnight swans. Achilles stood beside Patroclus at the helm of his own vessel, his copper locks streaming in the chill wind as his men rowed in perfect unison.

They'd left Achilles' bride, Deidamia, sobbing on the shore. Danae could not help but pity the poor girl, married to a man she probably would never see again. Lycomedes had been furious when Achilles announced he'd changed his mind and planned to leave for Troy with Odysseus. But there was little the old king could do to persuade him to stay, or hold him by force. The palace guard might outnumber the Myrmidons, but there was no comparison in their skill.

For most of the voyage, Danae haunted the prow deck, watching the familiar landmarks of the Aegean flow by. When they passed the isle of Imbros, her heart tightened with memories of the Argonauts: Tiphys and his beloved maps, Orpheus' music, and Ancaeus' rumbling laugh. All of them gone.

On the third day, the Bay of Troy snarled open before them. The fortress city was just as Danae remembered when she'd first sighted it from a distance aboard the *Argo*. Great walls of yellow stone towered over the eastern reach of the bay, a vast plain cut through with a thick vein of river stretching beyond.

'When we arrive, will you take me to my army?' she asked Odysseus.

'You will meet them soon, but first we must report to King Agamemnon with Achilles. I will introduce you as my seer, which will afford you access to the war council meetings.' He regarded her intently, brow furrowing. 'It is vital none but the Children of Prometheus soldiers discover who you are. Agamemnon's seer, Calchas, corresponds directly with the gods. They cannot know you are with the Greek army.'

Danae nodded, her jaw set. She recalled the golden amulets used by Polyxo and Dolos to commune with the Olympians and wondered if Calchas had such a device.

'While we are on Trojan soil, I will remain Dione.'

As they curved around the jutting lip of land opposite the city, the largest collection of ships she'd ever seen came into view. They clustered around the western side of the coast; full-bellied triremes anchored in the deep, built to carry entire armies and their mounts on multiple decks, and swift fleets of smaller one- and two-sail penteconters rested on the beach looking like fishing tubs next to the great warships. Beyond these vessels, another temporary city had sprung up. A patchwork of tents that stretched like barnacles along the shore, fifty deep in places. Flags hailing from kingdoms across Greece fluttered above their peaks, hazed by gusts of smoke rising from makeshift hearths.

As Odysseus' navigator steered their ship between the triremes, the wind changed, blowing over a cacophony of rumbling feet, clamouring voices, clanging armour and the bleating of livestock. Danae swiftly raised a hand to her mouth, the stench of animals and unwashed bodies clogging her throat.

Once their penteconter was beached, Odysseus instructed his men to report to the Ithacan quarter of the camp.

'Go with them,' he said to Hylas, Telamon and Atalanta. 'Dione and I will escort Achilles to the war tent.'

Atalanta crossed her arms. 'We stay with Dione.'

A burst of lightness sang through Danae's chest. 'I'll be fine.'

Atalanta's scowl deepened, but she conceded a nod.

Danae and Odysseus waited for Achilles to descend from his ship, with Patroclus and another Myrmidon soldier. He looked magnificent, clad in an embroidered tunic of cornflower blue, overlaid with a bronze breastplate. Jewels glinted at his wrists and ankles, and his hair was half braided and curled upon his head, the length of it left to tumble down his back in sea-teased waves.

Once their party was complete, they set off between the tents, down a path of sandy earth beaten into channels of hard mud by the tread of thousands of feet. Men huddled around campfires, some roasting spits of meat, some cleaning their armour, a few sparring between the dwellings. Several paused as the group passed, their eyes brightening at the sight of Achilles, then shifting to Danae, drinking in her cropped hair and long black gown.

Whispers began to follow them, soldiers trailing after them with hope-slackened faces.

'Achilles!'

'The best of the Greeks!'

'He has returned to the army.'

They stopped at a tent much larger than the others, the Mycenaean flag flying from its height, its awning guarded by two grim-faced soldiers.

'Shall we?' said Odysseus.

'After you, King of Ithaca.' Achilles curled into an exuberant bow.

Odysseus arched an eyebrow, then turned to the guards.

'Odysseus, King of Ithaca, and Achilles, best of the Greeks, seek an audience with King Agamemnon.'

One of the soldiers drew back the tarpaulin. Danae willed her face to remain calm as they stepped inside the cavernous tent.

Scented braziers hung from the sturdy wooden beams supporting the structure, yet they did little to mask the reek of stale sweat. A large table dominated the space, resting on a floor of mud-encrusted oxhides. A vast map lay unfurled across its surface, and bronze dishes cupping candles pinned the corners. A group of men were clustered around it, goblets of wine in their hands.

'. . . the city is too large to encircle. We may have blocked the Trojans from using their main gates, but my scouts spotted supply wagons coming in from the north of Mount Ida.' A man dressed in the armour of a general pressed a finger to the parchment. 'I've sent a company to discover the entrance they're funnelling goods to and cut them off. Then we'll starve the bastards out.'

An elderly man shook his head. He was dressed in a long maroon robe, his ebony skin creased with age, his curly hair entirely white. 'Diomedes, you are forgetting the most important principle of war: it must be undertaken only as a final resort. After all, thousands of lives are at stake. We must first sue for a peaceful return of Helen –'

'Look around you, Nestor.' A man with auburn hair and a sharp jaw flung his arms wide, spilling wine on the carpet. 'The soldiers in this camp did not sail all the way across the Aegean to sit idle in their tents then go home again. Troy must burn for what Paris did. What he took from me.'

'Menelaus is right.' A man with sallow skin and a hawkish nose turned to Nestor. 'We have been camped on their shore for months. The Trojans have had every opportunity to surrender Helen, yet they remain cowering behind their topless towers. They have brought war upon themselves.'

Nestor shook his head. 'I vehemently disagree. We are a hostile force, therefore it is our duty to initiate the customary peaceful negotiations before –'

Odysseus cleared his throat.

All five men turned. Odysseus bowed to the one standing at the head of the table who had his back to them.

'May the Twelve see you and know you, King Agamemnon. This is my seer, Dione, and Achilles, returned to us with his Myrmidons.'

Agamemnon turned. The ruler of Mycenae looked every inch the King of Men. There was no crown upon his head, no armour encasing his powerful body, yet every cord of muscle radiated violence. His long, dark hair was threaded with silver, as was his beard. His face was a clumsy mirror to that of his brother, his jaw heavier, his features less refined. Still, the familial resemblance was undeniable. Agamemnon and Menelaus: the brothers Atreides.

Agamemnon's small, earthy eyes flicked swiftly over Odysseus and Danae, then settled on Achilles.

'The best of the Greeks returns.' He desiccated each word until only sharpness remained.

Achilles met his gaze with an unblinking stare.

'Bow before your king,' hissed Menelaus.

Achilles did not. 'Let me make one thing clear: I will fight with the Greek army because it is the will of the gods. That is the only reason.'

Agamemnon glanced briefly at Danae. His lip curled. 'If you fight for the Greeks then you fight for me. Kneel, boy.'

Achilles still did not move. The men around the table tensed.

Despite the stale, humid air of the tent, Danae shivered.

Her eyes darted to the corner of the space and she started. A clutch of shadows stirred, revealing a sixth man who had previously been shrouded in darkness. He approached the table. The fluidity of his movements was at odds with the wrinkled skin hanging from his thin frame. He was dressed in a long black robe, his hair cut close to his skull. This must be Agamemnon's seer.

Calchas smiled, but there was no warmth in his watery eyes. 'King Agamemnon is blessed by the God of War, you would do well to remember that.' His voice rasped as though he'd swallowed altar smoke.

Anger twisted through Danae as she thought of the girl, Iphigenia, who had been sacrificed on this seer's false claim that it was the will of the gods. He must think himself so powerful, able to manipulate a king into murdering his own daughter.

As though sensing her rage, Odysseus subtly shifted towards her.

But before anyone else could speak Achilles replied, 'Send for me when you're ready to fight,' then swiftly exited the tent, followed by Patroclus and the other Myrmidon soldier.

'That boy is just as insolent as he was at Aulis,' said Diomedes.

'He is here and he will fight,' said Odysseus. 'That is all that matters.'

The sallow-skinned man made a disparaging sound in the back of his throat.

Odysseus raised an eyebrow. 'Do you disagree, Palamedes?'

'Respect for one's leader is paramount.' Palamedes regarded Odysseus with contempt. 'Something I wouldn't expect you to understand.'

While they spoke, Danae felt Calchas' unflinching gaze on her like insects crawling under her skin.

You will be the reckoning, said the voice. *He and all his kind will burn.*

The violence of it filled her with mettle. She would show this man what true power looked like. She raised her eyes and met his stare, life-threads singing through her limbs.

Hylas' fingers brushed her arm. Suddenly, she realized what she was doing and looked away, her life-threads retreating deep inside her. She must not listen to the voice.

'I meant what I said, Agamemnon,' said Nestor. 'I will not send my men into battle until all other options have been exhausted.'

'For the love of the gods, we were at war the moment that bastard stole my wife and gold!' Menelaus brought his fists down onto the table, rattling the candles. Hot wax splashed over the map of Troy.

'Brother.' Agamemnon placed a quelling hand on his arm. His voice grew low and dangerous as he addressed Nestor. 'You pledged your army to me.'

Calchas lingered at his master's side. 'Zeus himself sent a rainbow this very morn as a portent of war. Our campaign is blessed by the gods.'

Nestor faced the King of Men with an iron gaze of his own. 'I did pledge you my army. And I may be your general, but I am first and foremost the King of Pylos. I have a solemn duty to my people. I will not spill their blood without just cause.' Across the table, Menelaus' eyes blazed. 'Priam is known to be a man of reason. Allow me to ride to Troy as a peace envoy. If my attempts fail, I will order my men to follow your command. If you cannot grant me this simple ask, I and my ten thousand men will have no choice but to sail for Pylos on the dawn tide.'

Agamemnon ran a hand through his hair. His beady gaze

fell on the inked outline of Troy. He let out a long hiss of breath.

'Very well –'

'Brother –' interjected Menelaus.

'I have made my decision,' Agamemnon snapped. He turned to Nestor. 'You have two days. If Priam does not agree to return Helen, my brother's gold and additional reparations for the cost of launching this campaign, we will burn Troy to the ground.'

Nestor bowed his head. 'You have my thanks, King of Men.'

Danae's chest tightened. She caught Odysseus' eye, and to her surprise he winked, then announced to the room, 'I volunteer to accompany Nestor.'

She stared at him, biting the inside of her lip. What in Tartarus was he playing at? Peace was exactly what they wanted to avoid.

'Eager to leave us again so soon?' asked Palamedes, taking a deep draught from his cup.

Odysseus gave the hint of a smile. 'Given that I persuaded Achilles to return when he forswore setting foot on Trojan soil, I would think my negotiating power an asset.'

Nestor nodded. 'Odysseus' silver tongue would indeed be a boon.'

'I doubt even a wordsmith as adept as Odysseus will convince Priam to agree to our demands, but as you wish.' Agamemnon considered the King of Ithaca. 'Nestor, Odysseus and my cousin, Palamedes, will form the peace envoy. You have tonight to brief your second-in-commands should anything befall you behind those walls.'

The chosen envoy nodded.

Agamemnon waved a hand. 'You are all dismissed.'

Danae's heart hammered against her ribs as she followed Odysseus outside. The two guards, Sinon and Evenor, had been waiting for them and took up their usual haunt in Danae's shadow. They were all forced into a jog as the King of Ithaca hurried through the winding tracks between the tents.

'What have you done?' she hissed.

Odysseus barely glanced back at her. 'You will have to come with me, I cannot risk leaving you here. We will bring Hylas too –'

'Odysseus!' She grabbed his arm, and finally he spun around to face her. 'Why did you volunteer for the peace talks?'

He raised an eyebrow. 'I would have thought that obvious. To ensure they fail.'

'Wait here.' Odysseus gestured Danae into his tent, leaving Sinon and Evenor once more standing guard at the entrance.

Danae chewed her lip, looking around the inside of the makeshift dwelling. It was sparse compared to the grandeur of Agamemnon's war tent, housing only a pallet, a chest, a couple of stools and a table fashioned from two barrels and three short planks hammered together.

She padded over to the chest and heaved open the lid. It was filled with clothing, mainly tunics. Her brow furrowed as she delved in and pulled out a faded green dress. It smelt faintly of pine trees and a spice she did not recognize. As the length of the fabric unfurled, something fell from its folds. She stooped to retrieve it.

A horse carved from wood. A child's toy. Given the stains and smooth grain of its ears, it appeared to have been well loved.

A well opened inside her, the memory of Arius' first birthday and the figurine of Heracles that Santos had carved for him, dragging her into its depths.

Then a bout of raucous laughter pricked her ears, drawing her back from the darkness.

Hastily folding the dress and figurine back into the chest, she stepped towards the entrance of the tent, remembered the guards and paused, then crept to the rear and pulled the fabric away from the earth before slipping outside.

The tang of whetted bronze sharpened the air. There was a nervous pulse to the camp, the soldiers moving in clusters about the tents, grim-faced, limbs streaked with grime, waiting for the order that might end their lives before the next sunrise.

Danae navigated through the Ithacan dwellings, following the clamour she'd heard. She emerged into a small clearing where several pigs and goats were tethered in a makeshift pen. Benches had been dragged through the mud, upon which sat several rowdy soldiers. More crowded round the edges of the tents, passing skins of wine between them.

At the centre, straddling two benches, was Telamon, belting out an old kapeleion tune with a large amphora clutched in his hands.

> *On a moonlit night when the waves are clear,*
> *Drink to the Old Man of the Sea!*
> *Lost on the water, searching for land,*
> *Drink to the Old Man of the Sea!*

Every time Telamon called out the chorus line, the men raised their voices and swigged from their skins.

> *Trade him a fish, trade him a lover,*
> *He'll tell you the truth for a belly of plunder,*
> *Drink to the Old Man of the Sea!*
> *He'll appear as a seal, lion or tree,*
> *Wrestle him still and he'll spill for thee,*
> *Drink to the Old Man of the Sea!*

'Drink to the Old Man of the Sea.' A familiar voice, rough and rich, whispered in her ear.

Danae glanced over her shoulder and smiled. Atalanta proffered her a wineskin. She took it, her throat burning with the strength of the unmixed grapes. She coughed, but managed to splutter, 'Drink to the Old Man of the Sea!' in time with the crowd.

Atalanta patted her on the back. 'So, you survived the war tent.'

Danae leant close, murmuring, 'Odysseus and I are to enter Troy as a peace envoy with a couple of the other generals. We must ensure the talks fail.'

Atalanta's brow darkened. 'Surely Odysseus can go alone. You should stay here.'

But if the slippery cove strikes a deal
Be sure to keep an even keel
Or he'll drag you down down down
Until you drown drown drown

While the men chanted, Telamon tipped the amphora to his lips, clasping both handles, wine spilling down his chin to cries of, 'Drink to the Old Man of the Sea!'

'Odysseus wants me by his side,' whispered Danae. 'And I am more powerful than any man here, or any Trojan soldier. I can look after myself.'

Atalanta stared at her, eyes hard as marble. 'If you die in Troy, I will climb those walls, dig up your body and kill you all over again for being so damned stupid.'

Danae cracked a smile. 'I'll hold you to that.'

There was a crash, then a cry from the benches.

Danae's head snapped round. Telamon had dropped the amphora, shards shattered about his feet. His wine-stained jaw hung slack. Danae followed his gaze to a young man who had appeared at the edge of the crowd. He was tall and broad, his freckled cheeks stained pink from the chill sea breeze, his periwinkle eyes bright beneath a crop of flame-red hair.

'Ajax?' Telamon breathed.

The young man glanced about, bemused. 'Who wants to know?'

Telamon's mouth moved soundlessly before he managed to say, 'It's me . . .'

Ajax stiffened, realization dawning.

'What's this? A lovers' reunion?' called one of the soldiers.

Ajax's face ripened to the colour of the Ithacan flag, then he spun around and stormed away through the tents.

Telamon stood stupefied for a heartbeat, then he leapt from the benches and ran after Ajax.

'Is that his son –' Danae began, but Atalanta put a finger to her lips and tugged Danae after the two men.

They stalked the pair through the fabric dwellings, picking their way between taut ropes and groups of roaming soldiers until Atalanta pulled Danae behind a stack of barrels.

'Please . . .' Telamon called after the younger man, 'Ajax, wait!'

Ajax spun around, his muscular arms folded across his chest.

'You've . . . grown since last I saw you.' Telamon offered a smile. Ajax did not return it.

The silence screeched like a blade over stone.

'How is your mother?' Telamon offered.

Ajax's eyes darkened. 'You don't get to ask that.'

Telamon looked down at his feet.

'Why are you here?'

Telamon lifted his gaze. He hesitated for a moment. 'I've come to fight . . . I didn't know you'd be here.'

Moisture blossomed in Ajax's eyes. 'You shouldn't have come.'

Telamon braved half a step towards him. 'Please . . . son.'

Ajax flinched. 'Stay away from me, or I swear on the Styx you'll regret it.' He turned and stormed away, leaving his father staring after him, shoulders rounded.

Danae took a step towards Telamon, but Atalanta grabbed her arm, shaking her head.

Telamon dragged a hand across his mouth, then disappeared between the tents.

'He will need time,' said Atalanta. 'And a good drink.'

Danae looked back at the warrior, and it occurred to her that for the first time since leaving Delos, they were alone. Atalanta's hand still rested on her arm, her skin warm beneath the warrior's fingers.

Atalanta glanced down at her hand, then at Danae. She did not remove it.

Danae's lips parted, the air thickening with each breath. She knew she should speak, should move, but she could do neither.

'I did not lie with her.'

The moment shattered. Danae flinched from Atalanta's touch.

The warrior swiftly brought her hand to her side, fist clenched. 'The princess on Skyros . . . I didn't –'

'I don't care what you do.' Danae drew her cloak tightly around her torso.

Pain flickered across Atalanta's face.

Twin barbs of sorrow and satisfaction prised their way between Danae's ribs.

'I should find Odysseus.' She spun on her heel and stalked away, before she could utter another word she knew she would regret.

43. The Fortress City

The following dawn, under an iron sky, Danae, Nestor, Palamedes, Odysseus and Hylas guided their horses over the ford bridging the river Scamander, then rode onwards across the Trojan Plain. Danae could not fathom how Odysseus had convinced Agamemnon to allow Hylas to ride out with these generals. Another testament to his silver tongue.

Her jet-black cloak billowed behind her, whipping the flanks of her dappled mare. It felt strange to ride without having to tuck her legs back to accommodate wings. The loss of Pegasus, the horse she had once called Hylas, burrowed like a worm in her gut. She reminded herself that he was just an animal, yet somehow his abandoning her cut far deeper than Heracles leaving. Her throat tightened as she banished thoughts of the hero flying away from Delos on the back of her once loyal companion.

The winged horse's old namesake cantered ahead. She wondered if the fates had laughed as they took away one Hylas, only to deliver her another.

Sometimes she doubted that she had any choice at all; that no matter what she did, destiny would always correct her path, like a sailor tweaking a sail in a changing wind. A dark thread forever pulling her taut. No matter where she travelled, it would always drag her towards Olympus, sweeping everyone she cared for into its web. Perhaps this war with Troy was inevitable. It eased the heaviness in her soul to think that the lives of all those who would die might not rest solely on her shoulders.

The city of Troy seemed to expand as they charged towards it, stone towers stretching to pierce the clouds.

They slowed as they neared the walls. Specks of bronze glinted at them from high above, archers poised to rain down their arrows in a heartbeat. Danae's pulse quickened. She did not know if she had the power to protect them if all the soldiers let fly at once.

Nestor held up a hand, and they drew up the horses.

The archers were not their only greeting. Dangling on long ropes, suspended from the tops of the walls, were bodies.

'Shit,' muttered Palamedes.

'Who are they?' asked Danae.

Agamemnon's cousin glanced at her. 'The scouting party Diomedes sent out.'

Nestor sighed. 'This does not bode well.'

Odysseus' brow was studiously creased, eyes etched with practised concern. Only the barest twitch of his mouth betrayed him.

'What do we do now?' asked Hylas, eyeing the archers.

'We wait,' said Nestor.

Danae wrenched her gaze from the hanging bodies, and her eyes fell on an old oak tree, standing alone before the Scaean Gates, the main entrance to Troy. Its lower branches were hung with a myriad of figurines, jewellery and pieces of fine cloth. Painted vases leant against its thick, mottled trunk, and scrolls of parchment were tucked into the crevices of its bark.

'The oak is sacred to the Trojans,' said Odysseus, smoothing his horse's mane as it tossed its head. 'They believe it is connected to the fates. A twin of those holy trees that grow in the sacred grove at Dodona. They adorn it with gifts, like a shrine, hoping destiny will look kindly on them.' He winked at Danae so subtly, she almost wondered if she'd imagined it.

There was a thunderous crack, then the vast doors of the Scaean Gates rumbled open. Between the gap streamed a line of soldiers; swords sheathed at their sides, spears in one hand, shields in the other.

Danae grasped her horse's reins, while imagining herself sinking into the river of calm, and summoned her life-threads.

Odysseus drew his steed up beside her mare, hissing, 'Do not reveal yourself.'

Danae's jaw tightened, but she let her threads disperse within herself.

The soldiers halted, and a man whose crimson-plumed helm marked him as their captain came to stand before his infantry, eyes narrowed beneath his helmet.

'State your intent, Greeks.'

'We are a peace envoy. We seek an audience with King Priam.'

The captain met his words with a stony gaze.

'I evoke xenia,' Nestor pressed, 'Zeus' sacred rule of hospitality. We come as strangers seeking shelter and therefore must be permitted to enter Troy unharmed.'

There was a pause before the captain replied, 'I shall relay your message to our king.'

The soldiers retreated between the doors, and the Scaean Gates closed once more.

Time trickled by at an excruciating pace. Danae had no way of knowing how long they waited, for the sun's progress was cloaked by a persistent armour of cloud. She glanced up at the archers, their arrows still prone, and drew her cloak tight around her. If the Trojan guard atop the walls were tiring, they did not show it.

There was no denying winter's touch in the creeping darkness and the chill wind that bit to the bone. She caught herself thinking of the old lie, that Persephone must have returned to the Underworld and the earth now withered with Demeter's grief. She barely dared admit to herself that sometimes she longed to return to blissful unknowing. To put down the weight of truth and once more breathe the sweet ignorance of lies.

'If they grant us an audience, let Nestor do the talking,' Palamedes said pointedly to Odysseus.

'I will do whatever needs to be done,' countered the king.

Palamedes huffed out a breath. 'I know you, Odysseus. You are loyal to none but yourself.'

'I have pledged my army to Agamemnon just as you have.'

'Enough!' Nestor cut between the two generals. 'It is men's lives we hold in our hands. You would do well to remember that.'

Before either general could reply, there was a groan, and the great doors of the Scaean Gates opened once more. The captain and his men filed out.

'By the order of King Priam, I am to escort you to the palace. Dismount and remove your weapons.'

They did as they were bid, four soldiers relieving them of their horses and arms, while the others formed a barrier around them and turned to march the peace envoy into the city.

A crowd had gathered on the other side. As they entered the streets of Troy, Danae could see very little beyond the armoured bodies of the guards, but she could feel the hatred pulsing from the Trojans. She half expected their party to be attacked as the soldiers barrelled them through the streets, yet the people of Troy remained at a distance, their loathing radiating as though baked into the very stones.

The biting chill of the sea's breath was kept out by the high walls, its keen replaced by the rumble of the city. The air smelled of spice, stone, livestock and the occasional waft of roasted nuts. As the guards marched the envoy through the streets, between their heads Danae caught glimpses of merchants selling crates of fresh fruits, vegetables and barrels of fish, people bustling past with large vases of grain and smaller amphorae of oil and wine. Diomedes had been right; they must have a hidden supply route into the city.

Like Athens, the Trojan citadel was raised atop a hill in the northern sector. The wealth of Troy was evident from its buildings. Rather than wood, many were constructed from the same yellow stone as the fortress walls, but it was the palace that truly displayed the city's riches. Danae peered above the guards' heads at the twelve gold statues sitting atop the balustrades, fashioned in the likeness of the gods. The great building itself was lavishly painted, the intricately carved columns and roof friezes bright against the darkening sky. Two large fig trees grew from beneath the stones next to the entrance, their ripe fruit hanging like bruised raindrops aching to fall.

After climbing the acropolis's summit, the Greek envoy entered the palace through a pair of vast oak doors detailed with bronze. The guards finally peeled away, and they were greeted by the smoky perfume of incense, wafting from hanging braziers cut with patterns, their flames scattering diamonds of light across the tiled floor. Gilt chairs plumped with cushions rested against the walls, and more painted pillars lined the expansive corridor, guarding frescos of dancing nymphs in lush grottos with birds flying about their heads and lions prowling by their sides.

'I can see why Helen left Mycenae,' whispered Hylas.

There was a hiss and the clinking of metal. Then they were ushered at sword point down an expansive passage and shown into a large megaron, packed with richly dressed courtiers, many draped in jewel-coloured robes.

The cacophony of voices stilled as they entered, and silence crashed over the room.

Danae looked at Hylas and caught a flicker of her own trepidation reflected in her friend's eyes.

'The Greek peace envoy,' announced the captain of their guard.

Low muttering and murderous glances echoed through the room as the gathered Trojans parted, clearing a path to reveal a large hearth, framed by four saffron pillars. The royal family of Troy sat on a raised dais behind the fire pit, enthroned in high-backed chairs of bronze.

Danae squinted through the heady smoke, matching their faces to the descriptions Odysseus had given her.

King Priam presided from the central throne. He was elderly, his thinning white hair crested by a golden crown studded with sapphires. His cheeks were drawn and sallow, his hazel eyes yellowed with age. To his right sat Queen Hecuba, who appeared to be at least a decade his junior, her rich brown skin creased with worry, a matching gold band nestled upon her braided, silver-streaked hair.

On either side of the king and queen sat two younger men, their thick, dark hair worn long to the napes of the necks. The man on the left Danae assumed to be Prince Hector, leader of the Trojan army, from the scars on his muscle-bound limbs. Beside him was his wife, Andromache, a handsome woman with sharp, intelligent eyes. Prince Paris sat to the right of his parents, dressed in a fine tunic spun from emerald thread with a delicate golden trim, his entire body tensed with unfettered loathing. Danae's gaze slid swiftly over the twist of his handsome features, to settle on the woman next to him.

This, undoubtedly, was Helen.

It was rumoured that, like Heracles, she was the daughter of Zeus and a mortal woman, Leda, the former Queen of Sparta. If it were true, Danae could see nothing of her father in her features.

Objectively, Helen was perfect. Her face looked as though it had been carved from the purest white marble by a sculptor of divine skill. Her lips were full and flushed, her eyes large and honey-brown, framed by thick black lashes. Her hair was like liquid gold, threaded through with jewels that were dull in comparison to her beauty. Yet there lived in the princess a coldness that sapped her radiance. She seemed to Danae like an ornate shell. A once bright star extinguished, left with the bitter taint of what it cost to live in a world of men and look the way she did.

Danae found herself thinking of Atalanta. She traced the warrior's features in her mind, the tilt of her mouth, the ridges permanently etched between her brows, the scars that marked her battle-hardened limbs. She knew which woman she would prefer to gaze upon.

As the Greek envoy approached the dais, Paris placed a ring-encrusted hand over Helen's. She twitched away, threaded her fingers together and pressed them into her lap.

The tendons in Danae's neck tightened. Standing at the foot of the dais was a woman dressed in the crimson robes and matching veil of a priestess of Apollo. The memory of Danae's imprisonment at the hands of the priestesses in Delphi prickled her skin. Beneath the translucent veil, the woman's expression grew quizzical, and Danae realized that she was glaring. She drew a breath and tamed her face into a mask of calm.

'Bow,' whispered Odysseus as they reached the hearth.

All five of them lowered themselves to their knees, the guards fanning out behind them. In the silence, a trickle of sweat fled down Danae's neck, her head pulsing with the hearth-smoke. The nobility of Troy may be draped in finery, but beneath their jewels their eyes blazed with intemperate bloodlust.

'Three Greek generals walk willingly into my palace.' King Priam's voice was reedy, yet it cracked through the room like a whip. 'It would be a blow indeed to Agamemnon's army if I were to have you all executed.' He glanced at the guards, and they moved forward.

Danae's breath quickened. She shifted her weight ever so slightly. Then Hylas' fingers brushed against hers. A warning.

Nestor intoned the sacred greeting, then leant on Odysseus' arm as he heaved himself to his feet. 'I, Nestor, King of Pylos, Odysseus, King of Ithaca, and Palamedes, Prince of Euboea, come before you in peace with the hope to avoid war between our two peoples.'

Priam raised a hand, and his guards halted.

'You have already sent spies to infiltrate our city,' said Hector. 'How do we know this is not another attempt to glean information about our defences?'

'We swear on the waters of the Styx,' continued Nestor. 'All we seek is to return what was taken from the King of Sparta. The proof of our word will be in our ships leaving your shore never to return once this request is fulfilled.'

'Helen and I are married,' Paris growled. 'She is Trojan now, by law and in the eyes of the gods. Menelaus can find himself another wife.'

Before Nestor could reply, Odysseus stepped towards the hearth. 'King Priam, I would ask you to imagine that your own dear wife, or yours, Prince Hector, were snatched without your knowledge by a man you treated as an honoured guest —'

'He spouts lies straight from Menelaus!' Paris launched to his feet, then turned to his father. 'You know how Helen was treated in that brutal place. The Greeks want nothing but to tear down our great city and pillage the spoils of our wealth for themselves.'

Murmurs of assent rippled through the crowd. Queen Hecuba and Princess Andromache shared a glance, their mouths drawn tight.

While Paris spoke, Danae noticed Odysseus retreat behind the other Greek generals. She was reminded of Metis laying her lizard traps on Delos.

'My cousin, Agamemnon, is a reasonable —' Palamedes began.

But Paris would not let him finish. 'Agamemnon is a butcher, and Menelaus brutalizes women for sport. All Greeks are barbarians. We should burn them on Ares' altar and pour their blood in libation to the God of War!'

Inflamed by his words, several courtiers lunged at the Greeks, throwing themselves into the row of guards. Danae spun around as a man darted between the soldiers and barrelled towards her. Before she could act, Hylas was in front of her, pushing the Trojan back with his crutch.

'We claimed xenia!' cried Nestor. 'You cannot defy the laws of Zeus!'

'Enough!' At the sound of their king's voice, the Trojans grew still.

King Priam rose to his feet, glaring at the Greeks.

'I will speak with my councillors, and we will reconvene at dawn.'

Once more the gathered courtiers raised their voices,

forcing the old man to shout over them, 'Do you defy your king?'

At that the room quietened. Danae shared a look with Odysseus.

Then an elderly man, leaning heavily on a staff of twisted oak, emerged from the cluster of courtiers. He bowed his grey head to the dais.

'I, Antenor, offer my home tonight to the Greeks.' He glared at his fellow Trojans. 'I, for one, still honour the laws of hospitality.'

'So be it, until tomorrow,' said King Priam. 'Now get them out of my sight.'

44. Honoured Guests

Antenor lived not far from the palace in an imposing, two-storey house constructed from the same polished yellow stone as Troy's great walls. On the lower level, sky-blue pillars flanked an oak doorway stained red with lacquer, loomed over by small, square windows cut into the bricks like sunken eyes. Odysseus helped Antenor heave open the heavy doors, and the Greek envoy entered the spacious dwelling, while two palace guards positioned themselves outside, another pair heading to watch the street at the rear. Inside, the entrance hall was warm and smelt faintly of smoke and spice.

The Trojan councillor closed his front door with a sigh, resting a gnarled hand upon the wood.

'I apologize for the inhospitable welcome to my city. The threat of war has made people forget the expectations placed on us by the gods.'

'You have nothing to be sorry for,' said Nestor.

Antenor smiled as he propped his staff beside the door. 'Come, warm yourself by my hearth. I have many sons, but none now live under my roof, so there are rooms for all.' He raised his voice, 'Theano, my dear, we have visitors!'

A white-haired woman draped in a fine green dress appeared in the stone corridor. She stopped still at the sight of the strangers in her home, her eyes roving over their faces, their clothing.

'Who are these people?'

'Visitors to our city.'

Theano bristled. 'They're the Greeks, aren't they?'

Antenor looked surprised at her guess.

'Trust you to bring them to our house,' she hissed through her teeth. 'I've heard talk of nothing else all afternoon but the arrival of the enemy at our gate, and now they are under my roof!'

'They are guests of our king, we are honoured to receive them.'

Theano glared at her husband.

'My lady,' said Nestor. 'We are indeed amongst those who have besieged your shore and caused your city much grief. But we have come to you in peace with the hope of convincing Priam to return Argive Helen, so that no Trojan blood may be spilt. It is our dearest wish to sail back across the wine-dark sea and trouble your land no more.'

Theano's lips tightened. Her eyes settled on Danae, absorbing her short hair and obsidian clothing. Then she said stiffly, 'You are welcome in my home. Above all else we honour the gods.'

Odysseus grinned. 'As do we.'

'I'd heard tales of Trojan hospitality, but, Antenor, you have surpassed them,' said Palamedes, as a slave girl rubbed oil onto his feet.

They were all gathered round a roaring hearth. The stone floor was covered in animal hides, the walls draped in pastoral tapestries, and a veritable feast was spread upon several low wooden tables clustered around their lounging chairs. It was only when the food appeared that Danae realized how hungry she was. Plates of cured meats, cheese, bread, apricots and figs were brought to them by more slaves, each dish more tantalizing than the last. They had eaten for the most part in silence, barely pausing to wash the food down with gulps of watered wine.

They had seen no more of Theano, who, despite extending the comforts of her home, still seemed uneasy in their company and had withdrawn to her chamber.

'What think you, Antenor? Will Priam agree to our demands?' asked Nestor.

The old Trojan councillor gazed into the fire. 'Many in this city wish for Helen to return to Menelaus and be done with the whole sorry affair.'

'Surely Priam will bow to the demands of his people rather than risk war,' said Odysseus, as a slave refilled his cup. 'Many thousands will die, whoever the victor.'

Danae's wine suddenly tasted bitter on her tongue. She wondered how he could speak so easily of the deaths their sabotage would ensure.

'Were it that simple,' replied Antenor. 'You see, when it comes to Paris, Priam is rather indulgent.'

'Go on,' Odysseus prompted.

Antenor ran a hand across his mouth. 'When Queen Hecuba was great with child, she and Priam received a prophecy from Delphi. It foretold their unborn son would be the destruction of Troy. They were most distraught and knew that a terrible choice lay before them. Their child or their city. One life or thousands. They did what any wise rulers would do. When Paris was born the child was given in secret to a herdsman to be taken to Mount Ida and exposed on the hillside. The king and queen claimed the boy had not survived the birth and lived for years under the burden of the truth. When eighteen summers had passed, a young farmer arrived at the Scaean Gates who was the very image of his mother, Hecuba. It was revealed that the herdsman could not bring himself to leave the child to die all those years ago and so had raised Paris as his own. Priam believes the gods rewarded them by returning their son, and their eighteen years of sacrifice were enough to placate the fates. Unfortunately, Paris has proven himself to be vain, lustful and jealous, traits only exacerbated by the indulgence of his parents, who I believe have never shaken the guilt they bear for attempting to have him killed.'

'You speak very frankly of your royal family,' said Palamedes.

'Be not mistaken, I am, and always will be, loyal to Troy. I seek only to arm you with the knowledge to prevent this war.'

'And we are indebted to you.' Nestor reached across and clasped Antenor's hand.

Odysseus said nothing as he gazed at the flaming hearth. Danae wondered what schemes were percolating behind that furrowed brow.

'Come,' said Antenor. 'The hour is late. Let me show you to your chambers, I am sure you will all wish to rest before your audience with the king tomorrow.'

Barefoot, she walked upon the midnight sand. The ghostly grove outside Hades' palace lay before her, and beyond raced the dark waters of the River Styx. As she drew closer, the trees began to move, yet no breeze danced across her limbs. Their trunks were thicker than she remembered, their bark like silvery skin, branches reaching towards each other like outstretched arms.

She realized with a horrifying jolt that they were not trees at all, but people; their feet buried in the earth, wailing soundlessly at a sky they could not see.

She ran across the last stretch of ground, obsidian grains spraying behind her pounding feet. But when she reached the grove, the tree-like figures twisted away from her, hiding their faces.

'Don't be afraid, I'm going to help you!' she called, in a voice that was not her own.

A voice that whispered to her in the small, dark hours.
Heart racing, she raised her hands and saw pale, slender fingers.
It could not be.

Drain them, said the voice inside her head. A voice so like the one that had awoken with her power, yet different. Older, colder, hungrier.

Though a part of her screamed 'No!' another part growled with desire, and she found herself reaching towards the nearest person. Horror and excitement pounding in her chest, she wrapped her hands around their neck and began to drain their life-threads.

It felt wonderful.

Danae woke tangled in her cloak, her skin slick with sweat. She looked down at her hands in the stuttering candlelight and sagged with relief. They were her own familiar fingers.

She thought at first it was the dream that had roused her, then something clattered against the painted shutters of her bedroom window. Frowning, she paced across the room and flung them open.

'Psst!'

Danae gazed down both ends of the street. The Trojan guards were nowhere to be seen.

'Psst!'

She snapped her head around to see a cloaked figure emerge from behind a horse trough. The figure beckoned.

Danae hesitated for a heartbeat, then climbed through the window, landing softly on the ground below before slipping into the shadows, eyes darting about for the guards. The cloaked stranger hurriedly gestured her further down the street, then vanished into a narrow alleyway.

This might well be a trap, but mortal cunning was no match for a Titan.

Danae ran after them, then slowed, drawing her power into her fingertips as she stepped into the shadowy alley.

The figure was waiting for her.

Danae's limbs tensed as she readied herself for an attack, but the stranger simply drew back their hood and stepped into a sliver of moonlight.

It was the priestess of Apollo Danae had seen in the palace megaron.

'Forgive me, sister of the all-seeing eye.' The priestess's eyes gleamed in the cold light. 'We do not have long until the guards return, and I must speak with you.'

Without her red veil and priestess robes she appeared younger than Danae had first thought. Her tumble of raven curls hung loose about her face, her light-brown skin flushed with the chill of the night.

Danae drew herself up, adopting an air of authority. 'You distracted them?'

The priestess nodded, her shoulders twitching with nervous energy. 'I paid a pair of prostitutes to lure them away.' She spoke as though this was the most scandalous thing she'd ever done.

Danae blinked. 'What do you want with me, priestess?'

The woman swallowed. 'My name is Cassandra, I am the daughter of King Priam.' She drew a breath, then blurted, 'Helen wishes to return to Menelaus.'

Danae's heart sank through her chest. 'How do you know this?'

'She told me. She cannot bear the thought of so much bloodshed in her name. But my brother, Paris, will never let her go. So tonight, Helen slipped a sleeping draught in his wine. He will not wake in time for the peace talks tomorrow.'

'Why are you telling me this?'

Cassandra stepped forward, her eyes wide and shining as the moon. 'You must remind my parents what the oracle at Delphi prophesied all those years ago. Paris will be the ruin of this city. Please, make them remember. They do not listen to me.' Tears spilled down her cheeks. 'From one sister to another.'

Danae backed away.

'Please,' Cassandra begged, 'so many will die if you do not help me.'

'Who goes there!'

Danae spun on her heel. One of the palace guards stood in the street, peering into the alley. He drew his sword.

'Run,' Danae hissed at Cassandra. 'Go!'

Cassandra cast one last pleading look at Danae then threw up her hood and hurried away, to be swallowed by shadow.

Danae turned back to face the guard.

'It is I, the seer, Dione.'

'Come out here where I can see you.'

She did as she was bid, and stepped out into the street.

'Why would a foreign seer be skulking about in the dead of night?' The guard raised his weapon. 'Unless she's a spy.'

Danae's heart hammered against her ribs as she summoned her life-threads. She did not wish to hurt him, but what choice did she have?

But rather than lunging towards her, the guard stumbled. Blood trickled from the corners of his mouth, then he fell heavily onto the ground.

Odysseus stood behind him, breathless, clutching a blood-slicked dagger.

45. The Burden of Love

Hermes lay on his bed, staring at the ceiling. He had not moved for some time. A thin crack, the length of his arm, splintered the marble. He had never noticed it before. Around him, the chamber was in disarray. Brightly coloured fabrics and torn cushions lay strewn over the exquisitely carved furniture, feathers and jewels scattered across the floor.

A week had passed since Zeus took away his secret mission and gave it to his siblings. A week of living with the realization that he'd had a chance to earn his father's esteem, to finally rise above the other Olympians, to earn everlasting glory, and he had failed. His only consolation was that Zeus had been so consumed with quelling the threat of the dragon, Typhon, that he was yet to summon Hermes for punishment. But it would come, of that he was certain.

The beating of wings sounded from beyond Hermes' balcony. He tilted his head to gaze through the billowing gossamer curtains. Two horse-drawn chariots flew by, driven by an armour-clad Artemis and Apollo, no doubt leaving the palace to scour the land for the Titan girl on their father's orders.

Hermes squeezed his eyes shut, tears trickling down his temples.

Then his door creaked.

Blankets tangled about his armoured legs as he scrambled to sit upright, grabbed his helm from the pillow beside him and pulled it over his head.

Aphrodite stood in the doorway, a golden goblet clutched in her hand. Her copper hair was loose, tumbling over her freckled shoulders, her blush-pink chiton draped perfectly over every curve.

On any other day, the Goddess of Love visiting his chambers would have been a pleasure Hermes could only dream of. Now it only confronted him with yet another failure.

'You've been avoiding me.' Aphrodite walked unsteadily into the room and took a deep draught from the goblet in her hand. The scent of ambrosia wafted across the chamber. 'Where is my son?'

Hermes swallowed. Given all that had happened in the Underworld – Hades' and Persephone's deaths, the freed dragon – he hadn't given much thought to another attempt to convince Aeneas to give up his pledge to fight for Troy in the coming war.

Her face crumpled in the wake of his silence. 'Oh no, please . . . he's not . . .'

Hermes' eyes widened and he shuffled off the bed to stand before her. 'No, no! He's alive. He's well. Strong and brave.'

'Did you give him my letter?'

Hermes nodded.

Aphrodite's breath shuddered. 'And you told him about the war?'

'Yes.'

'Is he somewhere safe?'

Hermes looked down at his feet. 'No.'

The goblet tumbled from Aphrodite's hand, clanging on the mosaic floor, amber wine soaking into the strewn silks.

'Why didn't you take him away!'

'I tried to convince him to leave, but he wouldn't go! So, I gave him one of your amulets, told him if he was ever in need to find a bird . . .' He trailed off at the jewel-bright tears tumbling from Aphrodite's bloodshot eyes.

'It's all my fault,' she whispered.

Hermes blinked. This was not the response he'd expected. He shook his head. 'This is Ares' doing.'

She laughed, the sound brittle with pain. 'I was the one who whispered in Paris' ear that Helen was rightfully his. I told him they were moulded from the same piece of clay and fate had cruelly ripped them apart . . .' Her lip quivered. 'I should have known when Ares bade me do it violence would follow . . . he is the God of War after all.'

She slipped her hand into the pocket of her chiton and drew out a wooden figurine of a little dove, holding it to her breast. She swayed, her eyes closed, more tears seeping beneath her lashes.

Hermes desperately wished he knew how to comfort her. He wanted to place a hand on her arm, but his limbs felt as dull and immobile as bronze.

Aphrodite loosed a bone-weary sigh, then opened her eyes. 'You think I forsook Hephaestus' bed because of the injuries he sustained when Father threw him from Mount Olympus.'

'No,' Hermes said quickly.

'Yes, you do,' she replied sharply. 'Everyone does. But it's not true. Hephaestus stopped lying with me long before he was thrown from Olympus.'

Hermes' cheeks reddened. He wished she would stop talking.

She looked down at the little dove. 'No one has ever loved me like my mortal shepherd. Those few years with him are the only thing that has made this endless life bearable. Father has never stopped punishing me for running away, but I would do it again.' Her voice faded to a whisper. 'I don't believe we can keep turning our hearts over afresh. For me there was one person in all of creation, and I am prevented from seeing the fruit of our love.' Her tears flowed thick and fast. 'I am Aeneas' mother, I should be nurturing him, guiding him. He will have such a short little life, and I'm missing it. Sometimes it hurts so much I can't bear it . . .'

Hermes summoned his bravery and threw his arms around her. She stiffened, then melted into his embrace, resting her head on his armoured shoulder. Her body shuddered, her tears soaking his neck.

'What do we have here?'

Hermes sprung away from Aphrodite. Ares stood in the doorway.

His lip curled. 'Am I interrupting?'

'Don't be silly.' Aphrodite slipped the dove back into her pocket.

'Don't stop on my account.' Ares prowled into the chamber. 'I'm in need of some entertainment.'

Aphrodite recoiled from Hermes. 'Stop it, Ares. He's just a child.'

'You hear that?' Ares lifted the corner of a shredded cushion. 'You're nothing but a perverse little boy.' He flung it from him. 'You disgust her.'

The lump swelling in Hermes' throat threatened to break free.

Barging past his brother, he ran through the doorway, Ares' laughter hounding him down the corridor.

When Hermes finally returned to his chambers, he was relieved to find them empty. He pulled his helm from his head, crumpled to the floor in a heap of golden armour and sobbed until he ran dry.

He's just a child.

He lay on the tiles for some time, the clay cool against his burning face.

Perhaps he deserved this. He had failed his father, failed Aphrodite. Maybe Ares was right and he *was* nothing but a perverse little boy.

He could leave, fly away and live with Arachne in her forest. The thought eased his anguish for a heartbeat. But no, there was nowhere in the great expanse of earth, sea and sky that he could hide from his father.

Remember what you found in the Underworld, said the voice.

Hermes wiped his cheeks. Of course, after everything that had happened in the past week, he had forgotten.

He glanced around the chamber for the tell-tale shimmer of a shade lingering in the shadows, then crawled towards the bed. Reaching beneath the swathes of silk draped over the frame, his fingers found what they were searching for.

He pulled a tattered saddle bag into the light.

It had been a strange item to find in Hades' palace. On first inspection it appeared to be filled with useless tat. But his uncle had never kept anything that didn't serve a purpose.

Hermes removed his gauntlets and undid the clasp.

He upended the contents onto his bed: a knife, a few coins, a clay pipe and a pouch of herbs. He picked up the pipe and turned it between his fingers. The faded likeness of a golden tree was painted across the barrel. He sniffed the inside, wrinkled his nose and tossed it behind him. The herbs too he swiftly discarded.

Once more, he reached for the bag, his fingers prying around its depths. He paused. There was something still trapped inside. He turned the bag inside out and discovered an inner pouch sewn to the leather.

He drew out a ragged piece of brown cloth, wrapped around what felt like a roughly cut jewel. Swiftly peeling away the wrapping, he uncovered a shard of stone, all shining obsidian edges.

His pulse quickened, his palm warming beneath the worn cloth as his life-threads clustered into his hand.

A memory tugged at the far reaches of his mind.

Just after his father had made him divine, his brother, Apollo, had taken him to see Delphi.

'What do people ask the oracle?' Hermes had said as they soared above the holy city in Apollo's golden chariot.

'Anything they desire to know. Mostly it comes down to questions of power, lineage, infidelity, how to prevent an untimely death. Mortals aren't very imaginative.'

'And it always tells the truth?'

Apollo had smiled. 'In one way or another. The stone never lies.'

Hermes recalled a chamber, thick with sulphurous smoke and something trapped beneath the ground, cracked and glittering like a great black eye.

'Can *I* ask it something?' he'd said.

'No.' His brother's face had grown stern. 'Father has forbidden any of us Olympians to touch the omphalos stone. It would weaken us, drain our godly powers.'

The same fear that had pricked Hermes then returned as he stared at the shard of rock. It was a piece of the omphalos stone, he was sure of it. But if it was so dangerous, why had Hades had it in his possession?

His hand was aching now.

Touch it, said the voice.

Heart thundering, Hermes rolled the stone free of its cloth, onto his palm.

As soon as his skin touched the shard, he was yanked from his physical form, his consciousness plummeting into a void of nothingness. For a moment, there was only darkness.

Then terror like he'd never known engulfed him as his shimmering life-threads fled away across the blackness. He tried to reach for one, but he had no hand to grasp it. Instead, his consciousness lurched forward, dissolving into the strand and travelling along its length as it joined another, then another.

Shapes began to emerge. Hermes soared through the wings of an eagle, glinted in the eye of a bull and shot through the antennae of a butterfly as he raced through the tapestry of life. He was flying across the curve of a dolphin's fin when he remembered: he was meant to ask a question.

What did he desire the most? His father's approval? Aphrodite's love? Ares' envy?

He wanted all of it.

Suddenly the tapestry changed. The web of gleaming threads twisted, forming something new.

A city drawn in ever-moving lines of light. A fortress, its glowing towers stretching away into the darkness. Troy. Then the image shifted, the threads weaving into a clash of bodies, Aphrodite's son, Aeneas, falling back as a female soldier raised her sword against him. Hermes tried to cry out, but he had no voice to scream. The vision swirled again: the same battlefield, a different tangle of bodies. He searched for Aeneas but could not see him. Then a girl parted the throng, her short hair buffeted by an invisible wind. She stared at Hermes as if she could see him, then raised her hands, Poseidon's trident clutched in her fist. Life-threads streamed from her, leaching from the scene around him into her as she channelled her power.

With a gut-churning wrench, Hermes dropped the stone and returned to his body. He staggered from the bed, fell upon his hands and retched onto the tiled floor.

His insides emptied, he wiped his mouth and sat back on his heels, chest heaving.

Aeneas, Troy, the Titan girl, his uncle's trident. It didn't make sense. Yet, Apollo had said the stone did not lie. There must still be a way for him to redeem himself, even if the path was not yet clear. Perhaps he could save Aphrodite's son after all and defeat the Titan girl in one fell swoop.

Hermes looked to the darkening sky beyond his window and curled his hands into fists.

Of one thing he was certain: his destiny waited in Troy.

46. First Blood

Danae stared at the blood oozing from the Trojan guard's body, glistening in the moonlight like spilt ink.

She flinched as Odysseus grabbed her arm, pulling her to face him. Her gaze caught on the dark flecks splattered across his neck.

'What did she say to you?' His fingers dug into her flesh.

She ripped her limb from his grasp and backed away staring at the blade still clenched in his fist.

'How did you know . . .'

'I heard your window open. When I discovered you gone, I followed.' Odysseus pointed the knife at the guard. 'I slipped this from his belt while he threatened you.' He glanced about the shadowy street. 'What did that woman want?'

Danae drew a breath, her pulse still thundering. 'That was Cassandra, a princess of Troy. She told me that Helen has slipped Paris a sleeping draught to keep him away from the peace talks tomorrow. Helen wishes to return to Menelaus to avoid war.'

Odysseus digested her news, looking again to the slain guard. Then his head snapped up, his gaze sharp and bright as starlight.

'The guard attacked you in your chamber while you slept. I heard the commotion then pushed him out onto the street, where we fought. Before I killed him, he confessed he was sent by Paris to slay us in our beds. You will tell Antenor that, to avoid the wrath of Zeus, he must see us safely out of the city tonight.'

'What of Nestor?'

'Even he must agree that war is the only response to an attack on a chosen mouthpiece of the gods.' He paused, eyeing her. 'We will need to present them with signs of a struggle.'

After a breath of hesitation, she nodded. 'Do what you must.'

Everything seemed sharper in the moonlight. A city of cut-glass edges.

Antenor had been horrified at Paris' betrayal and agreed to lead the Greek envoy out through the city's old tombs to safety, the gates being watched night and day by sentries. Danae's torn dress and the guard's blood artfully smeared on her limbs by Odysseus had sealed the old councillor's decision. Nestor had been unable to hide his disappointment, but even he accepted that peace could no longer be salvaged.

Danae tugged her cloak tight around her as the chill of night chased Antenor and the Greek envoy through Troy's deserted streets. Her limbs thrummed with a hollow exhilaration born of danger and lack of sleep.

She could not banish the image of Odysseus slaying the guard from her mind. He had cut the man down as easily as scything wheat.

At a sharp hiss of breath, she turned to see Hylas grimacing as he strode beside her, leaning heavily on his crutch.

'Are you all right?'

'At night I wrap my leg in an ointment made from bitter root. It helps with the chafing. Didn't have time to before we left.'

'We can stop while you –'

'No.' Hylas set his jaw and quickened his pace.

The shadows seemed to stretch towards them with each turn, every new square crossed and alley traversed. Danae's eyes darted about so swiftly, the moon-brightened stones and their dark counterparts seemed to blur into monstrous shapes. She was not the only one whose nerves lay exposed. At one point a black cat leapt across their path, and Palamedes cried out then aimed a kick at the animal as it fled into the darkness.

She was acutely aware of how exposed they were without their weapons, and she was forbidden from revealing her power, Odysseus' order another collar about her neck.

Finally, they reached a building unmistakeable as a temple of Athena, given the bronze statue of the goddess presiding outside its columned entrance. Antenor ushered them into the shadow of a side wall and heaved open a plain oak door.

'This passage leads out through the old tombs. When the tunnel branches, take a right turn, then right again, and you will emerge onto a hill overlooking the Trojan Plain. My slaves will meet you there with your horses.'

Danae's pulse quickened. Tunnel. Underground. But she had no time to dwell on her fear as Odysseus, Hylas and Palamedes vanished into the passage.

'Thank you,' said Nestor, clasping Antenor's hand. 'I pray the gods look kindly on you. I'm sorry it has come to this.'

Antenor laid his fingers over Nestor's. 'I am too. I may well face punishment for helping you, but I will not stand by and see everything I hold dear torn down. Most of us Trojans are honourable people, we love the gods – remember that.'

Nestor nodded and disappeared into the passage.

Danae followed him, forcing herself to edge closer to her companions for fear of losing them in the gloom. Then the door shut behind them, and darkness reigned.

It was like being swallowed by the sea, yet instead of muffling sound, the blackness amplified all: the scrape of their sandals on the rough stone floor, the rasp of their breath, the blood pulsing in Danae's ears.

She tried to concentrate on the movement of her feet and the texture of the stone beneath her fingertips. Dry, crumbling. Not damp, like the Underworld. She held on to that difference, all the while her heart stammering with ever-increasing speed.

'Are we all still here?' Odysseus called after a while.

'Yes,' replied Palamedes and Hylas.

'Here,' said Nestor.

'Dione?'

'Yes,' she breathed, willing her voice not to betray her.

'We turn right.' Odysseus' words rang clear through the tunnel.

Danae did not know how she forced her legs to keep moving. Her thoughts raced so fast, they blurred into images she could not divine.

The group turned right again, and Danae stopped, her breath raking over her dry lips. She could no longer feel stone beneath her fingers but damp earth.

'No,' she hissed to herself between gritted teeth. 'Keep moving.'

Her leaden legs obeyed, and soon the terrain of the wall changed once more. She felt a groove in the earth, then a lip of stone. She lay her palms flat to the wall. The stone bore markings.

They must have reached the tombs.

In Danae's sight-starved mind, her imagination caught fire. She pictured the corpses coming alive and dragging their bones to dance with the living. She saw ghostly trees and people with no skin, the laugh of a dead man echoing through her skull.

Her legs gave way, and her lungs shrank to the size of

oranges. Lights flashed across her vision, sparks that elongated as they burst, stretching into glowing threads that scurried away in the darkness. Almost feverish with terror, she believed she had become trapped in the omphalos shard, her life fleeing from her until there would be nothing left but a sightless husk floating endlessly through time. All the while, her life-threads pulsed from her in waves, shooting uncontrollably into the earth.

'Dione!'

The ground shook, clods of earth and pieces of stone raining down on them.

'Dione!'

'Danae.' Her true name. Barely a whisper, spoken so close only she could hear. 'Danae, stop.'

Arms lifted her from the ground. She did not know when she had fallen.

'I've got her,' said Hylas. She clung to his voice, the warmth of his body pressed against hers.

'Run!' shouted Odysseus as the passage behind them collapsed with an almighty crash.

They hurried through the blackness, half sprinting half stumbling, Hylas' arm firm around Danae's shoulders.

Then the darkness shattered, and starlight bled through the cracks.

They emerged from the mouth of the tombs in a gust of dirt and dust, halfway up a hillside overlooking the fortress city. Behind them, the tunnel groaned like a dying beast, and they all fell to the ground as the last of the passage collapsed.

Beyond, the sea was like a sleeping beast, silver light dancing on its watery scales. The wind had chased the clouds from the sky, and the moonlit world was colder for it.

'What in Tartarus is going on?' called Palamedes.

'Poseidon, earth-shaker!' replied Nestor, unaware that his god's body rotted at the bottom of a lake on Delos.

'Dione,' Odysseus' voice rang out like a bell. 'Are you hurt?'

'I'm all right,' Danae called weakly.

'I don't like this,' said Palamedes, pushing himself to his feet. 'That was a god's doing back there. If not Poseidon, then one who clearly loves the Trojans and has set their will against us.'

'If a god wished us dead, we would not be standing here now,' said Nestor.

As the rest of them heaved themselves up, Odysseus moved towards Danae.

'Do you not remember what I said to you before we left the Greek camp?'

Frail as she felt, a rod of defiance straightened her spine. 'I remember.'

His eyes swept over her, searching.

'What say you, Seer?' Nestor staggered over to them. 'Did you sense the gods as we passed through the tombs?'

She was so weary she could barely think of a lie. 'Olympus looks to Troy, but the Twelve have not yet chosen sides. That was a warning.'

The wrinkles deepened between Nestor's brows as his thoughts turned inward, mulling over her words. Odysseus' frown remained, but he nodded.

'There!' Palamedes pointed to the city. Far to the right of the Scaean Gates, another entrance punctuated the great stone wall. It was difficult to tell in the moonlight, but it looked as though a crack had appeared at its centre. Then five horses emerged, two ridden, the rest tethered behind the leading pair.

'Praise the gods,' breathed Nestor.

Danae's heart lifted as the mounts charged towards them. But her elation was short-lived.

Hundreds of flames burst into light across Troy's battlements, then the dissonant clanging of bells rippled across the plain.

'Go,' shouted Odysseus. 'Get the horses!'

They pelted down the hillside, sprinting across the stretch of land towards the cantering horses.

Battered and bruised, the Greeks heaved themselves onto their mounts, untied the ropes that bound them together and set off across the Trojan Plain as the slaves retreated towards the city.

The drum of her mare's hooves thundered through Danae like it were her own heartbeat. Then another sound pricked her ears, a whistle cutting through the rush of the wind and clamouring bells. She looked back.

A swarm of arrows flecked the dark sky, their bronze tips glinting in the moonlight. Time slowed as they seemed to pierce the night then turn and fall towards the Greeks. Danae's eyes widened as the shafts gathered speed, plummeting downwards.

There was no time to think. Calming her breath, she imagined melting into her mind river, channelled a rope of life-threads into her hand and flung it at the sky. She would not lose control this time.

'Please, wind,' she whispered, 'carry them away.'

So, this is faith, she thought, as she watched the arrows continue to fall, the night sky webbed by threads of golden light. She was suspended somewhere between petrifying fear and a calm deeper than the widest ocean. Then the balance tipped, threatening to send her careering back into a maelstrom of panic. It wasn't working. Her unquestioning trust was going to kill them.

The tapestry of life flickered, threatening to vanish from her sight.

Then, just as she was about to force her will through her life-threads, the wind answered her plea. A power greater than herself surged through her, and her threads split, twisting across the sky as a blast of salty air scattered the arrows, sending them into a chaotic spin to land in an arc behind the horses.

Nestor laughed, a desperate expulsion of relief. 'The gods have spared us!'

Another fleet of arrows came, but their horses were now safely out of range. Odysseus looked back, his gaze settling on Danae. A thrill rippled through her at the realization brightening his face.

He may be a wolf, but she was a lion.

47. Light of Mankind

The sky was paling as the peace envoy returned to the Greek camp. At the sound of their horses, men emerged from their tents to stare as the group walked their mounts between the makeshift dwellings. None spoke, their faces grim. Odysseus, Palamedes, Nestor, Hylas and Danae were daubed with blood and dust, and Helen was not among them. It did not take a seer to divine that war was now inevitable.

By the time they tethered the horses and made their way to Agamemnon's tent, a procession of soldiers trailed behind them, waiting for confirmation of their fate.

The war tent bustled with the Greek allied army's commanders, all dressed in armour, as though they had already been told the outcome of the expedition.

Silence swept across the room, followed by Agamemnon booming, 'Well?' He wore a butcher's knife sheathed beside the scabbard of his sword.

Odysseus intoned the sacred greeting, then bowed his head. 'The Trojans betrayed us. Prince Paris attempted to have us murdered while we slept.'

'Is this true?' The King of Men addressed Palamedes.

His cousin nodded. 'We were forced to flee the city. We barely escaped with our lives.'

Nestor sank into a chair. 'Everything happened so fast. I still do not understand why Paris would do such a foolish thing. To break Zeus' sacred tradition of xenia . . .'

'The man is a godless bastard,' Menelaus grunted, a wild gleam in his eye. 'I will enjoy crushing his pretty face to pulp.'

'His reason does not matter,' said Odysseus. 'He attempted to murder a peace envoy.' He gestured to Danae. 'His guard tried to kill my seer and in doing so has enraged the gods.'

'We should have spoken to Priam,' said Nestor, 'given him a chance to —'

'Don't be a coward, old man!' The King of Ithaca rounded on him. 'It is done. And the gods themselves intervened when their archers tried to shoot us down,' he flung an arm towards Danae, 'is that not so?'

All eyes turned to her.

'Zeus himself spared us as we fled the city. I believe the King of the Gods now favours the Greeks.'

Agamemnon leant his fists upon the table bearing the map of Troy. 'That settles it. Nestor, you've had your chance at peace, now will you pledge your ten thousand men as promised?'

Nestor sighed. 'I will.'

Agamemnon straightened and looked to his gathered generals. 'Make sacrifices to Ares, then ready your men to march on the city with the next sunrise. We will crack their walls and ravage what lays within. My brother's wife and stolen treasure will be returned to him. The rest of the spoils are yours to divide as you see fit.'

The assembled generals bowed to their leader, then dispersed.

Danae watched Menelaus pace towards the tent's entrance.

'Do you not wish to know how your wife fares?' she asked.

Menelaus paused. Without looking at her he replied, 'Is she alive?'

'She is.'

He grunted, then swept out of the tent.

Odysseus turned to Danae as the last of the generals left and said softly, 'Come, it is time to meet your army.'

Hylas and Danae hurried to keep pace with Odysseus as he strode towards the Ithacan quarter. He led them to a large supply tent and drew back the curtain. It was packed with the Children of Prometheus members Danae had met aboard his ship alongside at least a hundred others, all shoulder to shoulder amongst the barrels, sacks and amphorae. Her heart lifted to see Telamon and Atalanta among them.

A hush swept over the tent. The men's faces glowed at the sight of her, as though she were a spark igniting the kindling of their faith. She caught sight of Sinon and Evenor in the crowd, beaming. As she gazed at her soldiers, some familiar, many strangers, for the first time since hearing Prometheus' prophecy, she truly understood what it meant to be the hope of mankind.

'I do not have long,' said Odysseus. 'I will have to brief the rest of the Ithacan force.'

'Is it time?' asked one of the men.

The king nodded. 'These are your orders: you will ride out with myself, the last daughter and the rest of the Ithacan soldiers. Once the gods descend, you know what you must do – shoot them down, draw them into the battle, then swarm them once they're on the ground, at least twenty men to each Olympian. Your mission is to support the last daughter in ending each of their lives.'

The gravity of what was about to happen settled into Danae's bones. She and these mortal soldiers had the element of surprise, but the false gods had powers, weapons, magically enhanced armour. She tried not to quake at the memory of how difficult it had been to vanquish Poseidon, how Metis had lost her life in the process.

She forced herself to stand tall. These men looked to her for hope, she could not show fear. She glanced at Hylas, then Telamon and Atalanta. Her comrades, her friends. They did not look afraid. As the Ithacan soldiers drew strength from her, she drew strength from them.

'Say something,' Odysseus murmured.

Danae paused. 'The fight will be hard. Possibly the hardest of your lives. The false gods are not easily slain. I killed Poseidon, and I watched Hades burn,' several men audibly gasped, 'but I could not have done it alone.' She beckoned Telamon and Atalanta to stand beside her, then placed a hand on each of their shoulders. 'Without these warriors, my corpse would be mouldering on a distant island. Hylas too has saved my life more times than I care to remember.' Hylas flushed to the tips of his ears. 'All of you are vital. You may not have powers like I do, but I need you, just as much as you need me. I cannot promise you will all survive. But I do know that each and every life on this earth is in danger while the false gods reign on Olympus. They have stolen from the Mother, they have stolen from us all. How many tears have been shed, lives lost, pain endured? It ends now. Tomorrow, when the Greek army rides out to meet the Trojan force, we will strike a blow so powerful that Zeus himself will weep.'

One of the soldiers fell to his knees. Many others followed in a cascade, all raising their hands to Danae with murmurs of 'Light of mankind'.

Yes, crooned the voice. *Yes!*

Danae let their belief wash over her. Then, all at once it was like a vice had been clamped around her chest. She backed away, lifted the tarpaulin and stepped out of the tent.

Swiftly, Hylas, Telamon and Atalanta emerged behind her.

'Are you all right?' asked Hylas.

Her hands trembled. 'Most of those men will probably die

tomorrow and they have no idea what waits for them. I have no idea! We should tell them the truth about the afterlife.'

'Don't lose your nerve,' said Atalanta. 'Like you said, we're all in this together.'

The energy thrumming through Danae's limbs quietened at the deep calm swirling in the warrior's eyes.

She rubbed the back of her neck and looked to Hylas. 'Odysseus knows what he's doing?'

Hylas nodded. 'I have never known his sources to be wrong when it comes to the gods. Like you said, the fight will be hard. But think how much easier it will be to pick off the false gods unsuspecting on a battlefield than when mounting an assault on Olympus.'

'He's right,' said Telamon. 'And we're with you, don't forget that.'

Danae's chest swelled with feeling as she took in their faces. 'I can't lose you.' She glanced at Hylas. 'Not again.'

'You won't,' said Atalanta. 'We've already taken down two false gods. The rest won't see us coming.'

Telamon laid an arm across the warrior's shoulders. 'Like stealing honey from a babe.'

Odysseus drew back the tent flap. 'Everything all right?'

'Yes.' Danae met his gaze, her shoulders squared.

'The men responded well to you in there.' He almost looked impressed. 'Be ready to move out at first light. And remember, it is imperative you do not reveal yourself until the battle with Troy is underway. Once the Olympians are lured down to the Trojan Plain my men will loose their arrows on the false gods. That will be your signal. Now, I must brief the rest of my army.'

As Odysseus paced away, Hylas touched Danae's arm. 'I've got something to show you. Come with me.'

*

Danae and Hylas headed deep into the depths of the Ithacan tents, soldiers hurrying about them, readying themselves for war.

'What makes you so sure you can trust him?'

'Odysseus?' Hylas glanced at her. 'He's more than proved his dedication to the Children of Prometheus. Don't you think?'

'It's just . . . in Troy he killed that guard as though he were nothing.'

Hylas scoffed. 'How many people have you slain?'

'Not since . . .' she paused, thinking of Persephone. 'I have not killed anyone who didn't deserve it since the Underworld. It feels different, now I know the three realms of the dead are a lie.'

Hylas slowed. 'Many will die before you reach Olympus. Good, honest people will lose their lives. This is what freedom for all mortals costs. Odysseus knows this. He is prepared to shoulder that burden.'

She looked at him, the man who aboard the *Argo* had been her closest friend. She remembered how fiercely he had defended Heracles when they sailed together, and wondered how he could give his faith so wholeheartedly to another after all the betrayal he'd suffered. Perhaps he was a fool, or perhaps he was the bravest man she knew.

'You haven't changed.'

Hylas glanced down at his wooden leg.

'You're still the Hylas I remember,' she said softly.

'I'm just playing the petteia board the fates have given me. As you are.'

Danae shook her head. 'I don't play as well as you.'

'You're still here, aren't you?' When she didn't reply he said, 'Come on, I think you'll like what I have to show you.'

They carried on walking past a row of tethered horses

tossing their manes and flicking their tails. Beside the mounts, a group of soldiers were washing and oiling their limbs ready for battle, while another cluster polished the bronze of their shields until they gleamed.

Danae and Hylas finally emerged onto a small clearing, scattered with makeshift pens for goats and chickens, surrounding a roughly assembled hut. Walls had been erected with planks of wood and sail tarp, and only half the roof was sheltered, the remainder open to the sky, belching plumes of black smoke into the air.

Hylas rapped on the doorframe.

There was a clang, followed by a stream of cursing from within.

'I told you, the spears will be ready by sundown. I'm only one man!'

Then the makeshift door was flung open.

The man before them was covered in soot, a thick leather apron tied around his stocky frame. His hands were buried in hide gloves up to his elbows, the rest of his copper arms covered in old burns. He wore a strange contraption on his head: a band that circled his cranium, upon which a row of small bronze levers stood out above his brow, each holding a tiny circle of what looked like glass. Danae gaped. She had never seen such a thing.

The rivets across the man's forehead deepened as he eyed the visitors at his door. 'Oh, Hylas, it's you and . . . ?'

'Daedalus,' Hylas inclined his head, 'this is the last daughter.'

Daedalus' thick eyebrows crept up his forehead. 'You're smaller than I imagined.'

Danae opened her mouth, but before she could reply, the man gestured them into his hut.

'Daedalus is one of us, Children of Prometheus,' Hylas said quietly.

The inventor frowned as Hylas limped through the doorway. 'Leg giving you trouble?'

Hylas grimaced. 'Yes.'

'Been getting it wet again, have you?'

'It's hard to avoid when you're travelling by ship.'

'And you've been cleaning it and maintaining the joint like I taught you?'

Hylas grimaced.

Heat seared Danae's face and stung her eyes as they entered the room. A forge had been set up beneath the open roof, with swords, spears, shields and an assortment of armour piled against the far wall. But it was Daedalus' workbench that drew her gaze. It was littered with intricate metal contraptions like the one strapped across his brow.

'As if I didn't have enough to do,' the inventor grumbled as he gestured Hylas into a chair. 'Give it here.'

Hylas eased himself down and loosened the straps of his leg. Daedalus whisked it from him and lay it on the workbench, before flicking one of the circles on his head device to sit in front of his right eye.

'Just as I thought . . .' He gently manoeuvred the ankle joint. 'Sea water's stiffened the hinges.'

'Can you fix it?' asked Hylas.

Daedalus shot him a glower. 'Course I can.'

'Are the items I brought you before ready?'

'One thing at a time,' the inventor mumbled as he worked on the wooden leg. 'So damned impatient.' He tinkered for a while then carried the leg back to Hylas. 'There, that should be better.'

As Hylas tightened the straps Danae crossed her arms, a groove between her brows. She could not tell if she found Daedalus' nonchalance endearing or irritating.

After securing the leg, Hylas used his crutch to stand and

took an exploratory couple of steps. He grinned. 'Much better. Thank you.'

Daedalus grunted, then moved towards the rear of his workshop. He took up something long and slim that had been leaning against one of the wooden walls covered in a length of cloth, and handed it to Danae.

Her skin prickled as her fingers closed around what felt like a metal spear. She tore the fabric away to reveal Poseidon's trident, whole and gleaming.

Hylas beamed. 'A weapon fit for the last daughter.'

'How . . .' Danae looked from him to Daedalus. 'How did you?'

'I brought it here from Odysseus' ship,' said Hylas. 'I thought it might help you in battle. The rest is all Daedalus.' He gestured to the inventor.

Daedalus wiped his brow with the back of his hand. 'Wasn't easy; I could tell as soon as the lad brought me the pieces that this was different. Gold's weak you see. We don't make weapons out of it, not because it's expensive, but because it's soft. This, though,' he sucked a breath through his teeth, 'this was different.' He seemed to brighten as he spoke, eyes sparking in the dark caverns of their sockets. 'It has been infused with something to strengthen it.'

Danae thought of the bronze medallion Metis had sent to Odysseus. The king said its homing properties were powered by his blood. Perhaps the Olympians used similar methods when forging their golden amulets. 'I think the gods pour their blood into their homing medallions, perhaps they did the same when forging their weapons. They can store power. I felt it, when I smashed the trident.'

'Yes,' Daedalus gestured excitedly towards the weapon, 'I thought something similar myself. Blood and power, poured together into the molten metal during the forging. I had to be so careful when I melded the pieces together not to upset the constitutional balance of the gold and render it useless.'

'What of the armour?' asked Hylas.

'That will take more time,' said Daedalus. 'It is delicately made, and I will need the right proportions to fit it to.' He looked at Danae.

For a breath she imagined herself encased in gold, striding towards Mount Olympus, the gods quaking before her.

'Tomorrow I must remain in my seer's disguise, but I will return after the battle. We can fit the armour then. There will be more fights to come.'

She gripped the stem of the trident with both hands and closed her eyes. She felt its presence waiting to be filled. She plucked a single life-thread and fed it into the gold. Once the connection was made the trident sang in her grasp, like another limb.

'Are you pleased?' asked Hylas.

She opened her eyes, smiling.

'I love it. Thank you, Daedalus. Thank you both.'

The inventor made a rough sound at the back of his throat and nodded once.

'You should keep it covered, don't let any of the soldiers see it,' prompted Hylas.

'Yes,' Danae murmured, running her hands along the gold before wrapping it back in its cloth. Then she paused. 'What became of the iron collar I brought from Delos?'

'You mean this?' Daedalus produced the collar from his work bench.

'I will need that too.' She reached for it.

'Ah,' the inventor's fingers lingered on the metal. 'I was hoping to run some experiments; it's a fascinating contraption, no clear locking mechanism . . .'

'If all goes to plan, you may run all the experiments you desire after the battle.'

Daedalus clung on for a heartbeat, then nodded and released the collar.

As they moved towards the doorway Daedalus added, 'If tomorrow goes in our favour, I'd like to speak more on what you know of the Olympians' weaponry.'

Danae looked over her shoulder. 'I know very little, but don't worry, I'll come back. I have a destiny to fulfil, remember?'

A shadow passed over Daedalus' face. 'I'll believe it when I see it.'

Danae and Hylas stepped out into the dusky camp, and the inventor slammed the door behind them.

'He is one of the strangest men I've ever met,' said Danae as they walked through the darkening tents.

'Because he didn't kiss the ground at your feet?'

She hit him gently with the end of the wrapped trident. 'He is one of us, yet in the presence of the last daughter, the only thing that seemed to interest him was divine weaponry.'

Hylas glanced at her. 'He lost his son.'

'Oh . . .'

'He and his boy, Icarus, were imprisoned by old King Minos of Crete, forced to serve him and only him. But Daedalus planned their escape, spent years fashioning two pairs of wings from the feathers of birds that landed on their tower. Once the contraptions were ready, Daedalus and Icarus flew away from Crete, over the sea. But there was a fault with Icarus' wings; the wax-like substance Daedalus had used to hold the feathers failed, and the boy fell to his death.'

'That's terrible.'

Hylas nodded. 'There's not much that moves him now, apart from his work.'

'Yet he is moved enough by our cause to fight the gods.'

Hylas paused. 'Of course. What did the gods ever do for him?'

By the time they returned to their tents the torches were lit, the last vestiges of sunlight dissolved into the wine-dark sea.

'Thank you,' said Danae, 'for everything. I don't deserve your friendship, but I'm glad I have it.'

Hylas stopped walking.

'What is it?'

He gestured to the tent beside him. 'This is mine . . . You could come in, if you like. Just for company. Unless you'd rather be alone?'

Danae bit down on the inside of her lip. 'There's someone I need to speak to.'

Hylas nodded. 'Of course.'

She hesitated for a heartbeat then stepped forward and drew him into a hug. He stiffened at first, then wrapped his arms around her. They held each other tight. All of a sudden, tears prickled Danae's eyes.

'I named my horse after you,' she whispered.

'What?' Hylas drew back.

She blinked the moisture from her eyes. 'On the Caucasus Mountains, one of Hera's winged steeds was left behind. He could have flown away but he stayed with me. I named him Hylas.'

His lips parted, colour blooming over his cheeks. Then he closed his mouth and nodded once.

Danae squeezed his arm. 'You should get some rest. See you at dawn.' Then she turned and walked away into the swathe of tents.

48. The Eve of War

Danae hurried past soldiers testing the fit of their armour and limbering their bodies, eyes bright and hard as their swords. It didn't take her long to find someone who could direct her to the tent Atalanta had claimed for the night, given she was a woman in a silver breastplate amongst a sea of men clad in bronze.

At Atalanta's dwelling on the outskirts of the Ithacan quarter, nervous energy twitched through Danae's fingers as she pulled apart the material hanging over the entrance.

Atalanta sat on a spread of animal hides, a bucket of water beside her legs, a wet rag in her hand. There was no other furniture, save for an upturned barrel that served as a table holding a squat candle melting into a terracotta dish. The warrior stilled as Danae entered the small space, like a creature disturbed in her den. For a breath, neither woman moved. Then Atalanta continued to wash the camp grime from her arms.

Danae set down the wrapped trident and collar. 'I thought you'd be drinking with Telamon.'

Atalanta scrubbed at a graze on her forearm. 'I'm saving the wine for our victory.'

'Saving the wine?' Danae's eyes narrowed. 'What have you done with Atalanta?'

The warrior scowled, but the side of her lip curled.

Danae summoned the courage to cross the space between them and sank to her knees. She took the cloth from Atalanta's hand and thrust it into the bucket, the salty tang of seawater rising up to greet her. She squeezed away the excess and began to wipe Atalanta's other arm. The warrior let her, eyeing Danae through heavy lids.

'If Artemis comes tomorrow, leave her to me.'

Danae paused, the rag dripping in her hand. The noise of the camp, the sea and the wind faded into the drum of her heartbeat.

'If you could ask her why she left you to the mercy of the raiders, would you want that chance?'

A muscle twitched in Atalanta's jaw. 'The only thing I want to hear from that bitch is screaming.'

Another question surfaced in Danae's mind, more words she didn't dare give breath. Instead, she said, 'I've been thinking about what Metis said – that she could bring Athena back to the way of the Mother.' She ran the rag down Atalanta's forearm. 'I wonder if all the Olympians need to die. Some might wish to embrace the path Gaia intended for her chosen Titans.'

'We have no other choice. They're too dangerous to be left alive. Anyone with that much power is.'

Danae paused. 'What about me?'

Atalanta looked up at her. 'You are different.'

Warmth spread through Danae's cheeks. She resumed washing the warrior's arm.

'If you're scared about tomorrow, don't be. Your power has grown stronger since we sailed aboard the *Argo*. I saw how you fought against Poseidon. And don't forget you've got some pretty good warriors at your side.'

Danae pushed away any thoughts of Atalanta riding into battle. 'Tell me about your home in Arcadia.'

Atalanta tensed as Danae ran the salt-sodden material over a half-healed gash across her shoulder.

'The Athenians might have their olive groves and treasure houses, the Thebans their plains of golden barley, but the forests in Arcadia are richer than any kingdom. In the woods across Mount Lykaion, there are no cities; no buildings of stone, no temples to maintain and no tithes to owe. We slept beneath the canopy, wet our lips with fresh springs and feasted on the abundance of the forest.'

'It sounds perfect.'

'It was.'

Danae recalled what the warrior had told her aboard the *Argo*: how a group of raiders had come to her forest and murdered her tribe of hunters. Her family. She continued to stroke the rag down Atalanta's arm, drinking in the ridge of each scar, the hard swell of her bicep.

'Did Artemis teach you to hunt?'

'No. That was Nephele. She was the most talented woman with a bow I've ever known.'

'That's high praise coming from you.'

'She had far more skill than I,' Atalanta said fiercely. 'She began teaching me to whittle my own arrows the day she found me.' A whisper of breath hissed between her teeth as Danae moved the cloth down to her mud-splattered calves.

'So, she stole you from your wolf pack . . .' Danae traced the cloth up to the bones of her knee, then higher.

Atalanta grabbed her hand. 'Enough.'

The warrior's onyx eyes seemed to burn in the light from the lone candle. Longing expanded through Danae's chest, but she dared not move. She half expected Atalanta to ask her to leave, then the warrior released her hand.

'Tell me about Naxos.'

The breath hitched in Danae's throat. She sat back on her heels.

'My family live in a hut by the sea. It's not much, but we have a yard, and for most of my life we kept goats and made cheese from their milk. When we had enough coin for the ingredients Ma would make the best honey cakes I've ever tasted.' She almost salivated at the memory. 'There's a dusty path that runs down from our gate to the beach and the cove where my father keeps his fishing tub. I learnt to swim in those waves before I could walk.' *And in those same waves my sister perished.* 'My brothers live nearby with their wives and babes, and beyond our village is Timon's apple grove, I used to steal his fruit . . .' she paused. 'It must sound dull to you.'

Atalanta shook her head.

'It sounds perfect.'

Danae's throat thickened. She wanted to talk about Alea, remember all the things her sister had loved and hated. She had touched on what happened to her sister on Delos, but there had been too much to tell to linger on her memory. And Danae did not know what would be unleashed if she opened that cavern.

'You're scared about going back,' Atalanta said softly.

Danae squeezed the cloth between her fingers.

'It is not easy to long for a past you cannot return to. The place remains, but you know it will never be the same. Because of that, I will never return to Arcadia.'

'Come to Naxos with me,' Danae blurted. 'When this is all over.'

The warrior shook her head. 'You won't see this face grow old.'

Danae's hands tightened into fists. 'You will not die tomorrow.'

Atalanta shrugged. 'You live the life of a hero and one day you run out of chances. Besides, you'll look like this forever.' She gestured at the entirety of Danae. 'You won't want me when I'm a withered crone.'

Danae gazed at her as the warm candlelight licked across her face. Even in the year they had been apart she could see a change, a deepening of the faint lines creasing Atalanta's eyes, her brow. She had never looked more beautiful.

'How old *are* you?'

The warrior rested her forearms on her knees. 'I have seen twenty-six summers.'

Danae raised her eyebrows. 'Must have been some rough summers.'

Atalanta flicked seawater at her.

Danae smiled, before silence reclaimed the tent. She looked down at the cloth in her hand.

'Did Artemis say she wouldn't want you when you grew old?'

'What?' Atalanta breathed.

The words pushed their way up Danae's throat until they spilt over her tongue. 'Was she more than just your goddess?'

Atalanta's face spasmed, and, like a creature emerging from the deep, the hatred born of poisoned love the warrior had harboured all this time unfurled into the light. Finally, Danae understood the conflict that had burned within Atalanta since desire took root between them. The mirror Danae held to the goddess who had ripped out the warrior's heart and smashed it beneath her gilded foot.

'I remind you of her, don't I?' Danae whispered.

Atalanta looked stricken.

'I'm not her,' she pressed. 'I know I left you once, but I will never abandon you again. I would never let anyone hurt you the way —'

With a snarl Atalanta pushed her back, knocking over the bucket. Seawater spilt across the ground. Danae scrabbled to her feet as Atalanta did the same. In the enclosed space, they prowled, their faces drawn and flickering in the candlelight.

Then Atalanta pounced, and Danae slammed into her, both women falling together in a heap of limbs on the animal hides. Danae gained the upper hand, squirming on top, but Atalanta twisted her foot around Danae's thigh and flipped her onto her back. Danae hit out, fists meeting flesh and armour.

'We might die tomorrow! Why won't you just admit . . .' Danae faltered as she tasted salt.

Tears dripped from Atalanta's face onto her own.

'Atalanta . . .'

The warrior let go and scrambled back, crouching as she wiped her cheeks. Danae remained kneeling on the hides, her breath shallow.

For a while neither of them spoke. Then Atalanta murmured, 'You are nothing like her. And I am glad.'

Danae reached across the space between them and took the warrior's hand, kissing her calloused palm.

Atalanta moaned. 'Danae . . .'

She drew Atalanta's hand upwards to the curve of her breast.

'Tell me you don't want this.'

'Oh, I want . . .' Another half-growled moan rumbled from the warrior's throat.

Danae pulled the other woman towards her. Longing ripped through her like fire as their bodies pressed together and they tumbled onto the hides.

Atalanta caressed Danae's breasts through the fabric of her dress, her nipples hardening at the warrior's touch. Then Atalanta's fingers travelled up, tracing the ridge of her collarbone to curl beneath the hard angle of her jaw. She lowered her head and kissed Danae's neck, each press of her mouth burning, teasing until finally those lips that Danae had dreamed of tasting met her own.

It was more than she had imagined. The sharpness of reality and the blaze of her senses sang through her body as Atalanta's tongue played with hers. Danae drank her in, hands prying beneath Atalanta's armour, struggling at the straps of her breastplate.

The warrior's kiss deepened, her fingers surging up into Danae's tangled crop of hair, raking her scalp. The breath hitched in Danae's throat, fear curling around her spine.

Suddenly, she felt not animal hide beneath her, but a chill marble slab. She was back in the Underworld, bound and gagged, her body no longer her own. Memory consumed her. It was not Atalanta's hands on her flesh, but Hades' fingers, bone-thin and cold, scraping across her head, sending shocks of unwanted pleasure through her body.

She punched Atalanta in the chest, a burst of life-threads exploding through her arm. The warrior flew back and crashed into the side of the tent, knocking over the barrel and sending the candle stuttering out into the dirt.

Shuddering uncontrollably, Danae scrambled around in the dark, unable to gather her senses.

Her mind was a roiling sea, her reason untethered. She was trapped again beneath the earth. She was going to suffocate. She was going to die.

Once her fingers connected with the fabric of the tarpaulin, she flailed her way to the entrance. Gasping for air, she knocked down one of the wooden poles and clawed her way out of the sagging tent. Behind her, Atalanta called her name.

Part of her knew she should stay, should try to explain what had happened to her in the depths of the earth, what Hades had done to her, but even outside in the fresh chill of the night air her mind screamed that she was being buried alive.

Stumbling to her feet, she ran.

Danae bashed into tent poles and tripped on tethers as she staggered through the torchlit tents towards the sea. Gazing up at the sky, she searched for the moon, the stars, anything to anchor her to the outside world. But the heavens were as dull as the earth, veiled by smoke-grey clouds.

She clawed at her throat, gasping for air, as she emerged beyond the line of tents and ran towards the ocean. The waves would save her. Once she reached the water, she would be all right.

Crashing to her knees, she moaned as the tide washed over her trembling limbs.

Breathe, said the voice.

Finally, air returned to her lungs. She remained where she'd fallen, kneeling in the sand, the cool water tugging at her dress. As panic slipped away, her thoughts returned to Alea, as they always did. She had raged at her sister for abandoning her, for not choosing to fight, but now she understood the draw of giving herself to the dark depths of the sea. She too longed to dance in the deep, let it wash away all her pain.

She was so weary, so bone-crushingly weary.

Escaping the Underworld had not freed her soul from the darkness. Now, she did not know if anything ever could.

Have faith.

Her heart ached as Metis' final words echoed through her mind.

She reached forward, pressing her hands into the tide-sodden sand. 'Gaia, where are you? Please . . . help me.'

She waited. But the guidance she craved did not come. Eventually, she rocked back onto her heels, shivering as the wind licked over her wet skin.

Atalanta's words lingered in her mind. She wondered what would become of her, once her destiny was fulfilled. Naxos had forever been a beacon, shining bright through the dark storm of her fate. There was so little left of the girl she had been. She wondered if her family would recognize the woman she had become. Would they look at her with horror when they learnt what she'd done to survive? The countless lives extinguished in the service of her destiny. And even if they did accept her, there would come a day when she would be alone once more; she'd weather time like a rock while they withered like fading blooms.

There was a shift in the air. The tide surged in rhythm with the wind, the rustle of the tents vibrating to the melody of the sea and sky.

Danae stiffened.

Something was emerging from the inky waves. In the darkness it looked like a creature from the deep, draped in long strands of seaweed.

She shuffled away from the water as the beast approached.

As it drew closer, she realized it was Achilles. His long copper hair was draped in tangled strands over his lithe frame. Free of the waves, he stooped swiftly to wrap himself in a leather kilt worn by the Myrmidon soldiers. Danae wondered how she hadn't noticed it lying there.

The young man startled. 'Seer, what are you doing?'

Danae wiped her hands. 'I could ask you the same.'

'I always swim the night before a battle.'

'Is that the secret to your skill?'

Achilles twisted his hair into a rope and wrung it. 'Perhaps. My mother taught me to worship the sea above all else. She said the ocean rewards those who honour its power.'

The face of Danae's father loomed so clear in her memory she was forced to turn away from Achilles.

'Do the gods trouble you, Seer?' Achilles lowered himself to the ground to sit cross-legged beside her. 'My father had a seer who went mad. The voices in his head were so loud he threw himself from a cliff.' The youth eyed Danae. 'Perhaps it's catching.'

She huffed a breath through her nose, a dull ache throbbing behind her eyes.

'I am not mad.'

Achilles shrugged. 'If you say so.'

They sat in silence for a while, staring at the ocean.

Then Achilles said quietly, 'My mother made me promise not to come to Troy.'

'Why?' Danae turned to study his profile in the gloom.

'Because she says I am to die here.'

'Why does she think that?'

Achilles plucked a shell from the sand, turning it between his fingers. 'She was told so, by the oracle at Delphi.' He met her gaze. 'What do you think, Seer, will I meet my end before the Scaean Gates?'

'I am no oracle,' she said softly.

'But you know the will of the gods. They favour you with their power, you have shown me as much.'

Danae wondered how many men he'd killed in battle. She wondered if fighting eased the burden of his fate.

'Sorry, I do not know.'

Achilles chewed his lip, then turned back to the sea.

'Mother also said that my legend will surpass even that of Heracles.' He spoke without passion, without hope, as though what he said had already come to pass.

'Do you not wish to live until your bones are weary? Have a family with the one you love?'

'Patroclus is all I have ever truly wanted. And I have always known I would never grow old.'

'You do not regret having to leave his side so soon?'

A frown marred Achilles' brow. 'He will have my legacy to comfort him, and we will be reunited in Elysium when he dies.'

A familiar ache rippled through Danae's chest.

'I'm sure he'd rather have you than your legacy.'

Achilles' frown deepened to a scowl. 'You are the strangest seer I've ever met.'

The hint of a smile pricked her lips. 'I've been told that before.'

He leant back, resting on his forearms, his sea-beaded face tilted towards the night sky. 'I see no point in fighting the fates. If I am to meet my destiny, I will do it on my terms.'

A warm breeze tousled Danae's hair, like breath against her chill skin. And there, through the gentle rush of the waves, a song. Perhaps the Mother had not abandoned her after all.

She pushed herself to her feet. 'Goodnight, Achilles, I will leave you to the ocean.'

Wrapping her arms around her chest, she trudged back towards the camp, the tempest of her thoughts finally lulled.

If Achilles could bear his fate with grace, so could she.

49. The Prodigal Son

Hera cracked her whip across the flanks of two winged chestnut mares. She gripped the handles of her golden chariot as the horses surged onwards, climbing higher in the azure sky.

The barley fields and evergreen mountains of Thessaly sprawled beneath her, the ripening land stained sunset shades of bronze and crimson. Far to her right, Ares' chariot gleamed as it peeled away towards the islands of the Ionian Sea. Ahead of her, Athena took a path over the Aegean coast. Hera had said she would scour the Peloponnese for the Titan girl, but instead of descending she continued south over the spine-like mountain range. Soon she passed over the emerald peaks of Mount Parnassus, and the wreckage of what had once been Delphi. Despite the efforts of Apollo's devotees to rebuild, and the pale stone buildings that had sprung from the blackened ruins, the land surrounding the holy city was still scorched and bare. The mortals may have forgiven Apollo's destruction, but the earth did not forget so easily. She drove her horses on, over the city of Athens, to the wide waters of the Aegean and the clutch of islands cradled in its swells. Finally, the Queen of the Gods steered her mounts down towards a small, rocky stretch of land.

The earth had seen two full turns of the moon and sun, yet Poseidon still had not returned from Delos. Her fear mounting, Hera had decided to go after him.

The lashing wind carried the stench of rotting flesh. Fighting to keep her chariot steady, Hera landed on the rough beach of a crescent bay. She alighted swiftly, staring at the mouldering carcass of Poseidon's sea-creature, Skolopendra. It had almost been picked clean, the beast's shell ravaged of soft flesh, its eyes long pillaged by gulls brave enough to face the wind.

Hera cast her gaze across the island, life-threads rushing from her armour into her gauntleted hands. It appeared to be all barren scrubland save for the stony hill at its centre. The earth was churned, great chunks of rock and trees lying discarded like driftwood amongst the yellow grass.

So, this was where Zeus had exiled the mother of his first child.

Hera's body turned against her, stomach roiling. She remembered pursuing another of Zeus' loves, Leto, as the woman fled across the sea, her belly swollen with the twins Artemis and Apollo. Leto had sought sanctuary on Delos, knowing it was the one place Hera could not bring herself to set foot.

Metis had haunted Hera each day of her eternal life. She may be the Queen of Heaven, but she had never been able to summon the courage to visit the only other woman who had truly stolen her husband's heart. Until her children's lives were threatened.

Leaving the horses tethered to the chariot, she began the climb up from the beach towards the island's lone hill. Clouds of spiny spruce littered her way, brightly patterned lizards scuttling between the shadowy cracks of lichen-stained boulders. The remnants of fine traps, like spider's webs, lay tangled between several of the rocks. Hera's nose crinkled with disgust. What a pathetic existence Metis must lead.

She paused near the crest. Nestled in a natural crevice sheltered from the wind was the wreckage of a small stone dwelling.

Heart already stammering from the climb, Hera began

pulling aside rocks and shattered pieces of pottery, their rough edges scraping the gold of her gauntlets, as she searched for the curve of a limb, a battered segment of armour, or the spokes of Poseidon's trident.

She paused, closed her eyes and breathed deeply.

The trident is not here, murmured the voice.

Hera's eyes snapped open. The voice spoke the truth; the weapon contained so many life-threads she would surely feel its presence.

She cast her gaze to the peak of the hill and resumed her climb.

The wind howled at the island's summit, a spread of yellowing grass and grey rock unfurling beneath her as she clambered to its height.

There were strange piles of stones dotted about the peak. She stared at one, then kicked it, sending the collection of rocks scattering down the hillside.

Turning to scour the island from her vantage point, to the north she spotted a lone verdant patch of land surrounding a small lake. She squinted. What appeared to be a rectangular mound of rocks lay by the water's edge.

Hera scrambled back down the hillside, sprinted through the crisping grass and sporadic bursts of hardy blooms, only slowing as she approached the rock pile. With trembling hands, she removed stone after stone until a body was uncovered.

Hera stepped back, eyes watering at the stench.

She was so small.

In the centuries that had passed since Hera last set eyes on Metis, she had transformed the woman's memory into something otherworldly: a magnificent creature, more radiant and terrible than the flaming heart of the sun. A woman so powerful, despite her transgression, she had kept a corner of Zeus' heart all for herself. But in death Metis looked fragile, her rags clinging to her bones, her hair thin and brittle. Just another corpse.

Hera had never visited Delos, not because she was jealous of Metis or afraid of her power, but because she believed that if she stood before her rival, she would be shown in unbearable clarity which elements of her own composition were so lacking that she could not hold her husband's love.

Now she would never truly know.

Suddenly, Hera felt like a young girl again, standing outside her new family's hut after being chastised by Kronos for refusing to eat the fish stew Rhea had prepared.

As the wind whipped her curls about her salt-stained cheeks, she turned to gaze across the island. If Metis had been buried and Poseidon's beast slain, it did not bode well for her brother's fate. Yet there was no body.

Her brows furrowed. How would the Lord of the Sea leave Delos without his creature? Surely he could not have swum to another shore?

She searched every stretch of the cursed island, scouring the cliffs for a glint of gold or the hum of the trident's power.

But there was nothing.

Heart leaden, Hera climbed back into her chariot and took to the sky.

When Hera returned to Olympus, she bathed in water scattered with rose petals, had her nymphs massage her skin and hair with scented oils, then donned her finest imperial purple gown. She finished her masterpiece by placing her golden sun crown upon her shining curls, then looked at the nymph waiting by her dressing table.

'I am ready. Take me to him.'

By the time they'd reached the cherrywood door in the

southern quarter of the palace, Hera's fingers had tightened into fists. Something inside her knew he would be here. Despite the danger closing in around them, and most of his children being scattered throughout Greece searching for the Titan girl, it all came back to this.

She nodded at the nymph, and the woman opened the door.

The room smelt sweet, like honey. Sunlight poured in from a round window hollowed into the apex of the brightly patterned ceiling, shining on a floor lined with colourful cushions. The muscles in Hera's neck tightened at the sight of the murals painted across the circular walls: Heracles decapitating the many-headed Hydra, Perseus saving the princess Andromeda from the jaws of the great sea-monster Cetus.

Marble pillars guarded these scenes, between which nymphs in pale-blue tunics stood vigil over two figures in the centre of the chamber.

Cheeks flushed, Hera dragged her gaze to the centre of the room.

Zeus lay across the cushions, reclining on his elbow. A child of around three years sat before him, playing with the fringe of a crimson cushion. The boy's auburn hair curled around his ears, his olive skin was lightly freckled, and his eyes were wide pools of cerulean.

Zeus always claimed the children he had brought to Olympus were cast in his image, but Hera could only ever see their mortal mothers.

Her husband looked up at her. 'You never come here.'

'I have news.'

Zeus' gaze flicked to the nymphs.

'Leave us.'

As one, they rippled from the chamber, their footsteps echoing off the marble walls.

The child watched them go, then his ocean-blue eyes fixed

on Hera. His lip trembled. He crawled towards Zeus, nestling into the crook of his torso. Gently, the King of the Gods nudged him to standing.

'This is Hera, the Queen of Heaven. You must bow before her.'

The boy blinked, looked once more at Zeus then clumsily bowed, before burying his face in Zeus' chest.

'She scares me,' the child mumbled.

Zeus laughed.

The warmth in his face almost shattered Hera.

'Has he shown any indication of powers yet?'

Zeus' brow darkened. A rod of satisfaction pierced her spine. It was petty of her, but wounding her husband was so tempting when every breath she took in this child's presence was an insult.

'He is still young. I have several new methods yet untested.'

She wanted to scream at him, demand to know how he could, after all these failed attempts, still labour under the delusion that he could pass on his powers to a mortal son.

'You have seven divine children,' she spat. 'Why is that not enough?'

Zeus rose to his feet. 'Because, wife, as I have told you before, their powers do not come from me. The Hesperides tree still holds the secret to what we are. It is the last hurdle to cementing our divinity. The Mother's final yoke around my neck.'

'Really?' her voice quivered, low and dangerous. 'Or is it that there are no more apples for you to give?' Outside, a cloud drifted above the window, and the light dimmed. She shivered, ready for the violence she always waited for. '*Gold that grows bears no fruit* . . . You may keep the tree hidden, but you cannot hide the truth from me. It has been centuries since you gave Hermes his apple. It was rotting, its gold dull.

I always wondered why you made him divine at such a young age . . . It was the last fruit the tree bore, wasn't it?'

She tensed, waiting for the inevitable explosion.

Zeus stared at her then lowered his gaze to the child. He reached out to brush a curl from the boy's forehead. 'You came with news.'

Hera sagged, steadying herself against a pillar.

'Did you not hear what I said?'

'Deliver your news or be gone.'

She drew a breath. 'Metis is dead.'

Zeus stiffened.

Hera wiped her mouth with the back of her hand, the lie she had practised tumbling from her lips, 'Poseidon told me he planned to fly to Delos in search of Prometheus' girl, for he believed Metis might aid her. Forgive me, I know you cared for the woman. I wished to shield our brother from your anger, so I kept his secret. But when he did not return, I flew to the island myself.' She paused. 'Poseidon has vanished, his sea-monster slain, and I discovered Metis' body buried beneath a heap of stones . . . Who else could have done this but the Titan girl?'

Zeus' chest heaved. He rose to his feet, his gold-flecked eyes clouding like a storm-swathed sky. Hera was struck by the strange urge to grab the child and run before he could unleash his fury and destroy the room.

'Metis, Hades, Persephone,' he said slowly, his former love's name weighted with just as much reverence as his brother and niece.

'Yes,' whispered Hera, tears escaping down her cheeks.

Zeus nodded to himself, focusing on the child at his feet. He placed a hand on the boy's head and ruffled his curls. A smile played about his lips.

Heart drumming, Hera took a step forward. 'One of your

brothers is slain, the other vanished. At this very moment your children are scattered across Greece searching for the girl. If they find her, they might well meet the same fate. What will you do?'

Zeus tilted the boy's chin. 'I failed with Perseus and Heracles; I will not make the same mistake with you.'

'Zeus?'

The King of the Gods lifted the child into his arms. The boy laughed.

'Do not shut me out,' Hera whispered. 'Not now.'

His gaze snapped to her. 'You forget that I made you, I made all of you. I am master of the Hesperides tree. I am the one who brought you to the holy mountain and fed each of you an apple. Every Olympian life is mine.'

'Then how did she gain her powers?' Hera whispered, finally daring to ask the question that had gnawed at her ever since the girl had destroyed the oracle at Delphi.

A shadow passed over her husband's face.

She sucked in a breath. 'You really don't know, do you?'

Zeus set down the boy and prowled towards her. Hera backed away until her shoulders bashed against the cool marble of a pillar. Zeus pinned her to the stone, taking her face in his hands. She shuddered as he pressed his lips to her mouth.

'I remember the first day I saw you,' he said against her skin. 'A terrified little thing. Helpless and alone. Who dried your tears, Hera? Who begged their parents to take you in?'

Hera shuddered.

'Who vanquished their monstrous father so we might rise up from the dirt?'

'He wasn't monstrous,' Hera breathed.

'Say that again,' Zeus said softly.

Hera's courage failed her.

'Without me, there are no gods.' He released her, the imprint of his fingers stinging like a scald. He smiled. 'Do not fear, my queen, one of my children will be our salvation.'

'Which one?' Hera rasped.

'The one that survives.'

Before she could respond, the peals of a bell rang through the sky palace. For a wild moment, Hera could not remember what the sound signalled; it had been so long since she'd heard it.

A guard flung open the door. 'Your divine majesties, Argus, the watchman, has rung –'

'That much is clear,' said Zeus, striding towards the door as a couple of the blue-clothed nymphs darted inside to tend to the child. 'Why?'

'Someone has arrived on Pegasus.'

'Poseidon?' Hera ran after her husband.

'No, my queen,' the guard replied as the three of them paced down the pillared corridor, 'a mortal.'

Hera's mouth tightened, her mind whirling with possibilities. It was forbidden on pain of death for mortals to approach Olympus unless escorted by one of the Twelve. Who in all the world would dare to break their sacred rule?

Hera's blood was pounding by the time they emerged onto a cloud-swathed terrace, lined with rows of trimmed cypress trees, a gilded fountain pouring intricate swirls of water along rivets in the stone floor.

Surrounded by a ring of spear-wielding guards was Poseidon's snow-white horse, Pegasus. The beast Hera had lost after her altercation with the Titan girl on the Caucasus Mountains. She moved closer, eager to see who it was that knelt upon the floor.

'Step back,' Zeus commanded the guards.

They obeyed, and Hera gasped.

The man raised his grizzled head, the effort of that alone sending tremors through his emaciated frame. He looked at them through eyes of sea, sunk into shadowy sockets. He was so changed, Hera almost didn't recognize him. Almost.

Heracles' gaze settled on Zeus, then his cracked lips parted to croak one word.

'Father.'

50. A Fallen Star

They marched with the dawn.

The blasted notes of salpinges rang through the air, the horns chased by the thunder of drums. The earth quaked, the River Scamander trembling in its banks, as the bronze leviathan of the Greek army surged across the plain, each helmet a shining scale, each sword a spine. Dust hazed the air, the city of Troy rearing through the tawny cloud like the skull of a rival primordial beast.

Danae's heart beat in her throat as she tightened her grip on her mare's reins, a small pack secured around her waist. In her other hand gleamed Poseidon's golden trident. Odysseus rode to her left, Hylas to her right. Behind them, amongst the Ithacan soldiers, the full force of the Children of Prometheus regiment followed on foot, their circular shields reflecting the rising sun. Ahead, in a vast patchwork of flags and metal, marched the rest of the allied Greek army: Achilles leading the charge with his Myrmidons in armour that shone brighter than starlight, followed by Nestor's ten thousand men, shaven-headed Spartans, Arcadians with their great ash spears, plumed-helmed Argives, Phocēans, Laconians, Cretans, Aetolians, Epeans, Salamineans, Minyans and Boeotians, all led by Palamedes, Diomedes and the other generals riding horse-drawn chariots.

Mirroring the force on land, a score of hulking triremes cut across the iron-grey waters of the bay, sailing towards the Trojan harbour. Between them, four sleek pentecontǎrs sliced through the waves, their hulls black as eels. Gulls soared about their masts, their caws joining the piercing sound of the salpinges, hailing the destruction to come. In the lead was Agamemnon's ship, its prow dominated by a gilded figurehead of Zeus, a golden thunderbolt stretched across his painted chest. The King of Men stood above the King of Heaven on the prow deck, a crimson-plumed helm upon his head, a matching cape billowing in the lashing wind.

Fighting to quell the roiling in her gut, Danae glanced back at the first row of soldiers. Telamon led a clutch of Children of Prometheus men, Atalanta another group, while the rest were scattered strategically through the Ithacan force. They had all received their orders the previous night. Once the gods were sighted in the sky, each group would focus on bringing them down into the fray with spears and arrows, then occupy them in battle while Danae delivered the killing blow.

Telamon caught Danae's eye and winked. Her lips twitched, heart lifting for a beat. Then her eyes slid past him to the soldier in the silver breastplate. Atalanta marched with a brow as thunderous as the clouds threatening to devour the rising sun. Knives glinted at her thighs and ankles, a broadsword was sheathed at her waist, and her trusty bow and arrows were slung across her chest. Danae's stomach tightened at the fresh dent at the heart of Atalanta's armour. There had been no time to speak of what had passed between them before she fled the tent. By the time Danae had returned to retrieve her weapons after conversing with Achilles on the shore, Atalanta had gone to prepare for battle.

Danae stared, willing the other woman to catch her eye.

I'm sorry.

I want you.

Please don't die.

'Dione.'

Reluctantly, Danae turned back.

Odysseus surveyed her from between the eye slits of his bronze helm. 'Once we cross the Scamander, you and Hylas will remain at the riverbank while our force marches on. You must wait for the gods to appear. Do not engage until they have all been brought to the ground and are embroiled in fighting our men. We cannot risk any of them discovering you are here while they retain an aerial advantage.'

'Understood.' Danae tilted her face to the sky, ever watchful for a glint of gold or the wings of a flying horse.

'Look.' Hylas pointed towards the bay.

The Greek warships had dropped anchor just beyond the cove shielding the Trojan harbour and its vessels. Their smaller penteconters slipped ahead between the triremes, rows of lights blinking into being on their decks.

Danae drew a sharp breath as a scatter of flaming arrows seared the air, igniting Trojan sails, decking and oars until the entire enemy fleet was blazing. Black smoke billowed across the plain, ash floating like blossom on the wind.

The Greeks had claimed the bay.

'It begins,' murmured Odysseus.

Danae squinted through watery eyes as Agamemnon raised his sword above his head, then brought it slashing through the air. A heartbeat later the salpinges were blown once more, their sound echoed by other horns within the marching regiments.

Full-throated cries tore through the air, as the first rows of soldiers picked up the pace and surged towards the topless towers of Troy. In different circumstances it would be foolhardy to attack such a well-defended city, but even a fortress such as Troy had never before been tested against an army of this magnitude.

Danae's pulse quickened as Odysseus urged his steed out in front of his men, raising his sword.

'Forward!' he cried, then led the charge.

There was no time to look back for Atalanta as Danae and Hylas were forced to ride after the Ithacan king.

The waters of the River Scamander churned beneath makeshift bridges fashioned from planks laid by the first soldiers to cross the plain. Danae pulled up her mare on the near bank as the fighters streamed past her, as though she were nothing but a rock in a current of molten bronze. This was where she and Hylas must wait. She gazed around frantically, then spotted Atalanta's silver breastplate on the far side of the river. Her ears thrummed with the war cries of thousands of men as her world narrowed to one woman.

Atalanta did not look back.

Danae clenched her jaw so hard she almost bit through her lip, then again tilted her face to the sky.

'Come on,' she breathed.

Beside her, Hylas held his horse still. He looked every inch the soldier, with his blade sheathed at his side, his breastplate gleaming under his navy cloak, his chestnut curls whipping his face.

'You should be out there, not waiting with me,' she called against the clamour of the men.

Hylas looked at her as though she were the only person on the battlefield. 'You should not have to wait alone.'

As the last of the Greek soldiers crossed the Scamander, movement aboard the ships drew Danae's gaze back to the bay.

It looked as though each trireme was raising an additional mast, with weighted wooden contraptions at their bases and bulbous cups at their tips. Soldiers scurried about the decks, straining with ropes and levers.

'What are those?'

Hylas smiled. 'Daedalus' invention.'

'What do they do?'

'You'll see.'

Danae watched, coughing as the wind-blown smoke from the burning Trojan ships raked her throat. The levers of Daedalus' contraptions were released to catapult clods of fire, metal and rock into the air, smashing into Troy's yellow stone walls. Brick and dust exploded on impact in a gritty burst. Some of the ammunition made it over the walls and the burning buildings within sent plumes of black smoke into the clouds above. A cheer rang out from the Greek army as they continued to surge towards the city.

After the initial volley, the walls were revealed to be scarred from the attack, but the triremes' weapons hadn't yet broken through.

'Damn,' Hylas cursed.

Danae's neck began to ache as her eyes darted from land to sea to sky in a wary cycle.

As the ship's vast catapults were reloaded, beneath her grip, the trident sang. She'd spent the last precious hour before dawn draining what little vegetation and sea-life she could find near the camp to imbue the weapon with life-threads. It had been intuitive, much easier than gifting the stick an ichor back on Delos. The gold had absorbed her proffered threads like a sponge. What's more, they felt amplified inside the trident, as though the gods-forged metal was some kind of echo chamber for their power.

Once more the catapults were unleashed, and once more the high walls of Troy remained impenetrable.

'I could blast through those walls.'

'No.' Hylas brought his horse between hers and the river. 'If the Olympians saw you, they would surely not risk falling into our trap. They might destroy the entire Greek army from the sky like they did at Delphi.'

Danae's chest tightened at the memory of the burning city. All those people murdered because of her. She clenched her jaw once more and set her sights on Troy and the masses of Greek soldiers now approaching the walls. It was impossible from this distance to tell where Atalanta and Telamon were, or to distinguish the squadrons of Children of Prometheus fighters from the rest of the Greek army.

The sky darkened, a fleet of arrows hissing from longbows behind the Trojan defences. There were cries from below as the Greeks hurried to raise their shields.

Not all were swift enough.

When the troops pressed on, there were gaps in their previously seamless ranks, the bodies of their comrades left to bleed out in the dirt.

As another hail of arrows pierced the sky, the allied force split, spilling around the base of the walls like a serpent coiling its prey. Vast as the army was, they could not surround the entire city, but they could cut off access to and from the main gates, keeping the Trojan army penned inside.

Again, many arrows found their marks, but the Greek army surged on, their number so great the Trojan's defences barely slowed them. Long ladders, each carried by upwards of fifty men, sprung from their ranks, soldiers scurrying like bronze beetles up their lengths. Several fell as swiftly as they rose, but not all. Danae gaped as some men leapt from the wood to clamber up the ropes dangling from the tops of the walls, still tied around the mouldering necks of Diomedes' scouting party. The Trojans hurried to cut the ropes free, but incredibly some Greeks made it to the battlements, tossing enemy soldiers from the tops of the walls until they were cut down.

'Shit,' Hylas breathed as a small group of Trojan soldiers suddenly appeared from a flanking position behind a crop of rocky hills to the south, smashing into the Greek force. They were a fraction of the Greek's size, yet they cut through their enemy's ranks like a blade through cheese.

'They must have been waiting,' said Danae, taking in the clash of bronze and bone while scouring the landscape. 'What if there are others?'

Far above, the bruised clouds finally opened, and rain pummelled the blood-churned earth.

Danae shielded her eyes, searching the sky. 'Where in Tartarus are they?'

'They'll come. Odysseus said they would.' Hylas' expression betrayed the conviction of his words.

From the harbour, another gust of smoke billowed across the plain, the blackened carcasses of the Trojan ships still smouldering in the rain. Despite the walls now being scaled by Greek soldiers, the triremes in the bay released another volley of fire, metal and stone, crashing into walls, destroying enemy and ally alike. Agamemnon stood above the figurehead of Zeus, wildly signalling the ships to launch their catapults again and again.

Hylas' eyes widened, the colour draining from his cheeks.

'Fuck this,' hissed Danae. 'I will not stand by while my men are needlessly slain. Atalanta and Telamon are out there, they need me.' She drove her horse towards the nearest bridge.

'Danae!' Hylas urged his steed after her. 'As one Argonaut to another, I beg you to listen to Odysseus!'

She paused on the cusp of the riverbank and looked back at him.

Something deep and raw flickered through his eyes. 'You made the right choice not coming back for me on the

Doliones' shore. Don't let your guilt force you to make the wrong one now.'

A rumble of thunder ripped the air.

Danae looked up, and moments later, lightning cracked the sky. She blinked frantically, trying to banish the light dancing across her vision.

Something gleamed against the dark clouds, flying directly over the battlefield.

Her heart suddenly felt too large for her chest.

Thunder ... lightning ... surely the King of the Gods himself had not come?

The trident's warmth burned her palm as it responded to the blood pounding through her veins.

Not now ... please not now. She couldn't face him yet. She was not ready.

She could see no chariot, nor any winged horses, just a solitary figure clad in gold, soaring like a bird through the storm-marred sky. Arrows and spears hurtled towards them, shot from the Children of Prometheus soldiers, but the god continued to circle above, avoiding their blows. She had never laid eyes on the King of the Gods, but something about the Olympian flying above her seemed wrong. They were too small and slight to be Zeus.

Suddenly another horn sounded, and from the east a second group of Trojan soldiers smashed into the Greek force.

The god too seemed to be distracted by this new addition to the fray, and finally one of the arrows found its mark. The Olympian dipped mid-air then hurtled down towards their attacker.

Danae's pulse slowed, then rapidly sped up.

Before Hylas could stop her, she kicked her horse's sides and cantered across the bridge.

She had seen battle before, fought bloodthirsty hunters on Lemnos and towering six-armed Earthborn on the Doliones' shore. But there was nothing that could have prepared her for this.

The crash of weapons, braying horses and guttural screams battered her ears. All around her, the men caught by arrows lay twitching in the dirt, armour smeared with earth and blood. Some still crawled towards Troy, reaching out as they groaned with the last of their strength. It became harder to find a path through them, the air thick with smoke and rain, and the metallic stench of open wounds and voided bowels.

She pressed on, towards the tangle of Greeks and Trojans battling before the Scaean Gates. Then her horse reared as a spear shot past her, burrowing into a Greek soldier's chest, blood spurting from the man's mouth as he fell. Danae gripped the saddle with her thighs, but with only one hand on the reins she couldn't hold her grip and slid back, thudding into the mud.

As she pushed herself up with the help of the trident, the mare galloped back towards the Greek camp. She was barely on her feet before a Trojan soldier came roaring towards her, sword raised above his head. Without pausing for breath, she swung the trident, its golden prongs connecting with the man's breastplate.

As though it was an extension of her arm, the trident released a burst of life-threads, amplified by the gold, which sent the soldier flying in a violent spin, twenty feet into the air.

Danae stared at the weapon and grinned.

No wonder the Olympians' powers had always seemed vastly stronger than her own with their weapons and armour. Then she thought of Metis, and of the raw power of Gaiasight. Danae had both.

Her hands tightened around the trident's shaft as she stared about the battlefield, then dived into the throng. Her eyes blurred with tears from the still-smoking ships as she scoured the mass of fighters for golden armour amongst a storm of bronze.

To her left a soldier's head was cleaved clean from his shoulders, another's chest ripped open by the spiked wheel of a chariot. Soon, she could no longer tell enemy from ally, the men's sweaty, ash-smeared faces all snarling like beasts in a lion pit.

So much power, said the voice. *All yours for the taking.*

She clenched her jaw as the trident seemed to sing in response beneath her hands.

A man fell in front of her, his throat slit, his life force seeping away into the dirt.

She paused, staring at the blood pooling beneath his head, her whole being aching with longing.

Then, through the din, she heard an unmistakable cry. Ignoring the voice, she leapt over the dying man and charged in the direction of the sea, weaving through the chaos.

The thunder rumbled, and another vein of lightning cracked the sky. With the lashing rain and dense black smoke, it was near impossible to see.

Channelling her will into the trident, she swung the weapon through the air, glowing threads streaming from the triple prongs to whip a clear path of air ahead of her.

The golden-armoured Olympian stood amongst the battling soldiers, an arrow protruding from between the join of the metal across their thigh. Children of Prometheus soldiers lay broken around them, bodies piled on one another like sacks of grain. A few remained standing, ready to sacrifice everything, while other Greek and Trojan soldiers fled in fear.

With a jolt, Danae caught a flash of silver nearby and

spotted Atalanta fighting sword to sword with a Trojan soldier with hair the same coppery hue as his battered armour.

For a heartbeat she was torn, but before she could make a move the god lunged towards Atalanta and the Trojan. They grabbed her by the neck, lifting her off the ground, then turned to the man she'd been fighting.

'Run, Aeneas! For the love of your mother, run!'

There was no time for fear or self-doubt. While the Olympian was distracted, Danae threw herself forward, swinging the trident like a club. The god was knocked off their feet, crashing into a mass of soldiers.

Atalanta gasped, falling to her knees, hands around her bruised throat.

Their eyes met, and Danae's heart swelled for a beat, before she turned and ran after the god.

She squinted against the rain, focusing on the Olympian through the torrent of droplets. They were already on their feet, a twitching soldier clutched in their fists as they sucked the man's life-threads into their body, healing their wounds.

She had moments.

Lungs screaming with the smoke, she sprinted, the trident gripped in one hand, her other reaching beneath her cloak. The god turned as she approached, eyes widening beneath a helm wound with a filigree of golden ivy. They were smaller than Danae had expected, shorter and with a much slimmer build than Poseidon. A dark smudge of blood trailed down their leg from where the arrow had been buried.

The drained soldier slid from the Olympian's grip as Danae drove the trident into the earth between them, with a shockwave that sent the god tumbling to the ground. As the Olympian hurried to their feet, she reached inside the pack fastened to her belt. The god lunged, clutching at the trident. Just as Danae hoped they would.

As their fingers closed around the shaft, she drew out the collar and snapped it around their neck. The god stumbled back, clawing at the iron ring with their gauntleted fingers. As they flailed, Danae ripped the golden helm from their head.

The face beneath was that of a pale youth, barely older than fourteen. He strongly reminded her of a young Philemon.

Lip quivering, Hermes, Messenger of the Gods and the Lord of Tricksters, sank to his knees in the bloody dirt.

'Please, don't kill me.'

51. A God and a Titan

When Hermes woke, he thought he'd drowned.

With each shallow breath, his lungs ached. The air around him felt heavy, as though he was suspended in tar. He tried to move, but his limbs were bound, his eyes smothered, his mouth gagged by what tasted like a filthy rag. Something cold and hard circled his neck.

Fragments of memory returned to him. He'd been hovering over the battle outside Troy when he'd been impaled by an arrow. He'd healed himself and killed a swathe of mortal soldiers, their feeble swords no match for his power. A woman in silver armour had been fighting Aeneas, just as the stone had foretold. Hermes had saved him.

Then *she* came.

Panic reached for him across the darkness. Fighting its smothering grasp, he delved within himself, searching for his life-threads.

He could not feel them.

Where are you? he screamed inside his mind. *Where are you!?*

But the voice did not answer.

As he squirmed, he realized that his armour had been removed and he'd been stripped down to the white tunic he always wore beneath it. He was defenceless, powerless and alone in the dark.

'He's awake.'

'Take the blindfold off.'

Not alone after all.

Searing light burned his eyes as the cloth covering his face was yanked free. Blinking, the inside of what appeared to be a shabby tent came into focus.

Two people stood in front of him: the fierce woman in battered silver armour who had fought Aeneas and a tall man with flame-red hair.

'I'm going to take off your gag,' said the man. 'You will not scream if you value your life.'

'Or your teeth,' added the woman.

Hermes nodded swiftly, then retched as the rag was loosened, the foul material raking over his tongue.

'You will regret this,' he spat.

The woman smiled. Somehow it was more fearsome than her scowl.

'Why did your family not come to the battle?' asked the man.

'It is over?'

The man snorted. 'It ended in a bloody stalemate hours ago. You've been out for almost a day. Answer my question.'

Hermes blinked the moisture from his eyes. How had this mortal known that his siblings intended to be at the battle, only changing their plans at the last moment when their father ordered them to search for the Titan girl? He would reveal nothing more to this man.

'I am a god. I am Hermes, son of the King of Heaven, and I will rain retribution down on you and all you love for daring to –'

'You will do no such thing,' said a third voice.

The woman and the man parted as another person walked into Hermes' frame of vision. Her slight body was draped in a long black robe, her dark hair clipped short around a strong-jawed face from which blazed a pair of oak-brown eyes.

He thought his heart might explode it was beating so fast. Hades' remains, charred and smouldering in the depths of Tartarus, stole unbidden into his mind. He squeezed his eyes shut, desperately scouring his body for a hint of his power. Still nothing. Wet warmth spread across his thighs.

'Answer his question. Why did the other Olympians not come to witness the battle?' The Titan's face was marred by a tangle of emotions he could not divine.

Finally, Hermes regained his voice. 'W-what have you done to me?'

Her lip curled. 'You can thank Hades for that collar. Feels like drowning, doesn't it?'

A sob lodged in Hermes' throat as he thought again of his dead uncle, then Poseidon. The Lord of the Sea would never willingly part with his most prized weapon.

'You killed Poseidon too . . .' he breathed.

Her mouth tightened. 'I will ask once more. Why did you come alone?'

Hermes' stomach plummeted through the ground.

'I . . .' He bit the insides of his cheeks. Surely his siblings would be looking for him by now . . .

Then cold realization trickled down his spine. He'd confided in no one, not even Hephaestus, about the vision he'd seen in the shard of omphalos stone, or his plan to fly to Troy. The rest of the divine children were far away, searching across Greece for the Titan girl, all unaware that she was here.

If both Hades and Poseidon had fallen against her, what hope did he have?

'Did it have something to do with this?' From behind her back, the Titan produced a small cloth-wrapped object. She laid it on her palm and peeled away the fabric to reveal the omphalos shard.

Hermes drew a sharp breath. She'd been through his belongings.

'Enough,' hissed the woman in the silver breastplate. 'Kill him.'

Hermes' heart lurched into his throat. 'No, please . . .'

The Titan ignored the other woman. 'Why did you come alone? Where are your siblings? Your father?'

Tears burned rivers of salt down his cheeks. He was a fool. He was such a fool.

'They will come . . . they will come for me . . .'

'Pathetic,' spat the flame-haired man.

Suddenly, the other woman drew a blade from her thigh and lunged towards him.

'Atalanta,' barked the Titan.

The woman paused, her knife dangerously close to Hermes' jugular.

'He is one of them. He killed countless soldiers. He tried to kill me and you,' she snarled.

'Step outside.'

Hermes cringed back, the hatred radiating from Atalanta's face scalding like a burning hearth.

'I said, outside.'

With a grunt, the woman withdrew her blade from his neck and paced from the tent.

The Titan's eyes raked over him before turning to the flame-haired man.

'Watch him.'

Then she too swept through the entrance.

Atalanta rounded on Danae as soon as she stepped into the daylight.

'Why the fuck is that thing still alive?'

'We need him.'

'The plan was to kill the false gods who came to the battlefield, not keep them as hostages.'

'There's been enough death for one day. Besides, he's more valuable to us alive. We still don't know why the other Olympians did not come. And with that collar on he's no threat.'

'How can you say that? He's one of them!'

'He's a boy!'

Atalanta's lip curled. 'Don't tell me you're fooled by his looks. He's just as flint-hearted as the rest of them.'

Danae drew a breath. 'We cannot go on like this.'

Atalanta folded her arms, the rise and fall of her chest betraying the schooled chill of her glower.

'Despite what we've been through together, in the war against Olympus I am your leader. You must follow my orders, like you once did with Heracles.'

Atalanta was quiet for a moment, then she huffed a sharp breath through her nose. 'Do you know why Heracles, Telamon, Dolos, Hylas and I worked so well together all those years?'

Danae waited.

'We never fucked each other.'

'Atalanta . . .' Darkness swirled at the edges of her vision: unspoken truths that might rip her apart if given voice. She'd made a choice like this before, standing in front of Heracles' tent at the foot of a snow-swathed mountain. Duty before desire. She could do it again. She must.

'You're right.'

Atalanta's eyebrows lifted in surprise.

'Ending the reign of thunder is what matters most. Anything that jeopardizes my ability to do that is . . . I cannot . . .' Danae swallowed the lump in her throat. She glanced down at the ground, churned to mud by yesterday's downpour, then raised her eyes to meet Atalanta's. 'I need you to swear that I can depend on you. That you will follow my orders as your captain. Just your captain. It is the only way this will work.'

The warrior gazed at her long and hard.

Part of her wanted Atalanta to rail, to fight for them, to drag the truth of why Danae had fled that night from the locked cavern of her chest.

Despite knowing it was for the best, she was crushed when Atalanta finally said, 'I swear it.'

Danae paced through the labyrinth of tents.

Above her, clouds wisped across the bone-pale sky like a fire's dying breath. Her black robe and cloak were soaked in mud up to her knees, like everything in the camp since the Greek army had returned the previous night, forced to call a stalemate with Troy before they dashed their entire force against those impenetrable walls. Groans wafted through the air from the scores of injured men left to heal in their tents, with nothing but a swig of wine to stave off the pain.

Beyond the Ithacan quarter, between the camp and the plain, a large trench had been dug. Hundreds of bodies lay within it, washed and stripped of their armour, ready for a journey to the Underworld they would never take. A ram had been slaughtered, its blood mixed with honey wine, water and barley. Libations for the dead.

In her disguise as a seer, Danae should have been with Calchas, prowling about the mass grave, intoning the funeral rites, but she had more pressing matters to attend to.

On reaching her destination, Danae flung open the awning draped over the King of Ithaca's tent.

Odysseus looked up at her. One of his eyes was swollen shut, a freshly stitched gash above his brow. He stood before a map of the Trojan defences splayed on the table, candles burning in small bronze dishes at its corners.

'Your plan failed,' said Danae. 'Only one god came to the battle.'

Hylas stood on the other side of the table, leaning on his crutch, his eyes flicking between Danae and the king.

'Things did not play out as expected, however –'

'Even now, you can't admit you made a mistake,' Danae spat. 'Your sources were wrong.'

Odysseus pressed his fingers into the edges of the map. 'Has Hermes revealed any useful information?'

Danae folded her arms. 'He had the omphalos shard. He must have recovered it from the Underworld.'

Odysseus loosed a long breath. 'It is good we have retrieved the shard, it will be invaluable in the war to come.' He glanced up at her. 'You should have told me about the collar.'

'You should not have promised me a plan you could not deliver.'

He stepped towards her. 'The men are talking. Some are saying they saw two gods fighting on the battlefield. I have done what I can to dispel the rumours and convinced Agamemnon their words were born of battle fever, but you should have taken greater care –'

'How many Children of Prometheus soldiers died?'

Odysseus grew still.

Danae repeated slowly, 'How many of my men did we lose?'

'Over two-thirds,' murmured Hylas.

She shook her head. 'So many lives wasted in a battle that did little to further our cause. You ask me why I didn't tell you about the collar – because something in me knew I could not fully trust you.' She unfurled her arms. 'Hermes hasn't yet revealed why he came alone, but if he divined my presence here through the omphalos shard, we cannot rule out that the rest of the Olympians know where I am too. Hermes may have merely been a scout, sent to confirm my location. When he does not return, others may follow. So when I leave this tent, I will take what is left of my army and your ship and sail for Olympus. Like I should have done the first day I set foot on Trojan soil.'

'You're angry, that is understandable, I am too. My sources have never been wrong before.' Odysseus' voice remained low and calm. 'But we must take stock, see what additional information we can press from Hermes before we make any rash decisions. Even if Metis were here to fight with us, two Titans against nine Olympians might still not be enough.' Odysseus ran a hand through his hair. 'As I have said before, there are too many of them to defeat in a direct attack on their palace. Even with the Children of Prometheus soldiers at your side. I have been contemplating alternatives: Achilles and the majority of his Myrmidons survived the battle; if we could convince him to fight with us against the gods –'

'His fate lies in Troy, mine on Olympus.' Danae curled her fingers into fists. 'Metis died so I could fulfil Prometheus' prophecy. She taught me many things, but I know I cannot do this alone. I wish I had another Titan to fight alongside, a whole band of heroes, or even a beast like Poseidon's sea-monster, but I don't. I can only hope the companions I do have left will be enough when the time comes.'

'This is a setback, but there are still more paths to take.'

'No, I'm done hiding from my destiny.'

'Sea-monster . . .'

Both Danae and Odysseus turned to look at Hylas. He was staring at the map of Troy, deep in thought. Then his gaze snapped up. 'What of the creatures from the Underworld spotted above ground: the dragon, the giants . . .'

Odysseus swept the idea away with a wave of his hand. 'My

sources reported Zeus has already disposed of the dragon. As for the giants, their whereabouts are unknown.'

Danae ignored him, staring at Hylas as his idea ignited a fire within her. She thought of Charon's loyalty, sparked after years enslaved to a cruel master.

'Our enemy's enemy . . . What if we recruited the giants?'

Hylas nodded. 'After centuries imprisoned in Tartarus, they will surely desire revenge.'

'Hylas.' Odysseus' voice was barbed with warning. He turned to Danae. 'Allow me to consult my sources before you take any action. I agree, it is too dangerous for you to remain in the Greek camp, so I suggest staying aboard my ship while I interrogate Hermes. Once we are fully armed with the enemy's intentions, then we can devise a new plan to whittle down the false gods before you storm Olympus.' He looked to Hylas for support.

But Hylas moved away from the table and came to stand beside Danae.

'All this time, you said the most important thing was ensuring the last daughter trusted you. You said our aim would fail if I did not convince her to do what you bade. I never doubted you. Not once.' He looked at Danae. 'I'm sorry, I should have put my faith in you.'

Danae's chest swelled. She turned to face Odysseus.

'Well, King of Ithaca, will you give me what remains of my army?'

Odysseus' eyes darted between them. It would have been impossible to divine his discomfort, were it not for the vein pulsing in his temple. Danae matched his wolfish stare, the truth an unspoken blade against his jugular. For all his cunning he was just a man, and she was a Titan.

Finally, he said, 'I have only ever sought to help you. Everything I have done has been in the service of your destiny.'

He paused. 'The Children of Prometheus are yours to command. I will not stand in your way if you wish to leave.'

Danae stood at the prow of Odysseus' sleek black penteconter. A sharp westerly wind whipped her cloak and bloated the sail behind her. Ahead, the dark waters of the Aegean swelled before the ship as they sailed out of the mouth of the Bay of Troy. Briefly, she closed her eyes and thought of her father.

We're sailing together.

Beside her stood Hylas, Telamon and Atalanta, and on the rowing benches sat the remaining three dozen Children of Prometheus soldiers, one man navigating the tiller. Still bound and gagged, Hermes was slumped by the stern deck, his hands tied to a ring beside the cabin door, glowering at Danae through red-rimmed eyes.

She looked at her companions, the three heroes who, despite everything she had done, everything they had lived through, were still standing beside her.

She drank in their faces, the determination blazing in their eyes, then looked to the crew.

'We sail for Lerna, one of the entrances to the Underworld. That is the mostly likely place the giants will have emerged from. From there, we will track their trail.' She drew a breath. 'You have all faced much peril, and there is only more to come. All I can promise you is that we will strive together, always, until the end. While the Olympians fight for themselves, we fight for all mortals. We fight for freedom, for a life lived beyond the tyranny of the gods. Remember, we have fate on our side. *When the prophet falls and gold that grows bears no fruit, the –*' She faltered as the men rose to their feet, melding their voices with hers.

'*The last daughter will come. She will end the reign of thunder and become the light that frees mankind.*'

She turned away, unable to hide the surge of feeling flushing her cheeks. Then a hand squeezed her shoulder.

'Ahh, Lerna,' said Telamon. 'So many fond memories: nearly being eaten by a many-headed hydra, being chased from the Underworld by a flock of murderous furies then taken prisoner by a deposed king . . . joyful times.'

Hylas came to stand on Danae's other side. 'We should consider how best to approach the giants when we find them. God-haters or no, they might take some convincing.'

Atalanta leant on the ship's rail. 'I vote we ply them with wine. Always helps with negotiations.'

'Once we've tracked them down, we'll find a way to win them to our cause,' said Danae. 'I have faith in us.'

She gazed across the shining expanse of ocean, cracked gold by the sparse rays of sunlight fighting through the clouds. Soon, land would appear on the horizon, and somewhere to the north, amongst the vast reaches of earth, was Mount Olympus.

Just for a moment, the wind turned, and a whisper of whistling song pricked her ears. She smiled.

Finally, she was ready to face her destiny. And she didn't have to do it alone.

Epilogue: The Day Prometheus Died

Far to the north-west of Greece, in the land of Epirus, lay the valley of Dodona.

Men used to say it was named after the river that flowed through the heart of the land, a gift from the Mother so her children would flourish. At the centre of this verdant valley nestled a grove of oaks. It was older than the gods. Older than the Titans. Older, even, than the dragons.

Before pilgrims flocked to Delphi, before coins were pressed into molten metal and buildings of stone towered over the plains, people would walk from far across the earth to lose themselves amongst those sacred trees and learn the secrets woven through their branches.

But that was long ago, before the old ways were forgotten.

Now mortals thought of fate as an immovable force, herding each person down a fixed path towards an inevitable destiny.

They were wrong.

But there was one man who remembered that the Moirae could be bargained with. For a price.

Zeus had resisted this journey for centuries, ever since Prometheus' poisoned words first reached his ears. He knew the cost of altering fate was always a devastating sacrifice. Yet now he found himself with little choice.

The trees murmured as he approached the ancient grove, his crimson cloak encrusted with ice from the Caucasus Mountains. Hours before, he had stood beneath a crag on the highest peak, Prometheus' corpse lying in the snow at his gilded feet.

Zeus slowed before the grove's towering trunks, staring into the gloom between them. The way was barred by hair-thin strands, gleaming as though spun from liquid starlight. His eyes narrowed. He unpinned his cloak and let it fall in a ripple at his feet.

Breath slow and steady as a moon-tide, he contorted his body between the gaps in the web, careful not to touch a strand with even the tip of a finger.

Three steps in, his foot crunched on the forest floor. He paused. Something lay splintered beneath his golden boot. The remnants of a comb fashioned from bone and pearl. He gazed at it for a moment, then carried on twisting through the strands.

A breeze shivered through the ancient trees, ruffling their leaves and jingling the offerings sewn to their branches.

Gifts for the Moirae, rusted and rotted with time.

Hours passed, and sweat trickled down Zeus' brow, stinging his eyes. His muscles ached like they had not done for centuries. There was a screech far above, and for a heart-rending moment he thought he had touched one of the strands. Then a dash of white flickered through the canopy. A snowy dove, its voice as harsh as its feathers were beautiful.

Quelling his racing heart, he pressed onwards.

Finally, he came to a clearing free of webs and was able to stand upright and stretch his limbs. In the centre was a vast oak, thicker and taller than its brethren guarding it from the world. Around its base, like a row of bronze teeth, was a circle of tripod cauldrons, their metal rims touching.

Zeus tilted his face to the torso-thick branches shrouded in darkness and waited.

An acorn dropped from the tree, tumbling into the belly of

one of the cauldrons. A clang echoed from within, chiming around the ring of bronze in a dissonant wave.

Out of the harsh, metallic chords came a voice, fractured in three parts.

What brings you to our grove, son of Kronos?

'Sisters of the sacred oak, I come before you to make a bargain.'

The branches above him shivered, and a clicking sound cut through the peals of the cauldrons.

'I wish,' Zeus continued, 'to change my fate.'

There was a cry like the ripping of the world, then the voices split.

The apple thief wants more time.

Greedy little Titan.

What will he give us?

Zeus raised his voice above the noise. 'Whatever you ask.'

The clicking intensified.

A strange sensation spread across Zeus' chest, a feeling old and forgotten stealing his breath.

Fear.

Leaves drifted down as the branches shook and three shapes descended the gnarled trunk.

Zeus stepped back as the first fate scuttled over the cauldrons. She was large as a wolf, her arachnid abdomen trailing silver thread in her wake. Her legs too were that of a great insect, but her arms were fashioned like a mortal woman's, her face a smooth opal, broken by a crimson gash of a mouth.

Clotho, the weaver.

The second fate slithered like a serpent, her sea-green body rippling like water. She had no limbs, only an oval moon-white face undulating before him, devoid of features except two round eyes, misted as the dawn.

Lachesis, the judge.

Lastly, a shadow slipped from the tree, drifting over the swells of bronze and along the ground. It slid up Zeus' armour, chilling his skin. The life-threads surging through his veins quietened, as though the third fate had reached inside his soul and quenched all that he was.

Then a voice whispered in his ear, *The fate you would change belongs to me, child of time. And I have waited so long.*

Atropos, the devourer.

Zeus' heart betrayed him, thundering in his armoured chest.

'I have walked the path of the Moirae, you must consider my bargain. That is the way.'

The darkness surged across his vision, and for a moment he thought it would consume him. Then Atropos retreated to prowl around him with her sisters.

He gasped, despite himself, as the surge of his life force returned.

Very well, the voices melded together once more, ringing in his skull. *Which thread would you have us cut in exchange for yours?*

'The one belonging to the girl Prometheus named the last daughter.'

A riot of hissing exploded through the grove. Zeus fell to his knees, covering his ears against the violent noise.

YOU ASK TOO MUCH.

'Please,' he gasped, 'I will do anything to change my fate. I will give anything.'

The hissing subsided, leaving a throbbing ache in his eardrums. He staggered to his feet.

He was alone in the grove. The Moirae were gone.

Rage boiled through his core. He was King of the Gods. He was denied by no one. Not even fate.

Drawing on the ocean of power he hoarded inside himself,

he sparked a shard of lightning into being, feeding the searing bolt until it spanned the width of the clearing, singeing the trees.

'You will take my bargain, or I will burn your grove to the ground.'

A shattered laugh echoed from everywhere and nowhere. The bolt in his hands died in an instant, his fire extinguished by a breath older than time.

Zeus' face spasmed into a snarl. He spun on his heel, turning his back on the Moirae's tree.

Wait.

A whisper of shadow played about his face.

What in all the world is most precious to you, son of Kronos? Do not lie, I will know.

Zeus fought against the dread stilling his tongue. 'My children.'

If the darkness had a face, she would be smiling.

I offer you this: there is a way to prevent the last daughter from ending the reign of thunder.

'How?'

If she is slain by a child of your blood.

Zeus' chest tightened. 'What will you take in return?'

Atropos enveloped him, caressing his cheeks. *Blood for blood. A child armed for a child sacrificed.*

He had known the price would be dear. It did not make the bargain any easier.

'Which child will you take?' he whispered.

That fate is yet undecided by Lachesis. It could be any, or none. It could still be you.

Zeus clenched his golden fist. He had lived too long and given too much to let human weakness stifle him now.

You know what you must do, said the voice inside his head.

Zeus gazed at the shining threads drawn across the trunks

beyond the clearing. So many lives taut with potential, so many lifetimes for him to mould in his image. So many more children still to be born.

'I accept your bargain.'

Atropos spun around him, thickening the air with midnight smoke. Through the blackness loomed Lachesis' misted eyes, and below it, a single silvery strand drawn taut. Ready to be cut.

As one the fates spoke, *It is done.*

Historical Note

The hymn sung by the Titans in Chapter 31 is a direct quotation of the first four verses of 'Hymn to Gaia, Mother of Them All' from the *Homeric Hymns*, translated by Jules Cashford.

Acknowledgements

Writing *Daughter of Fate* was a real labour of love. I so wanted to do the second instalment of Danae's story justice, hold her darkest, most challenging moments and her journey back towards the light with the same passion and care that went into crafting the first. Thankfully, after many months of drafting and re-drafting, a book emerged that I am proud of. I could not have done it without the support of the wonderful people around me. A big round of thanks is in order.

Thank you, once again, to my incredible agent Sebastian Godwin for your unending support, compassion and guidance. Thanks also to the dream team that is DGA; David, Heather, Aparna and Bianca.

To the UK team at Penguin Michael Joseph starting with my editor, Rebecca Hilsdon; I love working with you. Thank you for always getting the best out of my writing, and your unwavering positivity and passion for the stories I tell. Thanks also to the fantastic Jorgie Bain, Riana Dixon, Lily Evans, Courtney Barclay, and everyone else who's worked on this book. A huge thanks also to my wonderful US editor Dina Davis and the rest of the brilliant team at Hanover Square Press. And thanks to the rights team at Penguin Random House and the publishing teams and translators that have brought the first two instalments of The Dark Pantheon Trilogy to readers in other languages around the world.

Thank you to the immensely talented Tom Roberts for illustrating another stunning cover, to my wonderful sensitivity reader GiannaMarie Dobson and David Watson my copyeditor. Thanks also to my brilliant audiobook narrator,

Lucy Walker-Evans. I couldn't have wished for anyone better to bring Danae's story to life.

Thank you to all the writers whose friendship and support has meant the world; from the London crew to the PMJ gang and everyone in-between! And to all the friends and family who have supported my journey into writing and beyond – my heart is full.

To Sam, my rock and the only one I let read my first drafts(!), thank you for making me a better person and a better writer. You truly are a magical human.

To the booksellers who've championed this series, I am forever in your debt. And finally, to all the readers who have come on this journey with me, I'm writing for you now.